W9-BXU-926

CHELSEA
MANSIONS

ALSO BY BARRY MAITLAND

BROCK AND KOLLA SERIES

The Marx Sisters

The Malcontenta

All My Enemies

The Chalon Heads

Silvermeadow

Babel

The Verge Practice

No Trace

Spider Trap

Dark Mirror

MYSTERY

Bright Air

CHELSEA MANSIONS

A Brock and Kolla Mystery

BARRY MAITLAND

MINOTAUR BOOKS
NEW YORK

CHELSEA MANSIONS. Copyright © 2011 by Barry Maitland. All rights reserved. Printed in the United States of America. For information, address St. Martin's Press, 175 Fifth Avenue, New York, N.Y. 10010.

www.minotaurbooks.com

LIBRARY OF CONGRESS CATALOGING-IN-PUBLICATION DATA

Maitland, Barry.
    Chelsea mansions : a Brock and Kolla mystery / Barry Maitland.
        p. cm.
    ISBN 978-0-312-60066-2
    1. Brock, David (Fictitious character)—Fiction.   2. Kolla, Kathy
(Fictitious character)—Fiction.   3. Americans—Crimes against—
Fiction.   4. Russians—Crimes against—Fiction.   5. Police—England—
London—Fiction.   I. Title.
    PR9619.3.M2635C48 2011
    823'.914—dc22   2011020400

First published in Australia by Allen & Unwin

First U.S. Edition: November 2011

10 9 8 7 6 5 4 3 2 1

To Margaret

With grateful thanks to all those who have helped me in the writing of this novel, especially Margaret my wife, Dr. Tim Lyons, Lyn Tranter, and Ali Lavau and the team at Allen & Unwin.

We blinked into the bright sunlight, posing on the steps in front of the house, putting on big smiles for the camera. It was a perfect day, my sixteenth birthday, and in my beautiful party dress I felt like a butterfly newly born from the chrysalis of my old life. I had just made my first flight in an airplane, and was for the first time in a foreign country, and was meeting such fascinating people, who spoke to me as an adult.

"Say cheese," said the man holding the camera, a very distinguished-looking English gentleman, and we did. I was clutching the posy of flowers that Uncle Gennady had presented to me, with much ceremony, and as I stared at the camera I felt a hand squeeze my arm. I thought it was Mom or Pop, but when the picture was taken I turned and saw that it was Uncle Gennady. He was such a formidable man, his gaze so dark and brooding, that I felt a sudden chill, as if a wind had blown across the steppes and into the square.

ONE

THE GRAY-HAIRED MAN MADE his way slowly through the crowd, frowning with concentration, careful not to spill the two plastic flutes of champagne. A band was playing selections from Gilbert and Sullivan on the sunlit lawn ahead, surrounded by hundreds of people sitting on white plastic seats. It took him a moment to make out his friend among them.

"Here we are," he said, handing her a precious drink and sinking with a sigh of relief onto the seat beside her.

"Dear Emerson." She smiled at him, noticing the flush on his face. "Was there a huge line?"

"Not when they saw the prices. These cost more than our flights."

She patted his hand. "I'm sorry. I think you've had enough of this, haven't you?"

"Oh, don't worry about me. We'll stay as long as you want."

"I've had a wonderful day, but my feet are getting tired and I'd be happy to wander back."

He nodded, hiding his relief. He'd seen more than enough blooms to last the rest of his lifetime. A kind of numbness had set in somewhere inside the vast central marquee in front of yet another spectacular cascade of white or pink or purple flowers, and the rising temperature and crowd numbers had made him feel increasingly uncomfortable.

"You're not sorry I dragged you over here?" she asked.

"You know I'm not. I've enjoyed every minute. Though I do think you might have let me book us in at the Hilton."

She laughed. "But our place has so much more character."

"Oh, it's got character, all right—a manager who can't see, a concierge who can't speak, and a bellboy who can't walk."

"That's cruel, Emerson."

"But true. And you still haven't told me why you picked it."

"It's a secret, but I will tell you, when I'm good and ready."

"A mystery, eh? Won't you give me a clue?"

"It's a ghost story, but I won't say any more than that."

He laughed, then sat up and peered out over the heads of the seated crowd. "I thought I saw your admirer again back there. I took a picture, here."

She peered at the image on his camera, and made out the man in the dark glasses, taller than the people around him, with black hair slicked back. "Oh yes, that's him. He's rather sinister, isn't he?"

"Like a Mexican gangster. Can't see him now though."

"He's probably gone home to his luxury penthouse, which is what we should be doing. Come on."

They finished their drinks and got to their feet, feeling stiff now and tired, and threaded their way down the row of chairs and through the trees onto the avenue leading back to the entrance gates, becoming part of a solid stream of people making their way out onto Lower Sloane Street.

"No sign of a cab," he muttered.

"Doesn't matter. It isn't far. Do us good."

He doubted that. The question was whether they would have enough energy left to climb all those stairs at the hotel when they got back.

They crossed Sloane Square and continued up Sloane Street. There were fewer people on the footpath now and they walked at a steady pace together, her arm in his. Once, he recalled, a couple of decades ago, he had harbored fantasies about doing just this, running off to London or Paris with Nancy, their spouses none the wiser. He had never asked her. Would she have agreed? It was an intriguing question and one that he might put to her, late one evening over a bottle of wine. But now those spouses had passed away, and so had the lustful impulse. Now she was just a very good friend, as agreeable a traveling companion as anyone might wish for.

And as he formed that thought, a massive blow on his right shoulder sent him crashing to the ground. Dazed, head crackling with confusion, he lay on the concrete pavement aware of a harsh squealing noise that filled the air, and then abrupt silence. He tried to push himself upright but his arm and shoulder seemed to have no strength. He heard screams, human ones this time, and the sound of running feet. Someone was bending over him, asking if he was all right.

THE FIRST POLICE AT the scene were two officers from Chelsea police station in Lucan Place, who arrived at the same time as the ambulance. While one heard a confusing mixture of contradictory accounts from bystanders, staring with hands over their mouths, or talking into their mobile phones, the other spoke to the driver of the number 22 double-decker bus that was pulled into the curb. White-faced and jerky in his gestures, the driver was in absolutely no doubt about what had happened.

"After the Sloane Square stop the road ahead was clear. I crossed Cadogan Gate and noticed this bloke up ahead turn and see me coming, then start running, and I thought, you'd better get a move on if you want to catch us at Pont Street, mate."

"How fast were you going?"

"Twenty, twenty-five, no more, God's my witness."

"Go on."

"This runner dodged around the people on the footpath, then as I got closer he charged straight into this old couple. I saw one of them, the bloke, go flying, and I thought, you stupid bugger, look what you've done. Then . . ." The driver hesitated and stared for a moment at the policeman's chest, as if he could see a film unreeling in front of him there on the black protective vest. "Then the runner grabbed the other one, the woman, and lifted her up in his arms, like she was a baby, and spun her around and threw her in front of my bus."

"Hang on," the officer began, but the driver had buckled and was being sick over his boots.

TWO

"NANCY HAYNES, AMERICAN TOURIST, age seventy." The constable handed the passport to DI Kathy Kolla. Around them, the lobby of the casualty department was crowded, staff hurrying around members of the public seated in glum ranks.

"She died at the scene, yes?"

"Oh yes."

"Go on."

"Um . . ." He consulted his notebook. "On holiday with a friend, Mr. Emerson Merckle, both from the Boston area. The doctor's looking at him now. He was knocked to the ground in the assault and maybe dislocated his shoulder."

"We're quite sure it was an assault, not an accident?"

"Talk to the bus driver, he's here too. He described it vividly." The cop repeated the driver's story. "Two other eyewitnesses support his account."

He showed Kathy a diagram he'd made. "This one was walking southward on Sloane Street, toward the scene, twenty yards away, and had a clear view. Seemed reliable. The other was coming out of Grosvenor Court, standing on the steps, and happened to look in that direction. Again a clear view. The other pedestrians, and the people on the bus, were more confused. It all happened very fast."

"The assailant?"

"Tall man, according to the bus driver, maybe six-two or three, well built, IC1 or 2, black hair, dark glasses, dark clothes, black backpack. Could be a body builder—the driver said he picked up Mrs. Haynes like she weighed nothing. He kept running, up Sloane Street heading north."

"Not a bag-snatch?"

"No. Her bag fell onto the pavement. He didn't pick it up."

The bus driver was sitting hunched in the far corner, a plastic cup of tea on the floor at his feet. Kathy introduced herself and took him through his account once again. She was impressed by his conviction, but she'd heard many convincing but mistaken witness accounts before and so she pressed him. Surely the man might simply have pushed the woman aside, or stumbled against her by mistake? But he was unshakeable, speaking as if he still couldn't quite believe it had happened. "No, no, he threw her. The bastard picked her up and spun her around and threw her in front of me. I couldn't do a bloody thing." He shook his head.

When the doctors had finished with Emerson Merckle a nurse took Kathy in to see him. His left arm was in a sling, he had a large dressing on his forehead and he looked groggy.

"I'm Detective Inspector Kathy Kolla from the Metropolitan Police, Mr. Merckle. How are you feeling?"

He lifted his eyes to her with a bleak expression, unable to find the words to answer that. "The other officer said it was possible that Nancy was deliberately killed. Tell me that isn't true."

A retired businessman or professional, Kathy guessed.

"It sounds improbable, but several witnesses interpreted what happened in that way. We're doing all we can to find the man who ran into you."

"I thought that nothing could shock me any more. How wrong I was."

"Can you tell me anything about him?"

"Not a thing. One minute I was walking along the street, the next I was face down on the sidewalk. I heard the bus braking, but I didn't see anything of what happened."

"Okay. Can you give me some background, about Nancy and your trip over here?"

He shrugged wearily. "Nancy and I have known each other for many years. I was her accountant until I retired ten years ago. We both live in Boston, and since we lost our partners we've been traveling companions, going for weekend visits to shows in New York, or further afield, a couple of times overseas. This was our first trip to the UK together, although we've both been here separately in the past. We decided to have a week in London before going up north. Nancy was interested in her family history, and wanted to visit the place in Scotland where her mother's great-grandparents came from. That's where we were going tomorrow."

For a moment he lost his train of thought, derailed by some memory, before he roused himself with a cough and went on. "This was our day to visit the Chelsea Flower Show, which was the main reason for the timing of our visit. Nancy is . . . was a great gardener. She'd been really looking forward to this. We were at the gates when they opened at eight this morning, and spent the whole day there until we left at around four. We were both pretty tired, but we couldn't find a cab and decided to walk back to our hotel."

"Where is that?"

"Cunningham Place, the Chelsea Mansions Hotel. Nancy said it has character . . ." He stopped, swallowed and snatched a tissue from the box beside him and pressed it to his eyes. After a moment he sucked in a breath and said, "I'm sorry."

"So am I, Mr. Merckle. I should let you rest."

"No, no. I just want to get out of this place."

"They've said you can go. Shall I take you back to your hotel?"

He nodded. "I feel numb, like I just want to go to sleep and wake up and discover it was all a terrible nightmare." He looked at her. "How could somebody do a thing like that? There's no reason."

As they walked to her car, Kathy put a call through to the Chelsea police to check on progress in the hunt for the man. They had nothing new to report.

CUNNINGHAM PLACE WAS A small square in the area where the three golden postcodes, SW1, SW3 and SW7—of Belgravia, Chelsea and Knightsbridge—converge in inner west London. Despite the impeccable real estate location, Kathy thought it a rather gloomy place, its leafy central gardens overwhelmed by the six- and seven-story redbrick terraces that surrounded it. The grandest of these was Chelsea Mansions, forming one side of the square, its bulk enlivened by Dutch gables, decorative terracotta panels, white balcony trim and an impressive central portico. Most of it appeared to be taken up by private residences, but the end bay, sporting geranium baskets and a large Union Jack from its upper balcony, had an inconspicuous brass plate by its front door announcing *Chelsea Mansions Hotel, AA and RAC Approved*.

Kathy helped Emerson up the steps and opened the door, to be greeted by a strong smell of fried onions. A large woman was at the front desk, peering at a computer screen through glasses perched on the end of her nose.

"He-llo," she boomed, looking up, then her smile turned to a frown. "Emerson? Good heavens, what happened to you? Toby! Emerson's been hurt."

A figure hunched at her side turned around and peered up through opaque-looking circular dark glasses. "What's that, Deb?"

"His arm's in a sling. And he's hurt his head."

"My dear chap," Toby said, rising slowly with the help of a stick and coming around the end of the counter. "Have you had an accident?"

"It's Nancy," Emerson said with some effort. "She's dead." He sagged against the counter and looked as if he might crumple to the floor. Kathy stepped forward to support him and another member of staff appeared, Garry the concierge according to his badge. A man of few words apparently, he took in the situation, gathered Emerson up with little effort, pushed open a door marked *Guest Lounge*, and took him inside to a sofa. The receptionist, Deb, shouted down the hall to someone called Julie to bring a glass of water, and everyone crowded into the room while Garry expertly loosened Emerson's clothing and put a cushion under his head.

"And you are?" Deb turned to Kathy, who explained what had happened as Emerson began to show signs of life, sitting up with a groan and accepting the water that Julie, a plump black woman in a cook's apron, had brought in. It took several disbelieving questions before they all fell silent and stared in horror at Emerson. Finally Toby, sitting down beside him, put a hand on his shoulder and said, "This is absolutely appalling. My dear fellow, I don't know what to say. Such a fine woman. And in *Sloane Street?*"

He looked around at them all, shaking their heads in agreement, and Kathy felt as an almost tangible thing the wave of sympathy that flowed to Emerson, and beneath it something else, a sense of collective shame that such a thing should happen to a guest of theirs.

"We shall do everything we can to help, rely on that," Toby, who appeared to be in charge, went on. "You must be in total shock."

"A cup of tea," Julie suggested.

"No," Toby corrected her, "brandy. Garry, if you will."

Garry grunted and left the room for a moment, returning with a brimming glass which he handed carefully to Emerson, who hesitated, then nodded and took a sip. He coughed and mumbled, "I think we may have seen him, the man who did it."

"What?"

"It just occurred to me as I was waking up. When we were at the flower show we noticed a man who seemed to be watching us. We joked about it, that he was an admirer, stalking Nancy. Perhaps he was. It just struck me that he looked like the man the bus driver described. Look, I took a picture."

He pulled the little camera out of his pocket and switched it on, showing the last image to Toby, who studied it and passed it around the circle to Kathy. It certainly did look very like the bus driver's description.

"But that would be very strange," Deb objected. "I mean, you can't just wander in off the street to the Chelsea Flower Show. You have to book months in advance. We tried to get a ticket for a guest last week and it was impossible. So you're saying someone planned to go there ages ago, and when he got there picked another visitor at random and followed them out into the street?"

"Random," Julie said, rubbing her hands on her apron. "You can't fathom some people's minds."

"I'd like to get copies made of this picture, Mr. Merckle," Kathy said, "and I'd also like to take a look in Nancy's room with you, if you feel up to it."

"Of course. I'll finish this later if you don't mind." He gave Toby the brandy and struggled to his feet. They went out into the hall, where Deb handed over the keys to Nancy and Emerson's rooms, and Kathy and Emerson climbed the stairs, four full flights, to the top of the building. Emerson was gasping for breath by the time they got to Nancy's room, and sat on the edge of the bed for a while to recover.

"I told Nancy . . . we should have stayed . . . at the Hilton."

Kathy looked around the room. Homely would have been a kind description, shabby more accurate, the furnishings looking as tired as Emerson, like the relics of a Victorian family's house sale.

"Bit rough?" she said.

"Oh, splendid view, but those stairs . . . You didn't meet the porter. He has an artificial leg. He hauled our bags all the way up. And what is it with the English and plumbing?" His shoulders sagged.

"I'm sorry. Would you rather do this another time?"

"No, no, go ahead. What are you looking for, her drug stash?"

Kathy gave a little smile and opened the wardrobe. "So there's no possibility that Nancy knew this man?"

"Absolutely not. Oh God, how am I going to tell her family? She has sons in California and Oregon, and a sister in Cape Cod, cousins, grandchildren . . ."

"We'll do everything we can, and of course the American Embassy will want to help you with arrangements."

"Oh yes, I suppose so."

"There will have to be a post-mortem, and a report to the coroner. I'll keep you informed."

There was nothing in the least remarkable about Nancy Haynes' belongings, their very ordinariness a painful reproach. She had an account with the Citizens Bank in Boston, was reading Anita Shreve's latest novel, taking blood pressure and antihistamine tablets, and had an address book in which the only UK contact was someone called McKellar in Angus, Scotland.

"A distant cousin she made contact with. Like I told you, she wanted to check out her family roots. There should be some family photos she brought to show them."

Kathy found the pouch in the lid of Nancy's suitcase, containing a wad of pictures of children, family gatherings, studio portraits and some older black and white images of smiling forebears.

"They'll blame me, you know." Emerson sighed, staring at one of the photos of a family group.

"Of course not. There was nothing you could do."

"All the same, they'll think I should have protected her. Maybe if I'd tried harder to get a cab, or figured out how to pay for the bus . . ."

"You can't look at it that way. Was she well off?"

"She owns a valuable house in a good area of Boston, but she was short of cash. Net income last year was thirty-seven thousand dollars. I still do her tax returns. She invested unwisely a couple of years ago against my advice and her savings took a whack. But she was still adamant that we come on this trip."

Kathy got details of next of kin and returned downstairs.Toby was waiting for her in the hall, a determined set to his mouth. He stepped forward.

"Look, I didn't introduce us properly. I'm Toby Beaumont, the owner of the hotel, and behind the counter is Deb Collins, our manager and receptionist and mainstay of the operation. We were just discussing . . . it's hard not to feel a personal involvement with something like this. Of course you have hundreds of terrible cases to deal with, but this is so . . . intolerably unfair. What I'm trying to say is that we would like you to give us your personal assurance that Nancy's death will be pursued to the very utmost of the police capacities."

"Yes, I can assure you of that, Mr. Beaumont. We will do everything we can to solve this case."

"Right," he said doubtfully. "Thank you. Well, if there's anything we can do, you must let us know."

"Mr. Merckle has taken one of the pills the doctor gave him and is lying down for a while. He was supposed to be going on to Scotland tomorrow, but I think he may want to remain in London for a few more days. Can he stay here?"

"Of course, as long as he likes."

He didn't have to consult the computer. Business must be quiet, Kathy thought.

"I'm going to arrange for someone from Victim Support to contact him, and see what help they can give. Here's my card, and if anything occurs to you please get in touch."

"Yes, yes." Beaumont looked as if he wanted to say more, but then sagged as if defeated by it all, leaning more heavily on his stick. "The bastard was drugged to his eyeballs, I suppose. It's a shameful business."

KATHY RETURNED TO THE offices in Queen Anne's Gate, where the team led by Detective Chief Inspector David Brock was based. The Queen Anne's Gate annex was a few blocks north of the main buildings of New Scotland Yard, and unlike the modern headquarters was old, a hundred years older than Chelsea Mansions. The original terrace of townhouses had been converted into offices by openings punched through their party walls, so that the rooms were connected by a confusing maze of corridors and staircases. Which made the new critical incident command and control suite recently set up in one of the larger rooms look incongruous, with all those big touchscreen displays and computers supporting the latest HOLMES 2 suite for processing large volumes of information from major incidents. At first Brock had tried to ignore it, but of late he'd become enthusiastic, thanks mainly to Zack, the civilian operator who came with the machines and who made it all seem simple. Brock and Zack were there when Kathy arrived, along with most of the other people in the building, staring at a scene being played out in slow motion on the largest screen: a stream of pedestrians walking along a street, a red double-decker bus approaching. As they watched, someone drew their breath sharply, others shook their heads.

Kathy, standing behind them, said, "That's exactly how the bus driver described it."

Brock looked back over his shoulder at her. "The camera is above a doorway thirty yards beyond the scene. Here he comes . . ."

Kathy watched the tall dark-haired man emerge from the group by the bus and run past, below the camera.

"It's the man who was following them at the flower show," she said. "The woman's companion, Emerson Merckle, took a picture of him there." She handed Emerson's camera to Zack.

"Okay, now here's the interesting thing," Brock went on. "There's another camera at the bus stop toward Pont Street, a hundred yards further on."

Zack changed the picture, pedestrians walking past a bus stop.

"Nothing," Brock said. "He doesn't show up. There are no side streets. Where did he disappear to? Let's go take a look."

As they reached the front door Brock's secretary Dot caught them.

"The Press Bureau are after you, Brock," she said. "They need to see you as soon as possible, they say. So does Commander Sharpe. The American Embassy has been on to the Home Office."

"We'll be back in an hour. I'll ring them."

When they reached the car Brock said, "Let's make it quick, Kathy."

She switched on the lights and sped out into the London traffic, briefing him on the way about Emerson Merckle's account. When she had finished he took out his phone and started making calls. He folded it away as she turned into Sloane Street and came to a stop in front of the crime scene cordon.

A uniformed woman was setting up signs appealing for witnesses, and another was standing at the curb with a clipboard, speaking to a cluster of passersby. Other officers were door-knocking along the street. Brock spoke to the woman with the clipboard, then he and Kathy began to walk slowly in the direction the man had taken, toward the first camera, then on up the street to the second. There were no side lanes or obvious ways out.

There was a fenced park on the other side of Sloane Street occupying the center of Cadogan Place. Kathy looked at it and said, "He could have crossed the street."

"Yes, but he'd have been picked up by the second camera, unless he climbed over the railings and ran into the park. He'd have been pretty conspicuous doing that, but no one has mentioned seeing it." They stared across at the railings, shoulder height, with spiked tops like small spears.

There was one building between the cameras that was shrouded in scaffolding and plastic sheeting, with a builder's skip on the footpath, and they checked it carefully, but like all the others along the street its front door was firmly shut. A taxi drove slowly past and Brock took out his phone and called Zack. After a moment he snapped it shut again and shook his head. "No, there are no taxis on the CCTV footage, and all the traffic behind the bus was brought to a halt when it happened."

Brock's phone rang and he answered it as they walked back to their car. Kathy watched the frown, the scratching at his cropped white hair and beard as he listened, classic signs of Brock's impatience. "I really think that's premature, sir," he said, then fell silent as the caller gave him an earful. "Right you are," he said finally, and rang off.

He sighed. "The nation is on trial, the Met is on trial, we are on trial."

They climbed in, Kathy started the car, then paused. "Suppose someone was waiting up there, between the cameras, to pick him up."

"There's no parking. They'd be moved on."

"A builder's van? Or a motorbike, on the pavement behind the skip?" She started the flashing lights and took off.

Brock called Zack again, listened, then closed the phone with a thoughtful glance at Kathy. "The last vehicle to pass the second camera was a motorbike with two riders. Only it didn't appear on the first camera immediately before the assault."

"So it was waiting there, somewhere in between."

Brock nodded. "Zack's checking back to earlier footage to see how long before it came through the first camera."

"An accomplice."

"Two of them," Brock growled. "It doesn't make any sense."

WHEN THEY GOT TO the rear entrance of New Scotland Yard, Kathy assumed she was dropping Brock off, but he said, "They want you too, Kathy."

"Really? Why?"

He shrugged and she gave her keys to one of the men at the barrier and followed him inside, where they passed through the security check and took the lift up to Commander Sharpe's office on the sixth floor.

He looked older than she remembered from the last time she'd seen him, Kathy thought, as if the job was draining the color out of him. Probably he didn't have long to go before retirement. She wondered if Brock might be in line for the job if that happened, but then dismissed the idea; he'd loathe it.

Sharpe spoke briskly, outlining the pressure that was already building around them, then listened to a short briefing from Brock.

"So what are the alternatives?" Sharpe asked. "Terrorists? She was American after all."

Brock shook his head. "We've been in touch with Counter Terrorism Command, but she seems a very unlikely target, one among hundreds of thousands of tourists."

"Perhaps that's the point. A random victim, no American is safe, that kind of thing."

"And yet she doesn't seem to be entirely random." Brock went over the problem of access to the Chelsea Flower Show. "If that was the same man."

"What then?"

"It's too early to say, but if she was deliberately targeted we'd have to consider something relating to her home circumstances. Might she or her family be involved in something problematic in the States?"

"Ah." Kathy saw Sharpe's face brighten. He liked that idea. "And they decided to sort it out over here, well away from home. Was she wealthy?"

"Not according to her companion, Emerson Merckle, who's also her accountant," Kathy said. "She made some bad investments a couple of years ago."

"What's he like? Maybe he's been ripping her off and thought he'd get found out."

"There are a few things we should get the FBI to check on for us," Brock suggested quickly. It was always a worry when Sharpe wanted to play at detective. "But I really don't think a domestic angle is something we can even hint at in public. Not without evidence. Let's keep it simple."

"Yes, yes. I've been talking to the Press Bureau about that, and they're anxious for us to hold a press conference immediately to contain rumors. Let's get Marilyn in."

Marilyn was the senior media strategist with the MPS Press Bureau, and a woman of swift and decisive opinions. She came in and eyed Brock and Kathy for a moment, then nodded.

"Yes, just you two."

Brock said, "Wouldn't a senior figure, an AC, or Commander Sharpe, lend weight?"

She shook her head. "At this stage it would smack of panic. We're treating this as a highly professional but essentially routine response, right?"

Sharpe nodded.

"Do you really need me?" Kathy said.

"Absolutely. Bad news comes best from an attractive young woman." She gave Kathy a humorless smile that might have been ironic or sarcastic. "Brock, you first, with an outline of the facts and the police response. Rigorous, dedicated, no stone unturned. *Gravitas.* For Christ's sake nothing about Americans being safer in London than Boston, or Chelsea crime statistics or anything like that—it sounds defensive. You, Kathy, the human side—sympathy for the family, appeal for support from the public. Brief response to questions. We'll plant a final one for you to end on a positive note."

THREE

THE FOLLOWING MORNING A young man sat in a café in Edgeware Road reading a newspaper report of the murder in Sloane Street. At that moment a TV mounted up in the corner of the room began showing highlights of the police press conference on the same subject. He watched with a particular intensity as first Brock and then Kathy spoke to the camera. The waitress, approaching him with his order of bacon and eggs, put him in his late twenties. He had a rather serious, studious air about him with the glasses and the way he rubbed his jaw, studying the screen. Tall, dark, quite nice, but not her type.

"Fancy her then, do you?" she asked, thumping the plate down in front of him.

"Sorry?" The news moved on to something else and he turned his attention to her.

"The blonde cop. Reckon she's attractive?"

"Oh . . . yeah, I guess so."

"American, are you?"

"Something like that."

"They always put a blonde on to tell bad news."

"I hadn't thought about it, but you're probably right."

"I like the other one, with the beard."

"He's way too old for you."

"Yeah, but he's got a twinkle in his eye, don't you reckon?"

The man frowned, as if he found the idea mildly disturbing.

"Anyway, I'll let you eat your breakfast."

After he'd finished, he walked down to Marble Arch and crossed into Hyde Park. It was a fine May day, a cool breeze sending puffy white clouds scudding across a pale blue sky, and as he made his way deeper into the park, the grass as high as his knees, it seemed as if he might be far away in the countryside. Then he was crossing the broad path of Rotten Row, its sandy surface stamped with horses' hooves, and was plunged back into the city, making his way across Knightsbridge into Sloane Street before turning off into the side streets to reach the relative stillness of Cunningham Place.

A bell on the front door tinkled as he stepped inside, and a mature, rather intimidating-looking woman straightened up from a computer behind the counter and gave him the once-over.

"Good morning," she said.

"Good morning. I wonder if you have a room?"

"I'm afraid not. We're full."

"Oh."

"Four-oh-two's free." The voice came from behind the woman, and a man, previously hidden, appeared around her shoulder and peered at the stranger through darkened round glasses. "Canadian?"

"That's right."

"Yes, I can usually tell the difference."

"But four-oh-two . . ." the woman began to object, then shrugged. "Fourth floor. We don't have a lift, I'm afraid, but you're young and fit. How long for?"

"I'm not sure. A week? Maybe more. What's the rate?"

The two behind the desk had a brief whispered conversation before the woman offered him a price. It seemed very reasonable.

"Fine."

The man with the dark glasses suddenly leaned across the desk and thrust out his hand. "Toby Beaumont, proprietor, and this is Deb."

"John, John Greenslade."

"How old are you, John?" Toby asked.

"Twenty-eight," the man replied, a little puzzled.

"Ah yes." Toby nodded, as if something significant had been confirmed. "Bags?"

"I've been staying somewhere else, but this is the area I wanted. I'll bring them over later."

HE RETURNED IN A cab toward noon. As he made his way to the front steps he stopped for a moment to examine a large black limousine parked at the curb. It was a Maybach 62 Zeppelin, very new by the look of it. He'd never seen one before.

Deb introduced the concierge, Garry, saying he would be delighted to help with restaurant bookings, theater tickets and anything else John might need during his visit, although Garry, who avoided his eyes and said nothing, didn't give an immediate impression of delight. She also called Jacko, the porter, to carry John's suitcase up to his room, but when he saw how Jacko dragged his left leg John said he'd manage just fine himself.

He liked the room, a bit stuffy under the roof and probably unbearable on a hot day, but with a great view out over the square. He opened the window and the door to let in some air and began to unpack. The wardrobe door creaked as he hung his suit and a couple of shirts on mismatched wooden hangers, then stuffed his other things in the chest of drawers before sitting by the window and powering up his laptop. He checked his emails, then got into Google and looked up Maybach. The list price for a new 62 Zeppelin was 473,200 euros. He gave a little whistle.

Someone coughed. He looked around and saw an elderly man with his arm in a sling standing at the door.

"Oh, sorry," the man said. "I heard someone in here and I thought . . . well, I don't know what I thought." He had an American accent—New England, John judged, and watched as the man turned and went off down the stairs. But when John looked out of the window he didn't see him leave the building by the front steps below.

After ten minutes he locked the door of his room and went down. He spied the American in the guests' sitting room, reading a morning paper, and went in.

"Hi," he said.

The American looked up as if he'd never seen John before.

"We met upstairs just now," John explained, and they shook hands and introduced themselves.

"I'm sorry," Emerson said, "I shouldn't have interrupted you. I was a little confused. I knew the last person who had that room, you see."

John sat down beside him. "Was that the lady I read about?" He nodded at the paper Emerson was reading, folded to the report of Nancy's death: BIZARRE MURDER OF AMERICAN TOURIST.

Emerson nodded with a sigh.

"I'm really sorry about your friend," John said. "It must be terrible for you."

"Yeah. I still can't get my head around it. I woke up and thought, oh, it's a nice day, and then bang, it hit me."

He suddenly looked over John's shoulder and bit his lip. "Uh-oh."

John turned and saw the blonde police inspector outside in the lobby talking to Deb. She wasn't wearing the dark suit she'd had on TV, but a light shirt and pants, and she looked faintly flushed, as if she'd been running. Her features were rather lean, tending almost to severe, he thought, and he guessed that she didn't eat enough. Deb said something and the cop turned and came into the sitting room, smiling at Emerson, who gave a cautious smile in return and began to struggle out of his chair.

"Don't get up," she said. "I'll sit here."

John got to his feet. "I guess you two need to talk. I'll see you later, Emerson." He turned to the cop. "Hi, I'm John."

She nodded, making a mental note, he guessed.

KATHY SAT DOWN BESIDE Emerson, seeing the newspaper report by his side. "How are you today?"

"The shoulder's aching a bit, but the doc said that would happen. I've got painkillers."

"Have Victim Support been in touch?"

"Oh yes, a nice lady called in this morning. We had a chat."

"Good."

"And two people from the US Embassy."

"Uh-huh."

"And Nancy's son in California phoned to say he's flying out here right away to help me. I told him not to, but he insisted." He took a deep breath. "And about twenty reporters and photographers stopped by. The colonel wanted to chase them away, but they just needed a picture and a few words about Nancy, so I gave them that and they left."

"The colonel?"

"The hotel owner, Toby Beaumont. Ex-army, as if you couldn't guess. We heard one of the other staff call him 'Colonel,' so Nancy . . ."

He stopped and swallowed, then took a sip of water from the glass at his elbow and continued. "Toby wants to organize a memorial service for Nancy in the little church on the other side of the square. I've told him it isn't necessary, but he's determined. He says people want to do something to show how they feel."

"Do you want me to dissuade him?"

Emerson thought about it, then shook his head. "No, I guess it's okay. It's kind of him. He's talking about Sunday, after the morning service. I don't think there will be many people there."

"Right." Kathy hesitated, then said, "You know Nancy's family pretty well then?"

"Sure, I've known them for, oh, thirty years or more. I used to play golf with her husband, she and my wife were best friends, and I've watched their children grow up and leave home."

"I have to ask this. Is there any possibility, do you think, that there could be a domestic reason of some kind for Nancy to be killed? Something to do with her life back home?"

"Oh, you mean the mafia cousins in Las Vegas, and the huge life insurance the boys just took out on their mother?" He gave Kathy a weak smile. "You know, I did have that thought too, for a very brief moment. I guess we all watch too much TV. But it's just too ridiculous. Nancy is the last person on earth I could imagine this kind of thing happening to."

"Fine. I had to ask."

"Sure."

"Do you happen to know who will be the beneficiaries of her estate?"

He sighed, as if reluctant to go into it. "I do, as a matter of fact. A couple of years ago she asked me to act as one of her executors, and she asked my opinion about leaving specific small sums to her grandchildren and sister. Her two sons would be the principal beneficiaries, sharing her main asset, the house."

"How much is that worth?"

"Probably five million plus."

Kathy made a note of the name and address of Nancy's solicitor, thanked Emerson and got up to go.

In the hallway she saw the man who'd been talking to him earlier. He looked up from the leaflet for the London Eye that he was reading and said, "Hi again. I saw you on TV. Terrible business."

"You're staying here?"

"That's right."

"And you're American too?"

"Canadian. Look, I guess everybody says this, but I'd really like to help, if I can."

She nodded and showed him a copy of the photo from Emerson's camera. "You haven't seen anyone like this hanging around, have you?"

"Sorry, I've only just arrived. But I'll certainly keep my eyes open."

"Just so long as you don't try to tackle him if you do see him."

"No, I'd give you a call, I guess. If I had your contact details."

Kathy gave him her card. He seemed pleasant, but there was something odd about his manner, the rather intense way he looked at her. "What was your name again?"

"John, John Greenslade, from Montreal."

FOUR

WHEN KATHY GOT BACK to Queen Anne's Gate she again found Brock with Zack and another analyst in the new computer suite, heads down, checking maps.

"We've been tracking the motorbike on CCTV cameras. They headed north, Park Lane, Edgeware Road, then east to Camden Town, where we lost them." Brock took Kathy over to a screen with an enlarged map and pointed out the route.

"So far, none of the camera sightings we've got give us a clear view of the bike's number. We were tracking a yellow bike, possibly a Kawasaki Ninja, with two riders, and it took a while to see what happened."

Zack typed in a command and a film began to play.

"This is on the A503 heading north out of Camden."

Kathy said, "He's dropped the pillion passenger."

"Yes, we think somewhere near Camden Town tube station. The bike continues north with the single rider through Finsbury Park to Seven Sisters, where we lose him again. We're pretty sure he's ended up somewhere near by."

"Tottenham Green."

"Looks like it."

"So what do we do now?"

Brock said, "They must have been in touch by phone down in Chelsea, so they knew how to meet up after the murder. Then after they reached their destinations, in Camden Town and Tottenham Green, odds are they'd have been on their phones again, don't you think? So if we could trace two mobile numbers that are used in those areas at the critical times, we'd have them."

"Big job," Zack said.

"That's what computers are for," Brock replied. "And I've got a stack of paperwork on my desk. That's what humans are for."

It was late afternoon when Zack found it. A mobile phone had made a call from Chelsea soon after the time that Nancy and Emerson had left the flower show and begun walking up Sloane Street, and then fifty-two minutes later, shortly after the last sighting of the single rider, from Tottenham Green in North London. The number was registered to Captain Marvel.

"A comedian," Brock said.

"Yeah," Zack agreed, "but we know where he lives. The Quarry Estate. That's where the call came from."

Brock put a call through to CID at Haringey Borough Operational Command, covering Tottenham Green. It didn't take long to get an answer.

"Sounds like Danny Yilmaz," the inspector at the other end said. "He's used the name before. Drug courier, get-away driver. Murder's a bit out of his league though. Want us to pick him up?"

"Wait till we get there," Brock said. He grabbed his coat and turned to Kathy. "Come on."

AS WELL AS KATHY, Brock took Mickey Schaeffer, a detective sergeant who had recently joined the team at Queen Anne's Gate. He had an excellent record and seemed tough and intelligent, but Brock hadn't yet watched him in action and wanted to see how he'd perform. He left Kathy at the Tottenham police station to liaise with their inspector and went on with Mickey and two cars of local men to the Quarry Estate, a collection of three-story walk-up housing blocks spread out around the base of a pair of towers. Danny Yilmaz lived on the top floor of one of the walk-ups. There was no sign of a yellow motorbike in the parking areas outside, and they went up the stairs to Yilmaz's front door. Before ringing the bell, Mickey crouched at the letter flap and peered in. They heard the faint sound of a cough, the flush of a toilet, and Brock nodded to the copper beside him, who rang the bell. There was silence.

"Come on, Danny," Mickey called loudly through the slot. "It's the police. Open the door, please."

He repeated this, then nodded to a uniformed man who raised the ram he was carrying and swung it against the door, which burst open with a crash.

A cigarette was burning in an ashtray on the floor beside a rumpled sleeping bag. There was the sound of something breaking—crockery clattering to the floor. In the kitchenette at the back they were presented with the spectacle of a man's rear end struggling to squeeze through the narrow window above the sink, his flailing legs kicking plates off the draining board.

"Stupid bugger," Mickey roared. He grabbed the legs and heaved. For a moment there was no movement, but then the man shot backward into the room. He gave a shriek as his face connected with the window frame. Blood spurted from his nose as Brock caught him and they lowered him, howling, to the floor. Brock wiped a hand across his face, tasting the metallic tang of blood in his mouth.

Mickey said. "You all right, Chief?"

"Yes, I'm fine." Brock went over to the sink and ran the tap while one of the local cops behind him said, "This isn't Danny Yilmaz."

28

According to the Ugandan driver's license they found in the man's pocket, he was Peter Namono, a resident of Kampala, though he seemed unable or unwilling to confirm this as he sat moaning on the floor, clutching his bloody nose. One of the locals took a call on his radio and turned to Brock. "Our lads have picked up Danny Yilmaz. They spotted his bike outside the Haringey Sport and Social Club. They're taking him to the station."

Brock dabbed at the bloodstain on his shirt with a grubby cloth. "I'm getting too old for this. Next time I'll leave the exciting bits to you lot."

They all laughed.

DANNY YILMAZ WAS WAITING in an interview room when they arrived at Tottenham police station.

Kathy conducted the interview with one of the local detectives while Brock watched on a screen in an adjoining room. Danny was small, wiry, dark, with curly black hair that covered much of his face, which appeared prematurely aged. He seemed to be mystified by why he was there. Kathy cautioned him and asked him if he had given a lift to a man in Sloane Street the previous day. Sure, Danny said, it was all perfectly straightforward. He had his own courier services company, Shazam Limited.

"Shazam," Kathy repeated.

"Like in Captain Marvel, yeah?"

"Go on."

"This bloke hired me to give him a lift. Said he'd need me to be available for the whole day Thursday, from Chelsea, to run him around. I spent the day hanging out down by the river, waiting for him to call, dead boring, but he'd paid in advance. Then, about four he gives me a ring, tells me where to wait for him on Sloane Street, and to call him when I get there. Soon after he comes running out of nowhere, hops on the bike and tells me to get going, up to Camden Town tube station, where I drop him off. That was it."

"What did he look like?"

"Couldn't tell you. He had his own helmet in his backpack. I'd brought one for him, but he didn't need it."

"What else?"

"Um, dark gray shirt, jeans . . . oh, and gloves. He was wearing black gloves."

"But you'd seen him before, when he hired you, gave you the money."

"No, no, that was somebody else."

Something changed in Danny's posture and appearance. His expression of helpfulness became brighter.

"Who?"

"No idea. I only spoke to him on the phone. He said he had a friend coming to London, needed someone to drive him around for the day. Offered me twice my going rate, so I wasn't complaining."

"What name did he give you?"

"He didn't."

"How did he know about you?"

Danny looked mildly offended. "I have a website, don't I?"

"So you made yourself available for a whole day on the strength of a phone call from a man who didn't even tell you his name?"

"He paid in advance, didn't he? What else could I do? The cash came round by courier that afternoon."

"When did this happen?" Kathy asked.

Danny ruffled his hair, pondering. "Monday? Tuesday? Tuesday, I think."

"Two days before the job."

"Yes, that'd be about right."

"And you had a contact number for this client?"

"Yes, sure!" All eagerness, Danny pulled a phone out of his pocket and handed it over.

"This is bullshit." The CID detective at Kathy's side glared at Danny. "You'd better wipe that smile off your face and start telling us the truth, Danny. Who set this up? Was it your cousin Barbaros?"

"No, no, it's nothing to do with Barbaros. What's this all about anyway? What's this guy supposed to have done?"

The two police stared at him for a moment, incredulous, then Kathy spread some photographs of Sloane Street out on the table. "Whereabouts did you wait for the man yesterday afternoon?"

Danny looked at the pictures, then pointed at one, builder's scaffolding erected on the footpath. "That would be the place, I reckon. I pulled in between the poles."

"And how long were you waiting there?"

"Ten, fifteen minutes?"

"So you witnessed the murder."

"Murder?"

Kathy leaned across the table. "Not a hundred yards from where you were waiting, your mystery client grabbed a woman and threw her under a bus. *That* murder."

Danny looked shocked. "You're kidding me."

"And then he ran up to you and jumped on the back of your bike and you drove him away from the scene, making yourself an accessory to murder. *That* murder, Danny, the murder that's going to put you inside for twenty years."

Danny's jaw dropped, he shook his head. "Swear to God . . . I had my helmet on, didn't hear or see nothing."

The CID man gave a snort of disgust and half turned away, as if he couldn't stand much more of this.

Kathy said, "Who's the man in your flat?"

Danny shrugged. "Dunno. Friend of mine asked me to let him

sleep on my floor for a couple of days, till he gets a lift up north."

"What do you know about him?"

"Nothing. He doesn't say much. I reckon he's African, the way he talks."

"He doesn't seem to have any papers."

Danny rolled his eyes. "I don't know nothing about that."

"Give me the name and address of this friend."

He wrote it down and Kathy took this and his phone out to Brock. "What do you think?"

"He's giving us a highly edited version. He's scared, don't you think? More scared of his client than of us. Keep at him, Kathy. Charge him as an accessory to murder, that should focus his mind. And meanwhile, let's hope we can lift some of his client's DNA from his bike."

On their way back to the interview room the CID man told Kathy about Danny's cousin Barbaros Kaya, a more serious villain with a web of local connections. "I reckon he's got to be involved."

They charged Danny under the Accessories and Abettors Act and explained that, under the terms of the act, an accessory is liable to the same penalty as the perpetrator.

"Murder, Danny, that's what you're up for."

Danny demanded a brief.

The solicitor came quickly, almost as if he'd been waiting for the call. He had a short conversation with his client and they resumed the interview, going back over the ground, point by point, detail by detail.

"You said the man on the phone was arranging this for a friend *coming to London*," Kathy said. "Coming from where?"

"Dunno, he didn't say."

"What were his exact words?"

He couldn't remember, not really. The money? In used twenties, gone now to pay off some debts. The bag they were in? Who knows.

Four weary hours later Kathy brought the interview to an end. Danny had made only one slip, when Kathy pressed him about his passenger's exact words. Hard to say, Danny said, they were hard to make out, what with the helmet and his accent. He blinked as the word came out, realizing his mistake. What accent? Kathy pressed. British? Foreign? Danny shook his head but she detected a flicker on the second option. Foreign then, she insisted, and saw him go a little paler. What kind of foreign? But he blustered. He really couldn't say, it might have been Irish, Welsh, Pakistani, he had no idea.

He had given them nothing more of substance. The client's number on his phone proved to be unlisted and inoperative. Peter Namono was unknown to UK databases and there was no record of him entering the country. The local detectives were trying to trace the man who had arranged his stay with Danny Yilmaz and promised to talk to Danny's known friends and associates. Phone records for Danny and for Barbaros Kaya would be obtained. A team was checking CCTV cameras on all the stations of the Northern underground line serving Camden Town station.

LATER, TOWARD EIGHT, BACK at Queen Anne's Gate, Brock put his head around the door of Kathy's office.

"Time to go home," he said. "Fancy a drink?" The fact was that he couldn't get rid of the taste of that man's blood. He'd brushed his teeth and swallowed numerous cups of strong coffee, but it was still there, a faint noxious taint. Maybe Scotch would clear it.

The Two Chairmen at the end of the street was quiet when

they arrived, a couple of women on stools at the bar and a lone drinker in the far corner. Kathy sat at a table while Brock went to order, returning with a Scotch for himself and a glass of white wine for Kathy.

"Cheers." He felt the cleansing spirit burn down his throat and sank back into his chair with a sigh.

She wrinkled her nose in disgust.

"Wine no good?"

"Oh, it's fine, just what I needed. But I should have nailed Captain Marvel."

"Whoever he's protecting is a lot more scary than you or me, Kathy."

"It's frustrating." She looked up and noticed the single drinker in the far corner get to his feet and head toward the rear door. She had a brief glimpse of his face before he was gone and she frowned. He looked very like the Canadian from the hotel.

Brock, seeing her expression, said, "Had an idea?"

"No, I just . . . No, it's nothing."

Later, when she got home, still troubled by the thought of the man in the pub, she phoned the duty officer at headquarters and asked for a check on the Police National Computer and the Interpol databases. He rang back as she was reheating a Thai takeaway in her microwave. John Greenslade was not a name known to either system. She asked him to check the Home Office UK Border Agency. This time she did get a result. John Greenslade, a Canadian citizen with a Montreal address, had entered the country through Heathrow ten days previously as a visitor. His occupation was given as "university professor."

Restless now, she played with her meal without really tasting it and turned on her laptop. There was only one email of interest, from Guy, a short message that looked as if it had been written in a hurry.

Hi Kathy,

Hope all goes well with you. I'm okay, but the job has gone pear-shaped. Work has stopped, and they're moving me on, to Shanghai would you believe, where we've got a big project on the go. Sorry about the trip. Maybe we can meet up on the Bund. I think of you a lot. Stay safe.

Love,
Guy

She looked up at the envelope that had been sitting on her mantelpiece for quite a while now, containing a first-class air ticket to Dubai, and felt sad, thinking of lost opportunities and roads not taken. Then she roused herself and got up to take a shower. It would never have worked out with Guy anyway.

FIVE

ON SATURDAY MORNING JOHN Greenslade made his way down to breakfast in the dining room at the back of the hotel, overlooking a courtyard garden. He had learned from Deb that there were only seven guest rooms in the hotel, and three of those were occupied by semi-permanent residents: a young Australian woman lawyer, an elderly English woman who had been there since the hotel opened in 1996 and who was now rarely seen outside of her room, and a retired man originally from Nepal. Apart from Emerson Merckle and himself, the short-stay guests were two couples from Leeds, who came every year at this time for the flower show. They were in the dining room now, and gave him a cheery greeting. Once they picked up his accent they told him they'd done Canada, and described their trip there at some considerable length.

After breakfast he went back up to his room and worked on his laptop for a while. The BBC had a clip of the police press conference on Thursday night, and he downloaded this. After a while he got up and stood by the window overlooking the square. The Maybach had gone, its place taken by a red sports car. He peered down at it, trying to figure out what it was. A Ferrari Spider, perhaps.

Across the road he saw a figure sitting beneath the trees in the central gardens, and recognized Emerson's thatch of gray hair. He closed his laptop, picked up his keys and went out. At the front desk he asked Deb about the gardens and she explained that they were available for the use of guests by means of a key for the gate that the hotel could provide.

"Emerson's got it at the moment, John," she said.

"Oh, fine. I might go and say hello. It looks pretty nice over there."

As he went down the front steps he took a close look at the sports car. He was right, an F430 Spider, a beauty. He looked back up at the windows of the property next door, and saw an old woman glowering down at him from behind a curtain. John turned, crossed the street and pushed open the gate in the cast-iron railings.

Emerson didn't appear to have moved, hunched over something on his knees. As he got closer John saw that it was a pouch of photographs.

"Hi, Emerson," he called out, and the other man looked up, blinking to focus. "Am I interrupting?"

"What? Oh, no, John. Hello."

"It looked so pleasant in here. Private and secluded."

"Yes, it is."

"Are you sure I'm not intruding?"

"Not at all. Come and sit down."

John nodded at the photographs. "Nancy's?"

"Yes. She brought these with her. I was just . . . well, you know. I guess I'll have to give these back to her family, but I wanted to remember them."

"Is that her? She was an attractive woman, Emerson."

"Very." He said it with some feeling. "When she was younger she turned a few heads, I can tell you."

"Including yours, eh?"

Emerson smiled. "Well, we were both married then, to other people. But yes, I did admire her. And she was talented, very artistic. She painted in watercolors—New England landscapes mainly. They were much sought after. She sold them through a local gallery. Look."

He showed John a photo of people at a fancy-dress party. "That's Nancy as a bird of paradise. She made the costume herself, and the mask. Isn't it beautiful?"

"Oh yes. And that's you as the pirate chief, eh?"

"That's right." Emerson gave another wistful smile. "She made the parrot on my shoulder. We had a good laugh about that. She had a great sense of humor." He frowned suddenly.

"Sorry."

"Not at all, it's important to remember. She got her artistic talent from her mother. There's one of them together . . . here."

He drew out one of the older black and white pictures.

"Her mother was a professional sculptor, using her maiden name, Maisy McKellar. Nancy had been hoping to make contact with the McKellars in Scotland on this trip. Before Maisy married Nancy's father, Ronald, she worked with William Gordon Huff in California. Have you heard of him?"

John shook his head.

"He's mainly known for his statues of characters from the Old West—Indians and pioneers, that kind of stuff. There's a picture of Maisy somewhere . . . here."

A couple, their hair and clothes obviously in the style of the 1930s, stood arm in arm in front of a long reflecting pool, with a monumental arch in the background.

"Art Deco," John said. "It looks very Hollywood, don't you think? And that's Maisy with Huff?"

"I'm not sure. I guess it could be."

"They look a glamorous couple." John pointed to another photo. "And those are Nancy's grandchildren?"

"Yes, seven at the last count. I wonder what their parents have told them. *Your grandmother was thrown under a bus*. It's obscene, isn't it?"

"It is."

"The police have no idea why he did it. I suppose he was doped up on ice or some damn thing." He shook his head sadly.

"I'm sorry," John said. "This is upsetting you."

"Well, maybe it helps me to talk about it. Apart from the police, the only people I know in this city are in that hotel. They're trying very hard to help, but they do seem kind of odd."

"Yes." John chuckled. "They are, aren't they?"

"You've heard about the memorial service idea?"

"Yes, Toby told me. I'll be there."

"That's kind of you. It'll help to see a friendly face."

"Well, I'll get moving. See you then."

NOT MUCH MORE THAN a mile away to the east, Kathy was working in her office. She'd started the morning with a brisk swim in the baths in Pimlico, looking forward to an active day and, hopefully, a breakthrough. But on her desk she found a heap of accumulated paperwork awaiting her urgent attention, and reluctantly she sat down and started working through it.

A response had come in from the FBI during the night. They had spoken to Nancy's solicitor and confirmed that her two sons were her principal beneficiaries. They had also determined that neither had a police record and a preliminary search of both men's business and financial affairs had revealed nothing unusual.

But something had been fatally special about Nancy Haynes. If Danny Yilmaz was to be believed, someone had begun to arrange her murder within a couple of days of her arrival in London. Nancy must have been observed during that time, her movements tracked.

Kathy sent a reply to America, asking for a check on Emerson Merckle and information on Nancy's financial records, then turned to the forensic reports on Nancy's body and clothing and Danny's Kawasaki. There had been dozens of fibers, fingerprints and DNA traces, all painstakingly listed, but so far no matches to anyone apart from Nancy, Emerson and Danny.

After a couple of hours scanning incoming reports, Kathy rubbed her eyes and got to her feet. She went out to see how the CCTV team was getting on, searching for sightings of the killer on the underground, and picked up a mood of resignation.

"There are fifty stations on the Northern Line," Zack said with a sigh. "Not to mention connections to the Victoria Line, the Piccadilly, Circle, Central, District . . ."

"I get the picture. How about his ticket? Could he have bought an Oyster card with a credit card?"

Zack nodded, thinking. "We could get the numbers of all the Oyster cards that went through the Camden Town ticket machines at that time on Thursday . . . Leave it with me."

Kathy moved on, checking progress, feeling impatient, then returned to her desk. Mickey Schaeffer was at Tottenham, Brock at headquarters, and she wanted to be out of the office. One of the reports in the pile in front of her was by an officer who had spoken to organizers at the Chelsea Flower Show, which seemed to raise more questions than it answered. How had that worked, exactly? If the man that Emerson had photographed at the show was really the killer, waiting for his moment, had he planned to kill Nancy there among the crowds, and then changed his mind when he realized that they'd noticed him? The more Kathy thought about it, the more odd it seemed, a strange combination of planning and improvisation. Where had the man come from? Would a native Londoner have done it like that? Would they have relied on someone like Danny Yilmaz to make an escape? And how had he got into the flower show?

This was the final day of the show, she remembered; she could go and see for herself. She pulled on her jacket and headed out.

The street in front of the entrance gates was jammed with visitors carrying sun hats, backpacks and handfuls of maps and tickets, queuing to get in. As they approached the gates she saw them stare at the police notices posted nearby, appealing for witnesses with pictures of Nancy and the unidentified man, and whisper among themselves.

Among them were a few army veterans resident at the Royal Chelsea Hospital, in whose grounds the flower show was held, wearing the scarlet coats and black caps of the Chelsea Pensioners. She spoke to one who gave her directions to the organizers' office. Inside, a brisk woman finished a phone call and showed Kathy to a table in a corner of the tent.

"Yes, I spoke to a detective yesterday, Inspector," she said. "He wanted a printout of the names of all the people who bought tickets for Thursday, but he balked a bit when I told him there were forty thousand of them. And I doubt it would help anyway. Thursday's tickets were sold out two months ago, so he probably didn't pre-book."

"Then how did he get a ticket?"

"Probably from a scalper at the gate. I'm told the going rate is as much as two hundred and fifty pounds at the moment. The detective did try to speak to one of them, but I don't know how much success he had."

There had been no mention of that in the officer's report. "Are there cameras at the gate?"

The woman shook her head. They discussed the security at the show and the information on volunteers held in the computer, until Kathy decided there was no more she could find out. She thanked the woman and left. Outside she stood for a while at the entrance, watching the visitors streaming through. She saw no one trying to sell tickets, and after a while she returned to Queen Anne's Gate.

A number of messages had come in while she was away. A situation report had arrived from Tottenham Green profiling known associates of Danny Yilmaz and other possible criminals in the area. There were quite a few of them, but so far no connections to Thursday's events had been established. Peter Namono was not known to the police in Uganda, and appeared to be an unauthorized migrant. Apparently he had been in touch with a refugee advisory service in South London.

The Home Office had forwarded a request from the American Embassy for an update on the case, with a cover note demanding urgent attention. And a preliminary report from the coroner's office had been delivered. The autopsy had been completed and blood and tissue tests carried out in record time. Nothing new had been revealed and it was proposed to release the body to the family for return to the United States on Monday. Kathy sensed an all-round official desire to move on, to see a rapid and tidy end to an embarrassing and incomprehensible affair.

SIX

TUCKED AWAY IN ONE corner of Cunningham Place was a small, rather plain brick church. Built eighty years before the square was laid out, its modest spire had once stood out among the fields and hedgerows of the western edge of London, but was now overshadowed by its neighboring housing blocks. On most Sundays its congregation amounted to barely a dozen elderly people, but today they emerged through the porch to find a small crowd assembling outside in the sunshine.

As the vicar shook the hand of the last parishioner, Toby Beaumont mounted the steps with his two employees, Garry the silent concierge and Jacko the limping bellboy, all dressed in suits and ties, and introduced them to the priest as the ushers for the memorial service. Garry was carrying a poster-sized photograph of Nancy's smiling face, enlarged from a snapshot Emerson had provided, and received permission to tie it to one of the porch columns. Deb, Julie the cook and Destiny the maid followed, carrying huge bunches of flowers, and disappeared inside.

Kathy stood in the background in the shade of one of the large plane trees of the central gardens, watching the gathering. A few looked as if they were residents of the square, setting aside their Sunday papers to show their respect or see what was going on; some were media, including a TV camera crew and van; and others, lone men in suits mainly, appeared to be there in an official capacity. Several of these were clustered around Emerson and she speculated on which might be from the American Embassy, or representing the British government. Then a newcomer arrived, breaking into that circle to introduce himself, and Kathy recognized him with a start, his glossy bulk and prominent silk pocket handkerchief bringing back uncomfortable memories. Nigel Hadden-Vane, Member of Parliament, had figured in a previous case of hers concerning the criminal family of Spider Roach. Hadden-Vane had been instrumental in destroying the careers of both another MP and a Special Branch officer with whom Kathy had been involved. She wondered why he was here. Was he someone important in the Home Office now, or the Foreign Office? She would have to check.

They were moving inside, and Kathy followed, into the cool dimness of the little church. The organ was playing something solemn and classical, Bach perhaps, and she accepted an order of service from Garry and took a seat in a pew toward the back. She noticed Hadden-Vane say something to Garry, gesturing to a space in one of the front pews, before sitting down next to Emerson.

It seemed as if the congregation was complete and the service might begin, the vicar moving to the center of the altar steps, when he paused and stared down the nave toward the doors, and heads turned to look. Two men were entering, both wearing black suits, white shirts and black ties. One was of middle height and age, with curling hair at the back of his balding head and a conspicuous large gold watch on his wrist. The other was younger and much larger, built like a bouncer, elbows out, head shaved. There was something slightly alien and chilling about the pair of them, and the church went very quiet, the rustle of papers fading away, as Garry got to his feet and led them to the vacant seats at the front.

The service was simple and dignified: a couple of hymns, a couple of readings, some words from the vicar and a short and moving eulogy from Emerson. Then they were moving out into the silent square and across the street to the gates of the central gardens, where Julie and Destiny were waiting with trays of champagne and canapés. Kathy wasn't alone in noticing that the two latecomers remained in their pew until the church had emptied, and then strode away down the street.

"Who were those two?" she heard a woman asking Toby, who was standing with Emerson, shaking hands.

"Our neighbors, my dear." Toby raised an eyebrow.

"Oh, the Russians!" the woman said. "So *that's* them."

Nigel Hadden-Vane was working the crowd, Kathy saw, or at least that part of it which looked important, nodding vigorously, gesturing with his champagne glass, mopping his flushed face with his blue pocket handkerchief.

"Hello again."

Kathy turned and saw John Greenslade standing beside her, watching her intently, as if he'd been studying her.

"Hello. I didn't see you there."

"Oh, I couldn't stay away—Toby would never have forgiven me. He's done them proud, hasn't he? He deserves a medal, but I guess he's already got plenty of those."

Kathy couldn't decide whether he was being genuinely appreciative or mildly sarcastic. It was hard to tell with him, his quiet voice seeming to leave itself open to different interpretations, as if testing her response.

"Yes, he seems to have organized it with military precision."

"Exactly." John broke into a warm smile, as if she'd said something witty. "The whole team was up at three this morning, getting all this ready. I heard them from the top floor—that's where my room is. I'm a light sleeper, I guess."

"Are you getting to see a bit of London?"

Another smile, as if he was really pleased by her interest. "Yes, actually. Let's see, I've been to Tate Modern, the National Portrait Gallery, the Courtauld . . ."

"How about the Two Chairmen?"

He looked at her blankly. "I don't think—"

"It's a pub in Westminster, at the end of Queen Anne's Gate."

He stared at her, his mouth open. "Ah. You did see me. I was afraid you might have. How embarrassing."

Kathy stared back, saying nothing.

"I . . . was intrigued," he said at last. "I've had a bit to do with the police in Montreal—nothing nefarious, you understand. At least they haven't managed to arrest me yet." His grin faded as he saw her stony expression. "Yes, well, anyway, I was curious, how things were over here. You gave me your card with the address, and I went to take a look. Kind of enigmatic, I thought, the building, for a police office. Anyway, I fancied a beer and stopped at the pub down the street, and then you walked in."

When she still said nothing he looked down at his feet and scuffed the gravel. "No, that's not quite the truth. At least, not the whole truth. There was another reason."

"And what was that?"

He looked up with a frown and met her eyes. He shrugged. "Well, you know."

"No, I don't."

"You. I was interested in you."

You cheeky bastard, she thought. For a moment he seemed rather young and vulnerable. How old was he? Twenty-eight, she remembered from the immigration record. He made her feel older than her years.

"Inspector!"

She pulled her eyes away and saw Emerson advancing toward her, his hand on the arm of another man.

"I'd like you to meet Nancy's son, Martin Haynes, who's flown over from California."

They shook hands, and Kathy repeated the phrase that always seemed inadequate: "I'm so sorry for your loss."

"Thank you. This all seems very unreal."

"Martin flew over last night. He didn't get much sleep," Emerson said, by way of explanation.

Martin went on as if he hadn't heard him. "A service in a strange little church and then a garden party. I'm not sure what Mom would have made of it all."

"She would certainly have appreciated the flowers," Emerson said.

"Any progress with the case?" Martin asked.

"We're pursuing a promising lead, and we'll just have to see where it takes us. I'm confident we'll find the culprit."

"Are you?" Martin stifled a yawn.

"It looks as if the coroner will release Nancy's body tomorrow. I'll confirm it as soon as I can."

Emerson nodded. "The embassy are helping us with arrangements."

They parted and Kathy began to make her way out to the street. There was no sign of John Greenslade. On the way back to the tube station she passed Chelsea Mansions and took a quick glance up at the windows at the top of the hotel.

SEVEN

SHORTLY BEFORE TEN THAT Sunday night the front door in the central porch of Chelsea Mansions opened and a man emerged. He stood for a moment beneath the light, taking a deep breath of the warm evening air as if relieved to be outside. In his right hand he held a long, unlit cigar, which he gently rolled between his fingers. After a moment he looked carefully up and down the street, then descended the steps and crossed to the gate in the fence around the gardens. He transferred the cigar to his left hand, felt in his trouser pocket for the key with his right, and opened the gate. The darkness closed around him, the streetlights barely penetrating the thick foliage of the gardens as he followed the gravel path to the bench beneath the oak tree in the center, where he sat down. Searching again in his pockets he found the little guillotine and prepared the cigar, a Cuban Montecristo, which Shaka forbade him to smoke in the house. His lighter flared in the darkness, blinding him as he drew in the first breath of exotic smoke. He sat back with a sigh. In the distance he could hear the murmur of traffic on Sloane Street and Brompton Road, but here in Cunningham Place nothing stirred.

And yet, there was something, the faint sound of music coming from one of the windows around the square. The tune, broken by the whisper and rustle of the trees, seemed very familiar, but at first he couldn't place it. What was it again? He strained for the notes until suddenly he had it—Mussorgsky, of course, *Pictures at an Exhibition*, his father's favorite, and suddenly he was back in the apartment on Moskovsky Prospekt, his father leaning intently over the gramophone, beating time with an outstretched finger. "You hear them, Mikhail? Can you see them in your mind? Two Jews, Samuel and Schmuÿle. One is rich and the other is poor. Can you tell which is which?"

He was so engrossed by this memory that it was a moment before he registered the presence of someone else in the gardens, a dark shadow gliding silently to his side.

"Hello, Mikhail," the figure murmured, taking a seat beside him.

"We have things to resolve," Mikhail said. "Let me tell you how it will be." He spoke for several minutes, relishing the moment, punctuating his words with gestures with his cigar, its tip glowing in the darkness. When he finished he waited for a reply.

There was silence for a long moment, and then the other said, "No, Mikhail. *This* is how it will be." He felt an arm embrace him, and he made to pull away, offended by this familiarity. Then he froze as his eye caught the gleam of a blade. With some incredulity he felt its tip press hard against his breast, then a sharp pain as it pierced his fine cashmere sweater and entered his chest, once, twice, three times. The cigar dropped from his fingers and he heard a voice in his head say, "Yes, Papa, of course I know which is the rich one."

BROCK JERKED AWAKE WITH the phone ringing. He was sprawled across the sofa, the table lamp still burning, the second glass—or was it the third?—of medicinal hot whiskey toddy half full at his elbow.

"You all right, sir?" the duty officer responded to his hoarse gurgle.

No, he wasn't all right. He'd been feeling rough all day and was beginning to wonder if it might be swine flu—he'd neglected to have his shot, despite Suzanne's urging. He sat up, trying to clear his head. The place looked a mess, papers, books, CD cases, shoes, cushions all over the place. He looked around hopelessly for a pen and paper. At times like this he told himself that he needed more of Suzanne's disciplined presence in his life.

"Chelsea, sir. Cunningham Place. Fatality."

"Yes, yes, so what?"

"You know about it?"

"'Course I bloody know about it. Nancy Haynes. What is this?"

"Not Nancy Haynes, sir. Mikhail Moszynski. Fatal stabbing. Called in forty minutes ago. Kensington and Chelsea BOCU are asking for you."

"Oh . . . right." A calm descended on him and he found a pen next to the whiskey glass. "Get a car out here to pick me up, will you? Tell me again."

Before he got to his feet to take a shower, Brock speed-dialed Kathy's mobile. It took a while for her to answer—she was in a cinema with her friend Nicole, she explained, a late-night screening of Pedro Almodovar's latest. "I'm on my way," she said.

THE PATROL CAR DROPPED Brock by the entrance to the gardens in Cunningham Place and he was immediately struck by the scene, the bright glow among the trees in the center of the garden, the flashing lights of emergency vehicles, windows in the surrounding buildings lit up with figures staring down at the activity, and the throb of a helicopter moving slowly overhead.

He gave his name and walked in along a route defined by tapes toward the spot where lights and screens were being set up. At the center of the activity the figure of a man sat slumped on the bench. At first glance he looked like an actor on a bright stage, pausing in the middle of his performance, but then the dark stain across his chest and left leg brought the reality home.

A detective Brock recognized from the borough command came to his side and they shook hands. "Hello again," the man said. "So this is Mikhail Moszynski."

The way he said it made Brock glance at him. "Should I know him?"

"Russian, he married Shaka Gibbons a couple of years ago. You know, the model?"

Brock didn't know.

"Resident of Chelsea Mansions," the detective went on, indicating the building through the trees. "He owns most of the building. Stepped outside at about nine fifty to smoke a cigar here in the gardens. Apparently Shaka won't have smoking in the house. At ten thirty his bodyguard came out with a torch to check on him and found the body."

"He had a bodyguard?"

"Name of Wayne Everett, calls himself Mr. Moszynski's security agent and driver, on contract from . . ." He held his notes up to the light. "Shere Security. His boss arrived soon after us. They're both inside the house now with Shaka. Everett says he only felt for a pulse then stepped away. Looks like three puncture wounds to the chest. No immediate sign of the weapon, but I reckon we'll have to wait till daylight to search the gardens properly."

Brock grunted his agreement. His head still felt full of cotton wool. "That's where the American woman, Nancy Haynes, was staying, of course, in the hotel at the end of the block."

"Yes. As soon as I realized that I thought I'd better get you in straight away. There hasn't been a single homicide in this borough in the three years I've been stationed here and now we've got two from the same building."

They made their way toward the gates, discussing the steps that had been taken so far, when Brock saw Kathy coming through the checkpoint. He introduced her to the CID man and then sneezed.

"You all right?" she asked, but he dismissed it with a wave of his hand and the detective told her quickly what had happened.

"Shaka Gibbons?" she said. "She's his wife? This'll be huge. We'd better get the Press Bureau on to this right away."

As if in confirmation, the uniformed constable stationed at the victim's front door told them that Ms. Gibbons' manager had just arrived and been admitted at Ms. Gibbons' insistence. As Brock and Kathy passed him to go inside, the constable tugged down his protective vest and straightened his tie, as if expecting the cameras at any second.

Wayne Everett, the bodyguard, was waiting in the hall inside, looking grim, his bulk overshadowed by an enormous chandelier suspended from the high ceiling overhead. Another man was behind him, one foot on the bottom step of a grand staircase at the far end of the hall, murmuring into a phone. He now wheeled around and strode in front of Everett to face the detectives. He was Peter Shere, he explained, handing them business cards, head of Shere Security and responsible for all aspects of Mr. Moszynski's safety and that of his family while in the UK.

"Clearly there's been a shocking breach," he said angrily, and Kathy saw Everett behind him lower his shaved head a little further. "My immediate concern is to ensure the ongoing security of the family. Later we'll be carrying out a post-incident review. In the meantime, it goes without saying that we'll give you our fullest cooperation."

Brock pulled a wad of tissues out of his coat pocket and noisily blew his nose. "Do you have any reason to be concerned about the rest of the family?"

"No, but we had no immediate concerns about Mr. Moszynski either. He has a daughter, Alisa, living near Esher. I've sent one of our cars to bring her, her baby daughter and Mr. Moszynski's mother, who's been visiting them, back here. Alisa's husband, Vadim, is in Moscow at present. He's been informed and is flying back immediately."

Kathy was taking notes. "Is that the whole family in the UK?"

"Yes."

Brock said, "Let's hear what Mr. Everett has to say."

Shere waved his employee forward.

"I came on duty here at seven this evening," Everett said, voice subdued. "There's always one of us here with Mr. Moszynski twenty-four/seven, working twelve-hour shifts. I've been on this assignment for six months now without incident. I made myself known to him, established who was at home and carried out our regular security inspection of the whole house. Mr. Moszynski was having dinner with two guests in the dining room, and said that he would be remaining in for the night and wouldn't need to be disturbed again. After I'd completed my rounds I went down to the basement kitchen where Mrs. Truscott, the housekeeper, gave me a cold supper. I had no alcohol with the meal or at any other time in the past twenty-four hours and I request a blood test to confirm that."

Brock grunted impatiently. "Yes, yes."

"At ten twenty-five Mrs. Truscott returned from upstairs where she'd been checking to see if the dinner party needed anything. She informed me that Mr. Moszynski wasn't there, and had apparently gone outside to the square to smoke a cigar. This was strictly against the protocol we'd agreed with Mr. Moszynski, and I immediately took a torch and went out to check on him. The gate to the central gardens was open and I could smell his cigar as I went in. I found him sitting collapsed on the bench in the middle of the gardens. That was at ten thirty-two. I made out extensive bloodstains on his clothes and checked his throat for a pulse. There were no signs of life, and I immediately rang triple nine and our home base. I also rang Mrs. Truscott and told her to lock the front door and inform the other guests. I then waited with Mr. Moszynski's body until the police arrived."

He took in a deep breath. "I should add that Mr. Moszynski has done this twice before, to my knowledge, despite our objections. He told me he's very partial to a cigar after dinner, but Mrs. Moszynski won't allow it in the house or the rear courtyard. Ordinarily I would have been aware of someone opening the front door from the security system, which should have alerted me." He showed them a security monitor, like a large mobile phone, attached to his belt. "But this didn't happen. I assume that Mr. Moszynski disarmed it before leaving. He told me he didn't like me fussing over him when he went out for a cigar."

"I can confirm that," his boss said. "I had words with Mr. Moszynski about it, but he was pretty relaxed about security."

"What about the murder of the American lady at the end of the block?" Kathy said. "Didn't that concern him?"

Wayne Everett frowned at her. "Not as far as I'm aware. Why should it?"

"He knew her though, didn't he?"

Everett exchanged a glance with his boss. "I couldn't say."

"He went to Mrs. Haynes' memorial service this morning," Kathy insisted. "Your colleague was with him. Did he talk to you about that?"

"No."

"Who's been here in the house this evening?" Brock said.

Everett listed them: the cook who'd prepared evening meals

for the household had left at nine p.m.; the housekeeper, Mrs. Truscott; Mr. Moszynski's wife, Ms. Gibbons, who had eaten alone in her suite; Ms. Gibbons' business manager, who'd arrived within the past half hour at Ms. Gibbons' request; and Mr. Moszynski's two guests—his business partner Mr. Freddie Clarke and Sir Nigel Hadden-Vane.

"Hadden-Vane?" Brock stared at him, then at Kathy.

"Yes, he was at the memorial service this morning too. *Sir* Nigel now, is it?"

"Yes," Everett said. "He's the local Member of Parliament."

They went to speak to the wife first, in her suite on the first floor. As they mounted the stairs Brock felt oddly disoriented. From the outside the building appeared to be the series of townhouses that it once had been, with individual front doors, but inside the scale expanded, as if he'd drunk from Alice's magic bottle. They must have ripped out its guts, he realized, to build a palace inside the shell.

Shaka Gibbons was sitting on an antique chaise longue while a man leaned forward at the other end, whispering urgently into her ear. "Sitting" didn't really do justice to the elegant way she had arranged herself across the velvet fabric. Brock realized that he had seen photographs of her before, attending film and theater first nights, the races at Ascot. Now, in the flesh, he saw what a compelling presence she had: the sculpted African features, the pale caramel complexion, the attenuated limbs and fingers. And the East End cockney accent, softly spoken, which somehow gave the rest an edge, like a shot of rough brandy in a cup of exquisitely smooth coffee.

She pulled herself upright and the man at her side drew back. There was a smudge of mascara on her cheek and her eyes were liquidy. "This is my manager, Derek. Sit down, please," she murmured, and they sat.

"It's my fault, isn't it?" she said. "Forcing Mikhail out into the street to 'ave a cigar. What a bitch. That's what people will say. But it wasn't really like that. I 'ave asthma, you see, and the smoke fucks me up. But he could 'ave gone to his study, or the billiard room. They 'ave separate air-conditioning, he insisted on that. That's where he usually goes after dinner. But it was a warm night, and he liked the gardens, the space, the trees. He could imagine he was back in St. Petersburg, or wherever. And he probably wanted to get away from those two parasites."

"Parasites?" Brock cleared his throat. He felt suddenly very hot.

"Nigel and Freddie." She looked suspiciously at Brock. "You aren't going down with something are you? You 'aven't got the flu or something?"

Derek sprang abruptly to his feet and whisked a small aerosol can from his pocket and sprayed the air between Brock and Shaka. Then he took another container from his other pocket and approached Brock.

"Just for the hands," he said.

Brock looked at him as if he were mad.

"The hands? Please?"

Kathy held out her palms and Derek sprayed them, then turned back to Brock, who reluctantly followed suit.

"Are you aware of any threats made against your husband, Mrs. Moszynski?" he said.

"No. Of course people were jealous of him." She shrugged. "Freddie would know more about that." She was speaking more rapidly now, as if anxious to finish the interview.

"What about in Russia?" Kathy said. "Did he have enemies there?"

"The same, envy. He hated going back, the way people looked at him, because he was rich. Vadim takes care of things over there now."

"His son-in-law."

"Yeah."

"But he didn't mention any threatening letters, phone calls?"

"No, nothing like that."

"What about Nancy Haynes?"

Shaka looked blank.

"The American tourist who was staying at the hotel next door. Who was murdered last Thursday."

Shaka looked at her manager. "Did I know about that?"

"I don't know, Shaka."

"Your husband didn't mention it?" Kathy asked.

"No."

"He went to her memorial service in the little church across the square this morning."

"Did he? I thought he'd gone to the cathedral. He usually does on Sunday mornings." She turned again to Derek. "It is Sunday, isn't it?"

He checked his watch. "Not any more, darling." Then he added, to Kathy, "That's the Russian Orthodox Cathedral up the road in Knightsbridge. Very devout, Mr. Moszynski."

They were interrupted by noises from outside the room, the wailing protest of a woman's voice. The sound came closer and Shaka gave a groan.

"Sounds like Mr. Moszynski's mother," Derek whispered to Brock.

A small gray-haired woman burst into the room, her arms outstretched. Shaka got to her feet and reached down to embrace her mother-in-law. They kissed on both cheeks without much sign of warmth and the older woman swung round on Brock and hurled a stream of angry Russian.

"Sorry." Another woman, aged about thirty, had come into the room with a baby held against her chest. "My grandmother is upset. Baba!" she said sharply to the older woman, and then followed with some Russian. The old woman sank into a chair, put her face in her hands and began to sob.

Brock and Kathy went back downstairs, where Everett showed them into what he described as the library. Two men were sitting in leather armchairs on each side of a marble fireplace. They got to their feet and Nigel Hadden-Vane took a step forward. Brock saw a flicker of recognition cross his face as he introduced Kathy and himself. On their last encounter they had been adversaries by proxy, through the agency of other players, but the underlying agenda had been between Brock and the veteran criminal Spider Roach, whose part Hadden-Vane had taken. Whether he had done so in order to score points against parliamentary rivals, or for more sinister reasons, had never been resolved.

Now Hadden-Vane seemed subdued and cautious, eyeing Brock from time to time as Kathy put the questions. He explained that he had attended the memorial service for Nancy Haynes that morning in his capacity as MP for the borough. Mr. Moszynski, who was well known to him, had also attended and invited him back afterward for some lunch. As a member of the Parliamentary Business and Enterprise Committee, Sir Nigel had recently returned from an official visit to Russia to promote UK–Russian trade, and he and Mr. Moszynski had many things to discuss. Later they were joined by Mr. Moszynski's financial adviser, Mr. Clarke.

"Freddie," Clarke interrupted, putting out his hand, then offering Kathy his business card, with an address in Mayfair. Head shaved, with a gingery goatee beard and mustache, he looked far too young to be anybody's financial adviser.

The meeting had turned into a social occasion, Hadden-Vane continued. Mr. Moszynski was well known for his generous hospitality and the three men had remained together for supper, after which their host had left to smoke a cigar outside. He had given no indication of a threat against his life.

"Absolutely not," Freddie Clarke agreed. "This is just, well, unbelievable."

"Did he know Mrs. Haynes?" Kathy asked.

"No, no." Hadden-Vane shook his head. He was speaking carefully, as if to control a slight slur in his voice. Brock had noticed the glass and decanter of brandy on the small table by his armchair and guessed he was slightly drunk. "He attended her memorial service this morning to show his support, as a neighbor. He was extremely aware of his status as a guest in this country, and took it upon himself to behave as a model resident, supporting charities, local schools and the like."

Brock and Kathy continued questioning both men for some time, without getting any clearer idea of why Moszynski might have been attacked. Clarke sketched the international scale of his business dealings, but insisted that they were impeccably conducted and had attracted no personal or criminal antagonism.

"What about the Russians?" Kathy asked.

Hadden-Vane gave a dismissive wave of his hand. "There's too much hysterical nonsense made of all that. Every time some Russian expat has a turn it's a plot by the Kremlin and the FSB. Believe me, they're as embarrassed by those sorts of rumors and allegations as we are."

"Mr. Moszynski didn't exactly have a *turn*," Kathy said.

Hadden-Vane's eyes narrowed and a flush spread across his face. "No, and I should have thought it pretty obvious that the reason lies a good deal closer to home. There is clearly a psychopathic maniac on the loose in this borough, and the sooner the police focus on that fact the better."

Brock saw Kathy stiffen at the contempt in the MP's voice. "Two random victims from the same building?"

"And why not?" Hadden-Vane shot back, his voice raised

now and angry. "The papers reported where Mrs. Haynes was living. Why wouldn't he come back to haunt the place? Maybe he hates foreigners; maybe he hates Chelsea, maybe he hates the police. I don't know, but it's your job to find out, and put a fucking stop to it."

Behind him, Clarke looked down at his feet with a little smirk on his face.

THERE WERE PRESS AND TV cameras outside when they opened the front door, throwing a dazzling light in their faces. The night air was filled with a hubbub of shouted questions. The crowd parted reluctantly as they pushed through to the gate across the street and the relative calm of the crime scene.

"Sorry," Kathy said. "I almost lost it with Hadden-Vane."

"You did fine," Brock said.

"I wanted to hit him."

"That I would have liked to see . . . oh." A wave of nausea and dizziness suddenly overwhelmed him and he stopped and bent over, bracing his hands on his knees.

"You all right?"

"Dizzy." There was a bench nearby in the shadows, and he stumbled toward it and slumped down. "Hot," he muttered. "Is it me or is it very hot?"

The local CID man came toward them. "Everything okay?"

"My boss isn't well," Kathy said, sitting down beside Brock. He felt her cool hand on his brow and heard her intake of breath. "I think I'd better get him to a doctor."

"No . . ." Brock objected, but he found it suddenly hard to frame the words.

"We've got one here." The detective strode away and returned a minute later with a figure shrouded in a blue paper crime scene suit. He was the local forensic physician, who'd just completed a preliminary examination of Moszynski's body. Now he unfastened his bag and checked Brock's temperature and pulse. He asked Kathy and Brock a few questions and then said, "Looks like influenza, maybe swine flu. Have you been immunized?" Brock shook his head. "He shouldn't be at work," the doctor said. "Get him home to bed now and contact his GP in the morning." He searched around in his bag and said, "You're in luck." He pulled out a packet of Tamiflu tablets. "These will ease the symptoms."

"Come on," Kathy said to Brock. "I'll take you home."

"No," he croaked. "I'll get a cab. You stay here. You're senior investigating officer now."

"Take him home," the detective said. "There's not much you can do till morning. You'll need to be fresh then. I'll ring you if there's any results from CCTV."

"You're interviewing people in the square?"

"Of course, all under control."

Kathy turned to the doctor. "Anything you can tell us?"

"I'd put time of death at two to four hours ago, three puncture wounds to the heart, narrow blade, neat grouping, very precise."

Brock heard their discussion as if through a blanket. "Like an exercise in fencing school," he whispered.

Kathy put a hand under his arm and said, "Come on." As he got groggily to his feet he heard the detective chuckle. "He's probably given it to all our witnesses. See if you can spread it among the press on your way out."

They avoided the crowd around Chelsea Mansions and reached Kathy's car parked in the next street.

As he pulled the belt across his chest he gathered his breath and said, "Sorry, Kathy. Came on so fast. Feel so bloody helpless."

"A friend of Nicole's caught it, said it was like being poleaxed." She opened the packet of pills and gave him one with a bottle of water she had in the car. "One a day," she said, and started the engine.

Brock was silent for a while, his eyes closed, trying to think, and then, as they were crossing Chelsea Bridge, he said, "This is going to be big, Kathy. Did you hear what the press were shouting? *Litvinenko.* They think it's another political killing. MI5 will be involved, the Foreign Office . . ."

"Yes of course, I understand that." She paused. "You think it's too big for me?"

"Not the detective work, no, but the politics is something else." He coughed and tried to put some force into his words. She had to understand. "Sharpe will feel obliged to appoint a more senior SIO. Probably Dick Chivers."

"Superintendent Chivers," Kathy sighed. "Oh."

"Yes. He's got his own team. It won't be our case any more."

He watched her thinking about that. Would it matter to her? He had seen the look of distaste on her face as they'd been confronted by the gaudy opulence of the Russian's house. Perhaps she'd be happy to let Chivers have it. But *I* wouldn't, he thought.

There was a long silence as they drove on into South London. They were skirting Clapham Common when Brock spoke again. "It would only be for a day or two."

"Sorry?"

"The Tamiflu will sort me out in a couple of days. If we can hold them off until then . . ."

"How could we do that?"

"Nancy was going up to Scotland, wasn't she?"

"Yes, to Angus."

"Then an urgent lead has taken me away to Angus."

Kathy laughed in a way that suggested he was joking, or mildly delirious.

"It'll be all right," he insisted. "You can tell them I'll be back tomorrow night, then put them off till the next night . . ."

"You're not serious, Brock! Commander Sharpe would have kittens."

"You and I would be in constant touch." Then he sighed and closed his eyes again. "No, you're right, it wouldn't be easy, especially for you. Forget it."

There was a long silence.

"It'd be like sabotage, telling lies, undermining the system."

"Mm."

She was driving down his high street now, slowing for the turning beneath the archway into Warren Lane, and then he heard the tires drumming on cobblestones. They passed under the horse chestnut tree, huge in her headlights, and came to a stop outside his front door.

He staggered inside, up the book-lined staircase to the rooms on the first floor, and Kathy helped him to his bedroom.

"Thanks, Kathy. Too far for you to go home tonight. The spare bed's made up."

"Yes, sounds good. I'll ring Suzanne tomorrow, let her know."

"No, don't do that. She's gone to the West Country for an antiques sale." He could hardly get the words out now. "There are things she wants for the shop. I don't want her charging back here just for this."

All the same, Kathy thought. She'd probably get in trouble either way from one of them. The terms of Brock and Suzanne's relationship remained unclear to her. They loved each other yet preferred to live separate lives.

There was an alarm clock in the spare room, which Kathy set for five a.m., three hours away, wanting to be back in Cunningham Place at dawn, when the detailed search of the square would begin.

EIGHT

BY EIGHT THE NEXT morning it was becoming clear that they were unlikely to find any traces of the killer in the garden. A German shepherd from the Dog Support Unit had followed a trail out of the garden gate and across the street, but no further, and it was probably Moszynski's own. They would have to hope for fingerprint or DNA evidence that forensics may have picked up on the gate or bench, or on Moszynski himself. Another detective from the borough command, a DI, had taken charge of the scene, and briefed Kathy on the search that had been going on through the night for possible CCTV sightings, so far without a firm result.

Kathy phoned Dot at Queen Anne's Gate and told her about Brock's illness, and his plan to keep control of the investigation. She seemed unfazed by his Scottish deception, which, in the light of a new day, seemed increasingly unrealistic to Kathy. Together they went over the most urgent administrative tasks that would need to be covered, and Kathy asked her to send Phil, her usual case action manager, and DC Pip Gallagher, now permanently attached to the team, to meet her at the Chelsea police station as soon as they arrived.

They gathered there with borough command officers to plan

the next stages of the investigation and allocate manpower. The steps were familiar and predictable, everyone busy, but as the time passed and no tangible leads to the killer emerged, Kathy began to feel the same nagging sense of frustration that she'd been feeling about Nancy's investigation, as if they were missing something. It's the public interest, she told herself. The morning editions of the papers were full of it. It was like dancing naked on an empty stage.

She was on her way to Moszynski's autopsy, which had been pushed to the front of the longlist usual for a Monday morning, when a call came through from Marilyn at the Press Bureau.

"I can't get hold of Brock. Do you know where he is?"

"He's not available, Marilyn."

"Not available? I'm arranging a press briefing for one o'clock. Top priority. Commander Sharpe's agreed it with the Deputy Commissioner. Where the hell is he?"

Kathy took a deep breath. "In Scotland, I'm afraid."

She heard Marilyn splutter. "Did I hear that right? Another Russian oligarch gets murdered in London, every media unit from here to Vladivostok is hammering on our door, and our front man buggers off to Scotland?"

Kathy swallowed. "An important line of inquiry. But not for publication at this stage."

"Sharpe doesn't know about it, does he? I think you'd better talk to him, quick smart."

"Yes, I'll do that."

Kathy had been putting this off, but now, glimpsing the heavy machinery of senior management that had obviously been grinding away, she saw her mistake. As if to underline it, she got another call, this time from Dot.

"Sharpe's office is on the warpath, Kathy. Better give him a ring."

"Did you tell them about Scotland?"

"I thought I'd leave that to you."

Kathy felt a sudden spasm of nausea and wondered if she might have caught Brock's bug. She had an overpowering desire to tell Sharpe the truth, but she had already begun the lie and to switch stories now seemed pathetic.

Sharpe's secretary seemed reluctant to put Kathy through at first.

"He's in a meeting," she said. "He really needs to talk to Brock."

"That won't be possible. I'm leading the Moszynski investigation at the moment. I have to speak to him."

There was a short hesitation. "Hang on."

Then a male voice, harsh and impatient. "Sharpe."

"Sir, it's DI Kolla."

"Yes?"

"Concerning the Moszynski murder last night."

"Yes, yes. I need Brock to brief me *immediately*."

"I'm afraid he's been called away urgently, sir."

"Called away?"

"Yes, a critical line of inquiry, sir, which he had to attend to personally." Kathy hesitated, picturing herself hanging from a public gibbet. "In Scotland."

"*Scotland!*"

"Yes."

"I think you'd better get in here and tell me what's going on."

"Yes, sir. Can it wait for an hour or so? I'm on my way to Moszynski's autopsy."

There was a strained silence, then Sharpe said. "Just tell me, Inspector. What's he up to? What is this critical line of inquiry?"

"Nancy Haynes, the American tourist, was about to go on to Scotland when she was killed last Thursday. We learned of a substantial legacy up there which she intended claiming. This provides the first real motive we've had for her murder, and Brock felt it was so important that he had to pursue it immediately."

"But . . . for God's sake, that can wait. Moszynski's the priority now. *Moszynski*, not Haynes."

"That's what made it so urgent, sir. You see, if Haynes' death was indeed a planned murder, and not a random act, then Moszynski's murder may be simply an attempt to divert our attention and resources onto a much higher profile case, away from the real reason."

"The same killer . . ." Sharpe said. He sounded mildly skeptical but not entirely incredulous, Kathy thought. She hoped that a banal, domestic motive for Moszynski's death might have some appeal to Sharpe, at least enough to buy a day or two.

"How long before he gets back?"

"Hopefully tonight, sir, but I'm waiting for him to contact me. Unfortunately the castle's in a rather remote area, with poor mobile coverage."

"The castle?"

"The legacy, sir, a castle."

She wondered if she'd gone too far, then heard him muse, "A castle in Scotland . . ." and imagined the picture in his head, a turreted stone keep in the middle of a lonely loch among purple hills inhabited only by shaggy highland cattle.

"We were planning on Brock holding a press conference today."

"I wonder if that could be delayed, sir, until we have something concrete to report?"

"We'll get back to you. Let me know immediately you hear anything, understand? *Immediately*."

Kathy hung up and continued to the autopsy, which confirmed what they'd already assumed. Moszynski had died as a result of three stab wounds to the chest, one of which had punctured the left ventricle of his heart. The blade was sharp and narrow, about one centimeter wide and at least ten centimeters long. The assailant had most likely been sitting or crouching on the victim's right side, and would have been right-handed. His or her right hand and forearm would have been covered in blood.

Kathy went on to Queen Anne's Gate, where Zack had been busy compiling data fed into his computers from the teams in Chelsea and surrounding districts. Bren Gurney, the other DI on Brock's team, came in and asked Kathy how it was going.

"What's this about Brock going to Scotland?"

He laughed when she explained. "The old bastard! He's pulled a few swifties in his time, but this is a classic."

"It's not funny, Bren. I'm out on a limb on this. I had to tell Sharpe a string of lies."

Bren became serious. "Okay. How can I help?"

They went over it all again, the two murders, the lack of leads.

"That was a good story, Kathy, the castle in Scotland. You should write a crime novel."

"The great detective doesn't go down with flu in crime novels, Bren. Only alcohol poisoning and gunshot wounds."

"The crucial point is that you're connecting the two crimes. You're quite sure of that, are you? You're not just trying to stop someone else moving in and taking over one or both of your murders?"

"It's a hell of a coincidence if they're not connected."

"Yes, but the connection may not be crucial. There could still be two quite separate murderers, the second riding on the first to create a false impression of a connection, to muddy the waters. It might have affected his timing, but not his intent. And you've got to consider whether you wouldn't be better concentrating on Nancy Haynes' murder and letting someone else run the other. The Moszynski case is going to be a bastard. Everyone'll want a piece of it—Counter Terrorism Command, MI5, MI6. And what do we know of these Russians, the Litvinenkos and Patarkatsishvilis? Only what we read in the papers—that they were maybe killed by the KGB. This isn't our kind of case. Those other guys are experts; let them handle it."

Kathy nodded. "Yes, you're probably right. But that's not the way Brock sees it."

With ominous timing, Dot rang through to say that Kathy would be required to attend an interagency meeting at Marsham Street later that afternoon.

"Marsham Street," Bren said. "Home Office. I told you, didn't I?"

"And there's something else," Dot added. "We've just had a call from *The Times*. Apparently they received a letter this morning from Mikhail Moszynski, talking about threats to his life. They're couriering it over."

It arrived a short time later, a typed letter addressed to the editor of *The Times*, with Moszynski's letterhead and signature.

Dear Sir,

Recent correspondence in The Times *has focused on the economic performance of the Russian government. We must not lose sight, however, of big issues of human rights and threats to freedom of speech in Russia. Things have not changed since the murder of Anna Politkovskaya in 2006 by elements of Russian secret police for her criticism of the authorities. I too have been warned of threats to myself and my family by official elements who resent the success of expatriate Russian businessmen. Let me give good advice to your readers—do not be complacent about the situation in that great country.*
Mikhail Moszynski

The letter was dated Friday 28 May, the day after Nancy Haynes was killed.

"The envelope is also postmarked Friday," Bren said. "There's your motive, Kathy. Like I said, this is one for the security services, yeah?"

"But where does that leave Nancy Haynes?"

NINE

"BUT ONLY A SMALL oligarch," the man from MI5 said.

"A minigarch?" the Foreign Office representative suggested, with a wry smile.

They had all been assembled when Kathy arrived, the atmosphere relaxed and convivial, as if they'd just enjoyed a pleasant lunch together to which she had not been invited. The only ones to acknowledge her arrival were the second MI5 officer, a woman, who'd given Kathy a brief smile, and Sharpe, who looked stiff and uncomfortable in his uniform and who pointed to the empty seat by his side. Out of the corner of her eye Kathy saw that the MI5 woman was setting up a screen.

She sat down and Sharpe introduced her to a superintendent from Counter Terrorism Command, then leaned to her and murmured, "Any developments?"

"Only this, sir. Just came in." She handed him a copy of the letter to *The Times*, which he scanned with a frown.

"Well now," an avuncular man at the center of the table began, and the others fell silent. He was the only one with a name on a wooden holder in front of him, *Sir Philip Stafford, Home Office*, and Kathy wondered if he carried it around with him, or if he was permanently attached to that chair. "We should begin with a summary of the police investigation. If you please, Commander?"

Sharpe cleared his throat. "Our Senior Investigating Officer, DCI Brock, is unavoidably detained by an urgent line of inquiry, and I have invited his assistant SIO, DI Kolla, to stand in for him. I'll ask her to brief you."

Sir Philip smiled pleasantly at Kathy. "Very good. Inspector Kolla?"

Kathy wasn't sure whether she should get to her feet. She wished she had some kind of audiovisual prop like the MI5 people.

"Last Thursday afternoon, as you'll know, a seventy-year-old American tourist called Nancy Haynes was murdered on Sloane Street . . ."

It was the wrong opening, she sensed. They weren't interested in Nancy Haynes. After a few moments the two MI5 people put their heads together to discuss something in a whisper, while the man from the Foreign Office consulted his file of papers. Kathy hurried on to the Moszynski murder and had their attention again, but only for a short while, until they realized that the police had made little progress. They perked up again when she told them about Moszynski's letter to *The Times* and passed photocopies around.

The CTC superintendent said, "Is it authentic?"

"We're checking that now. *The Times* intend to publish it tomorrow."

"Other questions?" Sir Philip asked.

No one spoke for a moment, then the MI5 man, presumably the senior of the two, raised a finger.

"Sean?"

He spoke with a strong Ulster accent, his voice quiet but cold. "You seem to assume that the two killings are connected. Is that right?"

Kathy had the feeling she was being invited down a dangerous path. "Two victims within a few days, close neighbors."

"And how would you interpret that?"

"Our minds are open at the moment, but we are investigating Nancy Haynes' background . . ."

"You think that's relevant?"

"Of course."

Sean pursed his lips, then gave an impatient shake of his head. "Surely there's a much simpler explanation."

"I think we're getting ahead of ourselves," Sir Philip interrupted. "Let's complete the briefings before we debate theories. Do you want to tell us about Mr. Moszynski, Sean?"

"Sure." He nodded to his partner, who tapped on her laptop. "Mikhail Artur Moszynski." The screen came to life with a picture of the Russian, standing by the open door of a helicopter, dressed only in shorts and brandishing a cigar, a glass of champagne and a broad grin. The setting, on a dazzling white beach with palm trees in the background, was deliberate, Kathy guessed, shifting their attention away from parochial Cunningham Place to a more exotic and international context. At the same time she was trying desperately to work out what Sean's simpler explanation might be.

"Is that your chopper, Sean?" the Foreign Office wit asked.

"I wish. It's an AgustaWestland AW109 Power, eight-seater twin-engine, his latest toy this year, set him back six point three million US. Moszynski was a wealthy man, but still, as we were saying earlier, not in the same league as the big boys, like Abramovich or Berezovsky, though his story isn't dissimilar. He was born in St. Petersburg—Leningrad then—in 1957. His family weren't wealthy, but his father, Gennady Moszynski, had influence."

The MI5 woman was smoothly changing the image to follow Sean's delivery. A series of old photographs of Gennady and his family was followed by street scenes and aerial photographs of

Leningrad, as if the two of them had been rehearsing this all morning. Everyone was paying attention, including the FO man, who had now closed his file.

"Before the war Gennady rose through the ranks of the party in Leningrad and then moved to Moscow, where he became secretary to the Deputy People's Commissar of Culture. When the war started he returned to Leningrad, where he came to prominence during the siege of the city. In 1945 he was awarded Hero of the Soviet Union and was a member of Leningrad's Executive Committee for the next thirty years. This paved the way for his son Mikhail, who studied metallurgy at Leningrad Technical University in the seventies before going to work in a turbine factory. Mikhail also joined Komsomol, the Young Communist League, and became secretary of one of the city districts. With perestroika, he and a small group of insiders in the party began developing commercial interests, import-export through the port of St. Petersburg. These activities expanded when Yeltsin took power in 1991, leading to the first wave of privatizations in ninety-three to ninety-four. Mikhail and his mates set up stalls all over the city buying up the shares that the government had issued to workers in their own companies for a fraction of what they were worth, paying for them in vodka and cigarettes. By the late nineties Mikhail had acquired a major stake in the shipping company Rosskomflot, and was diversifying into other industries. Then when Putin became president in 2000 and started making noises about billionaires stealing the nation's wealth, Mikhail sold a number of his assets back to the government and began moving his money offshore. He also divorced his first wife, and bought the house in Chelsea, making it his permanent home in 2002."

Sean ran through some of his other properties and assets, and then outlined the Moszynski family members, including the celebrity second wife, Shaka Gibbons, whom Mikhail had wed two years previously. He came to a picture of Mikhail's son-in-law.

"Vadim Kuzmin, forty-five, also a native of St. Petersburg, and a former party lieutenant of Mikhail and Gennady in the eighties. In 1989 he was recruited by what was then the KGB, now the FSB, in the Sixth Directorate, which is responsible for economic counter-intelligence and industrial security. He married Mikhail's daughter, Alisa, in 2003, while she was studying at the London School of Economics, and he then moved permanently to the UK, although he maintains extensive contacts in Russia, and is thought to be still associated with the FSB. He flew back this morning on a private flight to Biggin Hill, where he got a lift in to Battersea heliport on Mikhail's chopper and went straight to Chelsea Mansions."

Kathy had an uncomfortable feeling that Sean knew very well that she hadn't been aware of that.

"So you've been keeping an eye on them, Sean?" Sir Philip inquired.

"With Tony's people, yes." Sean nodded at the CTC superintendent. It seemed as if everyone was on first-name terms except Sharpe and herself.

"And is Kuzmin significant for our purposes?" Sir Philip asked.

"It's possible, yes. The letter to *The Times* confirms our first reaction, and probably everyone else's, that Moszynski's murder was an FSB assassination, like Litvinenko. Yet Moszynski wasn't an obvious target. He had certainly made off with a large chunk of money that most of his countrymen, including Putin, would say belonged to the Russian people. But he wasn't too ostentatious with his wealth, didn't interfere in Russian politics and did contribute to a number of Russian charities, educational foundations and a hospital in St. Petersburg. Vladimir Putin came from St. Petersburg too, of course, and it's said that his family knew Gennady Moszynski, and it's always been assumed that the Kremlin didn't have a grudge against Mikhail. However, there's Vadim. He acts as Mikhail's agent in Russia, and is involved with a number of business and political groups, as well as the FSB. It's possible that he's been stirring things up."

Kathy looked at the thick file in front of Sean. The Security Service had been carrying out a parallel investigation to her own, and one that was smarter, better informed and backed up by a wealth of background of which she'd been entirely ignorant. She was out of her depth. Bren had been right. Let them have Moszynski.

At her side Commander Sharpe shifted in his seat. "Then what about Nancy Haynes?" He sounded as if he didn't really want to hear the answer.

"Ah yes." Sean nodded at his companion, and a new image came up. Two faces, side by side. "Nancy Haynes on the left, Marta Moszynski—Mikhail's mother—on the right." He really didn't need to say any more. They could have been sisters.

"You think it's a case of mistaken identity?" Sir Philip prompted.

"It's a distinct possibility. We could imagine that the killer was given a description and a photograph, that he was watching Chelsea Mansions, saw an elderly woman come out of one of the front doors, and assumed it was Marta."

"But why kill Marta Moszynski?"

"As a warning to Mikhail. When that failed they had no option but to go directly for him."

Kathy felt uneasy. Was that really possible? Why hadn't she thought of it, and seen the similarity? And yet, the images were misleading. The picture of Marta was hardly recognizable as the woman she'd seen at Chelsea Mansions the previous night. The face on the screen looked ten years younger; the deep lines had been brushed away, the complexion lightened, the hair given more color and body. Nancy Haynes, on the other hand, appeared older and more strained than the woman Kathy had seen in her photographs. It was probably a passport image, she guessed, the eyes blank, color bleached. And the two portraits were also enlarged to make the two faces look exactly the same size, but that too was misleading, for surely Nancy was taller and slimmer than the dumpy little woman who had run forward to Shaka, who had had to reach down awkwardly to embrace her.

Sharpe cleared his throat. "It sounds as if you've got it all worked out. I imagine you want us to hand the investigation over to you. We'll offer every assistance, of course."

"Good Lord, no!" The Foreign Office representative looked appalled. He glanced at Sean, who shot him a brief, grim little smile. Kathy saw it, and the thought flashed into her head, *They've agreed all this beforehand.*

"These are difficult times," the FO man went on. "Our relations with the Russian government are particularly sensitive on a great number of issues. We really don't want this to be seen as a *security* matter, not if we can help it. The local Member of Parliament was on the radio this morning saying that he believes there's a psychopath on the loose in Chelsea, and we really think that might be the best working hypothesis. Clearly a police matter, to be treated like any other local crime until evidence indicates otherwise."

Kathy could almost hear the conversation they must have had before the meeting. *Let the plod handle it. Calm things down.*

"Of course, if, in the course of your inquiries, you were to find leads pointing firmly offshore, then we would have to think again, but in the meantime, let's treat this case as you would any other murder in the capital."

"There is this letter to *The Times*, and we can't ignore what you've just told us," Sharpe objected. "What about international departures in the past eighteen hours? You've been checking exit points, I take it?"

Sean nodded. "Nothing obvious. No sudden departures of Russian embassy staff."

Sharpe glanced at Kathy, raised his eyebrows and said, "Very well, if that's the consensus we'll proceed as before. What about Moszynski's financial affairs? Should we be looking into those?"

"Oh, I shouldn't think so, Commander," Sir Philip said, gathering up his notes. "Not likely to lead to his murderer. So thank you all."

As they made for the door, Sean caught Kathy and handed her his card. *Sean Ardagh*. "Give me a ring when you need some help," he said.

"Thanks. Hold on, I'll give you mine."

"It's okay. I know all about you." He grinned and turned away.

On their way out Sharpe said to Kathy, "Heard from Brock?"

"No, sir. Not yet."

"Better tell him he's wasting his time, eh? Get him back here."

TEN

KATHY PARKED IN CUNNINGHAM Place and began walking toward Chelsea Mansions. The passersby that she had seen that morning leaving for work were now returning, glancing as they passed at the police tape draped on the fence of the gardens. As she approached the central portico she changed her mind, and decided to go first to the hotel. The bell sounded on the door and Deb Collins strolled out.

"Hello, Inspector. Thought we might get another visit from you."

"Yes, I'd like to have a word."

"I'm afraid you've missed Emerson. He flew back to the States this morning with Nancy's son."

"It was about the murder in the square last night."

"Ah yes. Your people called by this morning, but none of us saw anything useful. Poor old Moszynski, eh? Want to come through?"

She lifted the flap in the counter and showed Kathy into an office with a bay window overlooking the square. Toby was sitting at a table in the center, a bill held a few inches in front of his face, a glass of whiskey by his side. "Come in, come in," he said, getting to his feet.

Kathy looked around the room, neat and orderly. It didn't look as if there was a huge amount of business going on. There were framed photographs on the wall beside her and she took a closer look. Soldiers and tanks. Among them she made out a younger Toby Beaumont in desert uniform.

"You, Colonel Beaumont?"

"First Gulf War, 1991. Come and sit down. How can we help?"

"I was wanting a bit of background on your neighbors. Wondered if you could tell me anything about them."

"I'd have thought MI5 would know it all," Toby said.

"Yes, the official stuff. I was thinking more on a personal, day-to-day level."

"Gossip, you mean," Deb said.

Kathy smiled. "If you like."

"Oh, we can give you plenty of that, can't we, Toby?"

"How long have you two been here?"

"Since 1995," Toby said. "My great-grandfather bought this house when it was built in 1890. He was adjutant at the Chelsea Barracks down the road and wanted the family home nearby, and it's been in the family ever since. My father left it to my brother, who died in 1995 and left it to me. I'd recently retired from the army and was at a loose end. I looked at the place and thought, what the hell am I going to do with that on my own? Then I thought, a small, exclusive hotel—why not? But I knew I'd need someone to help me, someone absolutely dependable, and I thought of Deb. We'd met in Saudi, during the war." He nodded at the photographs. "I was on General de la Billière's staff in Riyadh and she was my liaison with the British Embassy there. The perfect choice, I thought, and I was right."

Deb chuckled.

"But you want to know about the Russians," Toby continued. "They arrived in . . . 2001, was it, Deb? Yes. The Mansions was eight separate properties at that time. Then two came on the market together, and Moszynski snapped them both up. Within two more years he'd got the rest, all except us. Made them offers they couldn't refuse. Tried to buy us out too, but I wasn't having any. Considered it, but I think what really stuck in my craw was when they decided to sell off the Barracks and redevelop the site for luxury apartments for more Russians, and I thought, no, bugger it, this is my home, my heritage, you can wait until I'm dead and gone, Mikhail, old chum."

"Only he beat you to it," Deb said.

"Anyway, the builders moved in. For over a year the place was in turmoil. They gutted it. Have you been inside?"

"Yes. Quite palatial."

"That's what we heard. We've never been invited in, mind you."

"So they keep themselves to themselves, the Moszynskis?"

"Oh, I wouldn't say that, not since he met Shaka. Plenty of entertaining, parties, just not for us. Letting down the tone of millionaires' row, we are. There'll be a huge funeral, I suppose."

"Rows, fights?" Kathy asked.

"Couldn't say. Completely soundproof now, that place. You do wonder how his old mum gets on with the new wife though, don't you?"

"How about the son-in-law?"

"Cold fish. Bumped into him once getting out of his Ferrari. He and the daughter live out in Surrey, but he's often here."

"Well . . ." Kathy checked her watch. "Thanks, I'd better get going."

They stood up. "Our MP was on the radio this morning, saying we've got a serial killer in Chelsea. Do you reckon he's right?"

"We don't know yet, Deb."

"That's what they want us to think, the people who killed

Moszynski," Toby said. "That's got to be political, and they used Nancy's death to make it look like a serial killer. That's my guess anyway."

"You could be right."

"You sound tired, dear," Deb said. "Must be taking it out of you, all this. Leaning hard, are they, your bosses? We know what that's like, don't we, Toby? When the proverbial hits the fan."

Kathy smiled at her. "Yes, it is a bit tense." She turned to find John Greenslade standing in the doorway.

"Hi, I thought I heard you."

"Hello."

"Well, your casebook's getting bigger all the time. Are you running the Moszynski case too?"

"I'm part of the team, yes."

"Come on, you're the senior investigator. I spoke to that detective you were with this morning in the square. That's what he told me. Homicide and Serious Crime Command, right?" He saw Kathy's eyes narrow and raised his hands with a smile. "No, no, I'm not stalking you, promise. I just look out of my window. How could I not? This is the most exciting corner of London right now."

"Leave the detective alone, John," Deb said, and to Kathy, "He's always asking questions, this man."

KATHY'S PHONE RANG AS she reached the foot of the steps outside the hotel.

"Boss? Pip Gallagher. I'm with the house-to-house teams in Cunningham Square."

"Yes, Pip? I'm in the square myself, outside the hotel."

"Yeah, I can see you. I'm to your left, in one of the flats on the east side. You got a moment? I think you might be interested in this. I'll come downstairs and let you in."

They met at the front door Pip had indicated and she led them up to an apartment on the third floor. An elderly man was sitting in an armchair by the window in the front room overlooking the square. At his side, Kathy noticed, was a folded copy of *The Times*, its crossword completed in neat, bold letters.

"This is Dr. Stewart," Pip said and introduced Kathy. "Could you tell the inspector what you told me, Doctor?"

"Indeed." The old man looked as if he was thoroughly enjoying himself. "I spend quite a lot of time in this chair these days, observing the comings and goings in the square. It used to be rather boring, but I must say that our Russian friend has livened things up considerably, especially since he married Shaka Gibbons. My goodness, the parties, the celebrities—Elton, Jude, Hugh. And have you seen their wonderful cars? That Ferrari! And the big black Maybach! Oh my . . ."

"Did you see something last night, Dr. Stewart?" Kathy asked.

He looked put out. "Last night? Oh no, I was fast asleep when all the drama took place. I didn't hear about it till my grandson phoned me this morning to tell me it had been on the news."

Kathy raised an eyebrow at Pip, who said, "Dr. Stewart thinks he saw Nancy Haynes visiting the Moszynskis."

"I don't *think*," he snapped, "I *know*."

Kathy looked at him, trying to assess how reliable he might be. He must have been eighty, or close enough, but his hands were steady, his mind and tongue sharp. "Tell me about it please, Doctor. This could be important."

"Very well. A week ago, last Monday, the twenty-fourth, I made myself a sandwich for lunch—tuna—and brought it here to my usual seat by the window. I saw Nancy Haynes come out of the hotel. I didn't know that was her name or anything about her until her death was reported in the paper on Friday, but I recognized her as having arrived in a taxi with a male compan-ion on the previous Saturday morning."

Kathy looked out of the window. There was a clear view across the corner of the square to the hotel, and the rest of Chel-sea Mansions beyond.

"This time she was alone. She turned right, and walked up the street there to the central porch of the Mansions, and climbed the steps. I saw her ring the doorbell and go inside."

"What was she wearing?"

"It was rather overcast and cool that day, and she had a light tan-colored jacket and a cream skirt. Smart but comfortable."

Kathy remembered a tan jacket hanging in Nancy's ward-robe. "I'm impressed by your memory."

"There's nothing wrong with my memory. And I was in-trigued, you see. Why would one of the hotel guests be visiting the Moszynskis? Surely any friend of theirs would be staying either with them, or in a much grander hotel than Toby Beau-mont's?"

"How long did she stay there?"

"Ah, that I can't tell you, I'm afraid. At least half an hour. But then, having finished my lunch, I had a nap, so I didn't see her reappear."

"Do you always have the same thing for lunch?"

"No, I have a routine. Cheese Monday, tuna Tuesday, roast beef . . ."

"But you said it was Monday and you had tuna."

Dr. Stewart stared at her, a momentary panic in his eyes. "No, no . . . You're just confusing things. Monday, it was definitely Monday."

KATHY WALKED UP THE street to the central portico of Chelsea Mansions, wondering what to make of Dr. Stewart's claims. The possibility that he had seen Nancy following this same route to Moszynski's front door was disturbing. If true, it was a crucial new element. What could she have wanted with him?

A male voice challenged her from a speaker on the wall and she told them who she was. After a moment a maid opened the door.

"I'd like to speak to Mrs. Moszynski," Kathy said.

"Mrs. Shaka or Mrs. Marta?" the maid said. Her eyes looked puffy, as if she'd been crying.

"Mrs. Shaka, please."

Kathy was shown into the same room in which she'd interviewed Clarke and Hadden-Vane the previous night. Now Shaka was sitting in one of the armchairs and a man was in the other, leaning toward her as if in the middle of some intense debate. Shaka looked up with irritation as Kathy walked in, and as the man turned Kathy recognized Vadim Kuzmin, Moszynski's son-in-law, from the MI5 photos. He got to his feet and made as if to leave, but Kathy spoke to him.

"Mr. Kuzmin? I'm Detective Inspector Kolla from the Metropolitan Police. I'd like to speak to you too."

He looked at her suspiciously. "How did you know my name?"

"I was told that you had arrived this morning. Can you tell me when you left on your Russian trip?"

"Last Wednesday."

"And when was the last time you were here in Cunningham Place?"

"Last Wednesday." The suspicious frown was still there, and Kathy wondered if it was a perpetual mask through which he viewed the world. "I called in here to talk with my father-in-law before I left."

"Are you aware of any threats to Mr. Moszynski, from people in Russia, perhaps?"

"No."

"We believe he wrote a letter to *The Times* newspaper on Friday, suggesting just that." Kathy showed them a copy of the letter. "Are you aware of this, Mrs. Moszynski? Did he discuss it with you?"

Shaka shook her head. "But he probably wouldn't have spoken to me about something like that."

"I don't believe this," Vadim said. "He never mentioned this to me, and I would know if there was a problem in Russia."

"The Aleksandrovs," Shaka said, "at dinner last month, they were going on about the FSB spying on their bank accounts."

"Expats!" Vadim snarled dismissively. "The Aleksandrovs are paranoid. It's nonsense. There was no threat to Mikhail. I tell you, I would know."

"Yeah, but maybe he wrote the letter for the sake of his friends, like the Aleksandrovs, that's what I'm saying, Vadim."

"Do you know this woman, Mr. Kuzmin?" Kathy showed him Nancy Haynes' photograph.

He shook his head.

"How about you, Mrs. Moszynski?"

"No, I don't know her. Who is she?"

"It's the American woman who was murdered last Thursday. She was staying at the hotel next door."

"That dump?"

"You're quite sure you've never seen or heard of her? Her name was Nancy Haynes." Kathy spelled it.

"No, I told you."

"Only someone saw her call in here last Monday or Tuesday, at around one o'clock."

"No, you've got that wrong. Why would she come here?"

"I don't know. I'd like to show your staff the photograph."

She shrugged. "Be my guest."

"I also need to ask them and both of you if you can remember any strangers hanging around in the square recently."

She continued with them for a while without getting any-where, then went to speak to the staff, beginning with Moszyn-ski's secretary, a middle-aged woman, elegantly groomed in an inconspicuous way, as if to blend into the grays and beiges of the decor. Her office seemed to be equipped with every latest business machine, yet Kathy had the impression that there was little work for her to do.

"Ellen Fitzwilliam," the woman said, offering her hand. Like the maid, she too looked as if she'd been crying, and there were crumpled tissues in the bin beside her desk. "This is so dreadful. I heard it on the radio this morning when I was having breakfast and I still can't believe it. People are saying that he was killed by the Russians, or by a serial killer."

"We really don't know at the moment, Ellen. You must have spent a lot of time with him. Is there anything that you can tell us?"

"Me . . . ?" She looked as if she hadn't expected the question. "Well, yes, I've worked for Mr. Moszynski for almost eight years now, but I can't think of any reason why someone would want to hurt him. He was a perfect gentleman."

"A good boss?"

"Oh yes. He was firm, very clear about what he wanted, but considerate too. When my mother was sick and I needed time off at short notice he was completely understanding. And he was just such an interesting man—he knew so many famous people. He started as a penniless apprentice, you know."

"Yes, an interesting family. How about his mother, Marta?"

"Oh, she's a character. Quite the matriarch. Of course she's had a very hard life. She's so proud of her son."

Tears began to form in Ellen's eyes. Kathy said quickly, "And his son-in-law, Mr. Kuzmin?"

"Ah, he is . . ." She seemed to have trouble finding the right word. "Very vigorous," she said at last.

"Vigorous?" Kathy looked at her, puzzled, and the woman colored slightly.

"A great sportsman. He likes shooting, and he plays football." She hesitated. "And very loyal to Mr. Moszynski, of course. Was there anything else?"

Kathy showed her the *Times* letter. "Have you seen this before?"

She frowned as she read it. "Friday . . . No, I haven't."

"Is there someone else who might have typed it for him?"

"No, I do all his typing. But he does sometimes write his own notes and letters on the computer. And that is his signature."

"Could you check your computer?"

Kathy stood behind her as she opened a file marked *Gen Corr* on the machine on her desk. "Nothing on Friday the twenty-eighth . . ." She tried the previous day and scanned the list to one marked *Times*, which she opened. "Here it is."

"Can you find out for me when it was written, please?"

Ellen tapped the keys and brought up the properties information on the document. It had been created on Thursday 27 May, at nine thirty-two p.m.

"Do you know when you left work that day, Ellen?"

She consulted her electronic diary. "Yes, I remember. I was taking my mother to the theater and I had to leave on time, at five thirty."

"So you wouldn't know who was here that evening?"

This time Ellen thumbed through a thick desk diary and said, "Mr. Moszynski had pencilled in that evening for a business meeting here at the house with his close advisers. He didn't say what it was about."

"His close advisers being . . . ?"

"Well, Mr. Clarke, Sir Nigel Hadden-Vane and I suppose Mr.

Kuzmin, if he was still here. I think he left for Russia around then."

"So Sir Nigel was a business adviser to Mr. Moszynski?"

"Oh yes, and on social matters too. They were very close."

Kathy moved on to show her Nancy's picture.

"Isn't that the American lady who was staying at the hotel next door?"

"You recognize her."

"Well, from her picture in the newspapers, yes, of course. We were shocked."

"We?"

"Mr. Moszynski and I. We talked about it. He was upset by the news."

"Why was that?"

"Because she was living right next door. He was like that. He got upset when the old lady across the square was hit by a car a couple of years ago. I had to send flowers every day to her in hospital. He felt things personally."

"But had he met Mrs. Haynes?"

"Oh no, he would have mentioned that."

"Someone said that they saw her call in here on that Monday or Tuesday."

"Here? No, they must have been mistaken."

"You're quite sure."

"Absolutely."

Kathy left her and went through the same thing with the other members of the household, without learning anything new. When she asked about the recording from the security camera at the front door she was told that the police had already taken it.

As she left she looked back up at the front of Chelsea Mansions, thinking of the palace inside, and the secret lives of houses. The problem was that it seemed hardly possible that Mikhail

Moszynski's killer had spent night after night waiting in the gardens on the off chance that his target would come out for a smoke. Someone in the house had surely tipped off the murderer, who must have been nearby, within, say, a ten-minute radius.

She got into her car and headed off across the river.

THERE WAS NO RESPONSE when she let herself into Brock's house in Warren Lane and called up the stairs. She had stopped at a Sainsbury's on the way, and put the bags on the kitchen table before going through to his darkened bedroom. All she could make out of him was a tuft of white hair above the blankets, and for a moment she had the terrible thought that he might be dead. "Brock?"

The figure stirred, grunted and whispered, "Kathy? That you?"

"Yes. Sorry to wake you."

"No, no . . ." He struggled to sit up. "Needn't have bothered."

"Has anyone else been in?"

"The doc. Dot rang him. He thinks it's swine flu." He swallowed, breathing heavily. "You shouldn't be here."

"I'd have got it by now. Anyway, I've had the jab."

"Good." He sank back against the pillows. "Feels like I've done fifteen rounds with . . ."

She couldn't make out the rest. "What can I get you?"

He shook his head.

"Soup? Hot drink?"

"Water," he croaked. "Then sit down and tell me . . ."

So she told him about her day. When she got to the end she was convinced he'd fallen asleep, and was just getting to her feet, when he muttered, "Or he's staying in the square."

"What?"

"Could see Moszynski go out, from a window overlooking the square."

He was right of course. They would have to trace everybody who could do that. But someone immediately sprang to mind. She thought of John Greenslade's comment, *I just look out of my window. How could I not?*

She began to tell Brock about him, but then stopped, listening to his breathing. This time he really was asleep.

Later, sitting at home in front of the blank TV, nursing a glass of wine, Kathy was glad he hadn't heard her account of John Greenslade. It hadn't been quite right, betraying the lack of resolution in her own mind. Her first impression of him on Friday morning, when she'd come upon him talking to Emerson in the hotel lounge, was almost of recognition, as if she'd met him before or seen his picture somewhere. She'd liked the look of him, his intelligent eyes and pleasant smile. She'd found him attractive, and perhaps he'd realized it and had tried to use it against her. For after that first meeting he had behaved like one of those murderers she'd heard about but never really encountered before, haunting the scene of the crime, trying to insinuate himself into the investigation, eager to help. Or was she reading too much into it? Was he just naturally curious and, as he'd claimed, interested in her? Either way, she thought she was going to have to find out more about him.

He'd described himself on his entry card as a university professor, so she googled Montreal University and came up blank. Then she looked for other Quebec universities and found him at McGill, where there was an associate professor in the field of Renaissance philology by the name of John Greenslade. Renaissance philology—what the hell was that? There was no photograph.

ELEVEN

TOWARD NOON THE FOLLOWING day, Tuesday, the first day of June, Toby Beaumont and Deb Collins were standing in the bay window of their office, watching the police activity in the square. Behind them, John put his head around the office door.

"What's all the excitement?" he asked.

"Police," Deb said. "At it again."

"What are they up to now?"

"Goodness knows," she replied, and turned back to her accounts. "The woman inspector, Kolla, has been next door at the Moszynskis' for a couple of hours now with some other serious-looking types. I suppose she'll be calling in here again."

"Mm. Makes the day interesting, I suppose." John glanced at the photographs on the wall. "Don't you miss the excitement of the old days, Toby?"

"No, old son," Toby said, with such a tone of weary resignation that both John and Deb shot him a cautious look. "Too old for that now."

John pointed to one of the framed photographs on the wall. "I was wondering who this young guy is? You've got several shots of him."

Toby turned from the window and stared at where John was pointing. "A very fine soldier," he said heavily.

"That cap badge—isn't that the SAS?"

Then John noticed Deb staring at him with a frown. She gave a little shake of her head and said, "And what can we do for you today, John?"

"Ah yes. I was thinking I should have at least one really good meal while I'm in London. I wondered if you could recommend somewhere around here."

"Yes, we've got a list. If you wanted somewhere really special you could try Frazer's in the King's Road. Expensive mind. Going on your own?"

"No, I thought I'd take a friend. Do you think we'd get in tonight?"

"I'll ring up for you if you like."

"Thanks."

They turned at the sound of the front door bell, and Kathy walked in.

"Ah, Inspector," Deb said. "We thought you might be paying us another visit."

"'Fraid so, Deb," Kathy said. "I'm going to have to speak to everyone again. Would it be possible for me to use the lounge?"

"Be our guest," Toby said. "We'll get you a pot of coffee."

"That would be wonderful."

"Could you do me first?" John asked. "I'm going to have to leave shortly."

"Fine."

They crossed the hall to the guests' lounge and sat facing one another. He looked at her expectantly as she took out her notebook and an electronic recorder.

"Well now, Mr. Greenslade, I have to inform you that this is an official interview which I'll be recording. Okay with that?"

"Sure."

She asked him his full name, age, address, employer and mobile phone number. "What are you doing here in London?"

"I'm attending a conference at University College on classical philology."

"Which is?"

"It's about the interpretation of old texts." He saw the doubt on her face. "Renaissance texts mainly." Then he added, "Quattrocento."

"Quattrocento," she repeated slowly, writing it down, making the word sound pretentious. He took a breath, wanting to explain, but she moved on abruptly. "And when did you arrive in London?"

"Monday the twenty-fourth, a week ago yesterday."

"How did you choose this hotel?"

"Well, I was booked into some place off the Edgeware Road that was one of the conference organizers' recommendations, but I didn't like it very much, so after a few days I moved here."

"When exactly?"

"Um . . . Friday it would have been. Yes, Friday."

"Why here?"

"Well, I read about Nancy Haynes' death and I was curious. The newspaper report mentioned where she was staying, and I wandered over to take a look, and thought, this is nicer than where I am, and asked if they had a free room, which they did."

"And it was free because it was Nancy Haynes' room."

"I guess so."

She let that hang for a moment, and he began to feel uncomfortable.

"Why were you curious about Nancy Haynes' death?"

"It just struck me as rather odd, I suppose."

"So you wanted to sleep in her bed?"

He felt a little jolt of shock. "No! Now you're looking at me the way I look at a student who's been caught plagiarizing or something. There was nothing macabre about it. I told you before, I've had a bit to do with the Montreal police."

"Yes, you did say that. What exactly have you had to do with them?"

"You don't believe me, do you? Look, why don't I give you the name of someone to call, and they can vouch for me, okay?"

He took out his phone and scrolled through his address book and handed it to her. "Paul Ledoux is a lieutenant in the Montreal Police Service, that's his office number." She wrote it down and handed back the phone.

"The conference has been a bit of a disappointment, not really my period, and I was looking for a distraction. I thought it might be interesting to be in the middle of a murder investigation."

"And is it?"

"Well, right at the moment it's a little uncomfortable, to tell the truth."

"Maybe that's because you're not being completely open with me, Mr. Greenslade."

He sighed, lowered his eyes from that accusing glare of hers and said, "Can I make a suggestion? Phone Paul Ledoux in a couple of hours when he gets in to work, and if you're not completely satisfied you can get out the thumbscrews. But if you are satisfied—"

He was interrupted by the sound of Kathy's phone. She glanced at the number and winced. "Excuse me," she said. "Better take this."

She got to her feet and walked over to the window, her back to him. "Sir?" He watched her listen, motionless, then shake her head and say, "I'm afraid he's still in Scotland, sir . . . Yes, I did tell him about the meeting, but he wanted to complete his inquiries . . . No, sir . . . Probably this evening, or tomorrow . . ." She took a deep breath and stared up at the ceiling, the phone clamped to her ear. Eventually she said, "Absolutely, sir, I . . ." She fell silent, snapped the phone shut and put it back in her pocket.

"Where were we?" she said.

"We were agreeing that you'd phone Montreal, after which if you weren't satisfied you would haul me in for further questioning, but if you were satisfied you'd have dinner with me tonight."

Kathy shook her head. "You've got a bloody nerve, John."

At least she'd called him John. "Yes, well, time is short. They're having a conference dinner tonight and I need an excuse not to go. I'd much prefer to eat somewhere nice with somebody who wouldn't want to talk about classical philology."

She nodded. "I can understand that."

"And I've had an idea about your case that I'd like to put to you. I thought of Frazer's in the King's Road."

"Frazer's?" She raised an eyebrow.

"You've heard of it?"

"Yes. I'm told it's expensive."

"Is that a problem?"

"I'd rather have a sandwich at the Red Lion."

"Are you serious?"

"Yes, and I'll pay for my own. Say six o'clock?"

"You are serious. Where is this Red Lion?"

"Parliament Street, not far from the Two Chairmen, which you know so well."

John left her to interview the next resident of the hotel. In the hall Deb called to him that she'd tried Frazer's and it was booked out. Did he want her to try somewhere else? He thanked her and told her not to bother.

WHEN SHE'D FINISHED AT the hotel Kathy checked the progress of the others in the square, and went through the lists they were working from. Several people had not yet been reinterviewed: Vadim and Alisa Kuzmin had returned to their home in Surrey and apparently Shaka had gone with them; Sir Nigel Hadden-Vane was tied up with parliamentary business in Westminster; and Mikhail Moszynski's financial adviser, Freddie Clarke, was working at his office in Mayfair. Kathy decided to start with him.

The place was hard to find, an inconspicuous door in a tiny square tucked away behind Curzon Street. The name on the small brass plate said *Truscott Orr*. It wasn't apparent what Truscott Orr did. The voice on the intercom was guarded, and when Kathy mounted the stairs to the small reception area she was confronted by a severe, smartly dressed woman who gave the strong impression that Kathy was intruding. Through an open door she caught a glimpse of two young men, not long out of school by the look of them, staring at computer screens. The woman spoke into a phone and led Kathy to another door.

Clarke had his sleeves rolled up, tie loosened. His striped shirt was enlivened by a colorful pair of braces, decorated with bears on one side and bulls on the other. Kathy wondered if you could tell which way the market was heading by watching which side he tugged.

"Ah, hello again. Er . . ." He glanced at the secretary who was hovering at the door as if reluctant to leave him alone with the detective. Rather as if she's his mother, Kathy thought. Clarke said, "Coffee, Renee? Thanks."

"Thank you for seeing me at short notice, Mr. Clarke," Kathy began. "There are a few points I need to clarify. First of all, can you just explain to me again exactly what your relationship was with Mr. Moszynski?"

He inserted a thumb under the bulls and said, "I advised him on his financial affairs."

"You are a financial adviser, then?"

"Yeah. Specialist in tax law."

A smart cockney spiv, Kathy thought. "So you weren't business partners, as such?"

"That too, but on a modest scale. I have investments in some of Mr. Moszynski's companies." He smiled encouragingly, as if to suggest he was an open book.

"Who are Truscott and Orr?"

"Founders of the firm, back in the seventies. I'm the sole director now."

"So you're familiar with all of Mr. Moszynski's business affairs?"

"I couldn't claim that."

"Could you describe them to me?"

"Mr. Moszynski came to the UK with substantial assets, which he has diversified through a number of holding and investment companies. He also set up several charitable and family trusts."

"I imagine it will be complicated."

"Oh yes."

"And his family will be relying on you to sort things out."

"In part. Ah, coffee."

Renee had appeared with a tray. "The boys are stuck, Freddie," she said.

"Oh damn. Could you excuse me a moment, Inspector?" He rushed to the door while Renee struggled to find a place to set the tray down among the papers heaped over every surface.

Kathy said, "My boss's desk looks a bit like that."

"Freddie is a genius," Renee replied stonily, defying her to deny it.

"At tax minimization?" Kathy said.

"At what he does."

"It sounds boring, but I don't suppose it is, with clients like the Russians."

Renee said nothing, seemingly not wanting to enter into a conversation, but also not wanting to leave Kathy alone in Clarke's office. She began arranging papers into piles, then stopped and turned to Kathy. "I read about the letter in the paper this morning. That's obviously the answer, isn't it? Like those other Russians. The KGB did it."

"Did Nancy Haynes ever come here, Renee?"

The woman's eyes narrowed. "Who?"

"The American lady who was staying next door to Mikhail Moszynski—the one who was murdered last Thursday."

"What's that?" Freddie Clarke had reappeared at the door.

Kathy repeated the question.

"Hell, no. Why would she? She certainly wasn't a client of ours. Why, are you trying to make some connection?"

"This is her photograph," Kathy said, showing it to both of them. "Have you ever seen her?"

They both said no, and Renee left.

"As you see, Inspector," Clarke went on, "I'm up to my ears at the moment. Was there anything in particular you were after?"

"I just wanted an overview of Mr. Moszynski's business affairs. I'm probably not asking the right questions. Maybe I should get our financial specialists to come and talk to you."

He frowned and tugged at the bears. "I'm sure that won't be necessary. I could give you a list of his principal companies and trusts, if you like. The most significant is RKF SA."

"Thank you." She thought a moment. "RKF as in Rosskomflot?"

He looked at her sharply. "That's right. You do know something of his affairs, then?"

"A little. Do you have company prospectuses, annual statements?"

He smirked. "These are private companies, almost all registered overseas. RKF is registered in Luxembourg, for example."

"Ah yes, of course. So what would Mikhail be worth, all up?"

"Oh . . ." Clarke shook his head with a frown. "Very hard to say."

"Roughly. Take a guess."

"Roughly . . ." He spread his hands. "Five hundred million? Six?"

"Sterling?"

"Dollars."

"And who will control that now?"

"I haven't seen his will . . ."

"But he must have discussed it with you."

"Various family members will inherit, but taken with her present holding in RKF, his daughter Alisa—Mrs. Kuzmin—will have a controlling interest, I believe."

"Not his wife?"

"Not under the terms of their prenuptial agreement. She will be generously provided for, but won't play an active part in the companies."

"And what role does Alisa's husband Vadim play?"

"He acts as Mikhail's business representative in Russia. Vadim has extensive contacts with government and business over there. Mikhail hasn't been back to Russia since his mother joined him over here."

"Was he afraid?"

"I've read the letter and editorial in *The Times* this morning, and I was a little surprised. Mikhail hadn't expressed those opinions so forcibly to me, but he was certainly uncomfortable about returning to Russia. He felt unwelcome there. Now look, if you don't mind . . ."

Kathy got to her feet. "Could I have your mobile number, Mr. Clarke? Just in case I have any more queries."

He looked reluctant, but wrote a number on the back of a card and gave it to her.

"Did you make any calls from Mr. Moszynski's house last Sunday?"

Clarke frowned. "Not that I can remember."

"What about anyone else? Did you see or hear anyone making or taking calls that afternoon and evening?"

"I don't believe so."

"Sir Nigel Hadden-Vane, for instance?"

"Em . . . actually, I think he did call his wife at one stage."

"Anyone else?"

"No. Now I really must get on."

KATHY DROVE ACROSS THE river and picked up the A30, heading south into Surrey. Beyond Esher she turned off the main road, following the satnav prompts. The traffic faded away and the houses, glimpsed through dense banks of foliage, became larger.

She turned onto a gravel drive toward an orange-brick, half-timbered Tudorbethan country house outside which a red Ferrari Spider was parked. A maid showed her into a living room overlooking a broad lawn at the back of the house. Two people were sitting on a sofa, Shaka and Vadim, just like the last time Kathy had seen them at Chelsea Mansions, almost like two people plotting. When they saw Kathy their faces shut down. Shaka's took on the distant, haughty look of a model on a catwalk, while Vadim's set into a hostile frown.

"Sorry to bother you again. I just need to check a few things with you. We need to establish a complete picture of where everyone was during the past week." Kathy went through her routine, recording their recollections of people's movements. Vadim had little to say, and looked increasingly impatient.

When they were finished, Kathy said, "Can you tell me who are the executors of Mr. Moszynski's estate?"

"We are," Shaka said. "The two of us." Had she sounded just a little too offhand?

"You and Mr. Kuzmin."

"Right."

"When was that arranged?"

She shrugged. "Soon after Mikhail and I got married, wasn't it, Vadim?"

He didn't reply, staring balefully at Kathy. She wondered if he'd learned that stare in the KGB.

"You'll have your hands full trying to sort out your husband's finances, won't you, Mrs. Moszynski? I gather they're complicated."

"He's not even in the ground yet," Shaka said coolly. "We're grieving. We haven't thought about it."

Kathy doubted that.

They heard Alisa's voice somewhere outside and Vadim seemed to rouse himself. He said, "We haven't shown Alisa the newspaper reports today. She is still very upset. Please be tactful."

When Alisa came in Kathy went through her questions, and as Moszynski's daughter spoke Kathy was struck by the contrast between Alisa and the other two. At thirty she was actually a couple of years older than Shaka, but seemed much more vulnerable. From time to time she wiped tears from her eyes, recalling something her father had said or done, while Shaka showed no emotion at all. Alisa's husband was fifteen years older than her, and Kathy thought that if she had known nothing about the three of them she might have supposed that Shaka and Vadim were the older generation, more worldly and hardened, and Alisa young enough to be their daughter.

When Kathy was finished she got to her feet and Alisa came over to her, head bowed, and said, "I don't know what I will do without Papa."

Vadim, whose impassive frown had hardly altered throughout the interview, showed Kathy out. At the front door she said, "Do you trust Freddie Clarke, Mr. Kuzmin?"

"What do you mean?"

"You'll be relying on him to access Mr. Moszynski's fortune."

He eyed her coldly. "Let me give good advice, Detective. Let the experts come up with the theories." He swung the door open and stepped back into the shadows, watching her go.

Let me give good advice, Kathy thought as she got into her car. It was a phrase from the letter to *The Times*.

TWELVE

KATHY WAS IN TWO minds about phoning Sean Ardagh, expecting a cool response, but he sounded brisk and helpful.

"A chat? Sure. Now?"

"If you can spare the time. Thanks."

"No problem. Let's meet in Victoria Tower Gardens across the road from my office. Give me an excuse to get out."

The gardens formed a long thin strip along the Thames Embankment close by Thames House, the MI5 building. Kathy spotted him straight away, on a timber bench, reading the *Evening Standard*.

They shook hands and he said, "So, how can I help you?"

"I think you know more about some of the people I'm looking at than I'm finding on the files."

"Could be. Who are you thinking of?"

"How about starting with Freddie Clarke."

Ardagh smiled. "The boy genius? Oh, they don't come any smarter than young Freddie."

"What's his background?"

"Classic East End barrowboy who turned out to be a financial wizard. Supposed to have a photographic memory, maybe high-function autism. He got a job as a messenger boy in the City and by the time he was twenty he was a star of the trading room, making money big-time. Then something happened, I'm not sure what exactly, probably upset somebody important. Anyway, he headed off to Luxembourg and joined Clearstream, the clearing house. You'll have heard of them."

"Vaguely."

"Look them up. At Clearstream he got to manage some of the big accounts of the Russian oligarchs. He did very well, but his mum got cancer and he wanted to come back to London. Mikhail Moszynski got to hear and offered him an exclusive deal to handle his affairs. He bought Truscott Orr for Freddie, who is now, what, thirty, thirty-one?"

Kathy scribbled in her notebook. The late afternoon was balmy, two children further down the park playing tag around their motionless parents. "So where will Mikhail's death leave Freddie?"

"Whoever inherits will be utterly dependent on Freddie to tell them what's going on."

"Really? Surely there'll be documents, contracts?"

"They say it's all inside Freddie's head. So if you're thinking of going after Mikhail's financial records, forget it. It's been tried."

"By you lot?"

Ardagh said nothing, face expressionless.

"Well, let's hope Freddie doesn't have an accident."

"Indeed. It's all immensely complicated, deliberately so. Mikhail was paranoid that the Russian government would try to take his money away from him. That's what Freddie was for, to build an impenetrable financial castle complete with false rooms, dead-end corridors, hidden passages and secret chambers."

"RKF?"

"That's just the gatehouse at the front that everyone can see. Behind it there's a maze stretching from Luxembourg to Bermuda to Labuan to Belize, and on and on."

"Freddie says Alisa will inherit the controlling share."

"Makes sense. Keep it in the bloodline. Mikhail would have wanted that."

"He says Shaka will be taken care of. But will she be content with that?"

"From what I've seen of her, I'd say she'll be sensible. She's like Freddie, another tower block kid. Her old mum still sells T-shirts at the East Street Market down in Walworth. And like Freddie, it's the game that drives Shaka, not the money. She wants to be the best, the most famous, the most glamorous."

"It sounds as if you've done quite a bit of work on these people."

"Not really. These are just my impressions." He gave a careless shrug, which Kathy didn't quite believe.

"How about Vadim?"

"Okay," Ardagh said, "your turn. What do you make of Vadim?"

"Cold, guarded, hostile. My guess was that he'd be quite controlling with Alisa."

"So you're thinking that he'll take effective charge of Mikhail's fortune, and therefore has a motive for killing him?"

"You must have had the same thought, surely?"

He nodded. "And the letter to *The Times* would point the same way, what with Vadim's links to the FSB."

"So you agree he could have been a party to the killing?"

"In theory. But you'd have a hell of a time trying to prove it." He thought for a moment. "And to be honest, it doesn't feel like the FSB to me. They're highly professional, using sophisticated encrypted phones, stuff like that. I can't see them having anything to do with a small-time crook like Danny Yilmaz."

"Maybe to put us off the scent?"

"Well . . . I could speak to Six for you if you like. I know someone who would tell me what they've got on Vadim."

"Thanks." Kathy thought he'd get more from MI6 than she would. "I'd appreciate that."

"Anything else? What about Mikhail's friend down the road?" He nodded along the length of the park to the tall Gothic edifice of the Victoria Tower.

"Parliament? You mean Hadden-Vane? He's been hard to contact today."

"He's got other things on his mind." He opened his newspaper and pointed to an article headed MP DENIES CASH FOR CITIZENSHIP CLAIM.

"That's him?"

"Here." Ardagh handed her the paper. "I'd better go. I'll call you if I get anything useful."

Kathy thanked him and remained on the seat, reading.

Sir Nigel Hadden-Vane has denied a report that he accepted a substantial sum of money from the murdered Russian businessman Mikhail Moszynski to facilitate his daughter Alisa Kuzmin's application for British citizenship, which was approved last year. He said that the claim, first made on westminsterwhistleblower.com, was completely without foundation. Sir Nigel was known to be a personal friend of Mr. Moszynski, and was a guest at the lavish wedding of Alisa Kuzmin in 2006 on Mr. Moszynski's private Caribbean island, Little Ruby Cay, in the Bahamas.

As she walked back through the park toward her car, Kathy passed Rodin's monumental sculpture *The Burghers of Calais*, with its six haggard figures standing in chains on the pedestal, and imagined Hadden-Vane up there, plump and sleek, among them.

"WHO'S BEHIND WESTMINSTERWHISTLEBLOWER.COM?" BREN asked.

"I think we'd better find out," Kathy said. "Zack?"

"I'll have a go," he said, without much enthusiasm.

Kathy had just described what she'd been doing, and one by one they'd made their reports. There wasn't much to be enthusiastic about. Information had been pouring into the HOLMES computer from interviews, records of phone calls made from the area around Cunningham Place, CCTV cameras, witness statements and calls from the public, but little of significance had so far emerged. Frustratingly, the camera over Moszynski's front door had been disconnected for several spells during the previous ten days while a new system was being installed, including the period on Monday when Dr. Stewart had claimed to see Nancy visit. About the only solid fact to emerge was that Moszynski's letter to *The Times* had passed forensic scrutiny and was considered genuine.

"The thing is," Zack said, "there didn't need to be anybody in the square to see him come out for a smoke."

"How do you mean?"

"Well, the killer could have had a camera hidden somewhere, watching the front door, and removed it once he was finished."

"He didn't have much time," Bren said. "My bet would still be on one of the people inside the house tipping him off."

"Not necessarily," Zack insisted. "Could be anybody. Could be Vadim."

"No it couldn't. He was in Moscow."

"So what? He could have arranged for the house security cameras to be relayed to his laptop, in Moscow or anywhere else. He could have watched Mikhail open the front door and phoned the killer as easy as if he'd been there on the spot."

Bren gave a groan. Kathy sympathized. She'd had the same sense of helplessness when she'd been talking to Sean Ardagh, who'd been so much better informed than she was. She wondered how Brock would have moved forward.

As if thinking the same thing, their action manager, Phil, who hadn't been told that Brock wasn't really in Scotland, said, "When's the chief getting back, anyway? Should be here I reckon."

"We need much better profiles of all the main characters," Kathy said forcefully. "Bren, get on to your friends in Fraud and Financial Investigations, see if they've done work on any of them—the Russians, Shaka, Freddie Clarke, Hadden-Vane. The money has got to be a big part of this."

SHE WAS LATE GETTING to the Red Lion, telling herself that she was stupid to come at all and should have phoned to cancel. John was standing by the bar, looking subdued. He glanced up and his face brightened as he caught sight of her, and she felt a little better. He showed her to a small table in the corner.

"What can I get you?"

"Just mineral water, thanks. I've got some driving to do."

She watched him blink away disappointment and say, "Certainly. Ice? Lemon?"

"Please."

"You didn't mean a sandwich here *literally*, did you?"

"Yes, I did. Sorry, I'm short of time."

"Of course." He looked chastened and hurried away.

He returned with her water and a pint of beer for himself. "Sorry, no sandwiches."

"Oh." She shrugged.

"Look, you've got to eat. Can't I buy you a decent, quick dinner?"

"Another time." She took a sip of water and sat back against the wall with a sigh, thankful to be off her feet. "So, how was your day?"

"Not as exciting as yours, I dare say. I went to the Summer Exhibition at the Royal Academy. Big crowds, but I enjoyed it."

"Good." Kathy looked around the room, checking. On reflection it wasn't a good idea meeting there, so close to Queen Anne's Gate. "What did you want to tell me?"

"Did you ring that Montreal number I gave you?"

"Sorry, didn't have time."

"Oh." He frowned down at his beer. "This was a mistake, wasn't it? I'm imposing on you when you're so busy."

She looked over and felt a little sorry for him, aware of the brusqueness in her manner. "Why don't you tell me about Chelsea Mansions? Is it a dump?"

"Well, it isn't the Savoy, that's for sure. I've no idea how it stays solvent with so few guests. But I like the people, Toby, Deb and the others. They're real characters and would do anything for you. They met in Saudi during the first Gulf War, he was in the army and she in the Foreign Office."

"Yes, they told me."

"And did they tell you that's where he lost his son?"

"No."

"Toby doesn't talk about it, but Deb told me today. Apparently he was with special forces. He disappeared somewhere out in the Iraqi desert. What made it especially tragic was that Toby was on the team at headquarters that planned the operation. He was keen for his son to go, to have a chance to see action."

"Oh dear."

"Yes. Deb thinks that's why he gave me a room. I'm the same age as his son was apparently, twenty-eight, and Deb says I look a bit like him."

"He has to like you to give you a room at his hotel?"

"Absolutely!" John laughed. "And what he charges depends on how much he likes you. My room's ridiculously cheap. That's what I mean about wondering how they stay in business. And that's why he feels so guilty about Nancy Haynes. He thinks that if he'd turned her down and she'd gone somewhere else she might still be alive. But according to Deb she wrote him this really charming letter about how she didn't want to stay anywhere else in London, and he said okay."

"Do you know why she wanted to stay there?"

"Good location for the Chelsea Flower Show, I imagine. So tell me, how did you come to be a detective?"

"Oh . . ." She didn't feel like going into it, but made an effort. "One day I was having a cup of coffee in a café. Across the street was a police station. I watched the people come and go through the doors—uniformed men, shirt-sleeved for the summer, chatting in pairs as they returned from their beat; people in civilian clothes looking like any other office workers, running down the steps to catch their buses; and, most of all, the uniformed women. I watched the way they moved through the evening crowds, and the way they spoke to each other. When I finished my coffee I crossed the street, followed three women constables up the steps, and asked the desk sergeant for information on joining up."

"Just like that? No regrets?"

"No. I felt like I'd come home."

He gave a puzzled smile. "I guess I'd have to know the back story to understand that."

But Kathy didn't want to say any more about herself. "You'd make a pretty good detective. You seem to be good at getting information."

"Oh, don't say that. My mother would kill me. She told me I could be anything I wanted, except a cop."

"How come?"

"She was married to one once—my dad."

"Ah."

"Yeah. So I became an academic, but still, I've always been curious about the police. I guess it must be the sense of comradeship that made you feel at home, the people you work closely with."

She laughed. "Not all of them."

"No, but, well there's that guy you were on TV with. Brock? Was that his name?"

"Yes, I've been on his team for a long time now. He's the best."

"Right. You must get pretty close, emotionally."

She stared at him, eyebrows going up, and he blushed. "Sorry, didn't mean to pry."

"Yes you did. Brock and I are colleagues."

"Right, right."

"So what would your Lieutenant Ledoux have told me if I'd got around to ringing him?"

"Ah, well, I've done some work for him."

"What, tutoring his kids, fixing his car?"

"No, no. Police work."

Kathy gave him a skeptical look and he hurried on. "My academic field is linguistics, studying texts, mainly from the fifteenth and sixteenth centuries. One of things I've specialized in is establishing authorship of unattributed fragments of writing. A couple of years ago they did an article about it in the *Montreal Gazette* and Paul Ledoux contacted me. He was working on a suicide that he suspected might be a murder, and wondered if I could tell if the suicide note left on the guy's computer was genuine. Looking at other things he'd done, I decided he hadn't written this, and appeared as an expert witness in court. It turned out I was right. Since then I've given advice in over a dozen cases in Canada."

"Forensic linguistics," Kathy said.

"Right. There aren't many of us about. The thing is, I heard about the Russian's letter to *The Times* this morning, and it occurred to me that you might need to authenticate it."

"We've done that."

"Oh." His face dropped.

"The notepaper, the signature appear to be genuine. It was typed on his computer."

"That's not what I look at. People can steal a piece of notepaper and copy a signature, but they can't impersonate another person's form of words, not perfectly. That's what I study: the text, its construction, vocabulary, use of idiom and so on."

"Yes, I understand that, but—"

"It just seemed to me a good idea no, *vital*, that you check that too. After all, if Moszynski didn't write that letter it changes everything, doesn't it?"

Kathy considered his bright, intelligent eyes. There was something quite disarming about his enthusiasm, like an eager border collie that knows exactly what needs to be done. She could have used a few more border collies on the job today. "It certainly does."

"And you don't really think the FSB is behind this, do you?"

"Don't I? Why do you say that?"

"Because Brock's in Scotland, isn't he?"

She blinked. "What?"

"On your phone in the hotel. Sorry, I couldn't help overhearing. You were talking about someone being in Scotland. It's Brock, isn't it, following up a completely different line of investigation? I had exactly the same idea myself."

"You did?"

"Yes. Emerson told me about Nancy's plans to contact long-lost relatives up there, and I wondered if there might be something in her past that led to her death. I guess it's my work that makes me think like that. I need to place the texts I deal with in the context of their past, because everything about them—language, ideas, themes—is shaped by that. You have to understand the past in order to interpret the present, like why you became a cop and I didn't. So anyway, what do you think? Will Brock agree?"

"Agree to what?"

"To me taking a look at Moszynski's letter. Or maybe he doesn't have to, if he's away in Scotland. You could commission me. I'm not expensive."

Kathy laughed.

"And it would look good on my CV. What we would need is similar samples—ideally other letters to newspapers. Do you know if he was in the habit of writing to the papers?"

A good question. "We can find out."

SHE FELT WEARY BY the time she got to Brock's place. Apprehensive, too—she had never seen Brock ill before, and it had been like a sudden revelation of his mortality. It had shaken her more than she'd realized, and as she raised the key to his front door she hesitated, remembering that first glimpse of him in bed the day before, and wondering how she would react if she went in and really did find him dead. Part of her would die too, she was sure of that.

"That you, Kathy?" The voice was hoarse.

She grinned, said, "Yep, it's me," and ran up the stairs.

He was sitting on the sofa in the living room, looking somewhat diminished in his old tartan dressing-gown, but with a little color in his cheeks.

"How are you feeling?"

"Bit better. Come in, sit down."

"What are those?" Kathy pointed to the files and crime scene photographs scattered around him.

"I got Dot to courier them over." He nodded toward the whiskey bottle on the side table. "Pour us a snifter, will you?"

"How about food?"

"Had some soup. Now, tell me what's been going on."

"Everyone's desperate for you to come back from Scotland."

"I'm planning on flying back tonight."

"Really? Are you up to it?"

"Sadly the bracing Scottish weather didn't agree with me, and I shall have a bit of a cold and look somewhat the worse for wear. But you've been covering for me long enough, Kathy. Tell me about today."

So she did, everything except her drink with John Greenslade.

"Zack's right," Brock said. "Soon we won't need to leave our screens to do our job. We'll be able to see what's going on inside every room and every car. But we still won't be able to see what's going on inside people's heads. And you're worried about what's going on inside Vadim Kuzmin's head, am I right?"

Kathy nodded. "He's a hard case, doesn't give much away."

"And Five can't give us any leads to Russian visitors we should be talking to?"

"Apparently not. We're running our own checks through the Border Agency, but so far nothing promising."

"So we're thinking of a domestic killer hired by someone like Vadim to do the dirty work while he's out of the country."

"Something like that."

"What about Captain Marvel?"

"Danny Yilmaz? We haven't got any further with him. The CPS are worried about going for the aid and abet charge on the basis of what we have so far, and the court granted him bail."

"And yet he's pretty much all we've got." Brock scratched his beard thoughtfully. "Tottenham have been looking into that cousin of his, Barbaros Kaya, but they haven't come up with anything."

"Yes."

"I think we should speak to Danny again. And Vadim, a formal interview. Let's work on both ends to find out who's in the middle."

THIRTEEN

EVERYONE SEEMED IMMENSELY PLEASED to see Brock back, Dot especially so. Brock shrugged off her solicitations with a grunt and a request for strong coffee. The truth was that he still felt half dead, and the effort involved in pretending to be normal seemed to sap what little energy he had. He sat alone for a while in his office, gathering his strength for the team meeting, then took a deep breath and put a call through to Commander Sharpe's office. He too was delighted to hear from Brock.

"You sound a bit ropey, Brock. Catch a bug on the plane? So how was the castle?"

Brock blinked, wondering what he was talking about. "Could still bear fruit, sir. But not as productive as I'd hoped. We're becoming quite interested in Vadim Kuzmin."

"The son-in-law, yes of course. The FSB connection. Is there a problem?"

"I wonder if a high-level request could be made for Five and Six to open their files on the man."

"We can but try. Leave it with me. There's been a hell of a lot of speculation while you've been away—TV, papers, blogs, questions in the House. Well, you'll know of course. Marilyn says we need to give them something. Maybe something on the Scottish angle? What do you think?"

"Not yet, sir. Could prejudice our inquiries."

Sharpe gave a growl like a pit bull with toothache. "Twenty-four hours, Brock. Give me *something*."

THE ENTHUSIASTIC MOOD IN the team meeting quickly went flat as Brock's unhappiness with progress became apparent. He listened with a frown to the reports from each of the groups and finally pointed at Emerson Merckle's photograph of the man at the Chelsea Flower Show, enlarged and enhanced until the pale scar down the left cheek of his brooding face was apparent.

"What happened to this man after he got off the motorbike at Camden Town tube station? We'll have to go over it all again, every station on the Northern Line, every camera, every eyewitness. Where does a man go after he commits a murder? Church, brothel, pub, betting shop, Turkish bath? There's got to be a trace of him somewhere. Kathy, I want you to take charge of this. Bren, you and I will go up to Tottenham and interview Danny Yilmaz again. Come on everyone, twenty-four hours. Give me something."

HE FELT BAD AFTERWARD, repeating Sharpe's demand without any clear hope of a result, and he felt worse when they finally had Danny Yilmaz sitting hunched in front of them in an interview room, waiting for his brief to arrive. There was something about the glare of the fluorescent lights, the indefinable smell in the stale air, the scrape of metal chairs on plastic floor tiles, that seemed deliberately calculated to make him feel nauseous.

"Danny," he said softly, "the tape's not running yet, nothing's going on the record, but before we begin I want to do you a good turn."

"Oh yeah, sure."

"We know you were lying to us. And we know why. It was a favor for your cousin Barbaros, wasn't it? And we know that it was Barbaros that you picked up on your bike after he killed that woman in Sloane Street."

Danny was eyeing him with a glassy, unfocused look and Brock felt his heart sink. This was absurd, a wild stab in the dark, and Danny knew it. But he had to press on.

"We can't prove it, not yet, but we know it's true. So we are going to make Barbaros's life hell until we do. We are going to rip his house apart and his car and that TV repair shop he owns, and his mother's house and your mother's house and everything they own until we find what we're looking for. So make it easy for us. Tell us where to look."

He sat back and waited. He sensed Bren beside him shift in his seat, probably thinking the old man had lost it. He was right, it had been a truly terrible impersonation of a cheap cop show interrogation, and when Danny told his brief there'd be trouble. Brock felt ashamed.

Danny lifted his head and stared at Brock, who thought he saw a flicker of panic in his eyes. "It was nothing to do with Barbaros," he said finally. "I swear. He was a Scotchman."

"The man on the phone or on the bike?" Brock said calmly.

Danny bowed his head. "The guy I picked up on Sloane Street."

"A Scotsman, you say?"

"Yeah. Well hard. Listen, it was nothing to do with Barbaros. You've got that totally wrong, I swear."

"We'll see," Brock said. "So where did he go when you dropped him at Camden Town?"

"I dunno. Back to Scotland for all I know."

"You think he came from there?"

"Well, he came from somewhere. That's what the bloke on the phone said."

"And you're sure the one on the phone wasn't the same man?"

"Oh yeah. The one on the phone sounded like a Londoner." He paused and slumped lower in his seat. "The one on the bike had flash shoes, Nike Air Jordans, blue with orange trim. Listen, I feel sick . . ." And then he turned his head and threw up on the floor.

They called the duty sergeant to look after Danny. "We'll leave it for now," Brock said. "Tell his lawyer he doesn't need to bother."

On the way out Brock phoned Kathy, passing on the information about the shoes and the Scottish accent. "It's possible he got the Northern Line from Camden Town to Euston, to catch a train back up north."

When they got into the car Bren said, "Smart work, Chief."

"It may be nothing. Anyway, I didn't deserve it."

Bren laughed, but didn't disagree.

"SCOTLAND?" ZACK SHOOK HIS head. "Is he having us on?"

"Apparently not," Kathy said, although the same thought had occurred to her. She began contacting the teams with the new information, moving some to Euston, Kings Cross and St. Pancras rail stations to check CCTV records. But it was Zack who first spotted the shoes, coming out of Camden Town tube station a few minutes after the killer had gone in, but this time on the feet of a man wearing a pale cream jacket and a cap.

"Got him," Zack said. "He must have put on the jacket and cap inside the station, and now he's heading north up Camden Road."

They picked him up again going into Camden Road rail station on the London Overground network, a couple of hundred yards away, buying a ticket and catching a train heading east.

Again Kathy called up the teams to check the stations along the North London Line—Caledonian Road and Barnsbury, Highbury and Islington, Canonbury, Dalston Kingsland, and then Hackney Central, where they retrieved images of him leaving the station and disappearing into the streets leading south.

Meanwhile the Scottish Crime and Drug Enforcement Agency had got back to them with an identification of the man at the flower show. His name was Harold Michael Peebles, thirty-six years old, known as Hard Harry Peebles, and his last known address was HM Prison Barlinnie, Glasgow, from which he had recently been released after completing a six-year sentence for manslaughter. A check confirmed that Peebles had been a passenger on a British Midland Airways flight from Glasgow to London on the morning of Wednesday 26 May. There was no record of him taking a return flight.

EVERYONE CONVERGED ON THE Hackney police station, where the CCTV coordinator began the search through local sources for the afternoon of 27 May. After an hour they had found one brief sighting on a bank security camera of the man in the blue and orange shoes, then nothing more. They moved their search to the following day, the mood of frustration growing among those who waited. Bren and the borough detectives were impatient to get out and canvass shops, pubs and betting shops with pictures of the wanted man, but Brock held them back, not wanting to spook him if he was still in the area. The trawl through camera footage continued through the twenty-eighth, the twenty-ninth, but in the end it was Glasgow that provided the answer. The office at Barlinnie Prison had run the word "Hackney" through their computer and come up with a next-of-kin address for one of the inmates in C Hall, where Harry Peebles had been housed. The address was for the man's sister, a Mrs. Angela Storey of 13 Ferncroft Close, Hackney. A check soon established that Mrs. Storey was divorced, childless and currently serving time in nearby Holloway Prison.

A helicopter from the Air Support Unit at Lippitts Hill was called in, giving them aerial surveillance. Ferncroft Close was a quiet residential cul-de-sac of just twenty houses in two terraces facing each other across a roadway jammed with parked cars. One end was blocked by a railway embankment and there was a rear access laneway running behind the back gardens of the terrace in which number thirteen was located. Brock called for an armed response unit and made his plans.

After his experience at Danny Yilmaz's flat, Brock didn't go in with the team, but instead watched from Queen Anne's Gate, through the helicopter's camera, the unmarked car and two white vans arriving at Ferncroft Close. There was a sense of unreality in seeing it unfold like this, like a computer game, with sound effects, a sudden burst of dogs barking coming through the headphones. Brock remembered other such raids in years gone by, when communications meant a shout and a dodgy radio.

THERE WAS NOTHING UNREAL about the raid as far as Kathy was concerned, sitting squashed up in the white van with a gang of uniforms. One of them was the operator for a device new to the Met, the Black Hornet, currently on operational field trials from its Norwegian manufacturer. Looking over the operator's shoulder, Kathy watched him open the small aluminum case that he was carrying and take out one of three tiny black helicopters, as small as a child's toy. They opened the rear doors of the van and the man released the device, which rose with a soft purr into the air. He settled back down with a control panel and screen, guiding the Hornet down the street to hover silently outside the windows of number thirteen, sending pictures back to the van. A neat toy, Kathy thought, but nothing could shield you from the reality of a forcible arrest, the shock of violent contact, the spontaneous decision that could take a life or ruin a career in a millisecond.

"No signs of movement on this side of the house," the Hornet operator intoned. He guided the machine over the roof and down to check the windows at the back. "Doesn't look as if anybody's at home . . . hang on. Upstairs room, far side. Curtains are closed and it looks as if . . ." He fiddled with the helicopter controls, moving it closer. "Yes, a light is on inside."

A stir went through the van, people easing in their seats, adjusting their equipment.

The Hornet operator looked at Kathy. "Boss?"

Kathy spoke into the radio to Bren in the other van, which was at the entrance to the rear lane. "Right," she said finally. "First crew straight up the stairs to that bedroom, second clear the ground floor. The others are coming in the back. Let's go."

The van lurched forward down Ferncroft Close and came to a stop outside number thirteen. Now the rear doors were thrown open and they were racing out, smashing open the front door, charging inside with shouts of "Police! Don't move!" Kathy pounded up the stairs, following the lead pair with their helmets and guns, and sucked in a deep breath as she watched the first man kick the bedroom door open, then come to an abrupt stop, staring inside.

"What?" She ran forward, and the smell hit her before anything else, a gust of hot, fetid air billowing out onto the landing. She pushed past the man and saw a figure stretched out on a narrow bed. A grotesque effigy of a man, bloated, cloudy eyes open and unseeing, skin green and mottled like a rotten marrow.

"Is that him?" Bren was by her side. Then he gagged and reached for a handkerchief to cover his nose.

Kathy called back over her shoulder, "No signs of life. Everybody out." She took in the rest of the room, an electric fire blazing away with both bars, a syringe and strap lying on a fluffy pink rug beside the bed, the headboard of the bed decorated with decals of fluffy teddy bears and rabbits.

She got on the phone to Brock. "He's been dead a while. Several days. Hardly looks like him, but there's that scar down his left cheek."

"I'm on my way."

FOURTEEN

THAT EVENING KATHY ARRIVED back at Queen Anne's Gate before the others and went to find Pip Gallagher. The young detective constable was at her desk, surrounded by photocopies and file notes.

"Sounds like I missed out on some excitement," Pip said. "We really got a result?"

"Looks promising. The man on the motorbike, dead in his safe house, OD'd by the look of it."

"Celebrating after a job well done, was he? Serves the bastard right."

"Got anything for me?"

"Yeah, boss." She shuffled papers together. "Grab a chair."

Kathy sat at her side and began to examine the pages Pip handed to her.

"Mikhail has written to the papers before, once to *The Times*, several times to the *Surrey Advertiser* and before that the *Esher News and Mail*, which has now closed down. There may have been others I haven't found."

"Funny place to write about the threat from the Russian government."

"Except that wasn't what he was writing about." Pip consulted her notes. "He was writing in support of the activities of various bodies—mainly the BHPS."

Kathy frowned, trying to think if she'd heard of it. "What's that, neo-Nazis?"

Pip laughed. "Not quite. The British Hedgehog Preservation Society."

"You're having me on."

"Straight up. Mikhail thought they were doing a wonderful job. Also the CPRE, the Campaign to Protect Rural England, and the PTES, the People's Trust for Endangered Species. He was a member of all three, apparently, and a generous donor."

"Esher is where his daughter lives."

"Yes. I spoke to the secretary of the local branch of HogWatch. They plot hedgehog sightings reported in by volunteers. Apparently Mikhail was a keen hedgehog spotter whenever he went down to visit his daughter."

Kathy was astonished. "You think you have an idea of someone, and then you come across something like this and realize you were thinking in stereotypes. The hedgehog oligarch. Nothing political? You're sure?"

"I've contacted all the national papers and the main London locals. Here are facsimile copies of the letters he sent." She handed Kathy a file. "I've also followed up on forensic linguists, like you said. Central registry has the names of two approved specialists, but one's in Japan for the next month and the other's in hospital having quintuple bypass heart surgery. So I gave them your Canadian's name and asked them to look into him. Was that okay?"

"Yes, fine."

"They checked him out and said we can use him if the other two aren't available. I've got the paperwork here that he'd have to sign." Another file.

"You've done well, Pip, thanks."

"I'd rather have been breaking that bastard's door down, boss."

"Next time."

BROCK RETURNED FROM HACKNEY, exhausted but quietly satisfied, and told the team to get themselves cleaned up, grab mugs of tea and assemble for a debriefing. Dot was waiting for him with a message from Commander Sharpe, who wanted to come over as soon as Brock got back.

Ten minutes later he was sitting in Brock's office.

"Brilliant," he beamed. "To be perfectly honest, Brock, I had severe doubts about that Scottish angle you were chasing. I should have known that you always have something up your sleeve. I still don't quite see what this has to do with Nancy Haynes' relatives though . . ."

"It turned out to be a bit more complicated than we first thought," Brock improvised. "There's still a lot of work to be done to tie Peebles to whoever commissioned the murders."

"Yes, but the important thing is that we have a result." Sharpe paused, looking at Brock more closely. "You look all in, old chap."

"I've had a bit of a bug, sir."

"Well, I think a simple press release. No need for interviews until you have some more answers."

"Yes, I agree."

Sharpe got to his feet. "I'd like to congratulate everyone personally."

"Of course." Brock led the way to the big room where they were all gathered and Sharpe said his piece, shook hands with Brock and left.

There was a buzz of satisfaction in the room, a sense of shared achievement, and Brock had to remind them that this was a good beginning, but only a beginning. Now they had to discover where Harry Peebles would lead them.

"Bren," he said, "tell us what we have from the house."

"Right." Bren got to his feet and stood in front of the board on which Peebles' picture was posted. Alongside he stuck felt-pen sketch plans of the layout of the two floors of the house in Ferncroft Close, and photographs of the bedroom.

"The body was found upstairs in this bedroom, fully clothed, with a syringe on the floor beside the bed on which he was lying. Fingerprints confirm that it is Peebles. Time of death is obviously important, but the body was not fresh. The medical examiner was cagey about time of death, because of the high temperature in the room. When pressed he suggested about three days ago, which would put it immediately after Mikhail Moszynski was killed. The light was on in the bedroom, indicating it happened at night. On the chest of drawers in the bedroom we also found a bag containing ten thousand pounds in twenties.

"The search of the house and garden hasn't yet found the knife that was used to kill Moszynski. But we did find a mobile phone in the pocket of Peebles' jeans. This is being given priority.

"The rest of the house looked as if Peebles had been living there for several days. Judging by the bottles, frozen-food packets and dirty dishes, it looked as if he was doing most of his eating and drinking there and not going out for meals. We've started door-knocking the street and surrounding area, including the local off-license and supermarket, and of course the CCTV cameras in the vicinity."

Bren paused, and Brock said, "Any other drugs in the house?"

"Not that we've found so far. But I did wonder if there could be a drug angle to this. Suppose Moszynski was using his companies to bring drugs into the country and had upset some locals, who decided to bring in an outside contractor to take care of him."

"Hm. What do we know about Peebles? Any gangland drug connections there?"

Kathy spoke. "We've got his record, and yes, plenty of drug connections. He was jailed twice for dealing and his last spell in Barlinnie was for the killing of a user who owed one of the big Glasgow drug gangs a lot of money. The Crown Office settled for manslaughter. Peebles was also a heroin user. He was on drug and alcohol rehabilitation programs while he was inside. No known connections to London dealers though. He told his parole officer about an offer of work in London, and was given permission to go south for a trial period of one week."

"Maybe Moszynski was moving into the Scottish market and upsetting people up there," Bren suggested.

"Anything else, Kathy?" Brock felt drained, remembering that he was due to take another Tamiflu tablet.

"We've been checking the cameras at Heathrow to see if Peebles was met off his flight on Wednesday, but nothing so far."

"Right." Brock stood up. "Well done, everyone. Go home and get a good night's sleep. We've got plenty to follow up tomorrow."

As he made his way out Kathy caught up with him and said, "One other thing. I thought I'd have the text of the letter that Moszynski sent to *The Times* authenticated."

"Haven't we done that already?"

"The notepaper and signature were passed by forensics, but we should make sure the language was his. We can compare it with other letters he sent to newspapers. But the thing is that the two specialists the Yard normally uses are both unavailable. There is someone else, a Canadian staying in the hotel next to the Moszynskis in Chelsea, where Nancy Haynes was also staying. He's had experience doing this kind of work for the police in Canada. In fact, it was he who suggested to me we should get it done. I thought I might ask him to have a look."

Brock gazed at her for a moment and thought he detected a slight awkwardness in her manner. It did sound a bit odd.

"Have I met him?"

"I don't think so, no. His name is John Greenslade, a professor of linguistics at McGill University. I've checked him out."

"So he's not a possible suspect?"

Kathy hesitated. "Well, I suppose no one in Cunningham Place is completely in the clear until we find whoever was paying Peebles. But it seems unlikely."

Brock frowned and rubbed his chin. "I remember the hotel, but haven't been inside. When I get on top of things I must go and take a good look. Okay, go ahead."

IT WAS ALMOST TEN o'clock that night when Kathy called in at Cunningham Place on her way back to her flat in Finchley. She might have left it till the following day, but told herself it would be another job done.

Deb was at her usual station at the front desk, the radio playing softly behind her. She looked up at the sound of the front door bell and cried, "Aha! Congratulations!"

Kathy hesitated. "Sorry?"

"It was on the news just now. A breakthrough in the Chelsea murder cases. You've got somebody."

"That was quick. Yes, we had a bit of luck today."

Toby had heard the noise and appeared, a glass of Scotch in hand. He raised it. "Well done. It was definitely him, was it, that murdered Nancy?"

"We believe so, yes."

"In heaven's name why? Drugs, I suppose?"

"We're looking into that."

"You look tired, dear," Deb said. "Can we get you something?"

"A drink?" Toby offered.

Kathy suppressed a yawn. "No, thanks. I just came to have a quick word with Mr. Greenslade, if he's in."

She was aware of them giving her quizzical looks. Toby lowered his glass. "He's surely not involved, is he?"

"No. There's just something he might be able to help me with."

"Really?" They eyed the files under her arm, then Deb said, "Yes, I believe he is in. Let me give him a ring."

She picked up the phone and dialed, and after a moment purred, "John, dear? You have a visitor," in such a suggestive tone that Kathy winced and wished she'd arranged to meet him at the local police station.

"Would you like to use the guests' lounge, Inspector?" Deb said. "There's no one in there."

"Fine, thanks."

When John appeared his hair was disheveled and he looked as if he'd been asleep.

"Sorry to disturb you so late," Kathy said.

"No, not at all. I was doing some last-minute editing on the paper I have to deliver at the conference tomorrow, and I fell asleep. It's one thing to nod off during somebody else's lecture, but falling asleep during your own is a very bad sign. So what can I do for you?"

"I've had approval to ask you to look at Moszynski's letter."

He straightened and his face lit up. "Really? That's great."

"I have some papers here you'll have to sign—the terms of your appointment and a confidentiality agreement."

"Sure."

He pulled a pair of glasses out of his pocket and Kathy watched him as he quickly scanned the pages. The glasses made him look older and more serious.

"Not a problem," he said at last. "Got a pen?"

He scrawled several signatures then said, "We'll need to get hold of some comparable things he's written in English."

She handed him the file. "We've found these other letters he's written to newspapers."

"Excellent." He pondered for a moment. "Do you know how he composes the letters? I mean, does he dictate them into a machine or to a typist, does he write a draft longhand, or does he type them on a computer?"

"We can ask his secretary."

"Yeah, that would be good. I'd like to know if someone else edited them before they were finalized."

"Do you need to speak to her yourself?"

"It might be as well."

He was giving his conference paper the next morning, and would be free after one p.m. Kathy said she'd arrange something for the afternoon and text him with the details.

"I do appreciate you asking me to do this. I was afraid you didn't trust me. Did you have to okay it with your boss, DCI Brock?"

"Yes, so don't let me down, John."

FIFTEEN

SUNDEEP MEHTA HAD HARRY Peebles' naked body on the stainless-steel table, carefully checking his arms and torso and between his fingers and toes for puncture marks.

"How long has he been out of prison?"

"Just over four weeks," Kathy said. "He'd been inside for six years."

The pathologist grunted. "I count five recent puncture marks, but the only way to be sure is to take his skin off and hold it up to the light. What's your thinking?"

"We'd like to establish his recent drug history. Get an idea how an experienced drug taker like him could have OD'd."

"Happens all the time, especially after a spell of abstinence in jail. His hair will give us his drug history, but the analysis will take time."

"What about time of death?" Brock said. Kathy glanced at him. It was the first time he'd spoken, and his voice sounded slurred. The very first time she had met him had been at an autopsy like this, with Sundeep Mehta presiding. There had been many since then. That first time she'd felt queasy, but now it was Brock who was looking gray.

"Give me a chance, Brock!" Sundeep protested. "I've hardly

begun. But by the look of him . . ." he gazed appraisingly at the corpse, "six days, seven?"

"No, no," Brock growled. "He killed someone on Sunday night, three and a half days ago. The room he was in was very hot."

"I know that." Sundeep consulted his notes. "Forty-two Centigrade. But still, bacterial action is very extensive. No flies in the room unfortunately. A few maggots would have helped." He reached for his scalpel.

Brock cleared his throat, and Sundeep looked up. "You feeling all right, Brock? You're looking . . ."

"Fine." Brock roused himself. "Had a touch of flu. Getting over it."

"Not swine flu, I hope." Sundeep looked at him severely over his face mask.

"Don't worry."

"Have you seen a doctor?"

"Mm."

"What did he give you?"

"Tamiflu."

Sundeep put down the scalpel and peered more closely at Brock. "How long have you had that rash?"

Brock touched his throat. "Just came up last night. Can we get on with the PM, please?"

But Sundeep wasn't to be diverted. He peeled off his gloves, put on a fresh pair and advanced on Brock. They looked a slightly comical pair, Kathy thought affectionately, old friends, the pathologist small and nut-brown against the larger, grayer bulk of the detective. Except that the expression on Sundeep's face wasn't comical as he unbuttoned the front of Brock's shirt, despite the other man's protests, and examined the scarlet blaze across his chest.

"Macula," he muttered. "Papular."

"What's that mean in English?" Brock grunted, brushing him off.

"It means . . ." Sundeep began, then shook his head and turned away to the phone on the wall. He consulted the hospital directory hanging beside it and made a call while the rest of them—Brock, Kathy and what could be seen of Sundeep's assistant beneath her plastic helmet and thick rubber gloves and apron—stood motionless, waiting.

"All right." Sundeep hung up. "It means that you're going upstairs to the fourth floor to see a friend of mine."

"No," Brock said. "This is . . ." He stopped, gave a grunt and slumped to the floor.

IT WAS ALMOST AN hour before Dr. Mehta emerged from the isolation ward. He looked worried and preoccupied.

"What is it, Sundeep?" Kathy demanded. "What's the matter with him?"

"Well, it's not swine flu, Kathy."

"So?"

Sundeep looked at her and his face formed an encouraging smile, which Kathy didn't find very convincing. "We aren't sure yet. There are many causes of maculopapular rash."

"Like what?"

"Oh, measles, rubella, typhoid . . ."

"Typhoid?"

"Has he been abroad lately?"

"No."

"In contact with foreigners?"

Kathy thought. "This started on Sunday night. We attended the murder scene of that Russian, Mikhail Moszynski, and Brock suddenly felt faint."

"Did he touch the body?"

"I don't know."

"Wait a minute." Sundeep disappeared abruptly back into the ward, and Kathy watched him through the glass panel, gesticulating to the doctor who was at Brock's bedside. As she watched them, Kathy guessed what they were discussing, and a chill formed inside her. After a few minutes Sundeep returned.

"You're thinking about Litvinenko," Kathy said.

He nodded. "Four years ago, Alexander Litvinenko fell suddenly ill in a sushi restaurant in London. It took a little while to establish that he had been poisoned with a radioactive isotope, polonium-210, in his tea. Polonium is invisible to normal radiation detectors, because it doesn't emit gamma rays, only alpha rays. It is highly toxic if swallowed—*or inhaled*."

"But . . . Moszynski was stabbed to death. You did the autopsy yourself."

"Yes." Sundeep was shaking his head.

"You think the stabbing was to disguise the real cause of death?"

"I don't know, Kathy. They're doing lots of tests. They want us both to give samples. When you've done that, go back to work and don't worry."

EASIER SAID THAN DONE. When Kathy got into her car she rang the number of the antiques shop down in Sussex owned by Brock's partner, Suzanne Chambers. Suzanne's assistant, Ginny, said that she was still on her tour of the West Country, attending auctions and sales, and gave Kathy the number of her mobile. Suzanne was devastated when Kathy told her what had happened.

"In hospital? He was feeling rotten when I phoned him on Saturday, before I left, but of course he said it was nothing."

"Saturday?"

"Yes. He thought it was just a cold."

Suzanne said she'd come straight back to London. She took down the address of the hospital and asked Kathy to ring again if there was further news.

Bren and his team had returned from a further search of the Hackney house when Kathy got back to Queen Anne's Gate and told them what had happened. She was still feeling stunned. "They can't say what's wrong with him, but it's not flu. They're doing tests."

"Like what? His heart?"

"I don't think so. They've put him in isolation, as if he's picked up something infectious. I had to give them a blood sample, and so did Sundeep."

Mickey Schaeffer gave a frown. "Do you think it could have something to do with the Ugandan kid in Danny Yilmaz's flat? He covered Brock with his nose bleed."

"I forgot about him. Where is he now?"

"They handed him over to Immigration."

"Get on to them, Mickey. Find out what happened to him. See if he's sick."

It was hard to concentrate on anything else, but while they waited Kathy asked Bren about Ferncroft Close.

"Neighbors can't remember seeing any visitors to number thirteen apart from Peebles. His are the only prints on the syringe and the foil of heroin. No indication where he got it from. Only his prints on the cash. Variety of prints elsewhere in the house, some probably the owner's, Angela Storey. We'll have to interview her in Holloway and get names of visitors we can eliminate."

"Nothing then?"

"Wouldn't say that." Bren gave his quiet smile, keeping the best for last. "The mobile phone. It's a prepaid job, again only his prints on it. It's made and received calls from just two numbers."

Bren handed her a note of the numbers. "One is another anonymous prepaid mobile. The other is a landline belonging to one Gloria Cummins with a Chelsea address. We know her." He handed Kathy a printout from the PNC.

"A prostitute?" Kathy skimmed down a string of aliases, cautions, arrests, charges and convictions.

"She's a madam now, and moved upmarket, running an escort service with a posh address and a stable of classy girls."

"Do we speak to her?"

"I don't know. I think there's something funny about this. Gloria seems an odd choice for a rough bastard like Peebles. You should check out her website, appealing to a better class of punters, and expensive. And she's in Chelsea."

"What are you thinking?"

"Maybe she's just an intermediary, a point of contact between Peebles and his client, maybe to hand over payments. And I imagine she'll be very reluctant to tell us anything. Her business depends on confidentiality. No, I think we should sniff around a bit first. And then there's the other number. Look at the timing of the calls—the day Peebles arrived in London, the evening of the day that Nancy died, and the night of Moszynski's death."

Kathy stared at the mobile number and felt a surge of adrenaline. "It's him, isn't it? The client, the one who ordered the hits. Peebles is telling him he's done the job."

"Looks like it."

"You don't think we can trace it?"

"That's priority number one. Leave it with me."

"Boss?" Mickey was standing at the door, looking worried.

"What?"

"Immigration are holding Peter Namono in a secure medical facility at the Gravesend detention center. They say he's sick, but they're still running tests to find out what it is."

"Right, thanks, Mickey. I'll let Brock's doctors know."

"Something else. I had to speak to Tottenham to find out where Namono was, and they told me that Danny Yilmaz had collapsed and been rushed to hospital too."

"Blimey." Bren was staring at Kathy.

Kathy got on the phone. Sundeep answered his mobile with a clipped, "Mehta," and listened in silence as Kathy told him. He got her to run through the sequence of events, then said, "Well, if it's the same thing, that would rule out the Russian as the source, wouldn't it?"

"You think the African might have typhoid or something?"

"We'll find out, Kathy."

Kathy hung up. They were all staring at her. They had heard her say *typhoid*, and were waiting for enlightenment, reassurance. She shrugged. "They're on to it. We just have to wait. So back to work."

She sat down with Bren and set about planning the next steps in the investigation, then left a message with Sharpe's office about Brock's illness, and finally returned to her desk and the new pile of reports that had arrived.

KATHY WAS IN THE main computer suite when Sundeep finally rang back. "We have a diagnosis, Kathy." His tone was neutral, Kathy thought, like someone giving the time or a weather forecast.

"Typhoid?"

"No."

"Thank goodness." She smiled at the others who were on their feet, listening.

"It appears to be something called MHF—Marburg Hemorrhagic Fever."

"Marburg? I've never heard of it. Is it serious?"

"I'm afraid it is. Very serious. If it is MHF—and there seems to be little doubt—we will all have to be isolated. You must make a list of everyone who has been in contact with Brock since that day. Also Yilmaz and Namono."

Kathy sat down slowly, fist tight on the phone cord.

"The Marburg virus comes from East Africa, Kathy. It was first identified in a German laboratory where they were working with African monkeys. Since then there have been a number of outbreaks in Africa. It's related to the Ebola virus."

"Ebola . . ." Kathy stared at the others clustered around. Someone whispered, "Oh fuck!"

Zack was tapping away on his computer, and when Kathy put the phone down he said, "Hell's bells."

They looked at him as he read from the screen in front of him, "*Marburg is a biosafety level-four agent. Transmission through bodily fluids . . . Early symptoms non-specific, including fever, head-ache, myalgia. After five days a maculopapular rash often present on trunk . . . Later-stage infection is acute and can include pancre-atitis, delirium, hemorrhaging, liver failure . . . Symptoms usually last one to three weeks until the disease either resolves or kills the infected host . . . There is no specific antiviral therapy currently available. Fatality rate from twenty-three to ninety percent.*"

Kathy felt dizzy. She took a deep breath and tried to pull herself together.

"Pip, Mickey," she said, "inform front desk that no one is to enter or leave, then contact everyone in the building and tell them what's happened. Tell them to tell their families to go home and put themselves in quarantine until we know more. Phil, I want a list of everyone who's been in physical contact with Brock, Yilmaz and Namono since last Friday. You'll have to con-tact Tottenham. I'll speak to Commander Sharpe."

She hesitated, then said, "Has anyone got any symptoms?"

There was a moment's paralyzed silence, then she said, "Okay.

Get on with it," and the room erupted, people running for the door and the phones.

Kathy put the call through to Sharpe's office, insisting on speaking to him immediately. As she waited to be connected, she remembered the rather awkward handshake that Sharpe had given Brock the previous evening. When he came on he listened to her report with little grunts of exclamation.

"You'll have to go into isolation, sir, and the Moszynski household, and probably most of our people at Tottenham."

"Good grief," he said finally.

SIXTEEN

THERE WAS A CONFUSED interval in which people tried to behave as if everything was completely normal, while they secretly
observed themselves and each other for symptoms—a gleam
of sweat, the pulse of a headache, a twinge of nausea. Locked
inside the Queen Anne's Gate offices, they were obliquely
aware of the turmoil going on outside as messages flew in from
Personnel, the Press Bureau and senior management. Toward
evening a team from the Hospital of Tropical Diseases arrived to
take temperatures and blood. Their appearance, in face shields,
impermeable tunics, leg and shoe coverings and double gloves,
gave rise to black, self-conscious jokes from the police and some
jittery looks between the civilian staff. Soon after the medics
left with their samples, shrink-wrapped platters of sandwiches
and cartons of soft drinks were deposited on the front doorstep
of the building, as if the occupants were plague carriers, which of
course they were.

Kathy and Bren, as senior officers on the premises, went
around the offices trying to exude confidence and encouraging
people to concentrate on the work they'd been doing. They
met up at Dot's office, where Bren was having a smile with Dot

about some trait of the old man that had always irritated her. Kathy watched them through the open door, Dot wiping a tear from her eye with a tissue and Bren, like a younger version of his boss, big and gentle, putting an arm around her and giving her a hug. Though Kathy and he were of the same rank, Bren had been an inspector for much longer and was senior to her, and it suddenly struck her that she shouldn't have taken over the way she had earlier. When he emerged from Dot's office Kathy apologized.

"Don't be daft," he growled. "You did well. We're a team, right?"

"Yes." She hesitated and then said, "You're worried about Deanne and the girls."

He nodded.

"I suppose I'm lucky," Kathy said. "I haven't got anyone close I could have given it to."

He gave her a look and said, "No, Kathy, I don't think that's lucky."

Later, Kathy rang John Greenslade's mobile. She explained quickly that she wouldn't be able to go with him to speak to Moszynski's secretary. She gave him the name and contact phone number and said he could speak to her on the phone. He said he would, sounding eager, and began telling her enthusiastically about his first impressions of the letters, but she cut him off and said she had to go. Then she added, "Are you feeling all right, John?"

"What? Yes, sure, why?"

"Um, there's a bug going around the office. I just hoped I hadn't passed it on. How about the other people in the hotel?"

"No, everyone's fine. But are you unwell?"

"No, I'm okay."

"What kind of bug is it? Swine flu?"

"Something like that. Let me know if you hear of anyone getting sick, will you?"

When she hung up she realized she hadn't asked him how his paper had gone that morning.

Feeling suddenly low, she forced herself to think about the next task. In the drawer of her desk were the four files, two from MI5 and two from MI6, that had been delivered that morning, for her eyes only, and reluctantly she unlocked the drawer and pulled them out.

She had never seen security service files on individual subjects before, and was impressed by their orderliness and terse insights. They followed a common format that she guessed had been developed over thousands of other such studies, with a physical and psychological profile followed by an ongoing biographical summary of the subject's career, backed up by sheafs of supporting material—agents' reports, photographs, transcripts of phone taps and conversations, photocopies of official documents, press cuttings, ticket stubs. She imagined that Mikhail Moszynski and Vadim Kuzmin were not really that important in the hierarchy of surveillance subjects, and that others would have much larger files, running to many volumes, but all the same, the scope was impressive.

She began with the MI6 file on Moszynski. It filled out the summary of his life in Russia that Sean Ardagh had given them, including his family background. There was a reference to a file on his father, Gennady, and to a KGB investigation into the family which had identified both Gennady and his wife Marta as Jewish. There was a rather detailed medical history of Mikhail which looked as if it had been taken from hospital records, noting a severe allergy to a number of common foods, particularly peanuts. His school record referred to his unremarkable academic performance and lack of interest in sports. The only distinguishing feature was a modest competence on the violin, which was apparently abandoned when he left school. Translations of other official documents also included his record of compulsory army service in the North Caucasus Military District and his academic record at St. Petersburg Technical University, where he met his first wife, with whom he had a son who died at birth, followed by his sole surviving child, Alisa.

Kathy had an impression of a rather gray and featureless youth until he joined the Young Communist League, in which he seemed to find a role as a back-room organizer and initiator of a number of money-making schemes. Then suddenly, in the early 1990s, the record seemed to come to life. There were pictures of him at the wheel of his first Mercedes, in a fur-collared coat at the gates of a factory surrounded by smiling men in overalls, and seated among men and women in evening dress at a banquet at which his wife wasn't visible. He had put on weight and become a kind of looming presence in these pictures, and had begun to indulge his taste for strikingly beautiful women and Cuban cigars (Romeo y Julieta or Montecristo for preference, the file noted pedantically). It was at this time that he began to appear in newspaper and magazine articles as one of the new breed of people of wealth and influence. After he left Russia in 2001 the reports thinned out to a few references from the Russian News Agency ARI until 2008, when his marriage to Shaka Gibbons produced a flurry of interest in Russian gossip magazines—*Maxim, Profil* and *Grazia*—with pictures of the two of them at movie premieres, Ascot and Wimbledon. No doubt new articles were appearing in Moscow and St. Petersburg on his murder and grieving widow, Kathy thought, just as they were in London in the pages of *Now, Hello!* and *OK!*.

To Kathy, however, the most interesting thing in the file was an assessment by an unnamed MI6 operative of Mikhail's relations with the Russian government. Despite his flirtation with the lifestyle of an oligarch, he had taken a lot of trouble to avoid giving offense or aggravation to the political hierarchy, and unlike some of the other Russian expats, like Berezovsky and Deripaska, had never been threatened with financial or criminal penalties. The report referred to a warm letter of appreciation from President Putin following a gift by Moszynski of money for new buildings for School No. 193 in St. Petersburg, where both had been students. It also speculated that the marriage between his daughter and the well-regarded FSB officer Vadim Kuzmin had been engineered by Moszynski to maintain a favorable impression in Moscow.

MI5's file on Mikhail Moszynski was much briefer and seemed to be a matter of routine, given his nationality and wealth. It dealt with his applications for UK residency and then citizenship for himself and his family, his lack of political affiliations, his membership of various charitable, cultural and social organizations, and listed his movements in and out of the UK since 2000. It also tried to grapple with his financial affairs, without, Kathy thought, much success. It listed the properties in Chelsea and the Bahamas as well as recent negotiations for a large country estate in Wiltshire. It also quoted a couple of estimates from the *Financial Times* of his net worth, of five hundred and fifty million US dollars in 2007 and four hundred and thirty million in 2009, but didn't attempt to unravel the structure of RKF SA or his other companies and trusts. Under the heading *Criminal history* was the entry *None*, with a footnote that his current accountant, Frederick Clarke, had been investigated by the Fraud Squad in 2003 without charges being laid.

Kathy slid the two Moszynski files aside and reached for Vadim Kuzmin's. She was rather pleased that both MI5 and MI6 had failed to record Mikhail's enthusiasm for hedgehogs.

She was wading through the MI6 briefing document on the

FSB Sixth Directorate to which Vadim was attached when Bren came in.

"Any news about Brock?" he asked.

"Haven't heard anything. What's up?"

"That mobile phone number that Peebles rang . . ."

"You've got a name?"

He shook his head. "No chance, but we've got the record of calls it's made in the past six months." He handed Kathy a print-out, a look of grim satisfaction on his face.

She scanned it, then frowned. "I don't understand. Only one number?"

"Right! Apart from Peebles' call to it, the phone has been used to contact only one other number, which it calls always on a Monday, between two and three in the afternoon."

"That's weird."

"Look at the number."

Kathy stared at it again, shrugged. "Should I know it?"

"It's Gloria Cummins. The Chelsea madam. It's her number. This bastard rings Gloria's knocking shop practically every Monday afternoon."

"Hell."

"Isn't that bloody wonderful?"

"What do we do?"

"Well, there's no point confronting Gloria. I spoke to the local boys. They know her well and confirmed what I suspected—she's tough as nails and won't give us anything on her clients if she can help it. If we approached her she'd just tip this bloke off, and then we'd be lost."

"So?"

"We tap her phone, listen in."

Kathy nodded. "So we have to wait. He doesn't ring every Monday though, does he? But he did last week." She thought. "That was the day Vadim returned from Russia."

"That's true."

Kathy shook her head in frustration. "By Monday we could all be in hospital . . . or worse."

"By Monday we might be begging to go to hospital. They're talking about sending in sleeping bags for us for tonight. I thought my days of kipping on the floor were over."

"That'll be fun. We'd better put an armed guard on Brock's stock of booze in the basement."

"Or drink it all ourselves first. What do you reckon, Kathy? By Monday we'll have reverted to savagery in here. *Lord of the Flies* in Queen Anne's Gate."

Kathy laughed and he ambled off. She went back to the file she'd been reading, turning to a picture of Vadim Kuzmin, apparently one he was proud of. He was standing among trees, hands on hips, a chilly smile on his lips, and dressed in the black uniform of the Spetsgruppa Vympel special forces which came under the control of the FSB, specializing in counter-terrorism and assassination.

IT WAS NEARLY EIGHT when Sundeep phoned again. He had some news, he said. The Marburg diagnosis had been confirmed. Brock and the others were reasonably comfortable and receiving the best possible care, and it was now a matter of waiting. The good news was that Kathy's test results, taken at the same time, had also come through, and she was clear, as was Sundeep himself.

"This is a good result, Kathy, the best we could have hoped for. We're very lucky that Brock kept himself pretty much to himself the last few days. You've seen more of him than anyone, so the chances are that the others will be okay, but they'll have to stay in isolation until we know for sure, probably some time tomorrow. But you're free to leave."

There was a smell of fish and chips coming from the entrance hall as the evening meals were brought in. A mocking cheer went up as Kathy appeared and relayed the latest from Sundeep, and Bren said something about rats leaving the sinking ship. By way of compensation she promised to visit the off-license and get them a case of red before she left.

On the way she stopped to buy an evening paper with the headline NEW SHOCK FOR SHAKA, reporting that the model had been put in isolation as a precaution after being in touch with someone infected with a mystery disease. Kathy wondered how long it would be before the full story broke.

AT THE HOSPITAL SHE found Suzanne sitting at an observation window looking into Brock's isolation ward. There wasn't much of him to see and he seemed to be asleep as a nurse, dressed like a mortuary assistant with face mask and double gloves, made notes on his clipboard.

The two women hugged and brought each other up to date. Suzanne said that she'd been told it could take another week before they knew if Brock would pull through. "They're contacting research teams in America and Switzerland that are working on new drugs which might help."

She looked strained, her face tight with worry, and Kathy thought, with a little tug of regret, that there would have been no one to look like that for her if she'd caught it.

As if she'd read Kathy's mind, Suzanne reached for her hand and said, "I'm just so relieved that you're in the clear, Kathy. They say you saw him most during the past week."

Kathy described what had happened and his refusal to let her contact Suzanne.

"Stubborn as always." Suzanne sighed.

"There's nothing that we could have done. Someone slipped

up when they identified the carrier—they should have warned us then. But even so, it would have been too late for Brock."

She regretted the choice of words, and began to add, "I mean . . ." but Suzanne squeezed her hand and said, "I know."

They sat together in silence for a long while until Kathy, exhausted by the events of the day, began to nod off. Suzanne roused her gently and told her to go home.

SEVENTEEN

THE COOL NIGHT AIR revived Kathy and as she went to her car she was suddenly possessed by a sense of energy and relief. Worrying about Brock had blocked out the thought of her own reprieve, but now its full force struck her. She was alive, out of danger, and suddenly very hungry. She hadn't touched the food that had been delivered to Queen Anne's Gate and now she felt an urgent need for a hot meal and company. There was a text message on her phone that she hadn't picked up, from John Greenslade, saying simply, *need to talk*. Her first instinct was to ignore it, but after a moment's reflection she keyed in his number.

"Kathy, hi, thanks for ringing back. I was worried about what you said, about a bug going around. Are you really okay?"

"Yes, John, I'm fine."

"Great. And I've had some thoughts on the letter."

She could hear music and laughter in the background, and imagined him at a conference function, having a good time. "You at a party?" she asked.

"'Fraid not," he laughed. "I'm in a pub. I'd invite you to join me, but it's a dump."

"I suppose you've eaten?"

"I had something that claimed to be a Cornish pastie. They

must have a special machine that turns pastry into bulletproof cardboard."

"Yes, they do. I haven't eaten all day. Can I buy you a glass of wine while you watch me eat? As a consultant, of course."

"You're on. Where?"

"Are you in Chelsea?"

"Yes, in Brompton Road. There's a Mexican place just across the street, nothing fancy."

She took a note of the address and rang off.

HE WAS THERE WHEN she arrived, waving to her from a corner table. There was a bottle of wine at his elbow, and he poured her a glass as she sat down. "Cheers."

"Cheers." She took a deep breath and sat back. "So how did your talk go today?"

"Fine, I think. Well, most of them stayed awake, I guess. Are you really all right? You look worn out. Hard day?"

"Oh, you know . . . Well, yes, it has been hard."

"Want to talk about it? I have signed the Official Secrets Act."

So she told him about Brock and the virus.

He looked horrified. "I've heard of Marburg. It's really serious, isn't it?"

"Yes, but I've been cleared, so I'm sure you've got nothing to worry about. Brock never actually came into the hotel, did he?"

"But you're so lucky."

"Yes, yes I am."

"That's just terrible about Brock. I can't believe . . . he could actually die."

He sounded so appalled, so concerned for someone he'd never even met, that Kathy thought he might just be being melodramatic, but when she looked at him she saw that he'd gone quite pale.

"All we can do is wait."

"Yes. That's so awful for you. And his wife? Is he married?"

"He has a partner, but they don't live together. She's been away and knew nothing about him being ill until I phoned her today. She's with him at the hospital now."

"What about kids?"

"No." She took a deep breath. "Well, come on, let's eat."

She signaled to the waiter, who came and took their order.

When he'd gone, John said, "You face this sort of thing every day, don't you? It makes my life seem absurdly sheltered. Sitting here like this, doing this job for you, I feel like a voyeur. If I can help, in any way . . ." He spread his hands helplessly.

"Well, actually it does help talking about it to someone on the outside, someone not personally affected." She hesitated, then added, "Maybe you should tell me something about yourself, apart from the fact that you're a university lecturer who does jobs for the Montreal police."

"What, like a dating site, you mean?" He put on a sugary voice. "I'm twenty-eight, single, an only child, and just *adore* cross-country skiing, classical opera and French food."

She smiled. "Good enough."

"What about you?"

"Me? Oh, I'm single and an only child too, but I've never skied, don't much care for classical opera and prefer Indian."

"Sounds like we're in trouble. But I like Indian too, and I'm sure we could work on the opera and skis."

"Anyway, this is a business meeting, remember? You said you had something to discuss."

"Yes, right. I had a good talk on the phone with Moszynski's secretary. She knew all the letters I mentioned to her except the last one, to *The Times*, which she hadn't seen until you showed it to her. The others she typed herself, either from dictation or from handwritten versions that Moszynski gave her. She's been working for him for eight years, since soon after he came to London. She got the job because she's fluent in both Russian and English and she said he always took great care with the wording of his letters, as if they might end up as evidence in a court of law—that's what he told her. At first his English was a bit rough, and she would suggest a lot of changes, but he was a good learner and gradually she came to make fewer and fewer corrections, especially for a formal document, like a business letter or one to the newspapers. She said she was surprised at the political content of *The Times* letter, but he had been quite preoccupied that Friday it was sent, because of the death of the American lady next door, so maybe that was the explanation. Maybe he thought the Russian government was somehow involved."

He paused and looked at Kathy carefully. "That's what the secretary was suggesting to me. Does it make sense, do you think?"

"Possibly. You could take that into account."

"Yes. Well, I did that, and I've come to a preliminary opinion I thought I might share with you."

"You haven't had long."

"No, and I'll need more time to set out a thorough argument, but I'm fairly positive. I don't think that letter to *The Times* was written by Moszynski."

"Really?" Kathy was surprised. She'd gone down this road in order to cover herself, in case the letter's authenticity was questioned later in court, but she'd never seriously doubted it. "Why do you think that?"

"There are several small departures from colloquial English usage—a couple of missing definite articles, like here . . ." He took a copy of the letter from his pocket and showed her: ". . . *elements of Russian secret police*, rather than *the* Russian secret police. The biggest departure I would say is toward the end, here: *Let me give good advice to your readers*. It sounds like a Russian gangster, doesn't it?"

"But he *was* a Russian gangster, John. Or at least a Russian businessman. And I've heard his Russian son-in-law use the same phrase."

"Okay, but he was very careful to avoid such mistakes in his other letters. They were correct to the point of being stilted. When I pointed it out to his secretary she said she didn't think he would have put it like that, though he might have said it in conversation. Judging from the other letters, especially the most recent ones, I would say that it was written by someone who knew how he spoke, and wanted to impersonate his speech in the letter."

Kathy reread the letter, frowning over the points he'd made. They seemed pretty insubstantial to support such a major conclusion. Also, it occurred to her that he was rather young to be held up as an expert in a field like this. How would he stand up to interrogation by Brock, let alone a barrister?

"Maybe he was just in a hurry," she said, "or upset, as his secretary said. Is there any way we can be more definite about this?"

He shrugged. "Get more samples of recent letters of his. Or get a second opinion."

"It's just that, as you said before, the implications are pretty serious. If you're right, it suggests that there was a plot by Moszynski's killers to implicate the Russian authorities."

She stopped talking as the waiter approached with their food.

They didn't discuss the letters further, as if they both wanted to avoid a subject that might lead to disagreement between them. Instead, he told her horror stories of Canadian winters and tales about the city where he lived and which he loved. He was good company, and Kathy was glad to have her mind taken off Brock's illness for a little while. John didn't forget though, and at one point, as they were considering the dessert menu, he suddenly asked her if she'd let him know if there was any change. "I just feel," he said, "that I'd like to shake the great detective's hand, if I get the chance, having come all this way." It seemed an odd way of putting it.

She said goodnight to him outside on the street and got a taxi to the tube station for the ride home to her flat in Finchley.

EIGHTEEN

THE LABORATORIES WERE SWAMPED, unable to cope with the flood of tests that were demanded. The offices at Queen Anne's Gate, the Moszynski mansion in Chelsea and the Tottenham police station remained sealed as quarantine sites, while Kathy felt herself in limbo, suspended between the normality of the past from which she was excluded, and a future that she dreaded entering. Each day she visited the hospital without learning anything new about Brock's condition. And each day she phoned the crew at Queen Anne's Gate and sensed a growing listlessness in their voices, despite Bren's attempts to sound positive. She based herself in a temporary office a few blocks away in the headquarters building of New Scotland Yard, where she took what comfort she could from the routines of paperwork and fulfilling telephone orders from the isolated team for treats—DVDs, pastries, chocolate, an electric wok, grapes, deodorant, Pringles. She imagined them finally emerging, pale and overweight, into the light.

She decided to check the reference in the MI5 file to Freddie Clarke having been investigated by the Fraud Squad, something that wasn't on the police PNC record. After making a few calls she got through to the inspector, now in Economic and Specialist Crime, who had been involved.

"It was during the investigation into the collapse of APGT in 2003, remember?" he said.

"Vaguely. Remind me."

"Big group of construction and materials companies that went bust, very suddenly, after racking up large loans. There was a suspicion of fraud and we investigated. I remember Clarke, very young bloke, working for a group of financiers who'd been involved in raising the loans. It took us a while to realize that he wasn't the office boy—he was the brains behind the consortium. Very difficult lad to pin down. Said next to nothing in interview and kept bugger-all accessible records. That's what brought us up against a brick wall in the end—no records of the crucial transactions that we thought may have been dodgy. The rumor was it was all locked up inside Clarke's head. He was the consortium's private Enigma machine. We couldn't crack it."

KATHY ALSO PAID VADIM Kuzmin a visit.

It was Friday afternoon, a light rain falling, and she had confirmed by phone that he was at home in Esher. When she got there he jerked the front door open with a violence that made her hesitate. He held her eyes for a moment with an icy glare, then waved his hand. "Come."

As soon as she was seated he began to interrogate her. What was this quarantine business? When she began to explain, he slammed his open palm hard on the arm of his chair and cut her off.

"No, no, no. This is just a ploy, to prevent my access to Mikhail's office and papers. This is an outrage, a hostile act."

Kathy waited until he'd finished, then spoke quietly. "Mr. Kuzmin, my whole police team is in quarantine. My boss is in an isolation ward and may die. This is a very serious emergency, nothing to do with your father-in-law's papers."

He curled his lip. "Then why are you free to come and go, Detective, eh?"

"I was the first to be tested, along with DCI Brock. We got the results back quickly, he was positive, me negative. But now the labs are overwhelmed. It will probably be another day or two before they can complete their tests. We just have to be patient."

His eyes narrowed and he regarded her as if she were a suspect who was more cunning than he'd first thought. "Marburg, eh?"

"Yes."

"I know this Marburg. We weaponized it in 1990."

"I'm sorry?"

"Soviet Ministry of Defense. I think you knew that."

"No, I didn't."

"Well, your security services do. Is that what this is about? You want this to look like the work of the FSB?"

"Sir, last Thursday week DCI Brock came in contact with a migrant from Uganda who was infected and is now also in hospital isolation. There's been no suggestion of FSB involvement to my knowledge."

"Really? Well there soon will be. Do you read the papers? First Litvinenko, now Moszynski, that's what they're all saying."

"Well, that's not really surprising, is it, in the light of Mr. Moszynski's letter to *The Times*?"

"If it's genuine."

"Do you have any evidence that it isn't?"

His eyes slid away, and for the first time he seemed unsure. "No."

"We've been told that he was upset the day he sent it, because of the murder of the American woman from the hotel next door."

"Of course he was upset. We all get upset when crime comes close to home."

"Is that all it was?"

"What else could it be? Mikhail was a sensitive man. Does

that surprise you? Russian oligarchs are just rich thugs, is that what you think? Wrong! Mikhail was a caring man, for his family, for his neighbors, for everyone. You know what he does when he comes here? He counts hedgehogs. That's right! He's worried they will be extinct. He cares about hedgehogs!" He gave a short bark of a laugh. "Also, people put crazy ideas in his head."

"How do you mean?"

"Oh, don't get me wrong, Mikhail was a brilliant man, brilliant. But he could also be gullible, with people he trusted."

"Which people?"

Kuzmin shrugged. "Rich men attract parasites, Detective, like dogs attract fleas. It's only natural."

Kathy recalled someone else using the word *parasites*. It was Shaka, she remembered, on the night of Mikhail's murder, referring to the two men sitting drinking downstairs. "People close to him, do you mean? Like Freddie Clarke?"

Kuzmin turned away, looking out of the window to the garden, where his wife was crossing the lawn, wearing an old raincoat and hood against the drizzle. "Freddie's all right. He was dedicated to Mikhail's interests."

"You're sure about that, are you? From what I hear, Freddie makes a habit of keeping things inside his head, rather than on paper. That must be a problem for you now. How will you know that he's telling you everything about your father-in-law's businesses?"

"If I ever think he's being less than honest, I'll let you know. Now you must leave."

Kathy stayed sitting. "Why don't you give me some names of these parasites you mentioned, Mr. Kuzmin? Maybe Mr. Moszynski was planning to expose someone. That could be a motive for his murder, don't you think?"

"But I thought the FSB did it?" Kuzmin sneered and walked over to the door. "Christina!"

The maid appeared and he said, "Please show this lady out," and walked away.

As Kathy got into her car she noticed Alisa further down the driveway, picking tulips from a bed. She turned at the sound of Kathy's wheels on the gravel, and Kathy pulled over and got out. "Lovely colors."

Alisa nodded. "They are nearly finished now. My father liked them very much. I hope to have some for Tuesday."

"Tuesday?"

"His funeral, at the Russian Orthodox Cathedral in Knightsbridge, provided the quarantine is lifted."

"Ah, I hadn't heard. What time will that be?"

"Eleven o'clock. You will be there?"

"I'll make sure I am. You were here at the house with your grandmother on the day he died, weren't you?"

"Yes, I wish so much I'd been with him."

"Did you speak to him at all that day, on the phone?"

Alisa looked away. "Yes."

"How did he sound?"

"All right."

There was something evasive about her reply. "Someone told us that he was upset that day about the death of the American woman from the hotel next door. Did he say anything to you about that?"

"No." She began fiddling with her secateurs. Looking at her, Kathy had the impression of a lost soul, and not just because of the loss of her father. It was as if she were trying very hard to please everyone with her imitation of an English wife, without really believing in it.

"But? Come on, Alisa. Something troubled you, didn't it? It's written all over you."

"He didn't mention the woman. But . . . he did say something strange. He said that if anything should happen to him I wasn't to worry. I could rely on Freddie to see that I would be all right."

Kathy got her to repeat the exact words he had used. "You should have mentioned this to me before, Alisa."

"Vadim said it wasn't necessary."

"You think your father knew he was in danger?"

"At the time I didn't think that, but afterward . . . I wondered."

"Did he say anything else to you that I should know?"

She shook her head. "He asked to speak to Baba—my grandmother. They had an argument, I think. I don't know what about." She checked her watch suddenly. "It's time to feed baby. I must go."

KATHY WAS ON THE road back to London, mulling over her conversation with Vadim Kuzmin, when a thought struck her. She pulled over into a lay-by and turned it over in her mind, then dialed Sundeep's number.

"Any news, Sundeep?" she asked.

"Nothing, Kathy. No change."

"Listen, do we know for a fact that Peter Namono was the original carrier?"

"What? Who else?"

"Could it have been Danny Yilmaz? I mean, in theory, can you tell which of them caught it first?"

"Well, probably not. They both seem to be at around the same stage in the progress of the virus, more advanced than Brock. But who could Danny have caught it from?"

"Good question."

She said goodbye, then rang Sean Ardagh.

"Hi, Kathy. I hear you're in the clear."

"Yes. Sean, I've just been speaking to Vadim again, and he

mentioned that the Russians weaponized the Marburg virus back in the nineties."

There was a short hesitation. "Yes?"

"You knew that?"

"I believe I did. Is it significant?"

His smooth tone annoyed Kathy. "Of course it is. They killed Litvinenko with some exotic radio isotope, so maybe now they're trying out another of their nasty tricks."

"Oh, come on. You've got the source—that Ugandan, right?"

"Maybe he caught it from Danny Yilmaz, not the other way around."

The MI5 man gave a soft, condescending chuckle. "Kathy, Kathy—what would be the point of that?"

"The *point*," she said, angry now, "is that our senior investigator and our only witness are now on the death list and the rest of our team is locked up in quarantine! Just about the most effective way you could dream up to screw an investigation, wouldn't you say?"

She heard him take a deep breath. "No, that's nonsense."

"Why?"

"They just wouldn't do a thing like that. Believe me, I know."

"It strikes me, Sean, that you know a lot more about this case than you're telling us."

"I know that there's absolutely no way that the Russians would release some indiscriminate biological weapon in the streets of London just to cover up Mikhail Moszynski's death. The idea is absurd. It would be tantamount to an act of war. It's just one of those unfortunate things that happen, Kathy, sod's law, a bit of bad luck. Now I have to go."

She hung up and thought about it. He was probably right, but his indifference still made her angry. This was Brock they were talking about, lying unconscious in an isolation ward.

NINETEEN

IT WAS SUNDAY AFTERNOON before she got the call from Bren that all of the laboratory tests had been completed, and everyone except Brock, Yilmaz and Namono was in the clear.

"I'm going home for a long hot bath and bit of home cooking, Kath," he said. "You've no idea how wonderful that sounds."

"You should take tomorrow off."

"No way," he said. "I want to be there when Gloria gets the call from Mr. X. I've told everyone to be there for a morning briefing."

"Okay, see you then."

She put the phone down and set off for the hospital again, but still there was no change in Brock's condition; he was feverish and looped up to a drip, oxygen and monitors.

AT THE MONDAY MORNING meeting Kathy had a long list of actions that she wanted taken to cover gaps that she'd identified in their investigation so far. She wanted the complete phone records of all the main players for the past two weeks re-examined, cross-referenced and analyzed. She also wanted the CCTV footage from Hackney, Tottenham and Chelsea searched once again for any third-party contacts that Harry Peebles and Danny Yilmaz may have had. There were a number of people to be re-interviewed, including the head of Shere Security, who had told her on the night of Mikhail's murder that they would be carrying out an internal review of what had happened. There were also family members to talk to again, but she wanted this left until after Mikhail's funeral, the arrangements for which they discussed.

"Oh and Pip," she added, "see if you can get some more samples of letters composed by Moszynski. Not necessarily to newspapers."

All of this was routine and background to the main event that they were all anticipating that afternoon. Bren confirmed that the tap on Gloria's phone had been authorized and established, and that they had been monitoring a stream of conversations from her business address in a small house in a quiet Chelsea mews.

"As far as we can gather, there are no girls at that address," Bren said. "It all seems to be done by phones and the internet. Gloria is the point of contact between the punters, who get to hear of her by word of mouth or through her website, and the stable of girls that she contacts and sends out to mutually acceptable addresses. She handles all the financial transactions electronically, and keeps tabs on the girls while they're working to make sure they're okay. She also handles their HRM issues."

"HRM?" Kathy queried. "What, pension plan, insurance?"

"Yes, exactly; their private health cover, gym, hair and beauty treatments, transport, security. She's got it all covered. We were working on building up a profile last week. It's an expensive operation, catering mainly to wealthy foreigners visiting or temporarily resident in London."

"How does Harry Peebles qualify?"

"He doesn't," Bren said. "I can only assume he was a favor for a friend."

"Well, let's hope we find out who this friend is this afternoon."

Despite the multitude of tasks, the time dragged until two fifteen, when the sound of an incoming call came over the speakers. A small crowd had gathered in the incident room to listen in, including a phonetics expert, Dr. Jenny Doyle, whom Kathy had arranged to be present.

"Hello, this is Gloria's Parlor." Gloria's voice was warm and seductive, just this side of a pastiche of a sexy callgirl.

"Hello, Gloria."

Bren and Kathy exchanged a frown, trying to identify the wolfish growl.

Gloria chuckled. "Hello, darling. Thought it might be you. Same as usual?"

"Four, if you please. Chloe free?"

"Let me check . . . Yes, that'll be fine."

"Excellent."

"Bye, darling."

The line went dead.

There was an expectant hush, then Zack spoke. "Yes, that was the mobile number all right."

"Where was he calling from?" Kathy asked.

Another long pause, then Zack said, "SW7 or SW3."

"Kensington and Chelsea," Kathy said. "Can you get a closer fix?"

"Give us a moment."

"Okay." Kathy looked up. "Back to work everyone. Bren, Mickey, Pip, Jenny, gather round. Let's see what we've got."

They sat around a table and listened several times to the recording of the telephone conversation, each making notes. Then

Kathy said, "What do you think, Jenny? What can you tell us about him?"

"Hm, nine words, that's all. Not much to go on."

"Best guess."

"Well, on the face of it it's Standard English RP—Received Pronunciation. Probably what we'd call Conservative RP, associated with older speakers of certain backgrounds, such as Home Counties, upper middle class. But it sounded to me like he wasn't using his usual voice. Did you get that impression? Like he was playing the part of a roguish Don Juan, for her benefit, as if this was a game they'd played before."

"Yes." Kathy nodded. "She seemed to respond in the same way once she recognized him. But you think he's a native English speaker?"

"Rather than Russian, you mean? The trouble is, RP is what's usually taught to people learning British English, and there's so little to go on with accent and register. That phrase 'if you please' sounds to me like a native speaker. But he may just be a good mimic."

Zack at his screens called back over his shoulder. "Within a hundred yards of South Kensington tube station."

"Can you track it?"

"Sorry. He's switched it off."

"Damn." Kathy looked at Bren, who was tapping his pen impatiently on the table. "What do you think?"

"What does 'four' mean?" he said. "Is he asking for four girls? Or is that code for the kind of service he wants? Or is the meet at four o'clock?" He checked his watch.

Kathy looked over to Zack. "Check Gloria's website, Zack. Does she advertise a Chloe?"

Bren shook his head in frustration. "I thought they'd confirm the meeting place, at least. They gave nothing away. It's as if he knew the line was tapped."

"Yeah, he's careful, isn't he?" Mickey said. "A phone he uses only to talk to Gloria, and then says as little as possible in a made-up voice."

"Yes, there's a Chloe," Zack said, and they went over to look at the images on his screen of a pretty, wide-eyed blonde girl. "Looks young, doesn't she?"

"Let's hope we've heard of her," Kathy said, and ordered everyone available to drop what they were doing and join in a search of the PNC database.

It was almost three thirty p.m. when they came upon Abigail Courtney Tierney, age twenty, charged three years before with four counts of shoplifting from stores in Saffron Walden. The woman in the police photograph lacked the make-up and hair styling of Chloe on Gloria's website, but the similarities were nevertheless striking. A check of her driver's license and phone records gave an address in a modern waterfront apartment block, just across the Thames from Chelsea, in Battersea.

They took two unmarked cars, arriving at the riverside development at three minutes to four. Kathy went to the entrance door and spoke on the intercom to a resident caretaker, who let her into the lobby, a place of glass and marble that might have served as an upmarket art gallery.

"We've had reports of a serial rapist operating in the area," Kathy said. "Targeting young women living alone. We're checking possible people at risk."

He took her into his office and gave her the names of three single women residents of the block, one of whom was a Ms. Abi Tierney.

"Do you know if any of them are at home at the moment?" Kathy asked.

A check of the security system showed that the alarms in two of the apartments were activated, whereas that in Ms. Tierney's apartment was switched off.

"I saw her come in half an hour ago," the caretaker said.

"Alone?"

"That's right. Lovely young lady. She's a model. You want to speak to her?"

"No, we don't want to cause panic. This may be nothing. Do any of these women bring men back here, do you know?"

"Well, I don't spy on them, but no, not really. Even Ms. Tierney, attractive as she is, doesn't have a boyfriend to my knowledge."

"Right. I noticed you've got a camera at the front door. I'd like to check your recordings if that's okay. Say the last couple of weeks?"

"Not a problem."

Kathy returned to the car with the disks and they settled down to wait. By five p.m. the only people to enter or leave the building were a young woman with two small children.

When they got back to Queen Anne's Gate they ran the CCTV images for the previous Monday afternoon. Once again, Abi Tierney had returned to the block mid-afternoon and not left again until seven that evening. But on the following day she had done the opposite, leaving her apartment at three thirty and returning at eight.

"That makes sense, doesn't it?" Kathy said. "If he wants a particular girl, it would be a bit late to phone up that same afternoon and hope she'd be free. Maybe he phones the day *before* the meeting. We'd better go through all of this footage and get a timetable of her movements last week. The appointment could be for four o'clock two days later, or three."

"If that's what 'four' means," Bren grumbled. "And if Abi Tierney is Chloe."

"Come on, Bren," Kathy urged. "Abi didn't get herself a luxury Thames-side apartment by shoplifting."

After an hour they had established that, as far as they could tell from the CCTV records, Abi could have kept a four p.m. appointment elsewhere on any day of the previous week apart from the Monday.

"Then we put a tail on her," Kathy said, "and identify all of her clients until we find something."

TWENTY

THE CATHEDRAL OF THE Dormition of the Mother of God and All Saints looked to Kathy more Italian than Russian. With its basilican front flanked by a stone campanile and not an onion dome in sight, it looked like a Tuscan hill town church that had inexplicably found itself dropped at the end of a London cul-de-sac beside a small park. When she arrived, the end of the street was crowded with mourners in dark suits and darker glasses, conferring together with that somber camaraderie that funerals inspire. She looked around and caught sight of one of her team standing discreetly to one side, taking photographs of them all.

Inside, the atmosphere was more as Kathy had expected, the dark interior glittering with the light of candles, perfumed by clouds of incense and reverberating with the deep mournful sound of a male choir. There were no seats, the mourners standing packed together in the nave, overlooked on three sides by a balcony. Kathy took an order of service sheet, printed in English and Russian, and found the stairs to the upper level from which she could get a view across the congregation toward the east end, where three bearded priests, wearing heavy silver and gold robes, stood in front of an altar and a paneled screen hung with icons.

They faced Mikhail Moszynski's coffin, around which his family clustered.

The harmonies of the choir subsided into an expectant silence, broken at last by the voice of one of the priests. "Blessed is our God," he chanted, "now and forever and to the ages of ages." There was a murmur from some of the crowd, and the priest continued, alternating between English and Russian.

It was an impressive service, Kathy thought, with its sense of ancient ritual, and most of all the spine-shivering voices of the choir, unaccompanied by any instrument, whose deep chords throbbed through the whole building and every body inside it. There was only one discordant moment, when the priest gestured to the family and both Mikhail's mother and wife got to their feet. Marta tottered and Shaka made to take hold of her arm, but the old woman shook her off with a hoarse cry, clearly audible in the silent cathedral, that sounded very like a curse.

Afterward, blinking outside in the sunlight, Kathy watched the people queuing to pay their respects to the bereaved family, all except Shaka, who was somewhere among a mob of photographers heading toward a limo. As Kathy wove her way through the crowd her ears were straining for voices, hoping to catch something.

"Inspector."

She turned to see John Greenslade at her elbow. Toby and Deb from the hotel were standing behind him, all three beaming at Kathy, like the best of friends, out for the day to see the sights.

"Hello," she said. "Didn't expect to see you here."

Toby's smile widened. "Wouldn't have missed it for the world. What about that singing, eh?"

"Yes." She turned to John and said quickly, "I'm getting some more letters for you."

"Great."

"See you."

She moved off to the edge of the crowd, where chauffeured cars were picking people up. From somewhere behind her she heard a woman's voice, flirtatious.

"And what about you, Nigel? Can we offer you a lift?"

And the reply, "If you please, darling. If you please."

Kathy held her breath and turned slowly around. An elegant female leg was disappearing into the rear door of a car, and following it, leaning forward as if he might pounce on it, was the bulky figure of Sir Nigel Hadden-Vane.

Kathy pulled out her radio and spoke rapidly to Pip Gallagher, who she knew was sitting in a car further down the street. "There's a black Mercedes coming your way," she said, and gave the registration number. "See where it goes." Then she made a call on her mobile to Bren, back at Queen Anne's Gate. "I think I've got him, Bren, our Mr. X. It's Hadden-Vane."

"Bloody hell. You sure?"

"Not a hundred percent. I think he's on his way to the function for invited mourners. It's in a club in Kensington. Pip's on his tail. I'm coming back."

THE PRIVATE FUNCTION CENTER was on a rooftop, landscaped with pergolas, pools and groves of trees, and with sweeping views across the city. In the streets below, unmarked police cars took up position and waited for the MP to reappear, which he did at three thirty p.m., bustling out of the front door as the taxi he'd ordered drew up at the curb. At the same time a call came through from the car waiting outside the riverside apartments in Battersea. "Chloe's on the move," the officer reported. "Catching a cab."

At Queen Anne's Gate Kathy and Bren watched the routes of the two taxis converge on West Kensington. Almost simultaneously the following cars reported their destination: the Wintergarden Hotel.

"I want pictures of them together in the lobby, if you can," Kathy said. "But don't let anyone see you doing it."

Bren swore under his breath. "You were right, Kathy. It is him. This is going to put one hell of a cat among the pigeons. I want to see Sharpe's face when we tell him. But even more, I want to see Hadden-Vane's face when we knock on that hotel room door."

Kathy shook her head. "No, Bren. We need more, much more. And he mustn't know we're on to him while we get it."

After a couple of minutes a report came back from one of the cars. "We've got a couple of shots of them together. They went up to the sixth floor. From the look on the receptionist's face he's a regular here. Shall we speak to her?"

"No," Kathy said. "Take pictures as they leave and follow them."

She took a deep breath and stared at Bren. "Why? Why would he want Moszynski killed? They were great mates."

"We know he's a corrupt bastard with some very dodgy friends, Kathy. Remember the last time? We knew he was tied up with Spider Roach, but we couldn't prove it."

"That's why we have to be careful. He made mincemeat of us the last time. He destroyed Tom Reeves' career and very nearly took Brock and the rest of us down too."

"Tom Reeves cut corners. He was a maverick, you know that. And Hadden-Vane destroyed him from behind the screen of parliamentary privilege. But he won't be able to hide from this."

"All we've got is a record of three very brief phone calls between Harry Peebles' and Hadden-Vane's mobile phones. We don't know what was said. We need further proof of contact between the two of them and we need a convincing motive."

Bren thought for a moment. "Maybe there're others involved. Vadim Kuzmin, for instance."

"A family coup, you mean? Yes, I've wondered about that."

"Maybe Vadim got Hadden-Vane to use his criminal contacts to do the deed while Vadim was safely out of the country."

Kathy nodded slowly. "That's possible."

"I just wish we could tell Brock," Bren said. "This would have him back on his feet in no time."

BY THE TIME SHE got to the hospital that evening Kathy was filled with a quiet sense of elation. For too long they had lived with the memory of Hadden-Vane's plot—his "Spider trap" as Brock had called it—to destroy a rival MP and in the process discredit Brock and his team. Now they were surely very close to getting the evidence that would finally expose him. She hurried into the hospital lift, imagining the look on Brock's face when she told him.

Suzanne was standing by the window looking into his cubicle, and when she turned around, Kathy was stopped short by the look of desolation on her face.

"Suzanne?"

"Oh, Kathy." Tears flooded down her cheeks.

"What's happened!"

"He's dead."

"What!"

"They've just taken his body away."

Kathy felt dizzy, hardly able to take in what Suzanne was saying.

"So sudden . . . I was with his mother . . ."

Kathy sucked in air, trying to hold herself together. "His mother?" Brock had never spoken of his mother.

"Such a lovely woman. Devastated, of course. I had to ring

for her husband to come. I had to tell him, Kathy. I had to tell him that Danny was dead."

"Danny?"

"Yes."

"My God, I thought . . . I thought you meant Brock."

"No, there's no change. But Kathy, you know what this means. They're all going to die. All three of them." She began shaking with uncontrollable sobs.

"No." Kathy wrapped her arms around the other woman and held her tight. "No, it surely doesn't mean that. Have the doctors said so?"

"I haven't spoken to them, but . . ."

"I'll do it." She made Suzanne sit down and told her to wait while she went along the corridor to the nurses' station, where she found one of the specialists.

There was no way of knowing, he said. Danny had had a sudden relapse, but Peter Namono was still stable, and so was Brock. They were doing everything they could. A new antiviral drug was being flown over from America. They could only wait and hope.

Suzanne was calmer when Kathy returned and passed on what she'd been told. Suzanne gave a weary sigh and wiped a hand across her eye. "I'm sorry, Kathy. I keep thinking the worst."

"When did you last have a decent meal? Not since last week, I'll bet. Come on, nothing's going to happen tonight. If he could he'd be telling us to get out of here and have a proper feed. I saw an Italian place down the road. How about it?"

Suzanne sniffed and began to form a refusal, then relented.

After the first glass of Chianti she gave a reluctant smile and said, "Thanks, Kathy. I did need to get away from that place. If he ever gets out of there I'll kill him for putting us through this."

Kathy nodded.

"I've been thinking about the work you do, the pair of you," Suzanne went on. "And I've thought about how alike you two are. That's why you get on so well, I suppose."

"I don't think we're alike at all."

"Oh yes you are. Both stubborn, like terriers when you get your teeth into something. Very loyal, but not always to the right priorities."

"How do you mean?"

"You both suffer from the same problem, what I used to call Brock's Paradox, the belief that you can only keep a relationship alive by not allowing it to reach its full potential."

Kathy sat back, feeling as if she'd been unexpectedly slapped.

"Oh, I'm sorry," Suzanne said. "I've upset you. Please, forget it. I've had so much on my mind and I—"

"Do you really think that's true?"

"About him, yes. Maybe not about you. Maybe you've just been unlucky with your men. What happened to the one who went to the Middle East?"

"He's moved on to Shanghai."

"Oh, that is rather inconvenient." She took another sip of her wine and then said, "That Canadian you're working with obviously thinks the world of you."

"What? John Greenslade? You've met him?"

"Yes. He came to the hospital a few days ago, Friday I think, with a beautiful bunch of spring flowers. He said he'd never met Brock, but just wanted to pay his respects. And then we had quite a conversation about you and the work he's helping you with. Quite star-struck, he was."

Kathy felt a blush creeping up her neck, and was saved from replying by the arrival of their vitello tonnato, the speciality of the house.

TWENTY-ONE

"LISTEN, I'M GOIN' FUCKIN" mad. Everybody wants me. I'm gettin' out of here."

Kathy listened to her ranting down the phone, about being cooped up in quarantine with her mother-in-law, about the press hounding her, about the stupid rumors they were printing, then said, conciliatory, "It must be terrible for you, Shaka, and I wouldn't bother you again if I could avoid it. Are you at home in Chelsea now?"

"No way. I'm goin' crazy in that house. I'm at Derek's office. The little shit's home in his bed, thinks *he's* sick now, so I'm hidin' out in his office."

"I'll come and see you there."

"I told you, I'm leavin'. Today."

"Just stay there. I'll be with you in a few minutes. I won't take up much of your time."

The agent's office was in Golden Square in Soho. In the taxi over there Kathy thought about the plight of Shaka, one of the most beautiful and admired women in the country who was being driven mad by the constant gaze of rapt attention. It was another paradox for Suzanne, she thought. They had parted the previous night on good terms, happy to have renewed their friendship, promising to keep in touch, and there had been a text message from her that morning, thanking Kathy for the meal.

Shaka answered Kathy's ring on the office door on the third floor. Several expensive-looking suitcases were standing inside.

"Where are you going?" Kathy asked.

"Little Ruby Cay. The driver will be here soon to collect me, so you'd better make it quick."

"All right. When I spoke to you on the night of Mikhail's murder, you described Freddie Clarke and Nigel Hadden-Vane, who were there in the house, as parasites."

Shaka shrugged. "Did I?"

"Did you tell Mikhail how you felt about them? How you didn't trust them?"

"They were useful. He used them."

"I know how he met Freddie, in Luxembourg, but how about Hadden-Vane?"

"Nigel got his claws into Mikhail as soon as he arrived, gettin' him invitations to the right places, introducing him to the right people. Mikhail needed that. Hell, he even arranged for us to meet. Mikhail saw a picture of me and said something to Nigel, and the next thing we were being introduced at a party. He was like Mikhail's pimp."

"He got girls for Mikhail?"

"I didn't mean it literally. It was just the way he acted, like a creepy pimp, buttering Mikhail up, arranging favors. I hated the way he flattered Mikhail all the time."

"And you told Mikhail that."

"Sure."

"And Nigel knew how you felt?"

"I didn't try to hide it."

"That would have made Nigel feel pretty insecure, wouldn't it?"

Shaka's mobile began playing a tune and she turned away to

answer it with a few curt words, then said, "The driver's here in two minutes."

"How does Nigel get on with the rest of Mikhail's family?"

"All right I suppose, all except his mother. He can't stand Marta."

"Why not?"

"Because she's a poisonous old witch. 'Nigel,'" she whined, "'You get me to meet Queen Elizabeth. Nigel, you get citizenship for Uncle Boris.' She's a fuckin' pain. Nobody can stand her. Even Mikhail had had enough."

"How do you mean?"

"Oh, they had a blazin' row."

"When was this?"

"Not long before Mikhail died. I was away on a shoot. It must have been the Tuesday or Wednesday of that week. He was very upset that evenin' when I got back. The old bitch had been givin' him a hard time about something, he wouldn't say what."

The buzzer on the office door sounded.

"Okay," Shaka said. "Gotta go."

"Have a nice break."

"Yeah, thanks. It was our favorite place, Mikhail and me. We were happy there. No paparazzi, no Marta."

"How about the parasites? Did they go?"

"Oh yeah."

"Aren't you worried about leaving now, Shaka? Aren't you afraid they may try to rip you off while you're away?"

Shaka gazed at Kathy for a moment, face expressionless, then said, "Vadim will keep them in line."

DESPITE SHAKA'S VIVID IMPERSONATION of Marta's spoken English, the old woman refused to speak to Kathy except in Russian, and an interpreter was called in.

Kathy began with a few words of condolence and a compliment on the dignity of the funeral service, but Marta, draped in a black shawl and wearing a large silver cross around her neck, listened to the translation with all the animation of a rock. A very tough old lady, Kathy thought, watching her. She'd been a teenager through the siege of Leningrad, of course, and had probably seen enough by the time she turned sixteen to harden the softest heart. She had married Gennady in 1950, when she was twenty-two and he forty-seven and already an important figure in Leningrad politics. Kathy wondered what had drawn the pair together. Was Marta once beautiful? Had she captivated the older man with her sparkling eyes and flashing smile? It was impossible to imagine now.

She had been hardened by tragedy, she said, in a growling Russian that sounded as if she were reciting some ancient saga, but nothing could prepare her for the loss of her son. He was a lion, a genius, a saint. Her only consolation was that he had left her a granddaughter and a great-grandson.

Kathy asked if she had any idea who might be responsible for her son's death.

Criminals, she said. English criminals. They were everywhere in the streets. You had only to look at television to know this.

"Could there have been anyone close to Mikhail who might want him dead?" Kathy asked.

Impossible. To know Mikhail was to love him, as a brother, as a father, as a son.

Kathy persisted. Did she trust Mikhail's friends? Freddie Clarke and Nigel Hadden-Vane, for instance?

Freddie was a genius and Sir Nigel a true English gentleman. They loved Mikhail and he loved them.

After a quarter of an hour of this, Kathy gave up. She thanked Marta, took the interpreter to the door and asked to see Ellen Fitzwilliam again.

Mikhail's secretary was feeding a paper shredder when Kathy was shown into the office at the far end of the building.

"Getting rid of the evidence?" Kathy said.

The woman looked at her in consternation, but then Kathy smiled. "Just joking. How are things going?"

"I'm just trying to tidy things up while Freddie—that's Mr. Clarke, Mr. Moszynski's accountant—while Mr. Clarke sorts out what's to be done."

"I've spoken to Freddie. I got the impression that Mr. Moszynski's business affairs were complicated."

"Freddie deals with all the financial matters. I mainly concentrate on social and charitable affairs, and his travel arrangements."

"I believe that one of our consultants, Mr. Greenslade, was in touch with you."

"Oh yes. I hope I was able to help."

"Certainly. He wondered if you had any more letters written by Mr. Moszynski, for comparison."

"I think he had copies of all the ones to newspapers . . ."

"Anything similar would do, provided it was composed entirely by himself."

The secretary frowned. "Then you do suspect that he didn't write the one to *The Times?*"

"Perhaps Mr. Greenslade didn't explain," Kathy said. "Both the coroner's and the criminal courts are very particular about the integrity of evidence, and we have to be meticulous."

"I see. Well, I'm sure I can find something."

As she began to scan through her computer, Kathy said, "Has Sir Nigel Hadden-Vane been keeping in touch since Mr. Moszynski died?"

"I haven't seen him here lately, but he was at the funeral."

"They had some disagreements recently, didn't they?"

Ellen looked surprised. "I was never aware of this."

"Wasn't Mrs. Marta Moszynski giving Sir Nigel a hard time?"

"Oh . . ." Ellen chuckled. "You've heard about that. Yes, she can be, well, difficult. I heard her . . . No, I shouldn't gossip."

"Ellen, this is a murder inquiry. You have to help me understand the dynamics here so that I don't go off on the wrong track."

"Of course. It's just that Marta can be quite imperious. She sometimes speaks to people as if they're her servants."

"Especially Sir Nigel."

"Yes, he does seem to cop it. I was shocked sometimes."

"What sort of things?"

Ellen dropped her voice. "Once I overheard him objecting to something she'd asked him to do for them, I don't know what, and she said that if she told him to lick her . . ."

Kathy watched Ellen's face go bright pink. "Yes?"

". . . her fat Russian arse, then he'd bloody well do it. Those were her words, Inspector, not mine."

Kathy laughed, and Ellen joined in, with a look of relief.

"Marta's got a pretty good command of English when she needs it," Kathy said.

"Oh yes. You don't want to get on the wrong side of her tongue."

"And she could be hard on Mikhail too, couldn't she? That Monday before he was killed, I believe they had a big row."

"Really? Monday . . . No, I don't remember that. But later that week, it must have been the Friday, the day after the American lady was killed, I know he was very upset about that, and she made some remark to him that made him angry."

"What sort of remark?"

"Oh, she came in here to get the newspaper, and it was open to the report of the woman's death—Mikhail had been reading it—and she made a rude comment about Americans, and he got angry with her."

Kathy waited while the secretary printed off half a dozen

more letters that Mikhail had composed, then thanked her and left.

IT WAS RAINING WHEN she stepped out into Cunningham Place, and she hesitated for a moment, pulling the collar of her coat up, before running to the end of the block and up the steps of the hotel. Deb, leaning on the counter reading the morning paper, gave her a broad smile.

"Hello, Inspector. How are we today? A bit damp?"

"A bit. I just want to drop off some papers for John."

"Ah, you've missed him. He went out for lunch twenty minutes ago to his new favorite pub, the Anglesea in Onslow Gardens. Know it?"

"No."

"They do a very nice pie and chips, John tells me. Very partial to his pie and chips is our John. Why don't you go and join him?"

Kathy checked her watch. "I might look in there on my way back. Thanks, Deb. See you."

She managed to find a parking space around the corner from the pub and found John seated at a corner table in the crowded bar, reading a copy of the *Spectator.*

"Hi," she said, and saw his look of surprise change to a bright smile. "I've got some more letters for you."

"Oh, great. Sit down."

"Better not stop."

"Have you had lunch? Come on, have a sandwich or something now you're here. The pies are sensational."

She shrugged off her coat. "Ten minutes then."

He hurried over to the counter and returned with a glass of mineral water for her. "Pies are on the way. How did you find me?"

"Deb told me this was your favorite pub now."

"Yes, Garry the concierge told me to try it."

"So he *can* speak."

"Occasionally. I think both he and Jacko are invalided ex-soldiers that Toby took under his wing. Anyway, he said this was the place, and I've seen the security guards from the Russians' house in here too."

Kathy showed him the letters. "I got these from Ellen Fitz-william."

"Ah yes," he said, putting on his glasses. "Yes, these should be okay."

"I was wondering, John. If you were right that Moszynski didn't write that letter, would it be possible to find out who did by analyzing other people's letters?"

"In theory, yes, it might be possible. Why, do you have a suspect?"

Kathy shook her head. "I was meaning more for the purposes of elimination."

He laughed. "That's cop speak. You forget, I've worked with cops before. When they don't want to tell you what they're thinking they start to talk cop speak, right?"

She smiled but didn't say anything. John got up in response to a call from the bar and returned with their pies.

"So you have got a suspect," he said.

"What I've got is at least three people who were close to Moszynski and who were in his house at the time the letter was written. So I would like to rule them out as suspects."

"That's fascinating. This would make an interesting academic paper."

"Except that you can't write it. You signed a confidentiality agreement, remember?"

"Okay, what can you tell me about them?"

"They were involved with Moszynski on a day-to-day basis."

"First language English?"

"For two of them. The other is Russian."

"Male, female?"

"All male."

"Not Shaka then. So we've got Vadim Kuzmin, Sir Nigel Hadden-Vane and one other, right?"

Kathy looked at him with surprise. "How do you work that out?"

"It's our favorite topic of conversation at Chelsea Mansions, and I noticed them both at Moszynski's funeral. And then there's this . . ." He opened the magazine he was reading and showed her a reference to Hadden-Vane's appearance before the Parliamentary Committee on Standards and Privileges to answer accusations that he had used influence to secure Alisa Kuzmin's British citizenship in return for hidden payments. "So who's the third?"

"Moszynski's accountant and financial adviser, a man called Freddie Clarke. Though it may be difficult to get samples of their writing."

"Formal letters would be best, but even emails, memos, notes might give me a clue."

"I'll see what I can do."

"Fine, and I'll look at these. You're right to be skeptical, of course, but I am fairly sure Moszynski didn't write that letter to *The Times*."

Kathy nodded, put some money on the table and got to her feet. "You were right about the pie. I'll be in touch."

BREN WAS WAITING FOR her when she got back to Queen Anne's Gate, his big ruddy face alight with energy.

"Take a look at this, Kathy," he said, and placed a sheet of paper on her desk reverently, as if it were a sacred text. "It's

Hadden-Vane's declaration of interests for last year, something every Member of Parliament has to put on the record."
Kathy read:

HADDEN-VANE, Sir Nigel Featherstone
1. Remunerated directorships
Director, Caribbean Timeshare Investments Limited
Director, Shere Security Limited

2. Remunerated employment, office, profession, etc.
Lectures for Anglo-Russian Investment Conference (Up to £5000).
In September 2009 I undertook a working visit to the Russian Federation, all expenses paid by the Anglo-Russian Business Promotion Council, who also paid me a fee (Up to £5000).

3. Gifts, benefits and hospitality (UK)
July 2009, guest of RKF SA at the Men's Finals at Wimbledon
16–18 October 2009, shooting in Inverness-shire as the guest of RKF SA.

4. Office-holder in voluntary organizations
Honorary Patron, Hammersmith Youth Employment Project
Honorary Patron, Wildlife Preservation Society
Honorary President, Haringey Sport and Social Trust

"So Moszynski took him shooting in Scotland," Kathy said. "Brock would appreciate that."

"The last item, Kathy." Bren stabbed his finger at it. "Haringey Sport and Social Trust. Care to guess who's a member of the youth club they run?"

Kathy stared at him. "Haringey . . . Not Danny Yilmaz?"

Bren grinned. "Got it in one."

TWENTY-TWO

IT WAS AFTER ELEVEN that evening when John Greenslade returned to Chelsea Mansions. Toby put his head around the lounge room door as he passed and said, "John, old chap, come in and join us. Deb and I are just having a nightcap."

"Oh, thanks, Toby. Sounds good." Judging by Toby's mellow tones and the level of the liquid in the Teacher's bottle, he guessed that this wasn't their first.

"Had a good day, dear?" Deb beamed at him, holding her glass up to the whiskey bottle as Toby poured.

"I've just seen a very scary movie, actually. Blood everywhere. I could do with something to settle my stomach."

"Quite enough of that in real life, eh?" Toby rumbled. "Especially in Cunningham Place." He handed John a brimming glass. "Cheers. Down the hatch. I see the inspector caught up with you." He waved a finger at the envelope John was carrying. "She called in here at lunchtime with it, and we told her she could find you at the Anglesea."

"Oh thanks. Yes, she had a quick pie with me on her way back to the office."

"No need to explain, old chap." Toby's smile inclined toward a leer. "You could have had a tumble in the hay for all we care."

They all had a chuckle over that.

"But John," Deb said, "what is this mysterious work you're doing with her? Or shouldn't I pry?"

"We're all friends here," Toby prompted. "In our past lives we've both signed more Official Secrets Act declarations than you've had hot pies, old chap. We know how to keep a confidence."

John gave a self-deprecating little laugh. "Oh, it's not such a big deal. In my university work back home I often have to look at the authorship of documents, or fragments of text."

"Like did Shakespeare or Francis Bacon write a particular sonnet?" Toby said.

"Right, or Guittone d'Arezzo and Guido Guinizelli in my case. But anyway, the Montreal police got to hear about it, and I've been able to help them in a few cases of contested documents."

"Aha," Deb said. "And now you're doing the same with Inspector Kolla."

"Moszynski's will!" Toby cried. "It's a forgery, is it?"

John laughed. "No, no, nothing like that. She just needs to be sure that something he wrote was genuine. For the coroner, you know."

"And is it?"

John hesitated. "I'm not sure that I can give a definitive answer at the moment."

"But you think it could be a fake?"

"I can't say."

"Interesting," Toby mused. "Bet it's the letter to *The Times*. It implicated the Russian government, which is what everyone wants to believe, but if it's a fake it suggests another motive. Sex or money."

"Sex?" Deb said.

"Well, in an earlier life, and after a few months in the Arabian desert, Shaka Gibbons might have tempted me to desperate acts," Toby said. "Here, let me top you up, old chap. All right, not sex. Money, obviously. Who could be after his money? The son-in-law, of course—he looks a ruthless bastard. And that weird accountant chappie that we saw at the funeral holding Shaka's arm. Who knows what he's been up to? And that slimy MP, Hadden-Vane, who's always there next door, day and night. He'd be in it for whatever he could lay his hands on."

John gave him a sharp look.

"What, got it right, did I?" Toby chuckled. "Not that difficult. It's a freak show next door, a fucking circus. We see it every day and we smile, don't we, Deb? The fabulously rich Russian, his crazy mother, the confused daughter, the sinister son-in-law, the glam wife . . ."

"Oh now, I like Shaka," Deb protested. "She's feisty, and beautiful."

"Yes, well . . ." Toby conceded. He fixed John with a glare, enigmatic through the dark discs of his glasses. "*The fault, dear Brutus, is not in our stars, but in ourselves, that we are underlings.*"

"What's that, Toby?"

"Time was, John, we were the masters of our fate, our wealth created by our own ingenuity and hard work. Now look at us—lackeys to every foreign crook and embezzler that turns up with a suitcase stuffed with roubles or dirhams. 'Let me take your bag, sir! Let me invest your lovely gold. Income tax? Good heavens no, sir, not for you. Citizenship? Any time you want! You like my house? Take it. A nice English girl? She's yours!'"

Deb laughed and patted Toby's hand. "Feel better now, love?" She turned to John. "He needs to let off steam, now and then."

Toby reached for the Teacher's. "Time was, John," he growled, "when I was a small boy, my family owned three of the houses that made up this block. My great-aunt Daphne, an independent lady of Fabian tendencies, ran a small hotel in number seven next door, catering to people of an enlightened disposition—she insisted on that. My uncle George owned number six, and my father this house, number eight. Numbers one to five were owned by respectable, hard-working families—a solicitor, a retired general of the Indian Army, a civil servant, a bank manager and the head of an advertising agency. Now we're the only ones left, clinging to the end of the Russian's juggernaut. Not that they haven't tried to push us out, eh, Deb? Every trick in the book. A refurbishment loan offered through a totally unconnected finance company that just happened to have been created by Moszynski's little rat of an accountant for the purposes of forcing us into liquidation. Then they used the courts, suing us for breach of contract, stuffing the pockets of *English* lawyers with their cash to pulverize us into submission. And they nearly succeeded, didn't they, Deb?"

"Yes, Toby." She leaned over to John. "They decided they had to own the lot, the whole block, but Toby wouldn't have it."

"You think I'm being paranoid, do you, John?" Toby said. "Then let me ask you this: what are the police doing, would you say? Come on, you're on the inside there. Tell us, what are they doing?"

"Well . . . I don't really know, Toby. Trying to solve Moszynski's murder, I guess."

"Exactly!" Toby nodded. "You've got it in one, boy. They're trying to solve *Moszynski's* murder. Not Nancy Haynes' murder. She doesn't count, does she? She didn't have a sackful of roubles to command our servile attention. She was a pensioner, for God's sake, a decent woman, but who gives a fuck about that."

"Toby, darling, I think it's time for bed," Deb said.

"True enough."

They drained their glasses and John said, "I didn't realize you'd had problems with the people next door."

"Actually, I liked Mr. Moszynski in many ways," Deb said. "He could be quite charming and considerate when he felt like it. But if he wanted something, and you were in his way, then God help you. Our rather shabby little hotel was an affront to his vision of his palatial residence."

"Will it be easier for you now, do you think?"

"We'll just have to wait and see, won't we?"

TWENTY-THREE

THE OWNER OF THE house in Hackney in which Harry Peebles had died was Angela Storey, who was serving six months in Holloway for the theft of seventy-eight thousand pounds from her employer, a car dealership. Kathy, wanting to know exactly how Peebles' use of the house had been arranged, went to see her, and found her to be a pleasant young woman, eager to talk about her situation.

"It was my own fault, I know. After Mum passed away I moved back home to be with Dad, and then when he died of a heart attack last year I was on my own. Dad left me the house, in Ferncroft Close, and a bit of money. It was the first time I'd had any to spare, and I went a bit mad. I started gambling on the internet, in a small way at first, then more and more. Soon I ran out of Dad's money but I didn't stop. I got into debt, only it was hard to meet the repayments on what I was earning in the office at Meredews. Then it occurred to me one day how easy it would be to create a new supplier account and pay myself a bit extra. I ended up with five false accounts before they found out. The money's all gone. Stupid really. Dad would be horrified to know that both Kenny and me are doing time."

"Kenny's your brother?"

"Yes, he's in Barlinnie Prison, in Scotland. It was the drugs with him. When Dad found out he disowned him, and Kenny left London and went up to Glasgow with a mate, a scaffolder like him, but they got into trouble up there. Anyway, when I got a message from him asking if a friend of his from Scotland could stay at the house for a few days I couldn't very well refuse, could I? I mean, by rights the house is half his anyway."

"Did you know this friend?"

"No. Kenny just gave me his name and I contacted Mrs. Taylor next door, who's got the key, to say it was all right for him to stay. It's terrible what's happened. A drug overdose, wasn't it? I should have known, I suppose, if it was a friend of Kenny's."

"I've got a book of photographs here, Angela, that I'd like you to look at and tell me if you've seen any of the men before, okay?"

Angela looked doubtful. "Will it get Kenny into trouble?"

"No, not at all. We just want to trace the people that Harry Peebles may have met while he was in London."

"Oh, I don't know . . ."

"I do appreciate your help, Angela, and I'll certainly report to the governor how cooperative you've been."

"Well, let's take a look then."

Kathy opened the album of mug shots and Angela began to scan them, slowly turning the pages. Eventually she stopped at one picture.

"Oh," she said with a smile. "I know him, but he would never have met with someone like Harry Peebles."

"How do you know him, Angela?"

"He was my dad's boss. My dad was a driver—a chauffeur, he insisted on calling it. He worked for Mr. Hadden-Vane for years."

"Really? Has he ever been to your house?"

"Oh no. But he knew where Dad lived, right enough."

WHEN SHE GOT BACK to her office Kathy found Bren leaning over Pip's shoulder looking at her computer screen.

"Hey, Kathy," he said. "Take a look at this."

It was an article from a local newspaper, three years old. The caption read, MP REWARDS CIVIC-MINDED YOUTHS beneath a picture of Hadden-Vane handing a certificate to a grinning teenager. In the background, clapping, was a group including both Danny Yilmaz and his cousin Barbaros Kaya.

"Brilliant, eh? The three of them together in the same photo."

"Yes. Can I have a word, Bren?"

They went into an empty office and Kathy told him about her visit to Holloway.

Bren grinned. "Well, now we have got him. We can connect him to both the killer and the bike-rider, and can establish that he had an opportunity to write the letter to *The Times* to put us off the scent."

"What about motive?"

"Something to do with money, I'd guess. Probably to do with the heat he's been taking over improper dealings with the Russians. Maybe Moszynski was about to come clean about something that would severely embarrass him."

Kathy nodded. "Maybe, but we have absolutely no evidence of that. And was he acting alone?"

"Vadim, you mean?"

"Maybe, or how about Freddie Clarke?"

"Yes . . ." Bren considered that. "Yes, if it's to do with money, he'd either be involved or have some idea of what's going on. But if he is involved and you ask him about Hadden-Vane's financial dealings with Moszynski, it'll tip them off."

"So we need to tap their phones, get hold of their emails, take a look at their financial records."

"The big boys upstairs are going to be very cautious, Kathy, after the last brush we had with Hadden-Vane."

"You're right. We'd be in a much stronger position if we could place him inside 13 Ferncroft Close, wouldn't we?"

"Yes, but none of the neighbors saw anyone else visit the house during that week that Peebles was there."

"We did find a number of unidentified fingerprints and DNA traces inside."

Bren nodded slowly.

"I thought I might have a word with Sir Nigel," Kathy said.

KATHY SHOWED HER IDENTIFICATION to the policeman on duty at the Cromwell Green visitors' entrance to the Houses of Parliament, and was directed to a reception desk from which she was escorted up stairs and along gothic corridors to the door of a secretary's office.

"Yes, I know he's expecting you," the woman said. "He is very busy at the moment, but he asked me to call him when you arrived. Would you just take a seat?"

After ten minutes Hadden-Vane arrived. He looked around the room then said to Kathy, getting to her feet, "On your own?"

"Yes, Sir Nigel." She offered him her hand, but he ignored it, or perhaps didn't notice.

"Thanks, Maureen." He lifted a thick stack of papers from the secretary's desk and turned to the door. "This way."

They walked at a fast clip down the corridor to another door. Hadden-Vane unlocked it and they entered a small office with bookcases filled with gold-lettered binders.

"Take a seat." He dropped heavily into the chair behind the desk, thumped the papers down in front of him and ran his eyes quickly over the cover sheet. "Right. What can I do for you?"

"We're trying to reconstruct Mr. Moszynski's movements in the days leading up to his death. I have a couple of timesheets here for the week beginning Sunday the twenty-third, and we'd be grateful if you could fill them in, one for your own movements and one for what you know of Mr. Moszynski's. If you could let us have them in the next twenty-four hours we'd appreciate it."

He frowned for a moment at the sheets of paper she gave him, then took a deep breath and puffed out his cheeks. "How's your boss?" he said, not looking up.

"DCI Brock? He's in hospital, in isolation. He contracted a virus."

"Yes, I heard. Is he out of danger?"

"Not yet."

He nodded slowly. It occurred to Kathy that he was tired. The bluster and showmanship of the other times she'd seen him were gone, and he seemed drained, like an actor between performances. The strain of recent days was taking its toll, she guessed.

"So who's in charge of the case?"

"I'm senior investigating officer, sir, reporting to Commander Sharpe."

"Really?" He seemed to consider this unlikely. "Busy work," he said finally.

"I beg your pardon?"

"That's what this looks like." He tossed the pages onto his desk and ran a hand over his face, rubbing his eyes. "Filling in time."

"I wouldn't say that. There are always a lot of routine procedures to go through in cases like this."

"But I thought you'd found the culprit?"

"It appears that he was paid to kill Mr. Moszynski. We need to find who by."

"And the American woman? Why would he kill her?"

"That may have been a mistake."

"A mistake?" He looked incredulous for a moment, then shook his head. "All right, I'll fill in your paperwork and have it faxed to you. Give me your number."

"It's at the foot of the sheet. Also, I'd like to arrange for an officer to come and take your fingerprints and a sample of your DNA."

"What?" Hadden-Vane seemed to focus on Kathy for the first time.

"For elimination. There were a number of traces on and around Mr. Moszynski's body in the gardens, and we need to eliminate the ones that may have been picked up from people he'd been in contact with."

"But you have the killer's body, don't you? You know which traces are his."

"We have to be sure he didn't have an accomplice."

He narrowed his eyes at her. "If there was an accomplice who has a police record, you'll know who he is. If he doesn't, the unidentified traces won't help you identify him, will they?"

Kathy began to argue but he shook his head abruptly and got to his feet. "No, sorry. Many of us are concerned about the indiscriminate taking and retaining of DNA by the police from innocent people, Inspector. I'll pass on that one. Now you must excuse me." He held the door open for her. "You can remember the way out?"

AS SHE MADE HER way across Parliament Square toward Queen Anne's Gate, Kathy pondered on the statues of famous men that she passed: Churchill, Lincoln, Mandela. She paused for a moment at the figure of Robert Peel, who had established the modern police force. All these men were remembered because they had successfully weathered crises of one kind or another, survived trials by fire. In comparison, nailing Sir Nigel Hadden-Vane was pretty small beer, only it didn't feel like that. She knew that a lot of people would be watching her closely once she declared her hand, some of them hoping she would make a mess of it, just as Tom Reeves had done. Taking on Hadden-Vane had cost him just about everything. She allowed herself a moment of weakness, to wish that Brock were there, then took a deep breath and made a phone call. When it was done she changed course toward Victoria Street and the headquarters building of New Scotland Yard.

On the sixth floor she made her way to room 632, where Commander Sharpe's secretary showed her straight into his office. He looked up from the report he was reading.

"Ah, Kolla. Take a seat."

That was the phrase Hadden-Vane had used, and she had a sudden chilling thought that all these important men were alike and would protect each other.

"Urgent, you said?"

"Yes, sir. I need to advise you of a development in the Moszynski murder case."

"Good, good."

"You may not think so, sir."

He arched an eyebrow at her. "Let's have it then."

So she did, and watched the eyebrows on his stern beaky face drop from surprise to foreboding as she described what had been discovered about Hadden-Vane.

"That man again," he growled at last. "But murder! You really think he'd go that far?"

"It depends on how desperate he was. At the moment we don't understand the motive. It may have been financial, and that might be hard to uncover without the cooperation of Moszynski's accountant, who seems to be rather secretive."

"So what can we do?"

"It would be helpful if we could establish whether his DNA

or fingerprints were present in the Hackney house where Harry Peebles was staying. Unfortunately he has refused to volunteer samples. So I'd like to arrest him on suspicion of involvement in the murder of Mikhail Moszynski, so that we can insist on him providing them."

"You can't just go around arresting people so as to get their DNA."

"I think we have reasonable grounds for suspicion, sir."

"It's all circumstantial, though, isn't it?"

"Yes, but from several independent circumstances."

Sharpe hesitated, unhappiness all over his face. "Leave it with me, Inspector. I'll consult a few people and let you know my decision."

Kathy bought a sandwich on the way back to her office and ate it while she dealt with some of the paperwork that had been building up.

After a couple of hours Sharpe got back to her.

"You won't get a decision until tomorrow, Inspector. In the meantime you might think about some other way of getting your evidence."

She talked it over with Bren and they decided that they would approach the Economic and Specialist Crime Command to request an investigation into Moszynski's financial affairs. The superintendent Kathy spoke to didn't sound surprised by the request and said he'd put a fraud team together, but warned that an investigation might take considerable time.

RAIN WAS SPLATTERING AGAINST the darkened windows and Kathy could hear the sounds of people leaving for the night when her phone rang. It was Suzanne, sounding both anxious and excited.

"There's been some change, Kathy. It seems that the fever has eased. I'm waiting to see the doctor to find out what happens next."

"I'll come straight over."

The cab made slow progress through the choked streets up to St. Giles' Circus. Beyond, traffic in Tottenham Court Road was hardly moving. Finally, itching with frustration, Kathy paid the driver and set off on foot. She was wet and panting from the exertion when she finally ran into the hospital and made her way to the isolation wards, where Suzanne was still waiting for the doctor.

The doctor looked somber and preoccupied when she finally came to see them. "The fever has subsided and his temperature is almost normal. He has regained consciousness and is breathing normally. Having survived thus far, we would expect recovery to be prompt and complete, but there is still the risk of further inflammation or secondary infections. We also have to carry out more tests to see if there's been any permanent damage to his organs, particularly his liver and eyes. We shall be monitoring this very closely. He is no longer infectious, and you can go in to see him, but please remember that he's lost a lot of weight and is very weak."

"Thank you, Doctor," Suzanne said, and then, as they made their way to the door of Brock's room, she turned to Kathy and whispered, "His eyes?"

They blinked open, pink-rimmed and bleary, when Suzanne touched his hand.

"Hello," he croaked, and Suzanne, overcome, burst into tears. "They tell me I've been ill."

"Of course you've been ill. You've worried us to death this past week."

"A week?" He gave a tiny shake of his head. "Can't remember."

Looking at the hollow temples and sunken cheeks, the skin as white as his hair and beard, Kathy thought of King Lear.

"How are you, Kathy?"

"Good." She pulled up a seat.

"Things are going well?"

"Absolutely. Everything's just fine."

The dark eyes regarded her for a moment, then he said, "You must tell me everything that's been happening."

"But not until you've got your strength back," Suzanne broke in.

He smiled at her and said, "How was Cornwall?"

After ten minutes his eyes closed and a nurse came and asked them to leave.

Outside in the waiting room a dozen people sat in various stages of agitation or resignation, some staring up at a TV monitor mounted on the wall. Suzanne began to ask what Kathy's impression had been when she stopped suddenly and pointed up at the screen.

"Look," she said. "Isn't that you?"

Kathy turned and saw a clip from the press conference they'd given the previous week, the camera focusing in close on her face. The sound was inaudible, but a ribbon of text scrolling across the bottom of the screen read: POLICE ACCUSED OF INCOMPETENCE AND "CAMPAIGN OF VILIFICATION." MP ADMITS USING PROSTITUTES. The picture had switched to Hadden-Vane, looking angry, then again to an image of a reporter beneath a dripping umbrella, talking to camera in front of the Houses of Parliament.

"I'd better find out what this is all about, Suzanne," Kathy said, feeling a small hard lump of anxiety forming in her chest. "I'll speak to you later."

TWENTY-FOUR

THE TRAFFIC ON TOTTENHAM Court Road had eased a little, but it took an age, standing in the rain, before a taxi responded to her signals.

When she got back to Queen Anne's Gate the place seemed so calm and normal, the duty officer giving her a cheerful wave, that she could almost have believed that nothing had happened. Then she opened the BBC online news on her computer. She clicked on *Breaking news*, and a studio newscaster began speaking.

"In a remarkable interview at his home late this afternoon, controversial London MP Sir Nigel Hadden-Vane admitted that he has been making use of the services of prostitutes for several years."

The image changed to one of Hadden-Vane, standing in a traditionally furnished living room, a sporting print of racehorses just visible on the wall behind him. A dignified-looking woman was at his side, sitting in a wheelchair.

"Three years ago my wife was seriously injured in a motor vehicle accident," Hadden-Vane declared, his voice resonant and somber. "It was touch-and-go whether she would survive, and though she did, she is now a paraplegic. Inevitably our lives required substantial adjustment, and one of the things that became impossible for us was to share our devotion to each other in a fully physical way. Accordingly, my wife suggested that I should fulfill my physical needs through the services of professional service providers."

A voice off-camera said, "Prostitutes? Is this true, Lady Hadden-Vane?"

"It is," she said, her words clipped and precise. "We had a problem, and we faced it in an open, practical way. Nigel has been going to the same agency now for over two years. I have met the principal of the company and several of her employees, and they remind me of the women who run the hairdressing salon I use—competent, enthusiastic and highly professional. There are many couples who must face the same dilemma that we faced, and I hope that by explaining this we can encourage them to discuss it without shame or reservation. The important thing is to be open and honest with each other."

"Is that why you are going public with this, Sir Nigel?"

"No, it is not. We regard this as a private matter between ourselves, and we would have preferred to keep it that way. However, I have learned that, during the course of their investigation into the murder of Mikhail Moszynski, the police came upon this information and intended to use it to implicate me in his death. I therefore decided to go public before they had that opportunity."

"Were you involved in Mr. Moszynski's murder?"

"Of course not. He was a good friend of mine and a good friend to Britain, too."

"Then why would the police want to implicate you?"

"Because the investigation by the Metropolitan Police Service has been badly mishandled. The team conducting the hunt for Mr. Moszynski's killers is inexperienced and has failed to make real progress, and is now flailing around looking for a scapegoat. As it happens, I have had dealings with them before, when

I exposed another bungled criminal investigation. They are seeking their revenge. I wouldn't be surprised if they were behind the scurrilous reports that have been circulating about supposedly irregular financial dealings between myself and Mr. Moszynski."

"They did track down the man who is believed to have murdered Mr. Moszynski and the American tourist Nancy Haynes though, didn't they?"

"He was a hired killer. The important thing is to establish who hired him."

"And do you have a theory about that?"

"It seems perfectly obvious to me and to everybody else apart from the police that the murder was commissioned by a dissident group within the Russian security services, just as Mr. Moszynski hinted in his letter to *The Times*. These people are experts in murder and espionage. It wouldn't surprise me if they have planted evidence to implicate me."

"And why would they want Mr. Moszynski dead?"

"To get hold of his fortune, to intimidate other Russian expats in the UK, and to damage relations between the Russian and British governments."

"Did Mikhail Moszynski pay for your prostitutes, Sir Nigel?"

"Certainly not." He gave a grim smile. "I have the receipts, VAT included."

"Thank you, Sir Nigel and Lady Hadden-Vane."

Kathy was conscious of phones ringing. One of them was her mobile. She checked the caller ID—it was Bren—and put it to her ear.

"Kathy! Have you heard?"

"About Hadden-Vane? I've just been watching it."

"What do you think?"

The truth was that she wasn't thinking very clearly at all.

"The bastard," Bren was saying.

"He was tipped off," Kathy said.

"Must have been. Where are you?"

"Queen Anne's Gate . . . Listen, Bren, I spoke to Brock."

"What?"

"Yes, he's conscious. He's very weak, but he sounded okay."

"That's great news." Bren sounded hesitant, as if he wasn't quite following her train of thought. "Maybe I should come in."

"Well, I imagine shit and fan are coming together as we speak. I'd better ring off."

What she wanted to do was watch the film clip again, but the phone on her desk was ringing insistently.

"Ah, Kolla, at last." Sharpe sounded breathless. "You're at Queen Anne's Gate?"

"Yes, sir."

"Are the press there?"

"Hang on a minute, sir . . ." She went over to the window and looked down into the street. It was deserted. "No, sir."

"Good. They're besieging New Scotland Yard. I'm on my way in. We'll come to you."

She didn't have a chance to ask who "we" were.

She checked her phone messages. Her friend Nicole was asking her to ring, and the caretaker of her block of flats in Finchley was letting her know that there were reporters outside, wanting to interview her.

Kathy opened up the BBC website again.

After half an hour there was a tap on her door and Superintendent Dick Chivers walked in. Another member of the Homicide and Serious Crime Command under Sharpe, "Cheery" Chivers was looking even more gloomy than usual. "Kathy," he said, offering his hand. "Bad business."

"Hello, sir."

In answer to the unspoken question on Kathy's face, Chivers said, "Commander Sharpe told me to meet him here." He unfastened his raincoat and gave it a shake. "Still pissing down."

He took a seat at one of the consoles and looked around. "You've had a technical upgrade. Any word on Brock?"

Kathy told him and a smile passed briefly across his face. "Excellent, excellent."

She stood there for a moment, then said, "Would you like a coffee?"

"Good idea," he said dolefully. "We'll need plenty before the night's out, I dare say."

After an awkward interval in which Kathy completed typing her observations on Hadden-Vane's performance, a call came from the front desk to say that Commander Sharpe had arrived and would meet them in the main conference room. Bren had also arrived, and was waiting in the front lobby when they went down. Together they made their way to the meeting room.

Sharpe was in his uniform, his hat and gloves on the table in front of him, looking as if he were ready to confront a riot or a press ambush. Marilyn from the Press Bureau was sitting at his side, typing furiously into a laptop.

"I've had words with the Assistant Commissioner on the way in," Sharpe said. "He agrees that we have little option. There will be a change of personnel. Superintendent Chivers will assume command of the investigations into the deaths of Haynes and Moszynski and all related inquiries. You'll make this your number-one priority, Dick. We need rapid progress.

"DI Gurney, you and your people will brief the new team and then be allocated to other commands."

Bren looked stunned. "Other commands, sir?"

"Yes. We'll work out where later. There's no shortage of opportunities."

"As a short-term measure?" Bren asked.

Sharpe gave him a barbed look of impatience. "Permanently, Inspector. The unit is no longer viable." He hurried on, "DI Kolla, you have twenty-three days of accrued leave entitlement. You will take this beginning noon tomorrow, after you've finished briefing Dick's team. I would strongly recommend, for your own convenience and ours, that you spend that time outside of London. In particular—and this is an order—I don't want you within a mile of Cunningham Place."

Marilyn was eyeing Kathy over the top of her large glasses, watching her reaction.

Kathy felt detached, as if seeing all this from a distance.

"Sir," she said, "I have prepared a detailed rebuttal of Sir Nigel's statements. I don't believe we need to overreact to—"

"*Overreact!*" Sharpe exploded, then thrust out his jaw and said, "Give your paper to Superintendent Chivers, Inspector. What I said stands." He took a breath, then continued, "We will announce a press conference at nine tomorrow morning, at which I shall make a statement. Marilyn?"

She handed out sheets, and they read.

The MPS views with grave concern the claims made by Sir Nigel Hadden-Vane on BBC television last night. We deny absolutely any attempt to embarrass or incriminate him. As in any murder inquiry, those people closely associated with the victim or present at the scene have been investigated in a vigorous but scrupulous manner by our officers, who have acted throughout with diligence and fairness. Our investigation has been hampered by elements of secrecy surrounding some of Mr. Moszynski's affairs, but the investigating team has made significant progress, including establishing the identity of the murderer. The team has also been hampered by the sudden critical illness of its leader, DCI Brock. As a result we have decided to appoint Superintendent Richard Chivers to overall command of the inquiry.

"That's all I propose to say to the press," Sharpe said.

"They'll ask about Kathy," Marilyn objected.

"That's all I shall say," Sharpe repeated, and got to his feet. "Now you and I should go to New Scotland Yard."

With a rueful look at Kathy, Marilyn stood up and followed him.

"Well," Chivers said finally, "sorry about that. Didn't know he was going to kick you lot out." His eye roved around the room as if working out where to hang his framed commendation certificates. "I don't know about you, but I'm going home to get some shut-eye. See you both here tomorrow, eh? Eight o'clock sharp."

When he'd gone Bren said softly, "Bastard."

Kathy blinked and sat up. "I feel sorry for him, stuck in the middle."

"No, Sharpe. He looked like he felt defiled just being here, like what he really wanted to do was raze the place to the ground and spread salt over the rubble. You were dead right, Kathy, they're overreacting, badly."

Kathy couldn't frame a response to that.

Bren looked at her with concern and said, "Come back and stay at our place tonight, Kathy. After a good kip and one of Deanne's hot breakfasts things will look brighter."

"Thanks, Bren, I appreciate it, but I'll head off home to lick my wounds. See you tomorrow."

She didn't go home to face the press mob. There was a change of shirt and underwear in her locker and a bed in the staffroom, and she just wanted to be alone to confront the reality of it all, to come face to face at last with something that had haunted her from the beginning: the possibility of stuffing things up so badly that her career would be over. *No longer viable.* Only it was worse than that, because along with her, Brock's whole outfit was going down. She had destroyed it, all of Brock's patiently nurtured team broken up, scattered across London. And she had to go and tell him what she'd done. A sudden wave of nausea rose up in her gullet and she got quickly to her feet, went out to the women's toilets down the corridor, and was sick.

SHE ROSE AT FIVE the following morning from the unfamiliar bunk, moist from a couple of hours of sweaty dream-filled sleep, had a shower and got dressed. Then she went to her computer and downloaded all the case files she could access onto a flash drive, and typed out the letter of resignation that she had been composing during the night.

She could hardly bring herself to look at them during Chivers' team meeting—Dot, Pip, Mickey, Zack, Phil and the others—as they gasped with disbelief at the news that they were to be moved on. When Chivers called upon her to speak she did force herself to meet their eyes as she accepted full responsibility for the way things had turned out, and commended them on their dedication. She told them the hopeful news of Brock's recovery and said she would be seeing him later that day to tell him what had happened, if he was well enough. Then she asked them to give Superintendent Chivers and his team every assistance to complete their work.

Chivers introduced his team, looking subdued, and explained how the debriefing would be organized.

At lunchtime, when it was all over, Chivers gave Brock's team the rest of the day off, saying they would receive text messages later as to where to report the following day. Bren suggested they adjourn to the Two Chairmen, and they all filed out, carrying bulging bags and backpacks. Kathy stood the first round, and waited until the moans became repetitive, then said she would have to leave them to go and see Brock.

When she got to the hospital and caught a first glimpse of him, sitting up against the pillows, sucking juice through a straw, her courage gave out. But he looked up suddenly as if he'd sensed her presence, and smiled and waved her in. That gaunt smile was the worst thing of all, she decided, but she choked back the sick feeling and fixed a smile on her own face and stepped forward.

"You look better today," she said brightly. "There's color in your face."

"I am feeling a bit more myself. Sorry if I was dozy yesterday. Suzanne's just popped out to do some shopping. How are you?"

"Umm . . ." She wasn't sure whether she should say anything, but then his eyes probed her and she launched into it. "It's been a bad twenty-four hours, actually."

He nodded. "Panic stations, eh?" He indicated the TV on the wall facing the bed. "I saw Hadden-Vane's performance, and Sharpe's press statement. But we've seen it all before."

She heard his reassuring, steadying voice, and wondered how she could tell him that it was worse, much worse.

"Sharpe has decided to put Chivers in charge," she said.

He frowned. "Well, can't be helped. In terms of his own accountability, Sharpe probably should have done it a week ago. You'll get on with old Cheery all right. Just play it by the book. That's what he likes."

"I won't get that chance, Brock. None of us will. He's brought his own team in. We spent this morning briefing them. We're being . . . dispersed."

"Dispersed?"

"Assigned to other commands."

A low growl rumbled in Brock's throat.

"And Chivers has taken over Queen Anne's Gate."

He looked startled, then slowly shook his head.

She waited, giving him a chance to say something before she broached the final thing. At last, when he said nothing, his expression unreadable, she took the envelope out of her pocket and said, "I've written my letter of resignation. I'll post it downstairs when I leave."

"You'll do no such thing," he said quietly. "A building's just a building and the team could benefit from a change for a while, but you're not going to sacrifice your career for that corrupt windbag. What on earth are you thinking of?"

"The team's being broken up permanently. Sharpe says it's no longer viable, and it's my fault entirely. I'm sorry, I was impatient. I showed my hand before I was ready. I deserved to be crushed. But you and the team don't. I've ruined everything you've worked for." She took a breath and shook her head. "I just feel so bloody stupid and inept. It's not as if I hadn't seen it all before. I let him do to me what he did to Tom Reeves—I set him up and then had him pull the rug out from under me, in full public view."

"This is nothing like what Tom Reeves did. Tom set himself up, getting evidence by breaking the law. I take it you haven't done that?"

"No."

"Good." He gave a sigh of exasperation. "Come on, Kathy, this isn't like you. You're tired, aren't you? But you're a fighter, and your instincts are spot on. You know as well as I do that that man is bent. I'll bet a pound to a penny that there's a ton of stuff about him and Moszynski that he's desperate to keep hidden."

Kathy bowed her head. "Yes."

Brock was scratching his beard. "That last bit about keeping the receipts, remember that? Bit odd, wasn't it?"

Kathy nodded. "I thought he must have primed the interviewer to ask that question."

"Exactly! That was his hidden confession. He couldn't help himself. The cock of the walk, preening himself in front of an audience of millions, he just had to say it. Moszynski paid for my tarts, but you'll never be able to prove it."

Kathy thought about it. "He's probably right."

"You'd better tell me everything that's been happening while I've been out of it."

So for the next couple of hours she did, taking him through the investigation step by step. He said little as she spoke, as if soaking it all in. At times his eyes closed and she thought he'd fallen asleep, but when she paused he'd murmur a question and she'd resume.

Finally Suzanne came back and put a stop to it.

"Don't worry, Kathy," Brock said as she got up to leave. "We'll sort it out." He really sounded eager, as if, having returned from the dead, the prospect of a battle ahead was invigorating. But all Kathy could feel was defeat.

TWENTY-FIVE

OVER THE FOLLOWING DAYS Kathy withdrew. She occupied herself with swimming, cleaning and repainting her flat, taking long walks and going to the movies. She wanted to avoid analyzing what had happened, but the world outside kept intruding, forcing her to confront it. For a start there were the newspapers, and radio and TV coverage, which she could hardly avoid, especially the Sunday papers which were full of the story. There was general respect for the Hadden-Vanes' confession, which was seen as brave and a welcome change from the hypocrisy that usually surrounded MP sex scandals in the UK. There was also much rehashing of the Russian question, and of the police investigation. There were even a few photographs of Kathy herself.

Then there was her friend Nicole Palmer, who worked in police records for the National Identification Service and whose partner was an MPS detective, and who told her of the rumors and opinions that were circulating within the force. There was general agreement that the higher echelons had failed to support Kathy as they should, and that breaking up the team was a disgrace. Kathy would have taken more comfort from this if she hadn't felt that Sharpe and his bosses were justified in the way they'd reacted.

Kathy also had calls from several team members—Dot, Pip and Bren—all anxious to know how she was coping, and letting her know where they had been posted. Most surprising was a call from Zack, who told her that they'd decided to keep him on at Queen Anne's Gate to manage the new computers. He offered to keep her informed of developments.

John Greenslade also called, several times, before she finally rang him back.

"Kathy! I'm so glad you've rung. I've been worried about you. Are you all right?"

"I'm fine, John, thanks. How are you?"

"Terrible. I'm feeling very guilty."

"Why's that?"

"It was all my fault, wasn't it? If I hadn't cast doubt on the letter to *The Times*, you wouldn't have turned your attention to the MP, and none of this would have happened."

"There was a lot more to it than that, John."

"All the same . . . I'd feel happier if I could talk it through with you, face to face. Would you do that? For an ex-consultant?"

She laughed. "From an ex-detective."

"They haven't kicked you out, have they?"

"Not yet. The resignation letter's in my bag."

"You mustn't do that, Kathy! Please, let's talk it through."

So in the end she agreed to meet him one day for lunch. But not yet. She wasn't ready for it yet.

She also met with Brock each day. Suzanne had now been away from her business for almost a month, and was having to spend time in Battle, commuting back up to London each evening to visit him in hospital. Kathy usually called in each morning, and after discussing whatever had come up of interest in the papers they might play a few hands of gin rummy, or a game of chess. But Kathy had brought him his laptop and copied her flash drive case records onto it, and inevitably his attention would stray back to the larger and more interesting puzzle of the murders in Chelsea.

One day he seemed particularly preoccupied, and finally said, "The whole investigation relies on one premise: that Peebles mistook Nancy Haynes for Marta Moszynski. But if that's not true, nothing else makes sense, does it?"

"No." Kathy felt a familiar reluctance to go over it all again, and picked up the pack of cards and began shuffling.

"How did you feel about that idea, when it was first suggested?"

"I didn't like it. I'd seen photographs of Nancy and I'd met Marta, and I didn't see much resemblance."

"Me neither."

"But we never met Nancy in the flesh. Maybe the photographs were flattering. Maybe she was more stooped in her everyday posture, when she wasn't posing for the camera."

"There must be some way to pin that down. Computer simulations? A reconstruction?"

"Well, it's not our problem now, is it?"

Brock looked at the cards she'd dealt him and played out the hand, then scratched his chin. "I've been thinking about Harry Peebles."

"Really?"

"Yes. He ordered a pizza delivery on his first night at Ferncroft Close, on the Wednesday, and again on the Thursday, but nothing after that."

"So what?"

"Then I had a look at his record. His manslaughter charge was based on a vicious assault with a hammer. He battered the man to a pulp—literally—and claimed self-defense. The year before he's believed to have thrown a teenager out of the tenth-floor window of a tenement block, but the sole witness disappeared and the police had to drop the case. And before that there was a string of assault incidents, all very violent and bloody."

"Yes?" Kathy couldn't see what he was getting at.

"All his victims have been physically mangled, Kathy. He likes to crush them, like throwing Nancy under a bus."

"Okay."

"But there's no record of him using a knife, and if he did I'm guessing he'd make a terrible mess with it. He has no finesse. Three precise, surgical stabs to the heart is not his style at all."

"Maybe he was told to do it that way, by someone who didn't want Moszynski disfigured."

"Well, that's a thought. Then there's Peebles' autopsy report. Sundeep is very wary of specifying the exact time of death, isn't he? That's when I collapsed, wasn't it, when we were discussing that with him, and reading between the lines, I'd say he's still not entirely happy with our later time, of Sunday night, after Moszynski's murder."

"He doesn't rule it out. The room temperature makes it difficult."

"I know, but still, I've always found Sundeep's instincts to be worth paying attention to."

Kathy sighed inwardly. What was he trying to do, take the whole investigation apart from the beginning again? The thought made her feel physically ill. She looked up and saw him regarding her with a faintly worried frown.

"Sorry," he said. "Just mulling things over. You're not still nursing that resignation letter, are you? Yes, you are, I can tell. Well, burn it. I forbid you to send it."

She gave a snort of amusement.

"I mean it." He picked up the pack of cards. "I wonder what Chivers is up to?"

Kathy said, "I could find out if you really want to know," and she told him about Zack.

So when she got home she rang Zack's number at Queen Anne's Gate. He sounded cautious, speaking so quietly she could hardly hear. "You calling on your own phone?"

"Yes."

"Get yourself a prepaid and ring me tonight after seven. I'll give you my private number."

She did as he asked, and when they spoke that evening she said, "You're being very careful, Zack."

"Got to be, Kathy. Chivers is very hot on security. We don't want him going through the phone records and seeing your number on the list again."

Then he brought her up to date. Everyone involved in the case was being reinterviewed, every camera re-examined, every phone record cross-matched. A fraud squad was working through Freddie Clarke's records. Two officers had been sent out to the Bahamas to speak to Shaka and two more to Scotland to track down Peebles' movements after he got out of prison.

"Sounds thorough," Kathy said.

"Oh, it is. The super is nothing if not thorough. He demands a perfect job."

Zack didn't like him, she could tell.

"Why are you telling me this, Zack?"

"Well, let's say that I trusted your nose for sniffing out something rotten, and that Hadden-Vane is rotten, yeah? And he's the one person we haven't spoken to again."

Hadden-Vane. When she put the phone down she pictured him again. And the dead—Nancy Haynes, Mikhail Moszynski, and Harry Peebles and Danny Yilmaz too—all dead, while he, improbably, rose above the carnage unscathed. She wondered if she was becoming obsessed.

THE PUB HAD A terrace overlooking the river, and they took a table by the wall looking directly over the water. It was a perfect June day, pale blue sky, sunlight sparkling on the dark Thames current across which a pair of two-man skiffs were skimming.

"Thanks so much for sparing the time," John said.

"I've got all the time in the world now." Kathy took a sip from her glass of wine.

"You haven't resigned, have you?"

"I'm on leave, stood down, not involved."

"I'm so sorry."

"Don't be. I told you, John, you had nothing to do with it. What about you? Shouldn't you be at your conference?" Kathy was aware that her words sounded brittle, and tried to make herself relax and enjoy this. It was a damn sight better than being in Queen Anne's Gate, she told herself, or moping about at home, but it just felt so unreal to be out and free during a working day.

"It finished last Wednesday, but I didn't want to go back home with this unresolved."

"Have you changed your mind about Moszynski's letter?"

"No, on the contrary. I studied those other documents you gave me and I'm more convinced than ever that he didn't write the letter to *The Times*."

"Has the new team been in touch with you?"

"No. Should I speak to someone?"

She shook her head. "Probably not. Send in your bill."

"How about your boss, Brock? Has there been any change?"

He seemed genuinely pleased when she told him, but then his frown returned. He noticed that her glass was empty, although he had barely touched his, and he poured her another.

"I just couldn't believe it when I saw that interview with Hadden-Vane on TV," he said.

"People seem to think it was honest and courageous."

"For her, maybe, but not him. I was quite impressed with him at Moszynski's funeral, but this was different. I thought it was the most devious and calculated performance I'd ever seen. Toby and Deb were outraged too. They'd come across him before, but it was the first time I'd really looked at him. You knew he was guilty, didn't you?"

A river cruise ship was passing, its open top deck crowded with people wearing dark glasses and sun hats. Some of them were waving, and Kathy felt a little surge of well-being, the first she'd felt in a while.

"I think," she said, "that if he was prepared to admit that much, and put his wife in front of the cameras to back him up, that he must have had something much, much worse to hide."

"Exactly."

"I also think that he moved so fast that he must have had it in mind all the time, as a contingency plan, if we got too close." She shrugged and gave him a smile. "But it doesn't matter what I think now."

"I like it much better when you're smiling," he said. "And it does matter what you think, at least to me, and to Toby and Deb. They're particularly upset that everyone seems to have forgotten about Nancy's murder. They think that you'd probably have solved that if Moszynski's death hadn't got in the way."

"I'm sure it hasn't been forgotten, John. Anyway, what are you doing with yourself, now the conference is over?"

"This and that. I'm helping Toby and Deb upgrade their computer software. They send their best wishes, by the way. They said they'd love to see you if you wanted to drop in for tea or something."

"Unfortunately I've been forbidden from coming within a mile of Chelsea Mansions."

John whistled. "That bad? Well, maybe I could keep my eyes open and tell you what's going on in Cunningham Place, if anything interesting happens."

It seemed that everyone wanted to keep her informed, while she didn't want to know. But when she got home later that afternoon, after a surprisingly good lunch and promises to catch up again, she thought about what they'd said, about Brock's questions about Peebles, and Toby and Deb's fear that Nancy's murder hadn't been properly investigated, and she forced herself to open up her laptop and load the case files, and begin to look at them afresh.

TWENTY-SIX

THE FOLLOWING DAY SHE took the laptop into the hospital with her. Brock was sitting up in bed, showing signs of impatience.

"I need to get out of here, Kathy, but they're being difficult. They say there's some residual infection and they have to keep me in for observation a bit longer. Really it's just that they've never seen Marburg fever before and they want to hang on to me, and prod me and test me like a prize specimen. I'm going mad just sitting around here."

"Well, maybe I've got something for you to think about. You asked what if Nancy wasn't mistaken for Marta Moszynski? The reason we've been assuming that is because we can't see any connection between Nancy and Moszynski other than the fact that they were living in the same block. But there was the thing that the neighbor, Dr. Stewart, said about seeing Nancy going up the front steps of the Moszynskis' place one day. I didn't put much weight on it, thinking he was mistaken, because no one else had seen her and there was no record of it on the camera mounted at Moszynski's front door.

"But I've been going over the log we made of all the people recorded coming and going on that camera, and there are gaps.

It didn't record Moszynski going out for his cigar the night he was killed, because he switched it off himself, according to the security staff. And there are two other times that week where there are gaps—for twenty-three minutes on Wednesday afternoon, and another for ninety-two minutes at lunchtime on Monday. We were told these were for maintenance. Those ninety-two minutes would have covered the period that Dr. Stewart saw her."

"Why would she visit?" Brock mused. "Did she know who lived there?"

Kathy shrugged. "No idea."

"Why would she go calling? To get Shaka's autograph for her granddaughter? Because she was interested in Victorian architecture? Or might she have been there before, at some time in the past? Maybe she knew the previous owners."

"We just don't know. We didn't take it any further. And if she went inside, could she have seen or heard something she shouldn't have?"

"And was it just a coincidence," Brock said, becoming more intrigued, "that the camera was switched off when she called? Or could it have been done so that there was no record of her visit?"

"Other people in the house would have seen her, the maid for instance, answering the front door." Kathy began to flick through the pages of the timetable they'd made of people's movements. "But, there's a thing . . ." She showed Brock the screen. "The maid went out at twelve forty-five, with the cook and the office secretary. Looks like they all had a lunch break together. Mikhail's driver and security guy was out too."

"What about family members?"

"Mikhail was at home. That's all."

A nurse came in to give Brock some pills and Kathy left for a few minutes. When she came back he had more questions.

"Wouldn't Nancy have phoned first to make an appointment? That would have given Mikhail time to make sure the house was clear and the camera switched off. Could there be a record of such a call? Would she have used her mobile, or the hotel phone? Wouldn't her friend Emerson have known something?"

"No, there doesn't seem to be a record of such a call on her phone or on Moszynski's phones, and Emerson had no idea. What I'd like to do is speak to the people in the hotel again, just make quite sure they didn't see or hear something."

He sighed with frustration. "It's all very well speculating, but we can't ask the damn questions."

"Maybe I can," Kathy said, "through John Greenslade."

"The forensic linguist?"

"Yes, he's still at the hotel and offered to help. The people there are upset that Nancy has been forgotten. I'm sure they'd be keen to tell us what they can."

"And you trust Greenslade's discretion?"

"Oh, I think so." She got out her phone and tried his number. He responded immediately.

"Kathy! How are you?"

"Hello, John. I'm with my boss, DCI Brock, at the moment. We were just discussing Nancy's murder, and we came up with a few questions that we thought Toby and Deb might be able to answer. Unfortunately, as you know, I can't come to them. I wondered if you might be able to arrange for me to meet them for an hour somewhere away from the hotel?"

Ten minutes later he rang back. They would meet her at The Parlor, in Fortnum & Mason, at twelve. "Will Brock be there?" he asked.

"'Fraid not. He's still stuck in hospital."

"That's too bad."

Brock was annoyed that he couldn't go. "Haven't been there

for years," he said. "Not since . . ." A memory seemed to trouble him for a moment, then his face cleared. "Enjoy yourself."

THEY WERE ALREADY THERE when Kathy arrived at the first floor of the Piccadilly store, the three of them at a table overlooking the street, examining menus with great concentration. They welcomed her with enthusiasm.

"This is such a treat," Deb said. "The hotel is like a jail. We pretend that we can't leave it and stay chained to the desk, when the truth is that Destiny can easily cope for a few hours."

Toby ordered a kniccurbocker glory and a bottle of wine, the others open sandwiches.

"We were utterly disgusted by what happened to you, Kathy," Toby growled. "Your principals should be shot. If they can't stand up to a bully like Hadden-Vane, God help us all."

"I think they had little choice under the circumstances, Toby, but thanks anyway. But stepping back has let me go over the ground again, and one gray area in particular that troubles me."

"What's that?"

"One of your neighbors told us that he'd seen Nancy calling at the Moszynskis' front door on the Monday or Tuesday, a few days after she arrived. We weren't sure how credible this was, but it raises the possibility that she might have had some connection with them that we don't know about."

"Oh, I don't know about a *connection*." Deb frowned. "She never mentioned anything like that to us."

"Which neighbor was this?" Toby asked.

"A Dr. Stewart, on the east side of the square."

"Oh, of course." Toby chuckled. "Did he tell you he writes murder mysteries? Never had one published. Gave me one to read once. Agatha Christie on steroids. He'd be lapping up the attention you gave him."

"You don't think he's a credible witness?"

"Let's just say that he's a lonely old man who would just love to be able to offer you a juicy clue. But can you seriously see him in a courtroom under cross-examination?"

Toby's face lit up as their lunches arrived and the towering confection of his kniccurbocker glory was placed in front of him. "Wonderful," he breathed. "I can remember the first and last time I had one of these. I hadn't been in the army very long, and I'd been on some godawful training course and was home on leave, and Ma brought me here. I can still taste that first mouthful. Just before they sent me off to my first war. The end of innocence."

"Which war was that?" John asked.

"Suez. A shambles."

"You were there? I was reading a book about it recently. It was such an interesting time, 1956—the Cambridge spies, the Russian invasion of Hungary, Castro landing in Cuba . . ."

Toby cut in, "Ancient history, old chap, best forgotten. I prefer to remember the kniccurbocker glories." He paused for a moment to taste and approve the wine, and they raised their glasses. "To justice," he murmured. "So, Kathy, anything else we can help you with?"

"Let's go back to the beginning. When did Nancy first contact you?"

"That was last autumn, as I recall," Deb said. "She wrote this extremely enthusiastic email about how she very much wanted to stay with us and hoped we could oblige."

"Would you still have a copy?"

"Should do, on file somewhere."

"Did she say why she picked Chelsea Mansions? Was it recommended by someone?"

"I don't think she said, just that she was dead set on staying with us. We could hardly refuse, she sounded so keen."

"And when she arrived, did she say anything?"

Toby shook his head. "Don't remember anything special." He spooned another dollop of ice-cream into his mouth.

"I think she said something about loving that part of London," Deb said. "She said it made her feel at home."

"Do you think she might have been there before?"

Deb shrugged and took a bite of her smoked salmon sandwich. "No, I think it was just a general statement. I think the real reason was that we were handy for the flower show and not too expensive."

"How about the neighbors? Did she know about the Moszynskis?"

"I think we did talk about them, didn't we, Toby? Or was that with the Leeds people? Someone had read about Shaka's wedding."

"That wouldn't have made the American news, would it?" Kathy said doubtfully.

"Oh, I don't know," John said. "We got it in Canada. One of those juicy news bites, 'Glamorous model weds Russian billionaire,' you know, like beauty and the beast.

"But I was thinking," he went on, "Toby, you mentioned that your aunt ran a hotel next door to your house at Chelsea Mansions. Is it possible that Nancy, or her parents maybe, once stayed there, and met the people down the street, and maybe Nancy thought she might try to trace them?"

Toby looked at Deb and they both frowned. "She didn't mention anything like that."

"Would it be worth seeing if you have any old records or photographs that might tell us something?"

"We had boxes of old family papers, but they got damaged by damp, down in the shelter."

"The shelter?" John asked.

"Our cellar. Pa built a bomb shelter for us in the cellar in '39,

227

before he went off to France with the BEF. Damn stupid idea really—if the house had been hit we'd all have been buried alive. But it's damp down there so we took what we could salvage up to the attic, next to your room, John. You're welcome to have a look if you want."

"Perhaps I might," John said. "History was originally my subject. If you really wouldn't mind, Toby?"

"Be my guest, old son. If you find any worthwhile photos, we might get them framed."

After they finished their lunch they lingered for a while in the food hall, and John took hold of Kathy's arm and steered her away.

"You think there might be some connection between Nancy and Chelsea Mansions?"

"I've really no idea, John, but it's an intriguing thought."

"It does kind of make sense. The holiday was a bit of a nostalgia trip for her—tracing the lost relatives in Scotland, that kind of thing. And she had brought old photographs with her. Emerson showed me."

"Yes, I saw those. I didn't take much notice at the time."

"I don't remember seeing any of Chelsea Mansions. They were mainly pictures of people. It would be interesting if any of those faces are up in Toby's attic, wouldn't it?"

"It might explain why she came to the hotel."

But not much else, she thought, as she waved them off in a taxi, the three of them looking like an affectionate family group, the elderly couple and their deferential, grown-up son, indulging the old man's passion for kniccurbocker glories. The sight of them together filled Kathy with a sense of futility. They hadn't been able to help, although they'd obviously wanted to, and the failure wasn't theirs, it was hers. She had been in a kind of shock since being dumped from the case, wasting time, clutching at straws like this, when the real questions lay elsewhere.

And the real questions were why Nigel Hadden-Vane had done it and how he'd managed it. They had caught sight of a couple of his connections to the killer and his accomplice, and sketched out a circumstantial case, but nothing more. How had he arranged it, making contact with the son of his old chauffeur in Barlinnie Prison to recruit Harry Peebles? How had he made contact with Peebles, given his instructions, paid the cash? The only person who might have given them an inkling was Danny Yilmaz, and he was dead.

On the way home she went over again in her mind that first interview with Danny. She remembered a slight change in his manner, an apparent eagerness to cooperate, when she began to question him about the man who had made the arrangements for the job over the phone. Did he know the caller? Was it Hadden-Vane himself, or had he worked through some other acquaintance of Danny's?

When she got back to her flat she went through the case files on her computer once again, searching for the newspaper photograph that Bren had shown her, of Hadden-Vane at the Haringey Sport and Social Club, handing out certificates. When she found it she stared at the faces, a dozen of them watching the ceremony. The quality was poor, the features grainy, but there was one other that seemed familiar. It took her a moment to place him, then she remembered. In the back row, face partially obscured, stood a man who looked very like Wayne Everett, the security man on duty the night Moszynski died.

TWENTY-SEVEN

WHEN SHE GOT TO the hospital the following morning, Brock was dressed and getting ready to leave.

"Kathy!" he beamed. "I was going to give you a call. They're letting me go home at last. Fancy a train ride?"

They caught a cab to Victoria Station, Brock opening the window to take in the smells of the city, untainted by hospital chemicals, and it was only when they were on the train that he began to speak of what was on his mind. He had been careful to choose an empty compartment, and as the train pulled out of the station he said, "Chivers called in to see me this morning. He brought me a book about preparing for retirement. I nearly threw it at him. Apparently he'd heard a rumor that I'd decided to go."

They were rumbling across Grosvenor Bridge, the chimneys and bulk of the old Battersea Power Station on the far side of the river, and hovering overhead a helicopter coming in to the heliport that Moszynski had used. Life goes on, Kathy thought.

"Did he say how his investigation is going?"

"I rather gathered that they haven't found anything more concrete to link Hadden-Vane to Peebles, nor a motive for him to be involved in either death."

"I might be able to help him."

"You got something from the hotel people?"

"No, they couldn't help. But afterward I was thinking about Danny Yilmaz, and wondering who else might have made the arrangements for Peebles' visit, if it wasn't Hadden-Vane himself. So I looked again at that picture of him at the Haringey club, and I recognized Moszynski's bodyguard, Wayne Everett, among the onlookers. And that makes sense too, because Hadden-Vane is a director of the company he works for, Shere Security."

Brock nodded, thoughtful. "I see."

"Should I tell Chivers?" Kathy asked.

"Hm, I think he'd regard it as just another circumstantial detail. So Everett was in the photo, so what? And it doesn't help us with the most important thing, the thing that's bothering him most: the motive. Why on earth would Hadden-Vane want to harm Moszynski or Nancy Haynes?"

They were passing through the densely packed terraces of inner South London now, the brickwork blackened with age and long-extinct coal fires. It was an area Brock had once worked as a young CID officer, and he said, "This feels like being in limbo, doesn't it? Watching life through glass."

"You could get away. Take a holiday, go somewhere nice with Suzanne."

"She's busy, and I'm supposed to check in to the clinic every day for tests. I could still be a walking time bomb, according to the specialist. So if you hear me ticking, watch out."

When they got off the train they stopped at the Bishop's Mitre on the way back to Brock's house. Brock ordered his habitual pork pie and pint of bitter, and Kathy watched him address them like a sacrament for a life recovered.

When they were finished she took a couple of sheets of paper from her bag and spread them out on the table. "This is our victim profile for Nancy Haynes. Thin, isn't it? I realized when I was talking to the hotel people how little we really know about her. We don't know why she chose Chelsea Mansions or if she'd been to London before, and we have only a vague sketch of her background and family structure. It didn't seem particularly relevant. Now I wonder. What if she had had some previous contact with Hadden-Vane?"

"I've been thinking the same thing," Brock said. "In fact I've been wondering if Sharpe might be right about you leaving London."

She gave him a puzzled look and he said, "Have you ever been to Boston?"

She hadn't. In fact she'd never been to North America, and at first she didn't like the idea of leaving. It felt like running away, and she objected that they could talk to Emerson and Nancy's relatives on the phone, but Brock wasn't having any of that.

"It's not the same, Kathy. You've got to see them on their home ground. Get the taste of it, where she lived, what kind of life she had. You know that."

So they went back to Brock's house and explored the idea, and when they'd finished Kathy got on the web and started to make some bookings.

ON THE TRAIN BACK to central London later that afternoon, Kathy called John Greenslade. He was at the Tate Gallery, viewing the Henry Moore exhibition, and they arranged to meet outside on the gallery steps. The sky was heavy with dark clouds when Kathy came out of Victoria Station and walked briskly down Vauxhall Bridge Road, and by the time she reached the river and turned along Millbank fat drops of rain were spotting the pavement. She ran up the steps toward the shelter of the portico and John stepped out to meet her with a smile, and it struck her with a sudden feeling of regret that she probably wouldn't see him again.

"Fancy a cup of tea?" he said.

"Okay."

They went inside and downstairs to the café.

"How have you been making out?" he asked, and she sensed a reserve about him, as if he'd resigned himself to getting nowhere with her.

"A bit of a loose end."

He nodded. "I would have called, but I figured you'd get in touch if you wanted to." He stirred his tea slowly. "And now you have. So what can I do for you?"

Kathy felt uncomfortable. "I really appreciate the help you've given me, John."

"Don't mention it. What do you need?"

"I wondered if you're going to stay in London for a few more days."

"I reckoned I'd stay at least over the weekend. Why?"

"If you had the time to look through Toby's old records that would be very useful."

"Yes, I said I would. In fact I made a start this morning. I found some old photo albums, family groups mostly—on a beach, playing golf, at a fair—the sort of things you'd expect, but I didn't come across anyone I recognized. To tell the truth, I don't really have any idea what I'm supposed to be looking for."

"I'm going to try to get hold of those photographs that Nancy brought with her, and I thought I could email them to you so that you could see if any of the people in those showed up in Toby's pictures. That would give us a connection."

"Email?"

"Yes, I'm going over to Boston. She may have had other photos, or letters which might tell us something."

John looked stunned. "I see. Are you back on the case then?"

"Not officially, no. But since they don't seem to be checking this angle I thought I would. Give me something to do. I'd be grateful if you kept it to yourself, though."

"When are you going?"

"Tomorrow."

"Have you been there before?"

She shook her head.

"I spent a month at Harvard last year. Hotels are pricey though. Have you got somewhere to stay?"

"A bed and breakfast in a place called Back Bay."

"Back Bay is nice. Very classy. You'll like it."

"It's where Emerson lives."

An awkward silence fell between them. She guessed what was going through his mind: *I could come with you, it's on my way home*. But if that was what he was thinking he didn't say, and she certainly didn't want to compound the problems she would face if Chivers found out what she was doing.

"I'm grateful, John, really I am," she said at last.

"It's a pleasure." He smiled stiffly. "You'll have packing to do. I think I'll take another look at Henry Moore."

At the door they shook hands and went their separate ways.

TWENTY-EIGHT

AS THE PLANE DROPPED through the clouds Kathy made out the ragged coastline and islands of Massachusetts Bay and, away to the south, the long crooked arm of Cape Cod reaching into the Atlantic. Soon she could see a harbor dotted with small craft, and wharves with the towers of central Boston behind, and then the plane was dropping into Logan International.

When she was finally clear of immigration she caught a cab into the city, giving the address of the bed and breakfast in Beacon Street. It was a solid brownstone house with a curved bow front to one side of the entrance steps. Two men welcomed her, gay she guessed, probably in their early forties, and showed her to her room upstairs. It was beautifully appointed and had a view out across the Charles River to the north shore beyond, lit up by the afternoon sun. Having assured her that they could help her with anything she needed, her hosts left her sitting by the window, feeling numb from the dawn start, the long flight and sudden immersion in this new city, and for the first time she was glad to have come, to have escaped the claustrophobia of London.

She had phoned Emerson Merckle the previous day to make sure he would be available, and had arranged to contact him as soon as she arrived, which she now did. He sounded pleased to hear from her, and suggested they meet for afternoon tea at a place in Newbury Street, just a few blocks away. She had a shower and changed into lighter clothes and set out through the leafy residential streets, across the broad boulevard of Commonwealth Avenue and on to Newbury Street, lined with fashionable shops, galleries and restaurants. As she approached the café she saw Emerson sitting at a window table, half a story above the street, gazing out at the passersby, and gave him a wave. He looked a little puzzled at first, not recognizing her, then smiled and got to his feet as she climbed the steps and went inside.

They shook hands and made polite conversation about her flight and where she was staying. She could understand him not recognizing her out of context, because he too seemed different, more confident and expansive in his own setting.

"You said you wanted to get to know Nancy," he said, "so I had to bring you to Newbury Street, her favorite shopping place. Sure, she went out to the malls, of course, but this was really what she loved, the boutiques along here."

"She liked clothes?"

"She liked shopping, the whole experience, for herself, for her children and grandchildren, for her friends. She bought me this shirt at a little place down the street here."

He paused, remembering. It was a very stylish shirt, Kathy noticed, brilliant white, with gold cufflinks and a dark tie and trousers so that he looked as if he'd come prepared for a formal interview, hair combed, cheeks pink.

"Afterward we'd meet somewhere like this and she'd tell me what she'd found. I look out of the window now and expect to see her walk by at any moment, with carrier bags full of her trophies."

"And she did the same in London?"

"Actually, no, not really. We did go to Knightsbridge, but that was about it, and frankly I was a little surprised. I was thinking about this after you called me. There were other things that strike me now, small things, but a little odd."

"Yes?"

"Well, we arrived in London on the Saturday, and the following day we took a boat down the river to Greenwich, but by afternoon I was feeling jetlagged and just wanted to lie down for a while before we thought about dinner. But she was more energetic, and said she'd go out for a walk around Chelsea. It was about seven that evening when she tapped on my door to tell me she was back, and when she came in I was aware of a peculiar smell. It took me back to my childhood. It was incense—my family were Catholics—and I asked her where on earth she'd been, and she laughed and said she'd been to vespers. I was astonished, because that just wasn't like Nancy at all, but she said she'd passed a cathedral and looked in."

"A cathedral?"

"That's what she said. I didn't think any more about it, until I got home and saw on the TV news about the funeral in a Russian Orthodox cathedral in London of that Russian who lived next to our hotel. I wondered if it could have been the cathedral Nancy visited, and if it was possible they had met there and that was why he'd come to Nancy's memorial service."

Kathy felt a stir of excitement. "It's possible. That cathedral is in Knightsbridge, not far from where you were staying. It's where he was a regular worshipper. This was one of the things I wanted to ask you, Mr. Merckle . . ."

"Emerson, please."

". . . Emerson. You left the day after Mikhail Moszynski was killed in Cunningham Place, and we didn't have a chance to speak to you again, but I wanted to find out if it was possible that Nancy could have had any contact with him."

"She never made any mention of a Russian, and we were together almost all the time, apart from that Sunday evening."

"What about the following day, Monday, around lunchtime?"

He pulled out a little appointments diary from his trouser pocket. "Monday, Monday . . . the twenty-fourth. That was the morning we did go shopping, to Harrods first of all. She bought some things in the toy department for her grandchildren. Then Harvey Nichols, then back to the hotel. What then?" He frowned in thought. "I was tired by the end of the morning and still a little disoriented by the time difference, and we decided to have a rest before going out to lunch. Why do you ask about that day?"

"Someone in the square said they saw Nancy call in next door, that day or maybe Tuesday, at lunchtime."

"Next door? To the Russians? She never said a word to me about it. I don't think I even knew she went out. Let me think . . . I read in my room for a while, and may have nodded off. Then I noticed the time, getting on for two, and went to see if she was ready to go. She was sorting some things on her bed, I remember— the pouch of photographs you saw. That was the first time I'd seen them. We went up the road to the department store in Sloane Square—Peter Jones—and had a late lunch on the top floor. Great views over London, I remember. She seemed very lively. I told her she had a spring in her step."

"But she didn't mention having gone out?"

"No, she didn't."

"But if she did, she may have taken the photographs with her?"

"I suppose it's possible."

"You said other things struck you as odd about your time together in London?"

"Well, she seemed a little secretive, now I look back, slightly out of character. It was only because she was usually so open that I noticed it as odd. Like the way she quizzed Toby at the hotel about its history, and his family, as if it really mattered. I knew her so well, you see. I knew what interested her—fashion, recipes, gardens, music. But not architecture, history, heritage."

"She spoke to Toby about that?"

"Oh yes. At least, I came in at the end of a conversation. That's what they were talking about."

"How did you come to be staying at Chelsea Mansions?"

"Oh, that was entirely her doing. When she first suggested the trip to me she had already decided on that hotel, said she'd found this 'darling little place' and I just assumed it was on someone's recommendation. When we got there and I discovered what it was like I asked her about that, and she was a little mysterious, as if it were a game. When I pressed her she said, teasing me, that it was a ghost story, and I assumed that whoever had recommended the place had told her it was haunted, and she wanted me to discover it for myself."

"And did she give any indication of knowing about the people next door?"

"None at all. It was only after I got home and read about the man's murder that I realized that I had heard about him before, because his marriage to that model had been in the papers a couple of years back. But we never saw them when we were staying in Cunningham Place, and the hotel people never spoke of them, at least not to me."

When Kathy had called Emerson from London he'd explained that he still hadn't passed on Nancy's pouch of photographs to her family, although he intended to send them to her sister Janice. Now he invited her to go back to his apartment to look at them. They finished their tea and stepped out into the street, where Emerson pointed out Nancy's favorite shops—The Closet, Marc Jacobs, Basiques—and Kathy had a vivid sense of the affront to the ladies of Back Bay that one of their number should be thrown under a London bus.

"Was there a lot of publicity over here about Nancy's death?" she asked.

"Oh yes, and her funeral was very big, at Trinity Church down the street there. Her husband Martin was a highly respected surgeon here, still very warmly remembered ten years after his passing, and the medical fraternity came out in force. Which I must admit gives me some qualms, talking to you like this."

"How do you mean?"

"It's one thing for Nancy to be taken from us by a random act of violence by a passing thug. That's part of the world we live in, shocking, regrettable, but unavoidable. It could happen to any one of us, here in Boston, or London, or anywhere. Why, just a couple of months ago, the old man who lives across the street from me was stabbed at a gas station over at Brookline, of all places. People shake their heads, pay their respects and get on with life.

"But you seem to be hinting at something else, Kathy, some reason behind Nancy's death that she might have been a party to. I'm not sure I'm comfortable with that idea, and I suspect that a lot of other people won't be either, especially her family."

"You want to know the truth, don't you, Emerson?"

"Do I? Will it help Nancy? Will it help her grieving family? Will it help me? Let's get this straight. You seem to be searching for some connection between Nancy and a Russian billionaire she'd never met. What on earth could that be? Had she discovered that her dead husband had been mixed up with the Russian mafia? Or one of her sons? Did they owe this man money? Had she gone to plead with him? You don't know, do you? You don't really know what can of worms you want me to help you open up."

They had crossed Commonwealth Avenue by this time, back into the grid of leafy residential streets beyond, with their brick-paved sidewalks and faux gas-lamp streetlights and dignified rows of red-brick terraces, and Emerson stopped at the foot of a flight of steps up to a porticoed front door. "This is where I live," he said.

"Emerson, if you really feel uncomfortable about this, I can walk away right now."

He shook his head. "No, you've come all this way. And anyway, I'd already decided to help you. I'm prepared to consider that Nancy went to London with some purpose in mind that she didn't share with me. But she wanted me along, and I think she would have told me eventually, if our journey hadn't been interrupted. And so I want to settle the matter, for her as well as myself. But if you're right, and depending on what you discover, I may ask for your tact and understanding."

They went inside to Emerson's apartment, which occupied the main floor of a building very like the bed and breakfast where Kathy was staying, with a similar generous bow front to the street. They sat at a table by the window and examined Nancy's photographs while Kathy took notes. Emerson was able to identify many of the people—Nancy's children and grandchildren, her husband and sister—but when it came to the older ones, early Kodak prints with faded color or shadowy black and whites, he was stumped.

"Her parents, I suppose; uncles, aunts, who knows? Janice would, of course."

He said it in a doubtful tone, and Kathy said, "Janice?"

"Janice Connolly, Nancy's younger sister."

"Does she live around here?"

"Provincetown."

"Is that far away?"

"It's at the far tip of Cape Cod, a fair distance, an hour and a half by ferry or three hours by road."

Kathy said, "I probably should go. Maybe you could give me her phone number."

Emerson hesitated, then said, "Let me ring her. She can be difficult sometimes."

He checked the number, picked up the phone and dialed. "Janice? It's Emerson. How are you?"

From his careful tone Kathy guessed they weren't warm friends, and it didn't take long before he got to the point.

"I have a London detective here with me who's come over to tie up one or two details about Nancy. There's some questions I can't answer and I wonder if you can help us . . . No, the police, Scotland Yard . . . Just background information, so they can close the case . . . Would you like to speak to her? . . . No? . . . Tomorrow?" He raised his eyebrows at Kathy, who nodded. "I'll drive her down. Shall we take you to lunch? . . . Oh, all right, say two o'clock, at your house . . . I'm not sure, a couple of hours? . . . No, all right, one hour. See you then."

He hung up and took a breath.

"Awkward?" Kathy asked.

"Very different from her sister. They didn't really get along, and she disapproves of me. Never mind, it's all arranged. She has some commitment for lunch but will see us afterward."

"You don't have to come, Emerson. I can hire a car."

He waved his hand. "It's my pleasure. I haven't been down there in years. The traffic will be bad this time of year, but we might take the old King's Highway and avoid much of it. Now you probably want to see in Nancy's house. I have a key. I think I told you that I'm one of her executors, and I'm keeping an eye on the place for the family—it's just down the street."

It was a three-story freestanding brick house on the corner of the next block, and Emerson waved to a neighbor who peered at them as he pushed open a squeaky gate and they made their way to the front door through beds of flowers whose blooming Nancy would never see. There was an air of stillness inside the house, the air tinged with a faint sweet trace of perfume, and

Emerson took in a deep breath of it, as if to capture the fading spirit of Nancy herself. He led Kathy on a brief tour of the rooms, returning to a dining room overlooking the back garden. Here there was a massive piece of mahogany furniture with a glass-fronted china cabinet set above drawers and cupboard doors.

"This is where she kept her papers and records," Emerson said. "I've been through it myself, looking for legal and tax documents relating to her estate. There are letters and private papers here too."

"I'd like to see recent correspondence, if I could. And any more photographs."

"There are some albums." He lifted out two books containing family pictures, all fairly recent. "I thought there were some older ones, but I don't see them . . . I'll have to persuade Janice to come and stay for a couple of days and go through all this stuff."

Kathy spent an hour reading letters, diaries and appointment books. She found copies of documents relating to the London trip, but nothing out of the ordinary and no references to anyone associated with the Moszynski household.

"Nothing," she said at last.

Emerson was seated opposite her at the dining table, going through a concertina file marked *Accounts*. "Yes," he said, "I'm familiar with all this from handling her tax affairs, and I'm sure there's nothing here that would interest you." He closed the file. "I do think you may be wasting your time."

She was inclined to agree as she returned to Beacon Street. She had borrowed the pouch of Nancy's photographs and on the way back took them to a business services shop that Emerson had directed her to, where she had them scanned. Later she sent an email to John Greenslade attaching Nancy's pictures, then checked her watch. The evening sun was shining bright across the Charles River but it was almost midnight in London. She closed the curtains, got into bed and fell fast asleep.

TWENTY-NINE

KATHY WOKE WITH A start, taking a moment to remember where she was. Reaching up to pull the curtain aside, she saw the sky lit by a pearly pink glow of dawn. Cars driving along Memorial Drive on the far side of the river still had their headlights on, and when she opened the window a cool freshness flooded in, along with the chirping of birds.

She pulled on a T-shirt, track pants and trainers and went quietly down the stairs to the front door. The street was deserted, its lamps forming a chain of glowing points beneath the trees away into the distance. She turned east toward the rising sun and jogged briskly along Beacon Street until it emerged onto the broad green slope of Boston Common, where other runners could be seen among the trees. She passed the golden dome of the Massachusetts State House and continued into the grid of narrow historic streets of Beacon Hill, then down between the towers of the financial district until she reached the wharves of the waterfront. She stopped there for a while at the water's edge, watching the early morning flights coming into Logan far across the water, before turning and heading back.

When she opened the front door she was met by a delicious

smell of cooking from the dining room. Looking inside she was hailed by Peter, the taller and more extroverted of the two owners, who invited her to sit down for breakfast. This morning his partner Tom, busy in the kitchen, was offering banana maple porridge with buttered apples, followed by sweet corn fritters with roast tomato and bacon. Kathy said that sounded wonderful.

It seemed like a propitious start to the day, made more so when she opened her laptop and found an email from London with several old photographs that John had discovered among Toby's documents. Some showed various of his relatives posing with other people Toby hadn't been able to identify, while a couple of others were of unknown groups standing outside Chelsea Mansions. Kathy put the computer into her backpack with her little Sony IC Recorder and a notebook, and got changed to meet Emerson.

It was Saturday, and they weren't the only ones with the idea of driving down to Cape Cod, but Emerson, at the wheel of his Lincoln Zephyr, was unperturbed by the traffic and Kathy felt pleasantly cocooned as they drove sedately southward, past Plymouth and on toward the Cape. After they crossed the Sagamore Bridge onto Cape Cod much of the traffic turned toward the warmer beaches of the south shores of the island, facing Buzzards Bay and Nantucket Sound, while Emerson took the old road along the north side, through a succession of small historic towns overlooking sandy bays and pretty boat harbors.

"Janice was married to a marine biologist based at the Atlantic Research Center up ahead at North Truro," Emerson explained. "He was drowned in a bad storm back in 2002, and Janice has stayed on in their house in Provincetown. It suits her out here. She loves the place, the white sand dunes and salt marshes, the beech forests, and she's a great hiker. She hates the city, not at all like her sister."

"You said they didn't get on?"

"They tolerated each other, I'd say. Janice is much younger—Nancy would have been eleven or twelve when Janice was born. Their father retired a few years later and he more or less reared the new toddler single-handed. The two were very close, whereas Nancy saw less of her father when she was growing up. There was the war, and then he was working for the State Department and away a lot. She was always more attached to her mother."

"The artist."

"Yes, Maisy was really a very fine sculptor. There are several of her pieces in the collection of the Museum of Fine Arts in Boston. Her husband was a diplomat. He died some time ago, but Maisy lasted until just last year. She was quite a character. I got to know her well."

They came at last to Provincetown, at the end of the road around the long curving reach of the island. They were too early to meet Janice, and Emerson took Kathy on a tour of the town, ending at a seafood restaurant overlooking the beach where they sat down for lunch.

As they were waiting for their order, Emerson, looking out to the boats in the harbor, pointed to a couple of swimmers with snorkels. "Well now, there's another funny thing. It's strange how your memory brings things up. When we were flying over to England Nancy asked me if I'd ever gone scuba diving. I thought it was an odd question, out of the blue. I told her no, and she said it would frighten her, diving deep under the water."

He shook his head as if to clear the memory. "Anyway, Janice lives just a couple of blocks away," he said. "Not far from where Norman Mailer used to live. Apparently they got on quite well. He probably recognized a fellow grump."

"This is going to be difficult, is it?"

"Well, don't be too disappointed if you get nothing. I'd buy her some flowers except that she'd know I was trying to butter her up and she'd take offense."

WHEN JANICE OPENED HER front door Kathy saw that he hadn't been exaggerating. She was dressed in old jeans and a faded T-shirt, and her gray hair was cropped severely short. Her eyes narrowed at the sight of them and her lips pursed tight.

"Emerson," she acknowledged grudgingly.

"Janice!" His joviality sounded unconvincing, and Janice flinched as he made to kiss her cheek. "Let me introduce the person I spoke about. Detective Inspector Kathy Kolla has been investigating Nancy's death."

They shook hands, Janice unsmiling as she scrutinized her visitor. She kept them waiting on the threshold just a fraction too long before inviting them in.

It was a timber house, its plain furnishings set off by clusters of natural objects—pebbles, sea-bleached flotsam, skulls of small animals—and also by framed photographs of blossoms, sea and dunescapes, birds.

"Beautiful photographs," Kathy said.

"Janice is a very accomplished nature photographer," Emerson said. "I expect she gets her artistic talent from her mother, eh Janice?"

She ignored him and indicated seats around a scrubbed pine table.

"You'd better show me your ID," she said to Kathy.

"Oh, I can vouch for Kathy, Janice," Emerson protested. "I met her in London, and—"

"All the same." Janice examined Kathy's Metropolitan Police pass and the business card she gave her. "I would have thought you'd have been accompanied by an officer of the state or federal police. I suppose they do know you're here questioning people, do they?"

"I'm just here in an informal capacity, Mrs. Connolly, clearing up a few loose ends so that our coroner can close the case. I'm relying entirely on your cooperation. You don't have to answer any of my questions if you don't want to."

"I won't," the other woman said decisively, and sat back with arms folded.

"We want to clear up the possibility that Nancy, or some other member of your family, may have had some previous connection to the place where she was staying in London, or the people who are living there now."

"What possible relevance could that have to her death? I understood it was a simple case of street violence."

"We're concerned by the coincidence that another person living in Cunningham Place, where Nancy and Emerson were staying . . ." Kathy noticed Janice's hostile glance in Emerson's direction, ". . . was murdered just a few days later. We need to rule out the possibility that there was any connection between the two crimes."

"Who was this other person?"

"His name was Mikhail Moszynski, a wealthy Russian businessman."

"Oh yes, you told me, Emerson, didn't you? I was upset at the funeral, and I don't think it registered. Well, what of it?"

"Are you aware of any connection?"

"Of course not."

"I have some photographs here on my laptop that I'd like to show you."

Kathy pulled out her computer and quickly opened up the file and began to show the pictures to Janice, beginning with individual shots of the Moszynski household, including Vadim Kuzmin, Nigel Hadden-Vane and Freddie Clarke.

"No, I know none of these people."

"Nancy took some family photographs with her to London. Perhaps you could just identify the people for me." They opened the pouch and went through the pictures, Kathy taking notes of the names of cousins, uncles, grandparents.

"I really don't see the point of this. Most of these are ancient. How can they possibly be relevant?"

"Nearly finished, Mrs. Connolly. Just a few more."

"Hang on," Emerson said, peering over Kathy's shoulder at one of the photos. "Isn't that Maisy?"

It was a picture of three adults and a teenage girl grouped together on the steps of a building, their eyes half closed against the bright sunlight on their smiling faces. Emerson was pointing at the woman who was standing between two men.

"I'm sure that's your mother, Janice."

Janice gave it another reluctant glance. "Maybe."

"And isn't that your father with her? And the girl—could it be Nancy?"

Janice gave a sigh of annoyance. "Very likely. So what?"

"Well, that looks a lot like Chelsea Mansions in the background, where we stayed."

Kathy looked more closely at the background, tall sash windows in dark brickwork, a black doorway with white painted surround. It might be Chelsea Mansions, she thought, or a thousand other similar places in London, or Boston come to that. "What about the other man?" Kathy asked. "Do you recognize him?"

"Obviously someone they met somewhere. I've never seen him before. And I'm not convinced that's Nancy. It's probably the other man's daughter . . . oh."

Something had struck Janice. She stared again at the photo. "That dress, it was Nancy's. I remember now, Pop and Mom took Nancy to London for her sixteenth birthday. I was only five. They left me behind with Grandma."

"When would that have been?" Kathy asked, but Janice waved her hand dismissively.

"This is nonsense," she said impatiently. "This has no relevance to you."

Kathy didn't press the point. She asked Janice to recall later trips made by Nancy to the UK. There had been two that she remembered, both with her husband, staying at the Hilton.

"And now I must ask you to leave," she said. "I have another appointment."

At the front door she added, "Your police must have a lot more time and money to spare than ours, if they can afford to send an inspector across the Atlantic just to check a few trivial details like this."

"Many thanks for your time," Kathy said evenly. "I'm sorry to have interrupted your afternoon."

"Dadgummed bitch," Emerson breathed when they got back into the car. It was such an uncharacteristic outburst from the gentlemanly Emerson, and said with such feeling, that Kathy had to laugh.

"But that *was* Nancy and her parents," he protested, "and they *were* standing outside Chelsea Mansions. I'm right, aren't I?"

"It's possible. I could get someone in London to check."

"If Janice was right and this was Nancy's sixteenth birthday, that would make it the twenty-sixth of April, 1956."

He slowly turned the car and began the long drive back to Boston. On the way Kathy sent a text message to John with the date and asked him to check the background to the photograph, then sat back to admire the well-maintained clapboard houses they passed in picturesque villages or set back among the trees of private acreages.

"You know what I find so upsetting?" Emerson said after a long silence. "The idea that Nancy might have kept it a secret from me. How could she have gone through that whole charade, choosing the hotel and all, and not told me the real purpose of the trip for her?" Then he added, "Unless it was something shameful. Do you think that could be it? Might she have wanted to revisit the scene of something bad, something embarrassing? Might she have been abused there, perhaps? Was she revisiting the scene of a trauma she couldn't confess to me?"

"It needn't be anything like that, Emerson. She may just have been a bit reticent about telling you that she wanted to revisit a happy memory from her past. Especially when she discovered that Chelsea Mansions wasn't the splendid hotel she remembered."

He gave a rueful smile. "I guess you're right. And if she was there in her teens it could have nothing to do with her murder, after all. Those other people in the old pictures are all dead and gone."

When they got back to Beacon Street he said, "Will you be leaving now?"

"I suppose so, yes. I'll have to check available flights."

"It seems a shame to have come so far and seen so little. Let me at least take you out to dinner at one of Nancy's favorite haunts. Nothing fancy, just a very friendly little Italian place down in the North End where we often went on a Saturday night. What do you say?"

"You've given me so much of your time already, Emerson, I'd feel guilty about taking more."

"Nonsense, it'd cheer me up no end. I'll phone Maria. I'm sure she'll squeeze us in when I explain. Shall we say eight o'clock?"

So she agreed, and spent an enjoyable evening with him, talking about all the places she should have seen, and would have to return to one day.

THIRTY

THE FOLLOWING MORNING PETER was already setting places in the dining room by the time Kathy came downstairs for her run. Today Tom was offering honeyed yoghurt with fresh berries followed by French toast stuffed with peaches. "He's a star," Peter said, seeing the look on Kathy's face.

This time she headed down through the South End and then east into Chinatown. As she pounded through the empty streets she tried to clear her mind. It felt as if she'd been here for a long time, much more than two days. That's what happened when you had a change of scene, she told herself, time expanded, became more generous. It had been a blessing to get out of London. It was absurd that she'd never been to America before—never been out of Europe in fact. Her work had constrained her, narrowed her focus. Was that why Guy's invitation to go to Dubai had seemed so appealing? What a disaster that would have been. No regrets there.

She returned to Beacon Street, skipping up the front steps, blood singing. After a quick shower she went downstairs and opened the dining room door. The smell of Tom's cooking hit her and she said, "Wow," then stopped dead, staring at the figure sitting at a corner table. He lifted his head and she said, "It *is* you," and John Greenslade got to his feet with a cautious smile. There was a suitcase on the floor beside him.

"Ah, you do know him then, do you, Kathy?" Peter said from the door behind her. "I wasn't sure whether to let him in. But he looked so forlorn, I thought I'd better give him something to eat."

She sat down at his table and asked what on earth he was doing there. He looked as if he hadn't slept, which, as it turned out, was pretty much the case, his flight being a nightmare, through Newark.

"There was something I needed to show you, Kathy, about the photographs," he said.

"Oh really?"

He registered her doubtful look and was rescued by the arrival of French toast and coffee, with Peter clearly trying to interpret what was going on. "Will he be requiring a room?" he asked.

"Oh, I think so, Peter," Kathy said. "Do you have one free?"

"We do. Next to yours as it happens." He arched an eyebrow and strolled off to talk to the couple from Iowa at another table.

"Well, this is a nice surprise," Kathy said.

"I'm relieved. I thought you'd be mad."

"I was talking about the French toast," she said, and watched his smile fade. "So what do you have to show me?"

"I'd need to get out my laptop."

"I suggest a shower and a shave and change of clothes first," Kathy said. "And maybe a couple of hours' sleep?"

"Not the sleep, but the other things would be wonderful."

Peter led him away while Kathy had another coffee and caught up on the news in the *Boston Globe*.

Later, in her room, John opened up his laptop and clicked to the image of the group in front of the building.

"First of all, that is definitely Chelsea Mansions. Each of the doorways is slightly different, and I'm certain they're standing in front of number eight, the present-day hotel, which in 1956 would have been the home of Toby and his parents. When I showed him the picture he had no idea who the people were, and thought they must have been staying at his great-aunt's hotel next door, but I'm sure you were right about them being Nancy and her parents. So then I began to look more closely at the unidentified man and I felt I'd seen him somewhere before. I looked through the other photos, and I'm pretty sure that he appears again in this one . . ."

He brought up the image of a couple standing in front of a long reflecting pool, with an Art Deco arch in the background. "I was struck by this picture when Emerson showed it to me in London. It's undated, but it looks very thirties, don't you think? The style of their clothes and hair, and the architecture. And that's Maisy, looking twenty years younger than in the Chelsea Mansions picture, and I'd swear that's the same man again."

Kathy stared at the two photographs, and at enlargements John had made of the two male faces. "I think you could be right," she said at last. "So, a long-time friend of Maisy and her husband Ronald." She shrugged. "Is it significant?"

"Well, then I tried to work out where the older picture was taken. Emerson told me that Maisy worked for the American sculptor William Gordon Huff, and I looked him up. I wondered if the man in the pictures might be him, only it wasn't. But I did find out that he did some monumental sculptures for the Golden Gate International Exposition in San Francisco, held in 1939 and 1940. Here are some pictures of it. And there, look, you can see the arch, and the long pool."

"Well done. So the man's probably American, but so what? The important thing is that Nancy and her parents visited Chelsea Mansions in 1956. Surely their friend isn't relevant?"

John held up a finger. "Take a closer look at this guy. Doesn't it strike you—the cut of his jacket, the haircut—that he doesn't quite look American? Or English? Now look at the London picture, that suit he's wearing. Look at the lapel. There's something there, a badge or something. I enlarged it and sharpened it with Photoshop, see . . ."

"A tiny star," Kathy said. "Five-pointed."

"What does that make you think of?"

Kathy felt a pulse of excitement. "A Russian?"

"Could be. I wondered if I could discover anything about Russians in San Francisco in 1939 or 1940. No luck. But I did find out that the main archive of material on the Golden Gate International Exposition is held here in Boston, at the Widener Library at Harvard. I thought we should go over there and take a look. So that's why I'm here."

To Kathy it seemed a forlorn hope, but she was intrigued, and so they packed up what they would need—laptops, notebooks, a small camera that John had brought—and set off along Beacon Street toward the center of the city. On the far side of Boston Common he led them to the entrance of the Park Street station of the T, the city's subway system, where they caught a train out to Harvard. The other people in their carriage were mostly young—a bearded youth in frayed jeans trying to sleep off a hangover, a cluster of young women with heads down swapping notes, and a couple sitting opposite, pressed together in dreamy contentment, looking as if they'd just got out of bed. Kathy was aware of John watching them.

The train emptied at Harvard Square and they made their way up into the sunlight, where John took her arm and led her across the street and through a gap in the older buildings on the other side and into Harvard Yard. A lane took them into a campus of treed lawns crisscrossed by paths and framed by simple four-story brick buildings, some of which John pointed out as they passed—Massachusetts Hall, built in 1720 and the oldest building in Harvard, and Hollis Hall, where George Washington had barracked his troops during the American Revolution. They turned into the central courtyard of Harvard Yard, where the more monumental buildings of Memorial Church and the Widener Library stood facing each other across a green.

John said, "Harry Widener was a Harvard graduate and book collector who died on the *Titanic*. The library was donated by his mother in his memory, and it's now the major library in Harvard, which has the largest university collection in the world. It's particularly strong in the humanities and social sciences, which is why we're here."

They climbed the broad flight of steps to the colonnaded entrance, where John showed his Harvard ID from his research visit the previous year. For Kathy to get access they were directed to the Library Privileges Office, where John managed to have her issued with a day pass as his research assistant.

The university was now in summer recess, and the library was relatively quiet. They found a couple of computers side by side in the Phillips Reading Room and began searching through the HOLLIS catalog. Kathy started with online descriptions of the exposition, which had been built on reclaimed land called Treasure Island in San Francisco Bay. It had been held to celebrate the recent completion of the Golden Gate and Oakland Bay bridges, and was open to the public for a total of twelve months through 1939 and 1940.

"Millions of people must have visited it," she said, peering over at John's screen.

"Yes . . . I'm looking for foreign delegations. It was supposed to showcase the culture of Pacific Rim nations, which would include Russia, I guess. They must have sent over an official party, don't you think?"

There was plenty of material in the catalog, and it was hard to be sure from the brief entries what much of it might contain. They divided up the list of catalog numbers they would have to investigate and set off for the stacks, up to American History which occupied the whole of level two, and began the long, slow task of skimming through every book, every leaflet and newspaper report, every photograph collection, every official document and memoir.

"HOW'S IT GOING?"

Kathy looked up, taking a moment to focus. Her writing hand felt as numb as her brain. She had no idea of the time.

"Two o'clock," John said. "Don't know about you, but I need a break."

"Yes." She blinked and rubbed her face with a hand that felt grubby with dust from old paper.

They went out, dazzled by the sunshine, and John took her to a café that he knew nearby.

"We're not getting anywhere, are we?" he said after they'd ordered sandwiches and coffee. They had found dozens of pictures and references to William Gordon Huff's statues, and to the Court of Reflections in which Maisy and the man had been photographed, but they'd come across no more images of her, nor glimpses of Russian visitors.

"There's all those Kodachrome home movies to go through," Kathy said. "And we haven't finished the newspaper reports."

They returned to the library, slightly refreshed, and went on with their hunt. After another hour without result, John went over to a computer station and began another search through the catalog. Eventually he returned to Kathy, her head bent over a collection of postcards, and said that he'd found some GGIE references in the Economics stacks in Pusey, an underground extension of the library, and was going down to take a look. Slightly mesmerized by the images in front of her, Kathy nodded and turned to the next page.

There was a sign on the wall above Kathy's carrel stating that cell phone and pager use was not permitted in the library except in designated areas, so she jumped and looked around in embarrassment when her mobile emitted a loud tune. She snatched it out of her bag and whispered, "Yes?"

"Kathy." It was John. It took her a moment to remember that he'd gone some time before.

"Yes?"

"I may have found something. Come down and see." He told her how to find him.

She took a lift down to the basement of Widener and came to the tunnel that John had described, leading to the Pusey extension, where she descended to its lowest level. He waved her over to his desk and showed her an ancient typewritten report by the GGIE Budget Committee on visitor numbers to the fair. At the back was a series of appendices, one of which listed international delegations.

"There," he said, and pointed to a paragraph headed *Union of Soviet Socialist Republics, official visit of July 16–30 1939 of Deputy People's Commissar of Culture, Varvara Nikoleavna Zhemchuzhina and 16 delegates.*

"So there were Russians there," John said. "For what it's worth."

Kathy was skimming the list of delegates' names, then said softly, "Oh, I think it's worth something, John." She pointed at one of the names: *Gennady Moszynski (Leningrad).* "Mikhail's father. That's who was with Maisy in San Francisco in 1939, and again with Nancy and her parents at Chelsea Mansions in 1956."

"Mikhail's father?" John repeated, looking at Kathy in astonishment. "How can that be?"

"I don't know, but it's important, isn't it? Nancy had a reason not just for revisiting Chelsea Mansions, but for meeting Mikhail Moszynski. Their parents had once been close friends, even in the middle of the Cold War."

"You think Gennady might have been based in the Russian Embassy in London in 1956?"

"It wasn't in the biography I was given, but I suppose it's possible."

"You have his biography?"

"It was in a background briefing paper on Mikhail Moszynski that MI5 prepared for us when we were investigating his murder."

"Do you think his father was a spy?"

"There was no suggestion of it."

"But anyway, that was over fifty years ago. What difference would it make now? What could any of that have to do with Nancy and Mikhail's deaths?"

Kathy didn't know, but that name on an old report had given her a shiver of revelation, the sudden sense of discovering the truth among all the confusion. "I've no idea what it means, John, but I think we might have earned our crust today."

He smiled at her. "This is exciting, isn't it? It's like how I felt when I identified a verse by Ariosto."

She smiled at his idea of excitement, and yet it was true; she felt as if she had caught a glimpse of a ghost, the ghost that Nancy had teased Emerson with. "Come on," she said. "Let's go and celebrate."

HE CHOSE THE PLACE, the best seafood restaurant in Boston he said, down on the waterfront where she'd come on her first early morning run. From their table by the window they looked out over the harbor as dusk turned the scene from gold to turquoise, and far across the water the lights of the planes dropped like slow-motion meteors onto Logan's island.

As they talked, it occurred to Kathy how many things there were to like about John Greenslade. He was attentive, amusing and a good listener. He persuaded her to tell him about her childhood, and as he listened so sympathetically she found herself admiring little things about him, his slender hands, his thoughtful frown, and the wry, self-deprecating crease of his smile that reminded her a little of Brock. He was attracted to her, she could see that, and she liked the caution and restraint that seemed to be attuning itself to her own. He was too young, though; the ten-year gap between them might be refreshing but it was also a barrier. His openness and enthusiasm made her feel cynical and old.

"Your turn," she said, wanting to return to safer ground. "Tell me about the Greenslades."

He looked suddenly serious, almost as if she'd said something to upset or offend him. Then he took a breath, a sip of wine and his face cleared. "There aren't any," he said. "Just me and my mother."

She looked at him, wondering what he meant, and noticed a tension that had gathered in the way he sat.

"The way she tells it, my father was in some kind of high-risk job. When she became pregnant with me she became afraid for her own and my safety, and ran away. She went to her sister in Toronto, and changed her name to Greenslade—'clean slate' was what she meant—and started a new life."

"Oh. He was abusive to her, your father?"

"No, no, not as I understand it. The danger came from some people he was dealing with, who wanted to get at him through my mother. She reached a point where she couldn't stand it any more and just took off. He didn't even know she was pregnant until her sister got in touch with him and told him. Her sister, my aunt, acted as an intermediary for a while, passing on messages and money he sent. But in the end my mother asked for a divorce and broke off all contact."

"Did she ever remarry?"

"No."

"And you've had no contact with him?"

"My mother always said that my father had died before I was born, but when I turned twenty-one she finally told me the truth, that she had no idea whether he was alive or dead. I felt it didn't matter. I mean, he'd had no more part in my life than an anonymous sperm donor. Now I'm not so sure."

"What a sad story. It reminds me a little of my boss, Brock. He lost his wife, from what I gather, in similar circumstances . . ." The look on his face stopped her.

She stared at him. "John?"

He couldn't meet her eyes, but gave a little nod.

"Brock is your father?" she whispered.

"Mum told me his name and that he'd been a policeman in London. She said it was up to me. I felt I didn't want it, this knowledge. For a long time I tried to ignore it. Then the conference in London came up. I tried to avoid that too, but they kept pestering me to give a paper . . ." He shrugged helplessly.

"That's why I got a room at Chelsea Mansions, after I read about Nancy's murder and how DCI Brock was in charge. I hoped I might get a look at him, get some impression of what he was like."

"And that night at the Two Chairmen," Kathy said, "and going to see him in hospital."

He nodded, looking miserable now. "I just didn't know what to do, what I felt—how *he* would feel."

Kathy reached out a hand to his. "I don't think you have to worry about that."

"Really?" He looked doubtful. "And then there was something else. He didn't come to the hotel, but you did. At first I wanted to find out from you what sort of man he was, but as I got to know you I found that I wanted to know *you* better . . . Which made things kind of complicated." He stopped, frowning down at the white tablecloth in front of him, and Kathy saw with some alarm that there was what looked like a tear forming in his eye.

"I'm sorry." He sucked in a deep breath and pulled his hand away to rub across his face. "I'm sorry. This isn't like me, I promise."

"It must have been very emotional for you."

"Yes. I was sort of prepared for that. What I wasn't prepared for was falling for his partner."

Kathy felt her face flush.

"You're an intimate part of his life, his professional life, and from what Mum said, that's the most important part. I thought . . . I was damn sure that would kill any chance I might have had with you."

"Oh, John." Kathy gave him an encouraging smile, but at the same time she knew that he was right. He was certainly a different person from the one that she had felt drawn toward just a moment before. Now he was Brock's son. How did she feel about that?

He roused himself and reached for the bottle. "I should have told you before, but I got cold feet. It was what we discovered this afternoon that made me face it, I think. Like me, Nancy went to London to confront something from her past. If only she'd ignored it, stayed at home in Back Bay, she might still be alive and she and Emerson could have been the ones sharing this meal here tonight. And you and I would never have met." He topped up their glasses and sighed. "So what should I have done, Kathy? Should I have ignored it too, that presence from the past?"

"I think," she said slowly, "that you probably felt you had no choice."

He gave a rueful nod.

A thought struck Kathy. "I wonder if Nancy felt the same

way. Do you remember the dates of the Russians' visit to San Francisco?"

"July 1939, wasn't it?"

"Yes, the sixteenth to the thirtieth of July. And Nancy was born on the twenty-sixth of April in the following year." She was thinking of the photograph of Maisy and Gennady in front of the reflecting pool, a strikingly handsome couple, arm in arm, eyes bright.

"Nine months," John said. "Wow, you could be right. An American romance."

THIRTY-ONE

SHE BLINKED HER EYES, hearing the dawn chorus clamoring through the curtained window. Then the previous evening came back to her, and John's revelation. His confusion had touched her, and she'd wanted to comfort him, but had held back, afraid that he would misinterpret her sympathy. She took a deep breath and sat up, wanting to be outside, running through the cool streets with the birds singing their little lungs out.

She slid out of bed and pulled on her running gear. Not too far, she thought, just down Beacon to the Common.

As she ran she replayed their conversation of the previous night, and then her thoughts turned to that other possible revelation, about Maisy and Gennady. It was such a tantalizing thought, which would explain so well why Nancy would have wanted to make contact with Mikhail, her half-brother. Perhaps too tantalizing, but easy enough to check, she thought. The path lab would have both their DNA. And if it were true, what did that mean? Why did they have to die?

She swerved around a couple of joggers coming in the other direction, and circled the Brewer Fountain to begin the run back.

Peter caught her in the entrance hall. "You are a popular girl, aren't you?" He nodded his head toward the dining room.

"Another early morning visitor demanding breakfast. I'll have to reserve a special table for your men friends."

Her heart skipped. Was Brock clairvoyant? She could believe it. "What sort of man?"

"Oh, a rather sinister type if you ask me. Irish—from the north, I'd say. Ulster, Belfast, that sort of thing."

She swore under her breath. No, it couldn't be.

"Tell me it isn't your angry husband, Kathy. I can't face bloodshed at breakfast time."

"I don't have one, Peter."

"Thank goodness for that. He saw you coming up the front steps, so you'd better go and say hello."

She opened the door and saw the lone diner by the window. He looked up and waved his fork at her. "Have you tried these chocolate waffles? Bloody brilliant."

"Hello, Sean." Kathy went over and sat down facing the MI5 man. "What brings you here?"

"You do, Kathy. You've been naughty."

"How do you work that out?"

"An American citizen has complained to the authorities about being interrogated on American soil by a British police officer."

Janice, Kathy thought. "Bit of an exaggeration. Hardly an interrogation. Just a chat."

"That's not how she saw it. She reported it to the Massachusetts State Police, who notified the FBI, who contacted us. And you should thank your lucky stars that they did, and that it's me sitting here rather than a couple of heavy guys from the Met."

"How did you find me?"

"I called Emerson Merckle from London. He was very helpful." He wiped his mouth. "Mm, I believe I'll have to have another serving of these. Sadly you won't have time. You have ten minutes to pack your bags." He gave a sniff. "And take a shower before we head off to the airport. So run upstairs and get on with it. And don't try to climb out of the bathroom window—the house is surrounded." He glared at her, then broke into a laugh. "You should see your face."

She hurried upstairs to John's room. He opened his door with a yawn, rubbing his eyes. "You've been out already? Boy, you're keen."

"Listen, John," she said urgently. "There's an MI5 officer downstairs, come to take me back to London."

"What?" He froze, startled. "Why?"

"I'll explain later, but I have to go straight away. I don't think he knows about you, so let's keep it that way. It would just complicate things. Will you be going back to London?"

He blinked, clearly still trying to get his head around what was happening. "I . . . yes, yes sure."

"Good. We'll talk when you get there. Sorry about this."

"Me too. Kathy, you won't tell Brock, will you? About what I told you last night? I have to do that myself."

"Of course." She leaned over and kissed his cheek. "It'll be just fine, you'll see. And thanks for coming over here."

The taxi was waiting at the door when she got downstairs. She found Peter and paid and thanked him, then hurried out. As she got into the cab she looked up and saw John's face at his window, then she slammed the door and they moved off.

"Pretty town, Boston, don't you think?" Sean said as they sped into a tunnel. "Wonderful what they did, burying that expressway by the harbor. You had a chance to get a good look around, did you?"

"Yes," Kathy said sourly.

"Mm. I'm never a great talker first thing in the morning either. But then, this is lunchtime for me, and I've been up half the night coming over here to get you, so you'd better get used to it and find your tongue."

Kathy saw the taxi driver glance at them in his mirror and she turned away and stared out of the window.

When they checked in at the airport Kathy was glad to discover that they wouldn't be traveling together; Sean was booked into business class, while she was in economy. He led the way to a café and bought them coffees and a hamburger for her. She thought she couldn't touch it, but after the first bite she wolfed it down.

"Better now?" he said. "So tell me all about it."

She'd had time in the cab to decide that she wouldn't tell him about Gennady unless it was absolutely necessary, her reasoning being that if Gennady had been a spy, and involved with MI5 or the Americans, it would probably be better to feign ignorance. But Sean Ardagh's sudden appearance had unnerved her. Had the FBI put a tail on her? Did they know about John, and their trip to the Widener Library?

"Yes," she said, "much better," hoping she sounded contrite and cooperative.

"So what possessed you to come out here?"

"I thought there was an angle that we'd overlooked, and that Superintendent Chivers might not be interested in."

"And that was?"

"I was puzzled by why Nancy Haynes had chosen such an uncomfortable hotel. Emerson complained about her choice—he could hardly climb the stairs to his room. I wondered if Nancy had had a particular reason, perhaps some family connection with Cunningham Place."

"Would that be relevant to her death?"

"Probably not. That's why it was never pursued, but it bothered me. When they took me off the case they told me to take a holiday, the further away the better, so I thought I'd come over here and try to satisfy my curiosity."

He shook his head with a sarcastic smile. "When you'd been told to keep your nose out of it. So what did you discover?"

She took him through her conversations with Emerson, their visit to Nancy's house and the trip to Provincetown to see if Janice could identify the people. "And then there was this." She opened up her laptop and showed him the group photo. "That looks very much like a teenage Nancy and her parents in front of Chelsea Mansions."

He studied it carefully, then said, "What about this other man?"

Kathy shrugged. "Janice didn't know who he was. Some family friend, I suppose. Or someone they'd met in London."

She was glad that he kept his cool gray eyes on the picture and not on her. It was disconcerting being on the wrong side of an interrogation.

"Can you put a date to this?"

"Janice thought it was around the time of Nancy's sixteenth birthday, in April 1956," she said, wanting to appear eager to help. "Her birthday was the twenty-sixth."

Now he did look at her, hard and for a long moment, studying her face for signs of duplicity. "So Nancy had been to Cunningham Place when she was a girl. So what?"

Kathy pursed her lips, trying not to overdo it. It was remarkably hard to appear innocent once every muscle twitch became self-conscious. "I don't know. I got my answer, I suppose, as to why she chose Chelsea Mansions."

"A nostalgia trip, you think?"

"Yes."

"And that's everything?"

"Yes."

"I'll need a full, detailed report of every minute you spent in the United States, with a verbatim account of your conversations with Emerson and Janice—particularly Janice. You were way out of your jurisdiction, Kathy, and you could have done a lot of damage. The Americans and ourselves, we have to cooperate on so many levels. We have to rely on people following the rules. You should have known that."

"Yes, Sean. I'm sorry. It was thoughtless."

"It was damn careless, that's what it was. You thought you wouldn't get found out."

She nodded, head bowed in contrition.

"I want that report when we land at Heathrow, with copies of the photos and everything. Put it on this." He handed her a flash drive. "We may have to give it to the Yanks, so try to sound as if you've got at least half a brain—your reasons for going, your reasons for not informing the American authorities, and especially the fact that you did it on your own, without reference to us. Be frank and open and penitent. Okay?"

"Yes. Will you be informing Commander Sharpe?"

He hesitated. "No, I'll leave that to you. Tell him if you want. Personally I'd let sleeping dogs lie."

"Thanks, Sean. I appreciate it."

"So you damn well should."

She did as she was told, composing the report on her laptop on the seven-hour flight home, trying to make her actions seem innocuous. Most of Sunday had to be invented, with John and the Widener Library edited out. He had insisted on paying for the harborside meal the previous evening, which was a blessing if they checked her credit card usage. Would anyone do that? She thought not, mostly reassured by Sean's response to her explanation, but she wasn't certain. What had she done to warrant a senior MI5 officer dropping everything and crossing the Atlantic to escort her home? Why hadn't he just phoned her and told her to get on the next plane? Had the Americans really been that annoyed?

She handed over the memory stick when they landed. Sean

had no luggage and they parted on the way to the carousels, leaving Kathy relieved that he wasn't going to confiscate her laptop, or take her in for more questions.

It was almost midnight when she got home, her day compressed by the flight across the spin of the earth, and she was in two minds whether to ring Brock. She decided she'd better. He was still up, restless from inactivity and excited by her outline of her trip. They agreed to meet the next morning in the city for breakfast.

THIRTY-TWO

BROCK SPIED KATHY CRADLING a mug of coffee at a table beneath a large poster of the female toreador Cristina Sánchez, who was poised, arms raised, to deliver the death blow with her sword. He noticed straight away that there was something different about her—Kathy, that was—though he couldn't identify at first what it was.

"Hello," he said.

She gave him a big smile, then jumped to her feet and planted a kiss on his cheek, which was quite unprecedented.

"Goodness," he said. "What have I done to deserve that?"

She laughed. "Well, we're off-duty, and it's a lovely morning. You're looking great. You've got some color back."

"Yes, I am feeling almost normal again." A delivery truck ground past outside, pumping diesel fumes into the café. The sky was overcast with a threat of rain, and it didn't seem to him like a particularly lovely morning. Her eyes were shining, her complexion subtly different. He remembered how low she had been when she left for America, but now her posture suggested optimism and energy, as if Cristina Sánchez looming over her had filled her with new life. "And you look as if the change has done you good too."

"Yes, it was what I needed, just to get out of London for a few days."

"So you liked Boston?"

"Brilliant. I'd have loved to stay longer, if Sean Ardagh hadn't stuck his ugly nose in."

"But it doesn't seem to have fazed you."

A waitress came to their table, and Brock ordered an omelette and toast, Kathy the full English breakfast.

"Well, I hope I convinced him of my abject contrition. He demanded a full report, which I had to write on the plane coming back. I've got a copy for you. There's no mention of you, of course. And I didn't tell him about identifying Gennady Moszynski in the photos."

"Why didn't you do that, I wonder?"

She hesitated. "I didn't think he was being open with me, about why he was there and what his interest in the case really was. I think they're involved somehow, perhaps with Vadim."

"Vadim?"

"Yes. Suppose Vadim is secretly working for MI5 or MI6 when he goes to Russia, and suppose they know, or suspect, that Vadim had a hand in the Haynes and Moszynski murders. Would they protect him?"

"I suppose," he said slowly, "it might depend on how valuable he is to them."

"That's what I think. So I thought I'd hold the Gennady angle back until we're more sure of our ground."

"Hm, a dangerous game, Kathy. But I'm impressed with your discovery. A great piece of research."

Brock noticed a faint trace of color appear in Kathy's face, and a hint of guardedness when she replied.

"Well, I did have some help."

"Ah, at Harvard? An American?"

"Actually no. It was that Canadian who gave us the opinion on the authenticity of Moszynski's letter, remember?"

Brock exaggerated his frown of confusion. "But . . . he was in London, wasn't he?"

"Yes, but I emailed him the photos that Emerson had, so that he could ask Toby Beaumont at the hotel if he could identify any of the people. And John—that's his name, John Greenslade—noticed the similarity between the man in the San Francisco photo with Maisy, and the one with the family group in the 1956 picture. So he hopped on a plane and came over to help me identify him. He had a pass for the Widener Library, where the archive was, and that's how we found Gennady. I couldn't have done it without him."

Aha, Brock thought. She was beaming an open smile at him, hands held palms up, like a magician who's just performed a neat trick demonstrating there's nothing up her sleeve.

"That was extremely public-spirited of him, to rush across the Atlantic just to give you a hand."

She had the grace to fully blush this time. "Yes, it was, wasn't it? He's fascinated by the case, and . . . he's a great admirer of yours, Brock. I'd really like the two of you to meet up."

Good grief, he thought, she doesn't need my approval. Surely she doesn't see me as some kind of father figure, does she? But he was touched all the same.

"And does he figure in your MI5 report?"

"No, I left him out too."

Brock nodded. Their food arrived and there was an interval while they sorted out salt and pepper and cutlery and began eating. Kathy seemed to be extremely hungry.

"Well now," Brock said when he'd finished, wiping his mouth with a paper napkin, "it was a brilliant discovery, but where exactly does it leave us?"

"Nancy nursed her mother, Maisy, in the last years of her life, before she died last summer. My guess is that they talked about the old days, and Maisy gave her the photograph and told her about Chelsea Mansions and about their friendship with a Russian official called Gennady Moszynski. Now, if you google 'Chelsea Mansions,' you get the hotel, but you also get lots of references to Mikhail Moszynski and his marriage to Shaka Gibbons. Imagine how astonished Nancy would have been. She must have been very curious to find out if he was related to her parents' friend."

"But why keep it a secret from Emerson? Why not talk to the hotel people about it?"

"Yes, that's interesting. Emerson wondered if there was something she didn't want to talk about, perhaps that she'd been abused or something like that."

"She looks relaxed enough in the picture, doesn't she?" Brock stared intently at the photograph. "I wonder if there's anything else it can tell us. If we had the original we could have got the lab to check it."

"I had the same thought. I brought the original back with me and gave Emerson a copy. Also, there's another interesting possibility," she said, and told him about the dates of Gennady's visit to San Francisco and Nancy's birth.

"Intriguing," Brock said. "But let's not jump to conclusions. And I'm not sure we could get the lab to check their DNA without alerting Dick Chivers."

"Yes, you're right." Kathy frowned. "Sean Ardagh seemed interested in the date of the photo."

"Fifty-six," Brock mused. "A big year for the spooks, I think. That was the year Burgess and Maclean turned up in Moscow. And the year Krushchev made a secret speech to the Party Congress, denouncing the cult of Stalin. People thought it would signal a thaw in the Cold War, but it didn't. There were riots in Georgia, then Poland and later Hungary, all put down by Russian tanks."

Kathy had her laptop out, looking up 1956 on the web. "Elvis released his first gold album," she said. "Jackson Pollock died in a car crash."

"What was happening in April?" Brock asked. "When Gennady was in London?"

Kathy searched for a moment. "Grace Kelly married Prince Rainier of Monaco . . . the first episode on CBS of *As the World Turns* . . . first demonstration of video tape . . . British navy diver Lionel "Buster" Crabb vanished in Portsmouth harbor . . . heavyweight champion Rocky Marciano retired . . . Got it. There was an official visit to the UK by the Russian leaders, Bulganin and Krushchev. On the twenty-sixth, the day of Nancy's birthday, there was a big banquet lunch held for them at the Mansion House in London. You can see a video of it."

"So Gennady was probably in the official party, and met up with Nancy's parents in Chelsea. How did they manage that, I wonder? They must have been in touch."

"But it's all so long ago." Kathy was scrolling down through the 1956 calendar. "And then in October there was the Suez Crisis. Toby mentioned that. He called it the end of innocence. He was in the army then."

"I wonder if he can tell us anything more about what happened that April."

"He told John that he didn't recognize the people in the photograph."

"Yes, but still, we might be able to jog his memory. I think it's time to pay a visit to Chelsea Mansions."

"I've been banned, remember?"

"Yes, but I haven't. You'd better stay out of trouble, Kathy. I'll do this alone."

BROCK PAUSED AT THE corner of Cunningham Place, gazing over at the bulk of Chelsea Mansions as if for the first time. He'd been hardly conscious of the place when he'd been there before, at night, his head spinning with fever. Now it stood, its brick gables glowing blood-red in the sun, with all the confidence and swagger of the late Victorian age. It was too overbearing for Brock's taste, too full of bluster, but he could see how it might appeal to a rich Russian whose father had perhaps told him as a boy about the grand London house in which he had once stayed.

He mounted the hotel steps and went in. Deb put her head around the sitting room door, her mouth full. She gulped, choked, then swallowed.

"Sorry about that," she said. "What can I do for you?"

Brock introduced himself and she cried out, "Thought I recognized you! Of course, on telly. I'm Deb."

"Hello, Deb. I wondered if Colonel Beaumont might be able to spare me a few minutes."

"Of course. We're just having a staff meeting—Toby!" She threw open the sitting room door and Brock caught a glimpse of people sitting on plump faded armchairs, holding mugs of tea and plates of cake.

It took a few moments for Toby to struggle to his feet and make his way out to peer at the visitor through the dark discs of his glasses.

"Detective Chief Inspector Brock, Toby!" Deb cried, as if she'd just conjured up the most wonderful treat.

"Ah! Of course. Welcome, welcome. You'll have some tea? Julie has made us Dundee cake. One of her best, straight from the oven. Come, come. Let's go into the office."

Brock followed him, a rather precarious figure leaning on his stick, but with the broad shoulders of a once powerful man. He indicated seats and said, "So we meet at last. Obviously we've been following events closely. John Greenslade will be very disappointed to have missed you—one of our guests, but of course you'll know all about that. He's disappeared somewhere for a few days. Taken a great interest in you, Chief Inspector. Yes, he will be disappointed. So what can we do for you?"

Deb bustled in with a tray. "Here we are. Do you need me too?" she asked hopefully.

"By all means," Brock said, "if you can spare the time."

"Certainly! I don't think the troops will mutiny while I'm away, will they, Toby?"

Toby chuckled. "We have a first-class team here, Chief Inspector."

"A family," Deb added. "And are you quite recovered now?"

Brock looked at her in surprise, and she explained, "John kept us informed. He went to the hospital to see you when you were in a coma, did you know that?"

"No. I had no idea."

"So how can we help you?"

"I should make clear that I'm off-duty at the moment, and this is just to satisfy my curiosity about some secondary features of the case that have been bothering me."

"Can't let it go, eh?" Toby nodded approvingly. "The new chap hasn't been to see us. What's his name?"

"Superintendent Chivers."

"Yes, that's him. Getting anywhere, is he?"

"I'm afraid I'm not up to date with the investigation."

"Cutting you out, are they?" Toby shook his head. "Turf politics, I suppose. So what are these secondary features?"

Brock took out the 1956 photograph and handed it to him.

"Yes," Toby said. "John showed me this. That's Chelsea Mansions in the background, right enough, but I couldn't tell him who the people were. Not that I could see the relevance, frankly."

"We've always wondered if Nancy had a particular reason for wanting to stay here," Brock said. "And it appears that she did. We've now established that this is Nancy in the photograph, aged sixteen, and those are her parents. So she'd been here before."

"Good Lord." Deb took the photograph for a closer look. "I suppose it could be her . . . But she never mentioned this to us."

"That's strange, isn't it? I believe your aunt owned a hotel here in Chelsea Mansions, Colonel."

He waved his hand. "Toby, please. Yes, my father's aunt, Great-Aunt Daphne, next door at number seven."

"So it's possible that these people were staying at her hotel. Certainly Nancy would have remembered being here with her parents. That's presumably why she was so eager to stay here. And yet, having come all this way, she didn't mention it to you?"

"That does seem strange," Toby agreed.

"Would you still have your great-aunt's hotel records, visitors' books, that sort of thing?"

"I'm afraid not. John had a poke around in our attic, but I don't think he came up with anything like that."

"Would you have been here at that time, Toby? April 1956?"

He frowned in thought. "Shouldn't think so. I was in the army by then."

"There was a visit by the Soviet leaders to London that April."

"Oh, I do remember that—B and K, Bulganin and Krushchev. The papers were full of it. I remember the *Daily Express* ran articles instructing readers on how to say 'Hello, how are you?' and 'Did you have a nice trip?' in Russian, in case they bumped into any of the official party in the street. But no, I'm sure I wasn't in London then. I would have been up at Catterick."

Brock wasn't altogether convinced by the way he dismissed the idea, but it was hard to read Toby's expression, behind those dark lenses. "Pity. I was hoping you might have been the photographer."

"Sorry, no. But look, this is ancient history. What's its relevance?"

He said it with a sudden vehemence, and Brock sensed an undercurrent of impatience, even anger in the man. Money troubles, perhaps. The place looked as if it was on its last legs.

"Why are you wasting your time with this?" Toby was going on, his voice hardening. "You and I both know what lies at the heart of it all. You had the answer in your hands. Money is what this is all about, the gangster Moszynski's money, and the sickness and corruption that flows from that."

"You didn't like him, did you? I believe he tried to cheat you."

"I detested him." Toby sat up straighter in his chair, sticking out his chin defiantly, and Brock had a glimpse of what he would have been like in the army, twenty years before.

"He was one of those men who have no history, no tradition. They are opportunists who exist only in the present, preying upon those around them and using their money to spread corruption. And at the heart of that corruption squats that poisonous toad, Hadden-Vane. You had him, Brock! You had him in your grip, and he slipped away, thanks to corruption!"

He reached for a folded newspaper and slapped it down on the table in front of Brock, who saw the picture of Hadden-Vane, beaming smugly at the camera, and the caption, *MP cleared*. The short article stated that Scotland Yard had confirmed that Sir Nigel Hadden-Vane was not considered a person of interest in the murders of Nancy Haynes and Mikhail Moszynski. An unnamed source claimed that investigations on British soil had now been concluded and that a request to send detectives to continue inquiries in Moscow and St. Petersburg had been rejected by the Russian government.

"You've been duped." Toby sank back into his chair. "Outflanked and outmaneuvered. The toad's too wily for you."

AND PERHAPS IT WAS true, Brock thought, as he walked back through Belgravia and Victoria. Or perhaps it was just the paranoia of an old soldier who had been defeated by the brutal realities of civilian life.

The officer at the reception desk at Queen Anne's Gate had been told to expect him, and immediately showed him up to his old office, where Superintendent Chivers offered him a coffee and a seat. Chivers seemed unabashed to be in occupation of Brock's old room. It was just an office after all, but still it seemed rather eerie, with the old clutter of books and papers swept away and someone else at Dot's desk outside, as if Brock were dead and returning as a ghost to see how the world was coping without him. Extremely well, seemed to be the answer.

"Yes, just putting the final touches to the report," Chivers said. "Then it's up to the politicians if they want to pursue it, which I doubt."

"So it was the Russians all the time?"

"Yes, a rerun of the Litvinenko case, except that they varied their method to hide the fact. No exotic poisons this time. They hired a local sub-contractor, Peebles, to do the dirty work."

"How did they get onto him?"

"Through Danny Yilmaz's cousin, Barbaros Kaya. We can't prove it, but we're sure he's had drug dealings with Russian mafia from the Caucasus. That seems to be the link. We think they were used by an FSB faction that wants to ingratiate itself in the Kremlin by bringing Moszynski's money back to Russia."

Brock wondered if Sean Ardagh had inspired this idea. "And will they do that?"

"That depends on which side of the fence Vadim Kuzmin chooses to jump. He holds the reins now. We've had the fraud boys working on the accountant, Freddie Clarke, but he's giving nothing away."

"And Nancy Haynes?"

"Peebles mistook her for Marta Moszynski. They wanted rid of her too—apparently she still has some influence with Putin because of her dead husband, Gennady Moszynski."

"The MI5 theory," Brock said.

"Yes." Chivers scowled at Brock, irked by his lack of enthusiasm. "You have a problem with that, Brock?"

Brock took the 1956 photograph out of his pocket and showed it to him. "This turned up. It's Chelsea Mansions, and that's a teenage Nancy Haynes and her parents. The other man is probably Gennady."

"What?" Chivers peered at it. "You sure?"

"Reasonably. Not so as it would stand up in court."

"Where did you get this?"

"Nancy's companion, Emerson Merckle, had a packet of her old photographs."

"Well . . . what am I supposed to make of it?"

"I'm not sure."

Chivers stared at it for a while, then pushed it aside and gave Brock a grim smile and shook his head. "Brock, you bugger, you always do this."

"Do what, Dick?"

"Try to complicate things. You're never satisfied with the simple answer. You've always got to look for a more complicated explanation, a more *interesting* and original explanation. Well, you're wrong. Remember Occam's razor, Brock—the simplest of two theories is to be preferred."

Brock hadn't seen Chivers so worked up. He seemed to have touched a nerve.

"My report is about to go to Sharpe," Chivers went on. "Don't muddy the waters, please."

"Fair enough." Brock put the photograph back in his pocket and got to his feet. "Thanks for the update, Dick."

Chivers showed him to the door. "Any time, Brock. You're looking well, by the way. Still on sick leave?"

"Another week, the doctor says."

"Best not to rush things. Not sure what they're going to do with this place. Someone said they were thinking of selling it. Shame if they did. Close to HQ but conveniently out of sight. I've become quite attached to it."

FEELING LIKE A DISPLACED person peddling a worthless trinket, Brock decided to give the photo one last try. He took the tube across the river to the Elephant and Castle and walked down to Amelia Street, where SERIS, the Specialist Evidence Recovery and Imaging Services unit, was based, and with them Morris Munns. Morris, whose myopic gaze through thick-lensed glasses seemed so at odds with his ability to conjure hidden information from crime scenes, grabbed him in a hug.

"We thought we'd lost you," he cried. "The Marburg Pimpernel. The lads ran a book on your survival. I lost a packet."

"You betted against me?" Brock said, shocked.

"It's called hedging," Morris chuckled. "Come on, you can buy me lunch while you tell me about this private job."

Over a Thai chicken salad Brock showed Morris the photograph. He peered at it, turned it over, sniffed it.

"Over fifty years old? So what am I meant to find?"

"The reason why this picture killed two people. No, I honestly don't know. Anything you can tell me about it. For instance there's a distinctive lapel badge on that bloke at the back. We think he may be Russian, the other three American, the background Cunningham Place in Chelsea. We don't know who took the picture. We believe the date is on or around the twenty-sixth of April, 1956."

"Okay. I suppose you'll say this is urgent, only I've got a backlog of weeks."

"Your other customers don't come back from the dead to buy you lunch, Morris."

After they parted Brock rang Kathy. He told her about Chivers' report and then, as he was about to ring off, she mentioned that John Greenslade was flying back from America that night, and could the three of them meet up for dinner the next evening? He wasn't wildly enthusiastic, but he sensed her eagerness and agreed.

When he got home he felt edgy and unable to settle. Later, after grilling a fish fillet for his supper, he sat in the window bay that projected out over the lane, watching the trains pass by in the twilit shadows of the cutting down below. He had a novel on his knee, but was unable to concentrate on it. Too many characters, he thought, none of whom he cared about, and too clever by half. Which was what Chivers would say about him. Quick and clean, was Chivers. Get the job done. Occam's razor.

THIRTY-THREE

MORRIS HAD RUNG BROCK in the middle of the following morning, arranging to meet him at a Latin American deli in the Elephant and Castle shopping center, the first covered shopping center in Europe back in 1965, and subsequently voted London's ugliest building, now awaiting demolition. It had a gloomy subterranean feel to it which depressed Brock's spirits, but Morris seemed perversely cheerful, sitting with a large bag of groceries by his side. Brock ordered a coffee and joined him.

"Can't stop long," Morris said. "But I needed to stock up for our samba party tonight."

Brock raised an eyebrow but said nothing as Morris took an envelope out of the carrier bag, extracted the photograph and laid it down on the table in front of them.

"It's printed on a Kodak Velox paper that was available from the mid-fifties into the sixties, consistent with your date. If the April twenty-six date is correct, the length and angle of shadows indicate the picture was taken at around four in the afternoon, this being Chelsea Mansions on the north side of Cunningham Place, right?"

Brock nodded, and Morris took some enlargements from the envelope.

"The lapel badge you mentioned is a five-pointed star, approximately ten millimeters across, resembling the gold star which Heroes of the Soviet Union were entitled to wear. The man wearing it has an area of scar tissue on his left temple which appears to be caved in, as if from an industrial accident or war wound. You could get a pathologist's opinion on that, and on some Soviet-era dental work he seems to be sporting." Morris pointed to a close-up of the man's smiling mouth.

"The other man, who you say is an American, appears to be rather well off and possibly involved in international travel and business. He's wearing a Rolex GMT Master wristwatch, the first watch to show two time zones at once, first released in 1954.

"The woman at his side is also well heeled, dressed in what looks to be a Dior A-line costume. But her taste in jewelry seems a little unconventional and artistic. The younger woman is carrying a posy of flowers—a mixture of what looks like roses and some other type, like Michaelmas daisies. She's also holding something else in her left hand . . ." He produced an enlargement. "Maybe a cigarette or spectacle case. She's much more informally dressed than the others, who look as if they've been to some sort of function."

"There was a banquet lunch for visiting Russians that day," Brock said.

"There you go then." Morris turned the photo over to look at the back. "Notice the faint brown smudge. It's a vegetable glue, as if there was once an accompanying note or card stuck to the back of the photo, so we did an ESDA electrostatic scan."

Morris flicked through the contents of his envelope to a gray photograph across which black lettering was visible. "ESDA picks up the faintest compression marks, in this case caused by something being written on another piece of paper with the photo underneath."

Brock read the message:

Dear Ronnie and Maisy,
What larks!
Love, Miles

"You're a magician, Morris."

Morris gathered the material up, put it back in the envelope and handed it to Brock. "Happy hunting, mate."

After he'd gone Brock remained at the table going over the contents of the envelope while he finished his coffee. Ronnie and Maisy were Nancy's parents, he remembered, but who was Miles? He examined the enhanced enlargements that Morris had made of the faces of the four people in the photograph, and he thought of Kathy's theory about Gennady as he studied them. The two American adults were long-skulls, tall and of slender build, whereas the Russian was a round-skull Slav, short and stocky. Brock looked at the girl's bone structure, the cheeks, the chin, and pondered. Finally he checked his notebook for the number of someone he knew well in forensic services. He got out his phone and made the call, asking for a special favor.

AS BROCK TURNED INTO Cunningham Place he saw two men emerge from the Moszynski entrance porch. One was the security guard, Wayne Everett, who hurried ahead to open the rear door of a Maybach Zeppelin for the other man, Vadim Kuzmin, who appeared angry and impatient. The limousine eased out of its parking spot and surged away at speed.

Brock continued toward the porch, climbing the steps and pressing the button on the entry phone. A female voice responded and he said, "Detective Chief Inspector David Brock, Metropolitan Police, to see Mrs. Marta Moszynski."

"One moment, please."

It took considerably more than that for the voice to come

back. It sounded anxious, and hesitant in its use of English. "I'm sorry. Mrs. Moszynski is not well enough to see you, sir."

"Tell Mrs. Moszynski I have information concerning her husband."

A hesitation, then, "Mr. Moszynski was her son, sir, not her husband."

"I'm talking about Mr. Gennady Moszynski, not Mr. Mikhail Moszynski."

"Wait, please."

Eventually there was a click and the door opened and the maid indicated for him to come in. As he entered the hall he was struck again by the scale of the internal transformation that had been worked on the original buildings. The whole of the middle house had been gutted to create a central atrium with stairs, lift and galleries rising through five stories to a glass lantern, with a multi-tiered lighting feature suspended within it. When he'd seen it before, at night, with the glitter of hundreds of tiny lights, it had seemed flashy but rather dazzling, like the foyer of an exotic gaming club. But now, with the lights turned off and no one around, it seemed merely overblown and pretentious.

He followed the maid across to the glass lift which rose with a faint hum to the third floor, where they walked around the gallery to overscaled double doors which the maid tapped, then opened. This was Marta Moszynski's private apartment, with a generous sitting room from which doors led off to other rooms. The old woman was sitting in an armchair by the windows overlooking the square, surrounded by a blue haze of cigarette smoke. She turned and regarded Brock's approach with a stubborn scowl that might have been modeled on Krushchev.

Brock took the seat facing her and said, "Good afternoon, Mrs. Moszynski. How are you today?"

She tapped her cigarette slowly on the heavy glass ashtray at her side. "What do you want?"

"I'd like you to tell me why Mikhail chose this building to live in when he came to London."

The question seemed to throw her, and she shook her head.

"Did his father tell him about it? Because Gennady was here, wasn't he?"

"You're crazy!" Marta growled, stubbing out her cigarette. "Go away."

Brock took a copy of the photograph out of his pocket and offered it to her. Reluctantly she reached out a knobbly hand and took it, then made a great play of picking up her spectacles from the small table at her elbow and putting them on.

"That's Gennady at the back, see?" Brock said.

She frowned and peered closer. "No."

"Yes. Here's a larger picture of his face. It was the twenty-sixth of April, 1956, and they were standing in front of this building."

"No," Marta repeated, and her head was shaking again, with movements so jerky and violent that Brock wondered for a moment if she might be having some kind of fit.

"And that's Nancy, the woman who was murdered just before your son. How do you explain that, Marta?"

"No . . . no, no."

"Could it be that Nancy—"

But Marta had lurched into movement, ripping the photographs into tiny pieces while she spat and cursed in Russian. She threw the scraps at him, screaming abuse, then turned and took hold of the ashtray at her side and hurled it too, with surprising force, straight at his head. He just had time to dodge and lift an arm, and he winced as the glass block hit his wrist. They were both on their feet now, Marta casting around for another weapon, when the maid burst in and ran to her. Abruptly the old woman's manner changed, and she began sobbing and gasping. The maid gathered her in her arms and eased her back down into the chair.

"You must go." The maid looked back over her shoulder accusingly at Brock. "She is not well."

"Do you need a doctor?"

"No. I will take care of her. Please leave now."

Brock hesitated, then nodded and turned to go. As he reached the door Marta hurled a parting curse at his back.

He waited for the lift, nursing his wrist. He was still jolted by the suddenness of her fury and its physical force. Now the silence in the deserted atrium made the whole episode seem surreal. The lift sighed to a halt at the ground floor and he stepped out, his heels squeaking on the polished marble floor. He took a few paces toward the front door, then stopped and looked around. In each of the flanking walls stood large doorways framed with classical pilasters and entablatures. He went over and opened a door to reveal a mirrored dining room in which a long table had been laid with porcelain and cutlery as if for an elaborate banquet. Another door opened into a huge sitting room whose walls were hung with contemporary art—Hockney, Freud, Hirst—and, bizarrely, hanging over the massive fireplace, a portrait of Mikhail Moszynski himself, dressed in the ruff and slashed doublet of a Tudor grandee, with a hedgehog at his feet.

On the far side of this room was another door, opening into a corridor. Brock was about to turn back when he heard the muffled whine of machinery from one of the closed doors up ahead. He went toward it and hesitated, his hand on the doorknob, listening. The whine became shriller for a while, then subsided again. It was a sound he'd heard before, but it took him a moment to remember it coming from Dot's office—a paper shredder. He opened the door.

The woman turned from the machine and stared at him.

There were tears running down her cheeks, and for a moment they stood staring at each other in surprise.

"I'm sorry to startle you," Brock said, and showed her his police ID. "Are you all right?"

Embarrassed, she wiped her hand quickly across her face. "Oh, not really. I've just been sacked. It's only to be expected really, but it was just so . . . abrupt. I'm sorry. I'm Ellen Fitzwilliam, Mr. Moszynski's secretary—former secretary."

"Tidying up?" Brock asked.

"Yes. I was sorting things out for Mr. Kuzmin, who's trying to make sense of it all for the solicitors, only he's decided . . . Well, anyway, he's just left, gone to speak to Mr. Clarke, if you wanted him."

"I imagine it must all be very complicated."

"Oh yes. And Freddie—Mr. Clarke—isn't easy to pin down. Was there something I can help you with?"

"I know you've been asked this before, but I'm just trying to tie up one or two details. I'm interested in Mr. Moszynski's state of mind in the days before he was killed. Were you working with him then?"

"Not on the Sunday when he died, but I did come in to work on the Saturday morning, and all through the previous week. I can't say I noticed anything terribly different about his manner. He seemed his usual self—brisk, businesslike."

"He went to the memorial service for the American woman here in the square on the Sunday morning. Was he upset by her death, do you remember?"

"Ah, yes, he did seem to be bothered by that—I told your inspector. He certainly read all the news reports about Mrs. Haynes' death, and got me to keep cuttings."

"He seemed personally affected?"

"Yes, I suppose so. He was certainly concerned about sending flowers for her memorial service."

"Was he?"

"Yes, he got me to order them on the Saturday, to be delivered to the church. He was quite particular about them."

"In what way particular?"

"About the type of flowers. I'll have the details in the file. Do you want to see?"

"Please."

She took a pouch of invoices and orders marked *May* from a filing cabinet and flicked through it. "Here we are."

Brock read the note. *One hundred pounds worth of roses and camomile daisies.* "Camomile daisies?" Brock murmured.

"Yes, he was particular about the daisies. It seemed an odd choice to me, but he explained that camomile is the national flower of Russia. Very thoughtful, don't you think?"

"Very." He looked through an open door on the far side of the room to what looked like a board room table, on which a couple of trays of sandwiches lay beneath plastic film, untouched. "Mr. Kuzmin miss his lunch?"

"Oh, yes. He and Mr. Clarke were supposed to have a lunchtime meeting to discuss the financial matters, but Mr. Clarke didn't show up. He wasn't answering his mobile phone, and when I tried to contact him at his office his secretary said that she hadn't seen him today at all. In fact, she hadn't seen him since he went out for a walk in Hyde Park yesterday lunchtime. But that's not unusual for Mr. Clarke. He gets bored and suddenly disappears without telling anyone, and then after a few days we get an email from Tokyo or Las Vegas or somewhere. Mr. Moszynski used to put up with it with a smile—he said Mr. Clarke was an eccentric genius. But Mr. Kuzmin isn't so tolerant. He started shouting down the phone at Mr. Clarke's secretary to see if his passport was still in his safe, and she checked and it had gone. Then Mr. Kuzmin got in a rage and told me there was nothing for me to do here and I was fired."

Brock shook his head in commiseration. "Bit fiery is he, Mr. Kuzmin? How does he get on with Sir Nigel Hadden-Vane?"

"Oh, pretty well. He tried to get hold of him, too, but the secretary at his parliamentary office said that he was in a committee meeting and would be tied up all afternoon."

Brock said he would find his own way out, and left the secretary to her shredding. He returned along the corridor and came to what looked like one of the original house staircases. He decided to follow it down into the basement, where the security control room was located, and as he descended he was aware of a change in the air, becoming cooler and tinged with the slightly acrid smell of fresh cement and plaster. Sure enough, the lower floor looked as if it had been recently abandoned by builders, with a heap of sand and a cement mixer blocking the way. Ahead of him a doorway had been roughly knocked through a party wall into what had once been the basement of the next house, and as he stepped through Brock found himself in a dusty, dark room that looked as if it hadn't been touched in a hundred years. He stopped, letting his eyes adjust to the dark, and then saw that the floor in front of him had been dug up, with the old stone slabs tilted up on end against the wall and the ground beneath excavated. He made out the dim line of an old earthenware sewer pipe. Planks had been laid across the earthworks to a doorway on the far side of the room, and he crossed and found himself in another cellar, the floor of which looked as if it had been similarly excavated and then filled in again. There was a closed door on the other side of this space, and when he tried the handle it opened into a carpeted corridor lit by fluorescent lights. A door to one side was open and he saw the equipment of the security monitoring unit inside. The room was deserted, a mug of coffee—Wayne Everett's perhaps—still warm on the table. The whole building had the air of an abandoned palace, half high-tech redoubt, half ruined excavation. He watched the screen for a moment as it flicked automatically from one empty room to another, before he continued along the corridor to a stair that took him up to the entrance hallway again. He opened the front door and, with a sense of relief, stepped into the sunshine.

THIRTY-FOUR

BROCK WAS EARLY, AND called in at a pub nearby to kill some time. The restaurant Kathy had suggested was an old favorite of theirs, a comfortable Italian place whose informality surely made it a good choice for a quiet friendly dinner. Yet Brock felt unsettled, as if Kathy were bringing an outsider into their relationship. No, that was absurd. He was glad for her, hoped this time it would work out. Lord knows, she had made some unfortunate, or unlucky, choices in the past. Was there a reason for that? he wondered. Something to do with her father's suicide, perhaps? Or with being in the police?

His eyes went to a TV screen in the corner where a wide-eyed German tourist was describing a suicide he had witnessed on Westminster Bridge that afternoon, a man jumping into the river. Brock was thankful that someone else would be dealing with it. He checked his watch again, sighed, sank his whiskey and said goodnight to the barman.

When he stepped into the restaurant he saw them straight away at his favorite table, with their heads together, laughing over something on the young man's mobile phone. Then they looked up and saw him coming, and both got to their feet, eyes bright and expectant. Brock shook the man's hand and tried to make an initial assessment. Firm grip, intelligent eyes, slightly wary. Fair enough. Not too smooth like that lawyer Martin Connell, probably not gay like Leon Desai, and apparently not Special Branch like Tom Reeves. So far so good. But what the hell had he been doing coming to see him, out cold in the hospital?

"Looked like you were enjoying a good joke," Brock said.

"Oh, yes." Kathy laughed. "John took a picture of the two guys who ran this B and B we stayed at in Boston. They were fantastic cooks."

Brock watched them as they recited some of the dishes they'd had. There was no doubt about it, the lad was smitten, casting surreptitious glances at Kathy. He wished that Suzanne were there to help him get through the evening and afterward carry out a considered post-mortem. She was expecting a full report on the phone when he got home.

They talked about Boston, ordered food, discussed the Henry Moore exhibition, ate, and several times he thought he noticed Kathy signaling to John with a questioning look or a raised eyebrow, and wondered what was coming. The young man was polite and deferential, but Brock had the feeling he was holding something back. Feeling a little more relaxed, he asked him about his work at McGill, and John became more animated and amusing, talking about his colleagues. Brock felt rather envious of the life he described, grappling with intellectual puzzles of—to Brock's mind—utter uselessness.

"So you're a kind of detective too," he said.

John seemed to flush with pleasure at that. "Yes, in a way. Maybe it runs in the blood."

Again that look from Kathy, and John bowed his head and took a deep breath, and Brock saw that he was about to say something that they'd already discussed. He had the feeling that this was the point of their meal together, and he felt a sudden irritation at the subterfuge, and a reluctance to share whatever confession they were about to make.

So he said quickly, "Well, I can't say I've solved our puzzle, but I did make a little progress." He noticed a shadow of disappointment pass across Kathy's face as he took out Morris's envelope. "Originally there was a note accompanying the picture of Chelsea Mansions. Its message was imprinted onto the back of the photograph."

He showed them Morris's ESDA image.

"Miles." John frowned as he read the signature. "That was the name of Toby Beaumont's son, who was killed in the first Gulf War." He told them the story. "But he certainly wouldn't have been around in 1956."

"Perhaps Toby named him after his own father," Kathy suggested. "He was living in that house in the background of the picture."

"That's possible," Brock said. "I had hopes that Toby might have taken the picture, but perhaps it was his father. Do we know anything about him?"

Kathy shook her head. John was examining the photograph.

"I showed a copy of that to Moszynski's mother this afternoon," Brock said. "She got very upset—tore the picture to pieces and attacked me. Nearly crowned me. She denied that it's Gennady."

John was nodding, a gleam of excitement in his eyes. "That's interesting. It could tie in with an idea I had. After Kathy left Boston I had to wait to get a seat on a return flight, so I went back to the Widener Library and did a bit more digging. I thought I'd try to find out more of what Gennady Moszynski's movements might have been in the UK during that 1956 visit, and I drew up a timeline of what happened."

With a slight show of embarrassment, like an overenthusiastic student trying to please his teacher, Brock thought, John drew a folded sheet of paper from his inside pocket and spread it out on the table.

"The official party arrived in the UK on a Soviet cruiser, the *Ordzhonikidze*, at Portsmouth on the eighteenth of April, and stayed for ten days, during which they had meetings and functions in London, as well as visiting Birmingham, Oxford and Edinburgh. This is what I've been able to make of their movements. But there was one thing that didn't go according to plan. Two days after the Russians left for home, MI6 announced that one of their operatives, a naval frogman, had disappeared near Portsmouth on the nineteenth of April, while testing some secret equipment. But the Russians then claimed that their sailors had seen a British frogman near the *Ordzhonikidze* on that day, and rumors began to circulate that the Russians had abducted or killed him. He was never found. His name was Commander—"

"Buster Crabb," Brock cut in, shaking his head. He felt disappointed. Was that what this dinner was all about, so that Kathy's new boyfriend could show off some crackpot conspiracy theory he'd come up with?

"You've heard of him?" John said.

"It's an old chestnut in this country, John, one of the great unsolved mysteries of the Cold War. There have been dozens of different explanations—Crabb had his throat cut by a Russian frogman, or was kidnapped and taken back to Russia, or defected, or even was murdered by MI6. Every couple of years someone comes up with a new idea. It's a waste of time."

John looked deflated. "I just thought, what if Gennady Moszynski was mixed up in that business and Nancy's mother had known about it and told Nancy? Wouldn't the Moszynskis want to shut her up? I mean, the Brits might not be so friendly if the word got out . . ."

"Then why kill Mikhail Moszynski? No, John, forget it. There's something much more personal behind this. Look at that photograph again, at the features of Nancy and Gennady. You were right about Nancy's birth date, Kathy. I asked the lab to compare the DNA samples taken from the bodies of Nancy and Mikhail. They were close relatives, brother and sister, with the same father—Gennady. That's the family secret that everybody's been trying to hide."

"Yes," Kathy said, "but . . ." She stopped as Brock's phone began to ring.

"Excuse me," he said, and flicked it open and listened. When the call was over he looked across at Kathy and said, "They've pulled Hadden-Vane's body from the river. Apparently he jumped from Westminster Bridge earlier this evening. Sharpe wants me at headquarters. Sorry, but I'm going to have to leave you."

AFTER BROCK HAD GONE they were silent for several long minutes. Finally John said, "Well, I sure blew that, didn't I?"

"I could see how difficult it was for you."

He shook his head in frustration. "I just couldn't find the words to tell him. All the time I felt like an idiot intruder, an amateur sleuth trying to impress real cops."

"It wasn't like that, John. He was a bit distant, but it was the first time you two have met and he's probably still feeling rough. He's usually warmer than that. You'll see."

"No. That bit about the frogman . . . Hell, he must think I'm a complete fool. And he's right. I should never have come to London, never have got myself into this situation."

"It was a good idea about Crabb. He shouldn't have dismissed it the way he did."

"He didn't just dismiss the idea, Kathy. He dismissed me. There's no way we're going to repeat this evening."

She reached across for his hand, which was clenched tight into a fist. "Come on, things will seem better in the morning. Let's have another glass of wine."

"No. Look, I need to be alone for while, to get my head around this. I'm sorry, Kathy, this is really difficult for me. I think I'll walk for a while, back to the hotel."

She withdrew her hand. "All right, if you're sure."

"I just didn't realize this would be so difficult."

He reached for his wallet and she said, "No, my turn. I owe you for that great meal in Boston."

"Seems a long time ago, doesn't it?"

She watched sadly as he walked away, turning at the door to give her a look of resignation, then disappearing into the night. It felt like a final parting, and she had to resist the impulse to go after him.

COMMANDER SHARPE WAS ALONE in his office on the sixth floor. He was watching something on a TV screen when Brock walked in, and clicked the remote in his hand to switch it off.

"Come in, Brock." Sharpe passed him a plastic sleeve containing a handwritten note, which read,

> *Dear Nigel,*
> *Take a look at this. westminsterwhistleblower.com has a copy.*
> *Freddie*

"This was in Hadden-Vale's mail today, inside a padded pouch that's currently with forensics. He opened it in his parliamentary office at around five this afternoon, and soon after walked out of the building to the middle of Westminster Bridge, where he jumped into the river. There were a number of witnesses.

"Presumably there was something else in the envelope, our guess is a DVD or flash drive with a recording of an interview with Moszynski's accountant, Freddie Clarke, which has since been released on the westminsterwhistleblower.com website." He nodded at the TV. "You'd better take a look."

The screen came to life with a title—SIR NIGEL FEATHERSTONE HADDEN-VANE, MP: THE TRUTH—then faded to the seated figure of a man, pale-faced and brightly lit against a dark, indistinct background.

"My name is Freddie Clarke. I am an expert in tax law and I was financial adviser to Mikhail Moszynski, who was murdered on the thirtieth of May. I am intimately familiar with the financial affairs of Mr. Moszynski and his family.

"Sir Nigel Hadden-Vane is the Member of Parliament for the district of Chelsea, in which Mr. Moszynski lived, and he became acquainted with Mr. Moszynski soon after he arrived here from Russia. Sir Nigel became a trusted confidant of the Moszynski family, advising on such things as legal and political matters and arranging access to important social occasions and to senior figures in politics and society, including cabinet ministers and members of the royal family. He was in fact instrumental in introducing Mr. Moszynski to his future wife, Shaka Gibbons."

Clarke's voice was mesmerizing, Brock thought, without emphasis or inflection, but punctuated in odd places by the sound of his labored breathing. He seemed to be holding himself together with great effort, as if under some kind of tremendous pressure, though it wasn't apparent what that might be. From time to time his eyes would flick away from the viewer to points to left and right, either to gather his thoughts or to look at someone behind the camera.

"In return for these services Mr. Moszynski donated money

to Sir Nigel's political party and paid for several trips abroad. These were declared in accordance with parliamentary rules. He also made much larger payments to Sir Nigel that were not declared, either to Parliament or to the Inland Revenue. These included a monthly retainer, a car, and miscellaneous expenses, including regular payments for prostitutes. I was engaged to hide these transactions from the authorities, which I did. However I have a mental record of them all, as follows . . ."

Sharpe flicked the fast-forward button. "There are several minutes where he just recites bank details, dates and amounts. He seems to have memorized everything."

The film resumed.

". . . Mr. Moszynski also made a number of loans to Sir Nigel on favorable terms, which Sir Nigel used to buy property and shares. Again I was asked to create financial vehicles to disguise these activities. However I did not advise Sir Nigel on his investments, since he considered himself an expert in these matters. Unfortunately he invested in the stock market in the middle of 2007 when it was at its peak, and lost heavily in the following year. In order to recoup these losses and repay his loans, Sir Nigel begged Mr. Moszynski to relax the terms of their agreements, which he generously did. However when Sir Nigel was still unable to meet his obligations he resorted to fraud. Mr. Moszynski's mother, Marta Moszynski, was particularly anxious that her son be awarded a knighthood, and Sir Nigel persuaded them that he could arrange this, if Mr. Moszynski undertook a program of charitable donations which Sir Nigel devised. These included wildlife conservation and youth support organizations. Two of these, the Hammersmith Youth Employment Project and the Haringey Sport and Social Trust, were in fact used by Sir Nigel to siphon off a portion of Mr. Moszynski's donations to finance Sir Nigel's debts. In March of this year I became suspicious and suggested to Mr. Moszynski that I carry out an investigation of Sir Nigel's financial affairs. It didn't take me long to discover hidden bank accounts into which donations to the two foundations had been transferred. The details of these are as follows . . ."

There was another toneless list of numbers and transactions before Clarke continued.

"When confronted by Mr. Moszynski, Sir Nigel claimed that these arrangements had been contrived for the convenience of the charities concerned and not for his personal gain, but I had proof that this was a lie. At the same time Mrs. Moszynski senior was putting increasing pressure on Sir Nigel about his promise to obtain the knighthood for her son, which he seemed unable to fulfill. These discussions were ongoing at the time that Nancy Haynes and Mr. Moszynski were murdered. I have no direct evidence that Sir Nigel arranged their deaths—in the case of Nancy Haynes in a mistaken attempt to kill Marta Moszynski—but there is no doubt that Mr. Moszynski was close to abandoning his support for him and could have made his life very difficult."

The screen went blank and Sharpe switched off the TV. He stared at Brock for a moment, then said, "I have to ask you, Brock, for the record. Were you involved in this? Or have you any knowledge of who was?"

Brock stared back, uncertain for a moment whether to feel insulted or flattered. He decided on the former. "Certainly not."

Sharpe gave a quick, embarrassed nod. "No, of course not. Had to ask. You may have seen the news reports of Dick Chivers' press conference yesterday, in which he announced the suspension of the police investigation into the murders, and specifically cleared Hadden-Vane of suspicion. In the light of these new developments, he's asked to be relieved of his involvement in the case. I have agreed. He's waiting downstairs and will go on extended leave once he's briefed you."

"Me?"

"I want you running the show again, Brock. You're up to it? Physically, I mean?"

"Yes."

"Get your team back to Queen Anne's Gate, quick as you can. I'm putting out a press release to give us some time. Obviously the fraud boys will be checking through all the banking information on the tape. Your job is to prove that Hadden-Vane arranged the murders."

"Do we know where Clarke is?"

"He hasn't been seen since yesterday lunchtime, apparently. We've no idea why he decided to go public on this. Conscience, perhaps. Dick will give you all the details."

BROCK FOUND CHIVERS SCOWLING into a coffee mug. He looked up and nodded.

"Musical chairs, eh? Help yourself to a coffee."

Brock did so and sat down. "Yes. Tough luck."

"I simply don't understand it. We were leaning on that little bastard for days, trying to squeeze something out of him, and he didn't say a word, not a hint. Then suddenly he's on the record with the complete works—bank account numbers, transactions down to the last penny. What made him do it?"

"We'll have to ask him."

"Fat chance." Chivers pushed a piece of paper across to Brock. "Seems he caught a flight to Athens this morning without telling anyone. He could be anywhere by now."

"Was he alone in that room where he was being filmed, do you think?"

"No idea. Why, you think he had help?"

"I don't know. What else have you got for me?"

Chivers indicated a neat stack of files. "Our records of interviews and daily summaries. You should find the paperwork up to date." He was famous for his paperwork, Brock thought.

"My team is at your disposal, and I won't be going anywhere for a few days, so you can get hold of me any time, day or night." Then Chivers reached into his pocket and laid down a bunch of keys. "Queen Anne's Gate. It's all yours again, Brock."

BROCK WALKED OVER TO Queen Anne's Gate, the files under his arm, through deserted streets. He opened the front door of the darkened building with the keys and made his way up to his old office. It looked unnaturally tidy and there was a faint smell of Chivers' aftershave.

He sat at the desk and dialed Dot's number. She lived in East Barnet, he knew, near the station in a house she'd bought with the husband who had died soon afterward of a heart attack, but Brock had never been there and had no mental image of the place. She answered almost immediately, a phone beside her bed or armchair, perhaps, and he told her what had happened.

"It was on the ten o'clock news, that he'd killed himself," she said. "I wondered what they'd do."

"Can you phone round the team and get everyone to Queen Anne's Gate first thing tomorrow morning, please, Dot? I'll speak to Bren and Kathy myself."

When he rang Kathy's number he wondered what he might be interrupting, but she answered immediately, sounding calm and slightly distant. After he'd told her of developments, he added, "That was a pleasant meal. Sorry I had to dash off. I hope John didn't think I was rude."

"'Course not. He's gone back to the hotel. I can contact him if you want to see him again."

"Not at this stage, Kathy."

JOHN GREENSLADE RETURNED TO Chelsea Mansions after a brisk walk that failed to clear his head of troubled thoughts and doubts. He said a quick hello to Toby and Deb, and went upstairs.

In his room he stripped and stood for a while under the pathetic dribble of warm water that passed for a shower, then lay on his bed, trying to decide what to do. To return to Canada having achieved nothing would be like a defeat, and yet he seemed to have boxed himself into a corner, making it almost impossible, he thought, to confront his father with the truth. The turning point had been his gaffe about the frogman, Commander Crabb. He had seen, in Brock's dismissal of the idea, any curiosity and interest that he might have had in John vanish. The only way to retrieve the situation would be to come up with something to make up for the mistake and establish himself as someone to be taken seriously. But what could that be?

He thought of the message revealed on the back of the 1956 photograph, and the signature "Miles." If Miles had been Toby's father or uncle, then the family's records might have confirmed it, yet he couldn't remember any such references in the boxes in the attic that he'd gone through. When he had searched them it had just seemed a bit of fun, something to bring him closer to Kathy, but now it took on a deadly seriousness. He wondered if he had missed something, and remembered Toby's comment about moving the records out of the basement where they had originally been stored. Perhaps some had been left behind, he thought. He should ask.

By the time he'd come to this conclusion the hotel was silent, the lights out. He decided to wait till morning, and to consult Toby first about his father. But he couldn't settle, and after an hour of restless turning back and forth on his bed he got up, dressed, and padded silently downstairs.

The door to the cellar was unlocked, and he felt inside for the switch for the light on the stairs and went down. He felt the sudden chill radiating from the rough old concrete columns and slabs that had been built down there in 1939 to protect its occupants from a direct hit on the house above. There was a smell of damp, and something else, something sour like old drains recently disturbed. There were a couple of tea-chests standing against the far wall. He went over to investigate their contents and found that they were full of old china, wrapped in ancient newspapers. Nearby was a bench with a few tools and boxes of rusty old nails, and beside it a rack of industrial shelving next to a solid door set flush in the wall. It had a large handle and two heavy bolts set in its steel face, as if it were the entrance to a bank vault or, more likely, a blast-proof inner shelter. And he noticed that the floor in front of the door was streaked with smears of muddy footprints.

He took hold of the handle, turned it and pulled. The heavy door creaked open, and a stronger smell of fetid air gusted out. The room inside was in pitch darkness, and it took him a moment to find the light switch on the wall outside, by the shelving. He turned it on and peered back into the chamber. The first thing he saw was a pick and shovel leaning against a side wall, next to a section of the brick-paved floor that had been dug up, with a pile of rubble and earth heaped beside the hole. The room was like a cell, he thought, imagining how claustrophobic it would have felt to be inside, feeling the thud and tremble of the building around you as the bombs fell.

Beyond the hole, on the far side of the room, was something

else, a piece of gym equipment perhaps, and John went in to investigate, skirting around the diggings. It looked like a bench that was higher at one end than the other, to form a sloping platform, and next to it were coiled several thick leather belts and lengths of rope, and a bucket containing a damp cloth. An unpleasant memory stirred in his head, a TV film of the torture of prisoners in Iraq, and an image of a man stretched out on such a contraption, feet up, head down, his face covered by a wet cloth onto which water was being poured to induce the sensation of being drowned. Waterboarding, he thought. But why would—?

Then John heard a sound from the cellar outside. As he turned to look, the light in the chamber was abruptly switched off. He heard the scrape of steel on stone and gave a shout as the rectangle of light from the doorway began to narrow. The heavy door slammed shut, plunging the room into absolute darkness.

"Hey!" He scrambled toward the door, tripping blindly over the bricks, and heard the bolts, one and then the other, being rammed home. When he tried the handle there was no movement. He beat his fists against the steel and yelled, and the sounds seemed to sink, deadened, into the mass of the material in which he was now entombed.

After a minute of shouting, kicking and banging on the door, he subsided with a groan. This was ridiculous. Who had locked him in? Not Toby or Deb, surely, nor Jacko with the artificial leg, or Julie or Destiny. Garry then, the silent one. But had he realized that anyone was inside the room? John thought back. Yes, he had definitely called out before the door closed. Was Garry deaf?

John shivered, suddenly very cold. He felt in his pockets and realized he'd left his mobile phone upstairs in his room. He swore out loud. What if Garry hadn't heard him? He'd probably been doing his rounds, locking up for the night, never imagining that there was someone down here. How long would it be before they wanted to get into this room again? A day? A month? He felt a skitter of panic in his chest. There was a spade and pick-axe, he remembered. Could he dig his way out? What else might be hidden in the corners of the room? A flashlight? Matches? He turned to blindly feel his way around and promptly stumbled onto the pile of rubble beside the pit. He reached out his hand and felt something smooth and hard and rounded, like an old copper cistern ballcock, perhaps. An old copper cistern ballcock with two holes, like eye sockets. And a row of ragged teeth. He dropped it, swore and fell backward, cutting his hand on something sharp and hard. Broken bones. "Dear God," he groaned. "What's going on here?"

AN HOUR OR SO later, John, hunched against a wall and shivering with cold, heard a faint sound from the direction of the door. He strained his ears and then heard another noise, a more substantial clunk, and then a heavy creak and a thin line of bright light appeared.

"Thank goodness!" he cried, and tried to scramble to his feet, but his knees had locked with cramp and he staggered, momentarily blinded by the sudden dazzle as the door was flung open. He made out the black silhouette of a figure against the light and began gabbling, "I thought I was here for good!" He laughed, seeing the figure's arm swing up toward him, as if to catch him. "It's all right, I can stand," he cried, and was felled by a shattering blow to the side of his head.

His face was pressed into the mud and someone was on his back, wrenching his arms behind him, binding them with tape. Then he was being turned roughly over and he felt a searing jolt of pain as if they'd dislocated his shoulder. He gave a scream that was abruptly cut off as tape was stretched across his mouth and wrapped several times around his head, his eyes. Fingers pinched his nostrils closed and he couldn't breathe. He began to struggle wildly, lashing out with his legs, and the hand released his nose. Now his ankles were being gripped, taped together, and he was being dragged across the floor and dumped awkwardly in a corner. Through the singing in his ears and the muffle of the tape he heard people talking. It seemed to go on for a while until he heard the bang of the steel door closing, and total silence. He tried to move his lips under the tape, but this had the effect of easing the tape up across his nostrils as well as his mouth. He froze, terrified he was going to suffocate.

THIRTY-FIVE

BROCK HAD WORKED THROUGH the night on the files, preparing his plan of attack. By five he was satisfied and had taken an hour's nap before waking to the sound of Dot in the outer office.

"Wanted to see what sort of mess they'd left the place in," she said when he put his head around the door, as if she were talking about squatters who'd invaded her home.

Brock yawned. The clean shirt and toiletries that he used to keep in the desk drawer were no longer there, and he'd just have to make do with a quick splash in the toilet basin. A lick and a promise, his mother would have said.

The team assembled quickly, talking together excitedly about the developments. Chivers' action manager was present too, to answer queries about the ground his team had covered, and his detectives were available if required.

Brock began with a brief summary of the facts surrounding Hadden-Vane's suicide, and then they sat in silence, watching the recording of Freddie Clarke's revelations. At the end of it, Brock asked Zack if he had any observations to make on the tape itself.

"Well, it's been edited," Zack said. "Nothing sophisticated, just a couple of places where there's a slight jump, as if a few seconds have been cut out."

"Meaning?"

"It could be that someone spoke, asked him a question maybe, and that's been deleted."

They replayed the tape to the places Zack indicated. "See?" he said. "His eyes have shifted as if responding to someone to the left, behind the camera."

Kathy said, "There is something different about his manner from when I saw him. He's very tense, keyed up. His eyes are staring and he hardly blinks."

"Drugs?" someone suggested. "Or fear?"

"What about the background?" Brock asked Zack. "Could you enhance it, get some idea where he is?"

Zack shook his head doubtfully. "Maybe if we had the original recording, but the quality of this is poor. I'll have a go."

Brock moved on to describe the lines of inquiry he wanted pursued. "We have to finish the job we were doing when we were taken off the case. We'd made connections between Hadden-Vane and the Haringey youth club and the house in Hackney, but we hadn't established how it was done. How did Hadden-Vane brief Harry Peebles? How did he pay him? The missing link may be the security guard, Wayne Everett. Kathy noticed him in the background of that newspaper photo you found, Bren. Could he have been Hadden-Vane's agent in all this? We need to go through all the CCTV footage again, and all the forensic evidence from Ferncroft Close, to look for his traces.

"Then there's Freddie Clarke. We need to find him, or at least discover the circumstances under which this confession was made. Is he to be trusted? What were his motives?

"We also haven't explored the possibility that Nancy Haynes may have presented some kind of direct threat to Hadden-Vane. It's hard to see how, but we ought to check that she didn't try to get in touch with him, speak to the people in his parliamentary and constituency offices, his wife."

Brock checked through the list in his hand. "One other thing. I went to see the people in the hotel yesterday, and I had the impression they were hiding something about their dealings with Nancy Haynes. They said she'd never mentioned staying in Chelsea Mansions as a girl, or shown them the photograph she had with her, which seems improbable to me. They admitted detesting the Russians next door, and I wonder if they might be trying to hide something else she'd told them, perhaps to protect her reputation? We'll need to talk to them again, but first I'd like a bit more background on them and their dealings with Moszynski."

He looked around the room. They were all fired up, debating options, throwing ideas around—all except Kathy, he noticed, who seemed preoccupied.

BREN GURNEY'S FIRST TASK was to speak to Wayne Everett. He bustled into the interview room with a file of papers under his arm and shook hands with the security man.

"Sorry to take up your time, Wayne," he said affably. "We need to speak to as many people as possible who knew Sir Nigel Hadden-Vane. I take it you've heard about his suicide?"

Everett nodded cautiously.

"How about the video of Freddie Clarke on the web, accusing him of fraud? Have you seen it?"

"Yeah. Jeez, what a shocker, eh?"

"You didn't have anything to do with that, did you?"

"What? No, of course not."

Bren chuckled. "Don't worry, had to ask. So what exactly was your relationship with Sir Nigel?"

"Relationship? Well, that's too strong a word. I knew him

because I worked for Mr. Moszynski, and Sir Nigel was a friend of his and often came to the house. Sometimes Mr. Moszynski got me to drive Sir Nigel home after a heavy evening, that sort of thing."

"How long have you been working for Mr. Moszynski?"

"Six months."

Bren paused and opened his file. With his heavy build and Cornish burr, Bren sometimes appeared slow and deliberate, and Everett waited, shifting in his seat as the silence dragged on. "Yeah," he said, "since December."

"As I said," Bren spoke at last, "we're anxious to talk to people who've had recent contact with Sir Nigel, and we came across this." He selected an enlarged photograph from his file and showed it to Everett. "That's you, isn't it? And that's Sir Nigel, yes?"

Everett looked puzzled. "Um . . . yeah. Could be. Where did you get this?"

"It was in the local paper, couple of years ago. Sir Nigel handing out prizes at the Haringey Sport and Social Club in Tottenham Green. Remember that?"

"Oh, yes." Everett gave an apologetic laugh. "Yes, I had met him before I went to work for Shere Security. In fact he got me the job there—it's a company that he part-owned."

"So Sir Nigel got to know you well enough to get you a job?"

Everett shrugged, not quite as nonchalantly as he might have intended. "Around then his chauffeur died, and I did a bit of driving for him, casual like. Then later, when I was looking for a regular job, he got me the interview with Mr. Shere."

"I see. Sir Nigel was a sort of patron of the club, wasn't he? We're wondering who else he knew there. Anyone else in the picture you recognize?"

Everett took another look. "Don't think so."

"What about this bloke?" Bren pointed to Danny Yilmaz.

"Face doesn't ring a bell."

"You sure? He's been in the news lately, name of Danny Yilmaz, died last week of something called Marburg fever."

"Oh, that bloke. Yes, I did read about it."

"So have you had any contact with him in, say, the last six months?"

"Absolutely not."

"That's his cousin behind him, Barbaros Kaya. Do you know him?"

"More by reputation. Bit of a tough guy, I've heard. But I haven't had any personal dealings with him."

Bren nodded. "Did you know Sir Nigel's previous driver then, the one who died?"

"I'd seen him around, yeah. I think his name was Bernie."

"That's right, Bernie. And he had a son and daughter called Kenny and Angela. Remember them?"

"I believe I do. Kenny went up to Scotland, I seem to remember."

"He did. Did you keep in contact with him?"

"No."

"What about Angela? She inherited Bernie's house. Have you visited her there?"

"No. I wouldn't have a clue where it is."

"Hackney, 13 Ferncroft Close. You quite sure you've never been there?"

"Quite sure."

"You didn't maybe take Sir Nigel there?"

"Not to Hackney, no, never." Everett was looking disconcerted now. "I don't get it. What's this all about?"

"The thing is, Wayne, with two recent homicides associated with Chelsea Mansions, we need to make quite sure that Sir Nigel's suicide wasn't, shall we say, assisted in any way. And we're also interested to trace Freddie Clarke and make sure his video was above board. You can appreciate that."

"Yeah, okay."

"But you knew Sir Nigel, you drove his car, were in close physical contact with him, shook his hand, may have touched his clothes. You see my point?"

"No, frankly, I don't."

"Your prints and DNA may crop up in the course of our forensic examinations, along with those of other people we'll want to trace. So we need samples of yours in order that we can identify and eliminate them. You'll agree to that, won't you?"

"Oh." Everett looked troubled. "Sir Nigel spoke to me about this. He had very firm views on the subject, and told me I should never agree to it unless it was absolutely unavoidable. He said there had been mistakes, miscarriages of justice."

"It really would help us, Wayne, and I can assure you . . ."

"No, sorry."

Bren sighed patiently. "That's a pity. We'll just have to do it the slow way. Now I'm going to need details of every occasion you and Sir Nigel came into contact during the past six months . . ."

"CAN YOU THROW ANY light on Mr. Clarke's confession, Mr. Kuzmin?" Brock asked. The two men were sitting in the library in Chelsea Mansions in which Brock and Kathy had first encountered Hadden-Vane and Freddie Clarke on the night Moszynski died, over three weeks before. In front of him, Vadim Kuzmin seemed tense and preoccupied.

"That's funny." Vadim gave a chilly smile and lit a cigarette. Apparently Shaka's prohibition no longer applied.

"Funny?" Brock said.

"Yes." The Russian inhaled deeply. "I thought you might be responsible, Chief Inspector. I understand you and Sir Nigel were old enemies."

"You must have had dealings with Mr. Clarke recently, in connection with Mr. Moszynski's business affairs. How did he seem?"

"Uncooperative, secretive, devious. My wife is an executor of her father's estate and the chief beneficiary. She was entitled to have full information about his assets and liabilities. I was trying to get Freddie to set down on paper all the details, but he seemed reluctant. He said it was very complicated."

"You argued over this?"

"Sure, we argued. It was intolerable."

"But you used to be a member of the FSB Sixth Directorate, Mr. Kuzmin," Brock said with a quiet smile. "You would know plenty of ways to get such information from a reluctant witness."

Kuzmin looked at him sharply. "I had nothing to do with that video."

"Really? I wondered, you see, because it struck me that the background to the film, the setting in which it was shot, reminded me of the cellars underneath this house. We're working on sharpening those background images."

Kuzmin shrugged, sucked again at his cigarette. "Good luck. Have you any idea where Freddie is now?"

"He took a flight to Athens yesterday morning. We don't know where he went after that."

"He's done this before, several times. He sits at his figures day after day until something snaps and he takes off. He has always come back before, but things are a little different now."

"You mean he might feel responsible for Sir Nigel's suicide?"

Vadim gave a derisive snort. "Who cares about that? No, I mean that he is now the only one who can lay his hands on half a billion dollars' worth of Mikhail's money."

This thought hung in the air for a moment, then Brock said, "We'd like to have access here to carry out a thorough search of the house, to make sure we didn't miss anything before."

"Sure, be my guest, take the place apart if you want."

Brock made a call to the team waiting outside in the square, then said, "It looks as if someone's been digging up the floors in the cellars. Do you know why?"

"Oh, that was Mikhail's next project, a huge swimming pool in the basement. They had to investigate the drains, to see how it could be done."

"Is Mrs. Marta Moszynski here?"

"No, she's with Alisa at our house. She doesn't like it here any more. It reminds her of Mikhail. It is painful for her. She is talking about going back to live in St. Petersburg. Is that everything?" He began to get to his feet, but Brock stayed where he was, watching the other man. He seemed as anxious as Marta to leave Chelsea Mansions.

"Not quite. In the old days, when you were all living in St. Petersburg, you knew Mr. Moszynski's father, Gennady Moszynski, didn't you?"

"What is this, family history time?"

"In a way, yes, it is." Brock reached into his pocket and pulled out the photograph. He handed it to Kuzmin, who, just for a brief moment, gave a look of recognition, Brock thought.

"What's this?"

"That's Gennady standing there behind the girl, isn't it?"

Kuzmin's eyes darted to Brock's face, then back to the picture. "Maybe." He said the word carefully.

"The girl is Nancy Haynes, the other two people are her parents, the building in the background is this building, and the date is the twenty-sixth of April 1956."

"Before my time," Kuzmin said dismissively and handed the picture back.

"You're not curious? Or do you already know what it means?"

"What are you talking about? What does it mean?"

"It means that, contrary to what everyone has been telling us, Nancy Haynes had been here before, she knew Mikhail's father and would surely have approached Mikhail."

"And you think this has something to do with their deaths? That's crazy."

"Gennady had met Nancy's mother before, in San Francisco in 1939. They became lovers. Gennady was Nancy's father, Mikhail was her half-brother."

Brock watched the man's impassive face. "You knew this?" Brock persisted. "Mikhail told you?"

Kuzmin shrugged.

"Nancy had recently lost the money she needed for the life-style she was used to. Did she ask for money from Mikhail to keep quiet about this family scandal?"

Kuzmin shook his head indifferently. "I don't know."

"What about Marta? How would she feel? Her revered husband, Hero of the Soviet Union, the father of an American woman. Would she have wanted rid of her, before she sold her story to the newspapers?"

That seemed to register with Kuzmin. "That old witch," he growled. "Who knows what she would have done? But what about Mikhail? Why kill Mikhail?"

"Yes indeed," Brock said. "Why kill Mikhail?"

BROCK LEFT KUZMIN AND went out to see how the search through the Russians' palace was going. They were looking for documents, letters, electronic records, anything that might throw light on the relationship between Hadden-Vane and the Moszyn-ski family.

Eventually he made his way down to the basement security

control center where Zack was working at the control panels, and took a seat alongside him.

"So what is all this stuff?" he said.

Zack looked up. "High-quality gear but nothing extraordinary. That's the controls for the motion sensors set up around the house, and this is for the window and door alarms. Then there's the CCTV stuff—the screen there linked to that DVR . . ."

"DVR?"

"Digital video recorder, which in turn is linked to that HDD—hard disk drive—which stores the images."

"Can we find out why the CCTV was switched off at exactly the times that we really needed it—like when Mikhail Moszynski went out for a cigar on the Sunday night he died?"

"The Shere Security people explained that, didn't they?" Zack said. "They said that Mikhail must have switched the recording off himself."

"The trouble is, Zack, that we may not be able to trust Shere Security—Wayne Everett in particular. How can we check this?"

"Well, either the system, or some key part of it, like the HDD, was switched off for that period, either deliberately or as a result of a tech glitch, or . . ."

"Or?"

"Or the system did record for those periods and was erased afterward."

"Can we test that?"

"Yes. Not here or at Queen Anne's Gate, but I can take the HDD over to technical support to take a look."

"Yes, do that."

Brock's phone sounded. Bren had something for them at Queen Anne's Gate. Brock contacted Kathy and got up to go. As he made his way out he passed an open door leading into the warren of unused cellars in which he'd seen evidence of digging. The walls in there were whitewashed brickwork, similar to what could be seen in the background on Freddie Clarke's video. He called Zack and reminded him to take a look.

As he stepped out into the square Brock saw a taxi waiting outside the hotel, the driver loading a suitcase into the boot. The hotel door opened, and he saw Deb, a coat over her arm, come trotting down the steps. When she reached the cab she turned and, seeing him, gave a wave, then she got in and the taxi moved off.

THIRTY-SIX

"I RECKON WE'VE GOT him," Bren said, nodding with satisfaction. He described what he'd established about Wayne Everett's earlier history with Hadden-Vane and the Tottenham youth club.

"He was Hadden-Vane's enforcer, and he made sure the club officers were kept sweet as he used the charity to divert his share of the money coming in from Moszynski. He knew Danny Yilmaz, and also Kenny Watson, who used to come to the club before he went up to Glasgow."

"He told you all this?" Brock asked.

"Yes. It took a while, but he finally agreed to let us have his prints and DNA. They're processing them now."

"Good. Does he show up on the CCTV records at Hackney?"

"We're still looking."

As Brock and Bren sat down together to go through the interview record in detail, Kathy at the next desk checked her phone again. Nothing from John. She tried ringing his number, but it was still switched off. She hesitated for a moment, then finally called the number of the Chelsea Mansions Hotel. It rang for a long time before it was answered with a tentative, "Hello?" She recognized Toby's voice.

"Toby, hello, it's Kathy Kolla."

"Ah . . . Hello, Kathy. What can I do for you?"

"I'm trying to get in touch with John. Is he in the hotel?"

"John? John Greenslade?"

"Yes."

"He's not here. I haven't seen him since yesterday."

Kathy frowned. "I was with him yesterday evening, and he said he was going back to the hotel. He should have got there about ten-thirty, eleven."

"No, he didn't come home last night—we presumed he was with you."

"Would you mind getting someone to check his room, Toby? See if he slept there?"

"It's a little awkward at the moment. I'm rather shorthanded. I'll ring his room, shall I? Hold on."

After a minute he came back on the line. "No reply, I'm afraid. He's not here."

Kathy rang off, feeling worried.

"Okay, Kathy?" Brock was looking at her.

"Not sure," she said, and told him.

"Probably nothing to worry about. But why don't you check the crime reports?"

"Yes, I will." She went to her computer and logged in. She worked through the accident and crime incidents from the previous night in the districts he would have walked through on his way back to the hotel, but none of the victims resembled him, and his name didn't crop up anywhere. Then, feeling a little foolish, she requested a check on passenger flights to North America. That too drew a blank. Well, she thought, of course he wouldn't have gone home without contacting her. She rang the caretaker of her block to see if he'd called in there, but again there was nothing. Then she decided she was being overanxious and got back to work on a pile of the documents they'd taken from Mikhail's office at Chelsea Mansions.

Brock came over to her side and said, "Did we find out any more about Toby Beaumont?"

"Yes, a little, about his father." She searched through the papers on her desk and found what she was looking for. "Well, not much. His name was Miles, so presumably he wrote that note on the back of the photo."

"And probably took the picture too," Brock said.

"Yes. Born 1910, Eton, Oxford, the army. He was sent over to France with the British Expeditionary Force in 1939 and evacuated from Dunkirk the following June. In September 1941 he joined the Special Operations Executive which had just been formed to carry out raids in occupied Europe. In 1942 he was parachuted into Greece as part of Operation Harling, which blew up the railway viaduct at Gorgopotamos and cut the railway line from Thessaloniki to Athens and Piraeus which was being used by the Germans to supply their army in North Africa. He subsequently returned to England, took part in D-Day and was awarded the Military Medal."

"A distinguished record, then."

"Very. Toby must have idolized him."

"So what did Miles do next?"

"Nothing. At least nothing we can discover. There are no records of him after he quit the army in 1946 as a full colonel, until he committed suicide ten years later, in November 1956."

"The time of Suez," Brock said. "The end of innocence— wasn't that what Toby called it? He was at Suez, wasn't he?"

"Yes."

They said nothing for a moment, Brock deep in thought. "So what was he up to?" he said finally. "This hero of wartime special ops who vanishes from the record, and then plays host to an

American diplomat and a senior Soviet party member at his home in London. What kind of *larks* was he up to?" Brock shook his head and got to his feet. "I think we've been mesmerized, Kathy, by the Russians. Let's go and have another chat with Toby."

As they made for the door they were called back by Zack, who had returned from taking the surveillance hard drives to the SERIS unit in South London.

"We've looked at that gap on the night of Sunday May the thirtieth," Zack said, "when Moszynski was killed. The system was checked at eighteen minutes past midnight, and it was discovered to have been switched off at nine-fifty-two p.m., just before Moszynski left the house."

"That's what the security people said."

"Yes, and that's what the copy that we took from the hard drive showed. But we've now had a closer look at the hard drive, and it seems that the system was actually switched off at six minutes past eleven. The previous hour and fourteen minutes had been recorded, but then erased."

"Aha." Brock leaned forward. "Wayne Everett. But is it possible to retrieve the missing time?"

"If you go to the computer suite I'll show you what we've got so far," Zack said.

They hurried there, where Zack typed on a keyboard and the screen in front of them buzzed into life, a crackle of white static at first, clearing to show the front steps of the Moszynski house and the street beyond. A car drove past, then a figure came out from beneath the camera and stood for a while at the top of the steps, the man's head and shoulders bathed in the porch light: Mikhail Moszynski. He looked to left and right up the street, then walked down the steps and across to the gate in the fence to the gardens on the far side, where the lower half of his body was visible as he fiddled with the lock, swung the gate open and disappeared off the top of the screen.

"Nothing happens for a couple of minutes," Zack said, and there was a buzz of static as the recording was fast-forwarded. "Now . . ."

The lower half of a figure emerged in the top left of the screen. It was wearing dark trousers, and against the background of dark foliage it was difficult to make out any detail. It walked quite slowly to the gate and went into the gardens.

"Another five minutes where nothing happens," Zack fast-forwarded the film. "Here we go."

The dark trousers had reappeared at the gate, and retraced their route out of view.

"There's nothing more for another twenty minutes," Zack said, "until Wayne Everett comes out and goes across the road, just as he said. There's no sign of him carrying a knife."

Brock was getting to his feet. "Come on, Kathy."

"You know who it is?" she said.

"Yes, so do you. Didn't you see the stick?"

THERE WAS A CAR standing at the curb outside the hotel when they arrived, its engine running. As they went up the steps the front door opened and Toby emerged, one hand clutching his stick and a briefcase.

"Hello, Toby," Brock said. "I'm glad we've caught you in."

"Oh." He glanced from Brock to Kathy and back. "I'm afraid I'm in a bit of a rush, Chief Inspector. Let's make it another time."

"Sorry, this won't wait." Brock advanced on him so that he had to back through the door. Looking over her shoulder Kathy noticed the driver get out of the waiting car. It was the concierge, she saw, Garry, the silent one.

They moved into the hotel office. Filing cabinet drawers were open, papers strewn across the table, as if there had been a hurried search for something, and Toby's photographs were missing from the wall.

"Where are you off to?" Brock asked.

"Can you tell me what this is all about?" Toby said, a touch of annoyance in his voice. "I really am in rather a hurry."

"Sit down, Toby," Brock said, and drew out a chair for himself.

They heard the front door slam shut and Garry came in and stood behind them in the office doorway.

"We've managed to decipher the CCTV footage shot by the camera on Mikhail Moszynski's porch on the night he died," Brock said. "It shows him going into the gardens, closely followed by yourself."

Toby stood there and stared, inscrutable behind the tinted glasses. "Really?"

"Yes. You stayed with Moszynski for about five minutes and then left. You were the only one in the gardens with him until the security guard went in there twenty minutes later and raised the alarm. Care to explain?"

"I think not."

"Very well. Toby Beaumont, I am arresting you on suspicion of involvement in the murder of Mikhail Moszynski. You do not have to say anything, but it may harm your defense if you do not mention when questioned something you later rely on in court. Anything you do say may be given in evidence."

Toby listened in silence to the caution, immobile as if on parade. Then he glanced at Garry and slowly sat down, facing Brock across the table.

"Very well. You want the truth, do you?"

"Yes."

"Mikhail Moszynski made my life hell. For some reason that I could never fathom, he was obsessed with this building, with Chelsea Mansions, and was determined to own it all. One by one he bought out the other owners until there was just us left. When I refused to sell he resorted to subterfuge. I needed money to carry out a much-needed modernization of the hotel, and one day a guest, a very plausible sort of chap, got talking to me about it. How much would I need? he asked. More than the bank was prepared to lend, I told him. It turned out he worked for a private investment company that specialized in loans for property developments of various kinds. We discussed the ideas I had in mind, and why the bank thought them too ambitious while I was convinced they would work. He thought so too, and a few days later he presented me with a proposal. It was exactly what I needed. I scanned the terms and noticed a couple of clauses that looked a little strict, but he assured me that his company was very experienced in this sort of project and understood the need for flexibility. I took him at his word and signed up, and the money was in my bank account the next day.

"Then the problems began. There were endless delays with the council over approval for alterations to the interior of a heritage building, by putting in a lift and so on. Good grief! I pointed out that the bloody Russians next door had gutted their heritage building and turned it into something from Las Vegas, but it made no difference. I discovered later that the poison toad, Hadden-Vane, had gone behind the scenes and used his influence and Moszynski's cash to fix the building inspector. Then there were extraordinary problems getting a builder. They would promise to tender, then back out at the last minute. Everyone we approached seemed to suddenly find themselves unexpectedly tied up elsewhere.

"The end result was that when the time came to start repaying the loan, we were hopelessly embroiled, the place a mess, no guests and no income. I failed to meet the first deadline for a repayment and when I asked for flexibility I was told that the letter of the contract would apply. Within a week we were rushed to court, where, surprise, surprise, Moszynski appeared as the owner of the loan company, backed up by a phalanx of barristers and solicitors. He didn't just want the first repayment. We were in default, he said, and so the surety on the loan, the building itself, was now his. He also demanded that I cover all his legal costs, amounting to a quarter of a million so far. When the judge mildly pointed out that this would ruin me, Moszynski nodded and said, 'So be it.'

"In the end the judge saved us. He didn't like the way Moszynski was using the law like an assault weapon. He gave me another week in which to fulfill the terms of the contract, and made Moszynski carry his own costs. Somehow we scrambled together enough money to settle the first account, and later arranged a loan from another lender and paid off Moszynski's debt in full. The hotel, as you see, was left unimproved.

"I tell you this, not by way of mitigation, but so that you understand the nature of this man, Mikhail Moszynski. If there was something he wanted, he was utterly ruthless and relentless until he had it.

"Well now, on Sunday the thirtieth of May we held a memorial service for Nancy Haynes. You were there, Inspector Kolla, and so, to my surprise, was Moszynski. I was even more surprised when he spoke to me and asked to meet with me in the gardens at ten o'clock that evening for a private conversation. I was inclined to tell him to go to hell, but I had learned to be cautious where Mikhail Moszynski was concerned.

"It was dark, and the others were concerned about my going. Deb wanted me to take Garry here with me, but Moszynski had insisted I come alone and I decided to comply. I am somewhat incapacitated of course, but not entirely helpless. I made my way to the gate and took a pace into the gardens, then stopped. I could see nothing. But then I smelled his cigar, and he called out to me, and I followed the gravel path to the bench where he was sitting.

"He seemed in a good mood, cheerful about something. Apart from the cigar I could smell brandy, and his voice was slurred. He said he had an interesting proposition to put to me.

"He began talking about Nancy Haynes, asking if she'd told me that she had visited Chelsea Mansions once before, as a teenager, staying with her parents at my great-aunt's hotel next door. I said no, she hadn't mentioned it, and he told me that she had met him at the Russian cathedral the previous Sunday, and told him about the visit. I hardly knew whether to believe him, because Nancy had given no hint of it to us, but then he said that she told him she had also met my father back then, and had developed a bit of a crush on him, and even had a photograph of him. He took it out of his pocket to show me, and though it was too dark for me to make it out, I was inclined to believe him.

"He then started talking about Nancy's murder, and how unfortunate it would be if further unpleasant consequences were to flow from that tragic event. Well, my ears pricked up at that—from the tone of his voice it sounded like a threat of some kind, and I demanded to know what he meant. Then he told me, as calmly as you please, that he would give me one final chance to sell the hotel to him, and if I refused he had it in his power to arrange things in such a way that the police would have incontrovertible proof that I, assisted by my staff here at the hotel, had murdered Nancy.

"Well, the idea was so preposterous, even for that megalomaniac, that I just laughed and told him he was drunk. I asked him, what would be my motive in killing her? He replied that he would tell the police that Nancy had revealed to him that my father had raped her on that visit, and she was about to make it public. He would also arrange for physical evidence of some kind to link me to the murder. He said that he rather hoped I wouldn't agree to sell, and that he could watch me being destroyed, and my staff along with me.

"And that's when I realized that he wasn't drunk, and that he wasn't a man to make threats he couldn't carry out. I also realized just how much he hated me, and that he would carry out his threat whether I agreed or not."

Toby sat up a little straighter in his chair and raised his walking stick in both hands. He gave it a twist and a tug, and the handle slid out to reveal a long slender blade. He laid it carefully on the table in front of Brock.

"My grandfather took this with him to the Boer War in 1900 as a young subaltern," he said, "although I don't believe he ever had cause to use it. But I like to think that he would have approved of the fact that I did. It was my duty to protect my staff, and as clear a case of self-defense as if Moszynski had held a gun to my head. The man was going to destroy us. I had no choice but to respond in the only way I could."

Brock said, "You're admitting to us that you killed Mikhail Moszynski."

"Yes."

It was a spellbinding performance, Kathy thought, all the more disconcerting for his utter coolness. She glanced back at Garry, standing with his back to the door, hands behind him. Was he armed? Was that why Toby seemed so unconcerned?

"When you returned from the garden, were you aware that you were being filmed?"

"Yes, I remembered the camera, so when I got back I asked Garry to fix it."

"How could he do that?"

"Oh," Toby said with a careless gesture of his hand, "when my father built the air-raid shelter in the basement he extended it under all three of the properties the family owned. They were interconnected, so that if there were a direct hit on one house, the people would be able to escape through to the basement next door. The openings had been sealed up since then, but I remembered where they were, and we made a way through. Garry simply went into their security center when the coast was clear, wiped the tape and switched the camera off."

"What about Freddie Clarke's confession and Hadden-Vane's suicide? Do you know anything about that?"

Toby gave a little smile. "It would be nice to think that I in some way encouraged the truth to come out, but I shan't say any more than that. And it was an excellent outcome, was it not, apart from poor Nancy's death? Moszynski dead, Hadden-Vane dead, the old witch Marta Moszynski running back to Russia and Freddie Clarke banished to who knows where. The whole damn viper's nest cleared out, and justice served better than I suspect you would have been able to achieve, Chief Inspector."

Kathy saw Brock glance back at Garry, still immobile and silent at the door, then reach into his pocket and take out his phone, but Toby leaned forward and shook his head. "No."

"I'm going to call for a car to take us into the station to formally record your statement. You gave it under caution. It's already valid in a court of law and you are still under arrest."

"No," Toby repeated, apparently quite unperturbed. "I don't think so. I haven't quite finished yet."

"There's more?"

"A little piece of personal history. It's rather painful to recall, but relevant to our situation. In 1990 I was in Riyadh, a staff officer at British Army headquarters preparing for the first Gulf War, following the Iraqi invasion of Kuwait."

Toby gave an enigmatic smile and, without moving his gaze from Brock's face, pointed to the wall to his left. "Over there was a photograph of my son, Miles, named after my father. He also was in Saudi, an officer with the SAS. Before the main hostilities began we hatched a plan to send some units across the border to pinpoint the mobile Scud missile batteries that we knew the Iraqis were deploying in the desert. Then we got intelligence that a senior Iraqi general, a close relative of Saddam Hussein, was personally supervising the deployment in a certain area, and we had the idea of sending a raiding party to capture or kill this man. It seemed a brilliant idea, like Colonel Keyes' commando raid to kidnap Rommel in North Africa in 1942. Some on the planning staff urged caution—it would mean penetrating deep into enemy territory, war hadn't yet been declared and the odds were formidable. But I was gung-ho. I was also responsible for selecting the unit to go, and I wanted my son to command it. It would be the making of his career, I thought, his one great chance for glory. I should have paid more attention to history—Colonel Keyes was killed in the raid on Rommel. And my son was killed in Iraq.

"Now, I want you to put yourself in my shoes, Brock. Imagine yourself as a father, ignoring sensible advice and sending your son to his death for a noble but doomed cause. How do you feel?"

"There's no point to this . . ."

Toby suddenly slammed his fist hard on the table, making his stick bounce. Behind her Kathy sensed Garry stir. "Bear with me, sir!" Toby barked. "How do you feel?"

Brock stared at him. "Devastated?"

"Devastated—exactly. You would never forgive yourself, would you? Now I put it to you that you are in precisely this same situation."

Kathy drew in her breath. Brock was frowning, as if he'd decided that the old soldier was insane.

"No," Brock said slowly. "I am not."

Toby gave a sudden radiant smile. At least his mouth was smiling, but what his eyes were doing behind the black discs Kathy couldn't tell.

"The day after Nancy was murdered," Toby said, "a young man called in here at the hotel, looking for a room. I liked him.

He reminded me a little of my son, the same enthusiasm, the same mischievous smile, and the same age as Miles was when he died. He was very interested in what had happened to Nancy. I assumed at first that this was just natural curiosity, but then I began to wonder. He went to some trouble to meet with you, Inspector Kolla, and to become involved in the police investigation. There was something about him that struck a chord with me, though I couldn't quite pin it down. It was as if he were trying to find something he had lost. Then he told us that you were critically ill in hospital, Brock, and that he had gone to visit you, and had waited outside your room for some time, and I thought I understood. I had lost a son, and he had lost a father. I put it to him, and he confessed that it was true. His mother, your wife, left you when she was pregnant, did she not? She went to Canada and refused further contact except, for a while, through her sister. When John learned the truth about his father's identity he felt compelled to come to London to meet him—you—only to discover you were now at death's door. However, you recovered, and I assumed he would have told you about himself, but apparently he did not. I wonder why?"

Kathy had watched Brock's expression freeze. He turned his eyes to her and she bit her lip and nodded. "It's true," she said softly.

"Ah, so *you* knew," Toby said to her. "Well, to the point. You, Brock, are in the position that I was in, though with rather more certainty about the outcome. You can go ahead and do what you believe to be your duty and arrest me, but if you do so you will know with absolute certainty, as I did not, that you will lose your son."

"What do you mean?" Kathy made to get up but felt Garry's hand on her shoulder, pressing her down. "What the hell are you talking about?"

"When he returned here last night, John became rather too

inquisitive. He found something he shouldn't, and I was obliged to take him into my custody. He's still alive, I should think, but he probably won't survive another night, which would be a shame. You have no chance of finding him without my help, which I will give you, by phone, two hours after Garry and I drive away from here, and provided you don't raise the alarm in the meantime. You can trust me on that. I give you my word. What do you say?"

"You can go to hell," Brock said.

"Brock, I think we should talk about this," Kathy broke in.

"Sensible woman," Toby said. "Listen to her, Brock. Just two hours. Garry and I will retire to the inner office there to let you discuss this in private, eh? You have three minutes to decide." He got to his feet and marched stiffly to the door which Garry held open for him.

Brock was staring at Kathy. "Is it really true?"

"Yes, John told me. I had to let him speak to you first. He was hesitant, uncertain how you'd take it, but we agreed that he'd tell you over dinner last night. Only it didn't work out for some reason."

Brock swore softly under his breath. "I think that was my fault. Dear God, Kathy! I had no idea."

"I know. I'm sorry. So what are we going to do?"

"We can't agree to this. The man's just admitted to murder. There was no evidence of a struggle, was there? He's a killer."

"And ruthless enough to let John die. We can't allow that, can we?"

"He's bluffing."

"I don't think so."

Brock put both hands to his face.

"Forget he's your son," Kathy said. "He's a member of the public whose safety depends on our giving a self-confessed killer a head start. We have no choice."

Brock took a deep breath and sat upright. He was about to speak when they heard the sound of a car starting outside in the street. Kathy ran to the window and saw Toby ease himself into the passenger seat and pull the door shut behind him. The car drew away from the curb. She turned back to Brock.

"They must have gone out the back way. What do we do?"

Brock nodded. "You're right, we have no choice." He seemed momentarily defeated.

"We could have them followed, but I think it's too risky. I'll get Zack to track them with cameras, shall I?"

She used her mobile to ring Queen Anne's Gate, speaking urgently down the line, giving them a description of the car and its number, then listened while they got to work.

"They've got them crossing the river on Chelsea Bridge," she said at last. "The roads are clear to the south. What do you think, Gatwick?"

Then, a minute later, "They're turning west on Battersea Park Road."

"The heliport?" Brock roused himself. "Come on, we've got to find John before they get away."

"How can we? They could have taken him anywhere."

"What could he have discovered that forced their hand?"

Kathy thought. "He'd been looking through their old records stored in the attic by his room on the top floor."

They hurried out to the front desk, where Kathy grabbed keys from the pigeonholes and they ran to the stairs. When they reached the top floor they opened the door to John's room. His bag was still there, the bed unmade.

"So he went to bed last night. Then maybe he got up and started searching the attic again."

They found the door nearby on the landing, opening into a narrow staircase that doglegged up into a cramped loft laced with rafters and beams. In the pale gloaming from a dusty roof light they made out boxes, piles of old books and several metal-bound trunks. They searched rapidly, peering into the dim recesses, accompanied by the muffled cooing of pigeons on the roof outside, but found no sign of John.

"I wonder," Kathy said, trying to suppress a rising feeling of panic, "if they made that tape of Freddie Clarke's confession? Perhaps John found some evidence of it."

Her phone interrupted her, and she whipped it out and listened. Toby Beaumont and Garry had abandoned their car outside the London Heliport terminal on Lombard Road and were boarding a waiting helicopter.

"An AgustaWestland AW109," Zack said. "The registered owner is Mikhail Moszynski's company, RKF."

Brock was thinking about what Kathy had said, the video of Clarke's confession, the glimpses of old whitewashed brickwork in the background, like the cellar next door. "Perhaps they brought Clarke here. We should check the cellar."

As they ran downstairs Kathy received another message. The helicopter's reported route was to Biggin Hill airfield in Kent, a fifteen-minute flight away.

They found the door to the cellar beneath the stairs in the ground-floor hallway, switched on the light and saw the flight of stone flags leading down. "John!" Kathy called. "Are you there?" There was only a dead silence.

At the foot of the steps they paused and looked around—a bench, some steel shelving, a box of tools, a bucket, pickaxe and spade. Nothing seemed out of place. Through an arched opening another room was bare, smelling of raw damp. They looked into a third room and a fourth, all empty.

"Nothing," Kathy said, feeling panicky.

"Beaumont was enjoying that, upstairs," Brock panted, feeling the chill of the place. "He was excited, hyped up, alive. He was back in Riyadh, in the war room—*gung-ho*, as he put it."

"Let's hope we can trust him. There's no sign of John anywhere."

"Someone's been down here recently," Brock said, pointing to footprints on the dusty floor.

Another call came in. "The helicopter is landing at Biggin Hill. There's only one plane preparing for take-off at present, a Cessna Citation Sovereign jet, fueled up, waiting on the tarmac for its final passengers. It's privately owned. RKF again." She listened some more. "It has a range of five thousand kilometers. Flight plan to Lagos, Nigeria. Zack is asking if we want flight control to hold it up."

Brock frowned. "We have no extradition treaty with Nigeria." He shook his head and kicked at the shovel in frustration, sending it skidding across the floor. Then he crouched down. Kathy saw that his kick had dislodged a lump of clay from the back of the shovel's blade. He felt it, damp and sticky.

He straightened and said, "No. Tell them to stop the plane. Put a vehicle on the runway. Don't let it take off."

Kathy stared at him in surprise. "Are you sure?"

"They've been digging," he said, "like in the cellars next door. But there's no sign of disturbance in here. So where were they digging?"

Together they paced rapidly around the other rooms again, scanning the floors and walls, examining the brickwork, but could see nothing. When they returned Kathy took another call from Biggin Hill; the pilot of the Cessna was asking what was going on and the control tower wanted to know what to tell them.

Brock groaned. "Tell them . . ." he began slowly, and at that moment Kathy's eyes focused on the steel shelving in front of her. "Wait," she said. She stepped forward and heaved at the shelving, sending it crashing to the floor. As Brock looked at her in astonishment she pointed to the white wall behind the shelving, which wasn't brickwork but a panel of white board.

Together they pulled the board away to reveal a metal door with a steel handle and two heavy bolts. Kathy reached for them, then abruptly stopped, noticing the wires that led from the bolts to a large flat cardboard box which had been taped to the center of the door.

"They've booby-trapped it," she said, taking a careful step back. "What is he planning to do, blow the whole building up?"

Brock said, "Call the bomb squad, Kathy." As she made the call she watched him walk away, looking back to the stair and round again at the wall with the sealed door, scratching his beard. When she hung up he said rapidly, "This is the side of the house facing the Moszynskis, right? And Toby told us that he had found a way through to their basement. So we may be able to get into this room from the other side, from the Moszynskis.'

They ran up the stairs, along the hall and out into the street, Kathy on her phone again, shouting for back-up. When they arrived, panting, at the Moszynskis' front porch there was no answer to their urgent pounding on the door.

"The place is empty," Brock gasped. "They've all left."

As they waited for help there was another call from the air-field. A Colonel Beaumont had asked for a message to be relayed. Chief Inspector Brock was running out of time, he'd said. The plane must be allowed to take off immediately, or he would not answer for the consequences. Kathy looked at Brock for a response, but he said nothing, staring fixedly down the street from where the sounds of police sirens could be heard.

Brock shouted at the crew of the first car as they jumped out, and they brought up a ram and began slamming it at the edge of the door. The door was very solidly built, and it seemed to take an age before it finally splintered and burst inward.

"Kathy," Brock said, "one of us will have to stay at the hotel and take the bomb squad down. I'll do that. You go with these lads. There's a door behind the glass lift on the other side of the hall that gives access to a stair to the basement. You'll find tools down there you may need, pickaxes and sledgehammers. Let me have the Biggin Hill number and I'll stay in touch with them."

Kathy gave it to him and then led the uniforms, joined now by a second squad, across the hallway. She followed Brock's directions, running through the cellars, leaping over excavations and piles of debris until they came up against a solid brick wall with no openings. "Okay," she panted, "we need to work our way along this wall, left and right, into the rooms next door, until we come to some sign of a way through."

It wasn't long before they found it, a panel, encrusted with layers of old whitewash. They ripped the panel apart with a crowbar to reveal a heavy steel door beneath, like the one next door, but without a handle. "Handle must be on the other side," Kathy said.

A few blows with sledgehammers convinced them that they would never penetrate it that way. "We'll have to go through the wall," one of the men said. "Stand back!" and two of them began an assault on the brickwork to one side of the door, sending splinters of brick flying.

As they worked, Kathy imagined the bomb, just a few yards away from them now, steadily ticking toward whatever deadline Toby Beaumont had set. She turned away from the noise of the sledgehammers and called Brock. The bomb squad had arrived, he said; he was with them now, examining the box with some kind of equipment they'd brought; they could hear the pounding of the hammers, ringing through the brickwork. She turned at the sound of a shout as a blow finally punched a small hole through the wall. "Shouldn't be long now," she yelled into her phone.

They steadily worked at the hole, smashing it larger and larger until it was wide enough for a man to slide through. Then they stopped and looked at Kathy. She called for a torch and stuck her head and shoulders through and turned it on. The beam flashed around the chamber, picking up a mound of soil and bricks, a shovel, but no human figure. Her heart sank. They would be too late now. They would never find him. "This isn't it. He's not here," she cried, and then thought she heard an answering sound, a distant moan. She twisted her head, straining, and called out, "Hello!" and there it was again, not much more than a whisper. She pushed her head further in and turned the beam down at the floor, and saw a figure directly beneath her, bound in tape and covered in broken bricks and dust, a mop of dark hair she thought she recognized. "Hell!" she said. "We could have killed him." She clambered through the hole, swept the debris off him, and began to rip away the tape. At the same moment a door on the other side of the chamber swung open and Brock stood there and the room was flooded with light.

THIRTY-SEVEN

THEY STOOD ON THE hotel steps and watched the stretcher with John, wrapped in a silver thermal blanket, face covered with an oxygen mask, being wheeled to the ambulance.

"Are you sure it's true, Kathy?" Brock said. "He wasn't just shooting you a line, was he?"

"About being your son? No, it's true all right. I'd bet Moszynski's millions on it."

And it was only then, in the strange aftermath of frenzied action, that the impact of Toby Beaumont's revelation fully struck him. John Greenslade was his son. It had always been there, in the back of his mind, wondering if this day would come, and how it might happen, but he could hardly have imagined this.

His mind went back to a nightmarish day in April 1981, the day his wife Alice left him and the day Brixton, down the road, exploded in flaming anarchy. Neither event had really surprised him. It was almost a month after that before he discovered that Alice had gone to Canada to stay with her sister Tess, although even then Tess had been reluctant to admit it. "She just wants to be left alone, David," Tess had said. "She's terrified." But that was absurd, just histrionics, he'd told himself. It was many years before he discovered that Spider Roach had been threatening her. She had left without a word, and he'd had no inkling she was pregnant. It wasn't until after he had signed the divorce papers Tess passed on to him three years later that she finally let him know that Alice had had a baby boy.

And now what?

He reached for the phone and dialed Suzanne's number. She was astonished, then delighted by his news, and wanted to jump in her car and drive straight up to London to be with him, but there was so much to do now, and he needed time to think, and they agreed in the end that they would get together at the weekend.

WHEN THEY FINALLY LET them in to see John, he was sitting up in bed, his head bandaged and a drip in his arm, but his expression was alert.

"John, how are you?" Brock said, going to the side of the bed, and something in his manner must have alerted John because he shot Kathy a quick, uncertain glance, and Brock said, "Yes, Kathy told me. You really are Alice's son?"

"Yes, and yours I believe."

Brock was lost for words for a moment, then he growled, "Hell of a way to find out."

There was an awkward silence, and then they both began to laugh.

"We'll have time to talk later, but right now you'd better tell us what happened to you."

So John told them the story. "I really did think I was going to die down there," he said finally. "It was the skull that really freaked me out. I thought, someone else died here, and now it's my turn."

"There's no skull down there, John. We both had a good look around the cellar before we left, and the sloping plank you mention, that you thought might be for waterboarding, that was there, but no skull and no bones."

John looked at Kathy, who nodded in agreement.

"There was a smooth lump of stone among the debris," Brock said. "Perhaps that's what you felt."

"No! Look, I saw it, when they returned and there was light. It was a grinning skull, with eye sockets and a row of rotten teeth."

Brock shrugged. "Well, the main thing is that you're alive and reasonably okay. I'd have hated to have to tell your mother that I'd got you killed on our first encounter."

John smiled. "She'd have said it was only to be expected. But there was a skull, Brock . . . Kathy, don't you believe me?"

She shrugged. "We'll get a thorough forensic search made. If there was anything there we'll find traces."

On the way out Brock said, "It's amazing what the human mind comes up with under extreme stress."

THEY DECIDED TO WAIT until the next day to interview Beaumont and his team. There had been four of them on the plane—Toby and Deb, and the two men, Garry and Jacko. There was no sign of the two other women members of their staff, Julie the cook and Destiny the maid, and Brock ordered a search for them. From the bomb squad they learned that the cardboard box had contained nails and a lump of clay, the "bomb" no more than a dummy, presumably intended to delay any possible searchers.

Brock arranged for the luggage on the plane to be taken to Queen Anne's Gate and a room cleared for the contents to be laid out and thoroughly searched. Apart from clothes and toiletries, they found a number of those things that people might take with them when leaving for an uncertain future from which they don't expect to be coming back any time soon. They all had photographs of family and friends; Deb had an embroidered sampler that looked quite old, a locket of what looked like baby's hair, a collection of letters and a can of mace; Garry and Jacko had both taken pistols and ammunition, and Toby his swordstick. They were all carrying a great assortment of medications.

Of more pressing interest was a pouch in Toby's luggage containing fifteen pages of typed notes with bank account details, access codes and balances, together with two copies of a DVD of Freddie Clarke's interrogation, uncut and almost three hours long.

And in the middle of Toby's suitcase, packed between the neatly folded tropical suit, shirts and regimental tie, was a striped plastic beach bag containing one human skull, the bones of two hands and pieces of perished black fabric.

"Oh," Brock said.

SHARPE CALLED HIM IN the following morning. "This reads like some kind of bizarre crime novel," Sharpe said, tapping his report. "You sure you hadn't been drinking when you wrote it?"

"Unfortunately not," Brock said.

"Amazing. And he really is your son?"

"It seems so."

"Good grief." Sharpe gave a rumbling laugh. "Well, I should congratulate you. I'll have to buy you a cigar." He seemed to find the situation highly amusing. "So, a very satisfactory result all round . . ."

That's what Toby Beaumont said, Brock thought.

". . . Marta Moszynski persuaded or forced Hadden-Vane to organize the killing of this embarrassing offspring of her dead husband, and Beaumont killed Mikhail Moszynski in a quite unrelated act of retaliation for the Russian's threatening behavior."

"Mm." Brock nodded doubtfully.

"Come on, Brock, it may not be exactly what you expected,

but it's an excellent result. No grand conspiracy, no involvement of the FSB. The Foreign Office and MI5 will be delighted. They've been keeping a very close eye on us, demanding daily updates. I'll pass your report by them before we go public on anything."

"It's only a preliminary report, sir. We'll start interviewing Beaumont and his crew this morning, and I've ordered a forensic search of the hotel. There are many other details that need following up."

"Fair enough, but the main thing is that the documents and DVD you found should allow the fraud boys to track down the money. I'm sure everyone's going to be very happy to hear that."

"Beaumont was probably able to squeeze other information out of Freddie Clarke. He'd certainly found out how to requisition the company helicopter and jet."

"Yes. Waterboarding is a horrifying experience, I understand. I imagine Clarke would have told them anything they wanted to know. Is he still alive, do you think?"

"Well, he certainly boarded that Athens flight. My guess is that Toby would have left him access to enough of Moszynski's cash to keep him quiet for a long time."

Sharpe nodded. "The only jarring element is these damn bones in Beaumont's suitcase. What the hell is that all about?"

"We don't know. I'll be interested to hear his explanation."

"Yes, well, until we do find out I think we might take that out of the report."

GARRY AND JACKO REFUSED to speak. Deb said only that she had nothing to add to whatever Toby said.

"Toby has confessed to us that he murdered Mikhail Moszynski," Brock said. "That puts you in the position of an accessory, Deb, liable to the same punishment as him. You've just spent one night in jail, and it's going to be like that for the rest of your life. Do you really owe him that much? He's told us his version, now we'd like to hear yours."

She flushed slightly and said, "Toby speaks for all of us, Chief Inspector. I have nothing more to say."

Toby himself was quite willing to talk. He sat there facing Brock, looking defiant.

"Well, you kept your nerve, Brock, I'll grant you that, but you put your son in jeopardy. You gambled with his life. How do you feel about that?"

"I did what you did, Toby," Brock said.

"Oh no, not the same at all. I gave my son a chance at glory, you just didn't care."

"Glory? Not much glory in all this, is there? You stab an un-armed man to death, try to take off with his cash, and end up putting your three loyal companions in jail for the rest of their lives."

Toby flared, his face turning puce. "They had nothing to do with this. I did it alone. They are innocent!"

"They were in the plane with you, and now they refuse to talk—they say you speak for them. Only one way a jury's going to interpret that. They were after the cash, just like you."

"I couldn't leave them behind, with no future . . ."

"Well, they certainly haven't got one now."

"Perhaps . . . perhaps if I agreed to cooperate fully with you, you might be more sympathetic to their position."

"I don't think you've got much to negotiate with, but you can start by telling us about the skull and bones in your luggage."

"Ha!" Toby sat back with a grim smile, his composure return-ing. "I thought that would set the cat among the pigeons. You've probably been wondering about that all night, eh?"

Brock folded his arms and stared at him. "Let's have it then."

"My grandfather was an officer in the Fourth Army in the First Battle of the Somme, in the First World War. In July 1916 his company was involved in a frontal attack on the German lines, from which he was the only survivor. He was never quite the same after that. When he next returned home on leave, my grandmother came into the dining room one day and found a centerpiece on the dining table comprising a human head and pair of severed hands. She summoned my grandfather and asked him what it meant, and he explained that it was a souvenir he had brought home from the front, comprising the remaining body parts of a young German infantryman he'd killed."

He paused. He was enjoying himself, Brock thought, enjoying the looks on their faces. "What happened?" he asked.

"Grandma instructed their butler to dispose of the remains, and called the family doctor. Grandpa ended up being treated for shell shock at Craiglockhart Hospital in Scotland, and the butler buried the remains in the cellar. This became a family legend, as you can imagine, passed on from generation to generation of children under the covers after lights-out. According to the legend, the ghost of the dead German still haunts number eight, Chelsea Mansions." Toby gave them a toothy grin.

"So what was he doing in your bag?"

"You may know that Moszynski was planning to build a swimming pool in his basement, and started digging up his drains. That caused problems with ours, and we had to look at what was going on. That's when we found Fritz. Up to then I didn't really believe he existed. Anyway, I wasn't quite sure what to do with him, but when we had to leave in a hurry I thought I'd better not leave him there. I was planning to give him a decent burial in our new home."

"Which was?"

"We hadn't really decided yet."

"Hm. You have a long family tradition of service in the army, don't you, Toby?"

"Indeed."

"Your father?"

"Oh yes. He was with Special Ops during the war. Did amazing things in Greece, behind enemy lines."

"And after the war?"

"Returned to civvy street, import-export."

Brock opened his file. "Let's get back to your little adventure, Toby. I want every detail, every nuance. Begin with the arrival of the Russians in Chelsea Mansions."

WHEN THEY BROKE FOR lunch, Bren joined them for sandwiches.

"Heavy going?" he asked. "You look knackered."

"Beaumont's going strong," Brock said, stretching his shoulders. "Only too eager to talk, justify himself. Hasn't even asked for a lawyer."

"How does he explain the skull?"

Brock told him and Bren laughed. "What a story, eh?"

"Yes. We'll have to see if forensics support it. How have you got on, Bren?"

"Mixed. We haven't been able to find a match for Wayne Everett's fingerprints at Ferncroft Close yet. We're still waiting for the DNA results. We have tracked down the two women on Toby's hotel staff. Destiny, the maid, is on holiday in Morocco with a friend, and Julie the cook is staying with her sister in Nottingham. She's on her way here, expected about two."

"Good."

"So Beaumont's story hangs together then?" Bren asked.

"Yes," Brock reached for a sandwich. "It's consistent. You agree, Kathy?"

"There's only one major discrepancy that I can see," she said. "The report from the forensic linguist."

"John Greenslade?" Bren said, eyes lighting up. "There's a rumor going round about him, Brock . . ."

"It's true, Bren. It seems he is my son. We'd never met. Apparently he got himself involved in the investigation so that he could get to meet me."

"Blimey. Is it a secret?"

"Obviously not. But, no, Bren, I'm delighted. Of course I'm happy for everyone to know. If anyone's interested."

"Oh, they're interested," Bren said with a grin.

"Anyway . . ." Brock cleared his throat. "What about his report, Kathy?"

"He was convinced that the letter to *The Times* wasn't composed by Moszynski. If that were true, then presumably it was written by Moszynski's killer to suggest that the FSB were behind his death. Now we know that Toby could have sent someone—Deb perhaps—into Moszynski's house to type the letter on his computer, using his letterhead and copying his signature. But if so it means that he didn't kill Moszynski in a fit of spontaneous anger on the Sunday night—he must have been planning it since at least the Thursday evening."

"*If* John is right." Brock sighed. "It's not real science, Kathy, it's intuition, guesswork. It's too little to turn the case inside out."

"Well, I think we should press Toby hard on it. His story seems too self-serving to me. Maybe he saw Nancy's death as an opportunity to mask his murder of Moszynski."

They ate for a while, then Brock said, "I'd better give Sharpe a ring, bring him up to date. I think we'll change around this afternoon. Kathy, you talk to the cook when she arrives, find out what you can. Bren, you and I will continue with Beaumont."

THIRTY-EIGHT

"SO WHAT IS THIS all about?" Julie said. "Everyone's been so mysterious. They just said it was very urgent."

A car had been waiting at St. Pancras to pick her up from the Nottingham train and speed her to Queen Anne's Gate, and she looked flustered and slightly disoriented, but not displeased at this unexpected attention.

"Can you just tell me how you came to be in Nottingham, Julie?"

"Well, when Toby sprung it on us that he was closing Chelsea Mansions and we didn't have a job any more, I decided to go and stay with my sister for a while."

"When was this?"

"The day before yesterday, Wednesday evening."

"What time, exactly?"

"Um, about seven, dinner time."

After Hadden-Vane's suicide, Kathy thought, but before John had returned to the hotel.

"Why was he closing the hotel?"

"Because he'd got a good offer to sell, he said, and the buyers wanted a very quick settlement. He was ever so apologetic about the short notice, but he made up for it handsomely with our severance payout. Very generous he was. And so thoughtful. He bought Destiny two tickets for that Moroccan holiday she'd been going on about, and wanted to give me an overseas trip too, but I said I'd like to spend some time with my sister first. We had to pack up that night and leave first thing Thursday morning."

"What about the guests?"

"Well, they'd all gone, all except Mr. Greenslade, who'd returned unexpectedly from America."

"When did the others go?"

"That same day, Wednesday. Toby had to compensate them too. Why, have there been complaints? Is Toby in trouble or something?"

"He is in trouble, Julie, but not over that. You see, he's admitted to us that he murdered Mr. Moszynski."

Julie's jaw dropped, the whites of her eyes growing huge. "No! I don't believe it."

"It's true, I'm afraid. He was stopped from leaving the country on a plane with Deb, Garry and Jacko. They're all in police custody now. Toby has been quite open about what he's done."

"The others were going with him? Well! The army connection, of course. They were always close, those four."

"Tell me about your time working for Toby, Julie."

"I won't say a word against him. He was always a perfect gentleman. I do know that Mr. Moszynski provoked him something dreadful. He must have just snapped."

She'd started at Chelsea Mansions five years ago, she explained, and described her life there. She had lost her home and been very depressed after a bad divorce when they took her in, and Toby and Deb had been a blessing for her.

"I still can't believe that he would kill Mr. Moszynski. Are you sure he's admitted it? He did get upset with them, but who wouldn't, arrogant pigs that they were. Toby always tried to do the decent, civilized thing. Like, when that MP, Hadden-Vane, came visiting, he'd keep his driver waiting out there in the square for hours on end, and Toby would say, 'Come on, Julie, let's take the poor chap a cup of tea and a slice of your fresh-baked cake,' and we'd go out together and Toby would stay with him for a chat. That's how considerate he was."

"Hadden-Vane's driver?"

"Yes, he died a couple of years ago. Can't remember his name."

"Toby would probably pick up some gossip about the neighbors, I suppose?"

"Oh yes, always came back with a titbit or two."

"Did Toby get to know any of the other staff next door?"

"No, I don't think so. Garry did a bit."

"Really?"

"Yes, he liked to go down the Anglesea with one of Mr. Moszynski's security men, Wayne. Poor Garry, is he in trouble too?"

"We'll have to see."

"Doesn't say much, but he feels things. Very loyal to Toby. Devoted."

"Toby's very proud of his army connections and his family, isn't he?"

"Oh, yes, it's a long tradition. Those photos on his wall, the generations."

"Did you ever hear the American lady, Nancy Haynes, ask about them?"

"The one who was murdered? Oh, I don't know. She was certainly very friendly with Toby and Deb, very open and chatty. Her companion, the man, was quieter, didn't say much."

DURING THE AFTERNOON BROCK was called out of his protracted interview with Toby to answer a phone call from Commander Sharpe.

"Anything new, Brock?"

"Not really, sir, no."

"I'm putting out a press statement. I'll get a copy to you now to have a look at. Tell me if there's anything you're unhappy with."

"Right."

"And Sean Ardagh has been on the phone to me. They're interested in those bones found in Beaumont's luggage. Foreign Office are worried the Germans will be offended if his story is true and gets out. Ardagh wants us to hand them over to his people for testing. More secure, he says, and they have some new fancy equipment we don't have. You don't have any objections, do you?"

"Our labs are perfectly capable . . ."

"Of course, but I want to appear cooperative. I've told him yes. He's sending someone over."

When he hung up, Brock thought for a moment, then rang Sundeep Mehta. "Sundeep, have you tested that skull and bones we sent over yet?"

"I've made a start, Brock, but I've a hundred other things to do."

"MI5 want to take them from us to carry out their own tests. They say they have better equipment."

"Really? First I've heard of it."

"They're sending someone to the lab right now. Could you hold them off for long enough to finish your work?"

"Not really. I had more tests scheduled later this afternoon. Is there a problem with MI5?"

"I don't know, Sundeep. I'm just naturally suspicious, you know me."

"I'll do what I can."

IN ANOTHER PART OF Queen Anne's Gate, John was giving Kathy a detailed statement describing what had happened to him.

"Are you sure you're up to it, John?" she asked. The large dressing had gone from his head, revealing three stitches and an area of inflammation on his temple. She peered at it. "Does it hurt?"

"Only when I theorize," he said.

"Been doing much of that lately?"

"A little. Toby's lying, isn't he?"

"You think so?"

"I believe he wrote that letter to *The Times*. Which would mean he planned it all days before."

"Yes, I pointed that out to Brock."

He saw the expression on her face. "He didn't buy it?"

"I'm afraid not."

John put a hand to his forehead and winced. "That's what I mean. That's when it hurts."

"You don't have to prove anything to him, John."

He shrugged. "Fancy a drink later?"

LATE THAT EVENING, EXHAUSTED from the day's interrogations, Brock sat at his desk nursing a whiskey. It wasn't the letter to *The Times* that was bothering him, but another anomaly. According to the phone record, Harry Peebles had made a call to Hadden-Vane's mobile about an hour after Mikhail Moszynski was murdered, just as he had after Nancy Haynes was killed. But why would he do that, if he hadn't killed Moszynski?

Brock called up the record of Bren's interview with Wayne Everett on his screen, and began to go through it once again. When he'd finished he brought up the transcript of Kathy's interview with Toby's cook, Julie, that afternoon. Then he poured himself another Scotch.

THIRTY-NINE

"NO, THIS ISN'T RIGHT." Bren sat back, shaking his head.

"What's that?" Kathy looked up. She'd had another Saturday morning swim and she felt invigorated, her hair still damp.

"Brock ordered some forensic checks last night. They've got them all wrong. Is he here?"

At that moment the office door opened and Brock stuck his head in and growled, "Morning." He looked rumpled and bleary, as if from a late night and possibly a hangover.

"Your forensic results just came in, Brock. They've stuffed them up."

"Oh?" Brock frowned, as if trying to remember what he was talking about.

"Yes, the fingerprints from Ferncroft Close. They reckon they've got a match, but not to Wayne Everett. It's obviously a mistake."

"Ah." Brock came in and sat heavily on a chair. "That coffee smells good."

Kathy got up to fetch him a cup.

"It's a beautiful June Saturday morning," Brock went on. "They'll be setting up the stumps on village cricket pitches all over England. Thank you, Kathy. Just what I need." He took an appreciative sip. "They've got a match to Garry, I take it."

Bren looked surprised. "Yes, how did you know? They must have mixed them up."

"No. Sundeep was right all along, about Peebles' time of death. He died on the night after he killed Nancy Haynes."

"What? But he couldn't have!"

"Because he phoned Hadden-Vane three days later, yes. Except that he didn't—Garry did."

Bren began to frame a protest, but Brock went on. "Our case against Wayne Everett is circumstantial. He knew all the players—Hadden-Vane, Danny Yilmaz, Kenny Watson up in Barlinnie and his sister's house in Ferncroft Close—but we have no witnesses, no camera or forensic evidence to link him to the murder. Someone else who knew Wayne could have got that information from him, and used it. Yesterday Toby's cook Julie told Kathy that Garry and Wayne were drinking buddies."

"So . . ." Bren's brow creased as he digested this, "you're saying that Garry discovered that Wayne was acting as Hadden-Vane's fixer to arrange Nancy's murder, and then, when Toby killed Moszynski, he used that knowledge to frame Peebles for the second murder, by going to Ferncroft Close where he discovered his body and phone, and sent a further message to Hadden-Vane. All within an hour of Toby killing Moszynski. Pretty smart work." Bren sounded skeptical.

"Yes, unless they'd planned it that way all along."

"Eh?"

"There's another way of looking at it, Bren. Garry wasn't the only one from the hotel getting pally with the staff next door. Julie told Kathy that Toby had made friends with Hadden-Vane's old chauffeur, Bernie Watson, when he was alive, taking him cups of tea when he was sitting out there for hours waiting for his boss. I think they'd been spying on the Moszynski household for years, hoping to get something to use against them."

"Well, yes, but . . ."

"The thing is, we now know Garry was in the house at Ferncroft Close, but we don't know when. You're suggesting that he went there at the very end, after the Moszynski murder, but he could equally well have been there from the beginning. He could have been the one who arranged for Peebles to come down and murder Nancy Haynes."

"What, you mean he could have been working for Hadden-Vane?"

"No, Bren, for Toby. Freddie Clarke's confession would have ruined Hadden-Vane financially, politically and socially—that's why he jumped off Westminster Bridge. But it didn't provide any evidence that he was involved in murder."

"But why would Toby want Nancy dead?"

Brock shook his head. "I don't know. But I've always felt that those two murders, although they were so different, were part of the same story. Nancy Haynes tossed a bomb into the works when she came to London. I don't know what it was, but we'll find out."

Kathy, who had been silent up to now, decided she might as well get her two bob's worth in. "And that would mean that John was probably right about the letter to *The Times* being a fake."

Brock gave an impatient little frown. "Maybe so," he conceded. "But you mustn't let your feelings get in the way of your reason, Kathy."

She stared at him in astonishment. "*My* feelings?"

Brock blinked and looked embarrassed for a moment, then said quickly, "Bren, we need to find out exactly where Garry left his traces at Ferncroft Close, and whether any of them were overlaid by Peebles'. I'm also wondering if Garry may have killed Peebles with that overdose. It always seemed very convenient that he died before we could get to him."

As they began to discuss procedures, Kathy turned back to her desk and got on with her work.

JOHN HAD MOVED TO another hotel, not far from Chelsea Mansions. When Kathy called on him that evening she found him ironing a shirt.

"Catching up with the laundry?" she said.

"Helps me think," he replied.

"Have you been doing much of that?" The truth was that she had half expected him to be gone, back home to Canada.

"A bit."

"Not theorizing though, I hope."

He smiled. "Yes, that too. I've been making my head hurt."

She noticed a pile of books and pamphlets on the table. She looked at a title. "Imperial War Museum?"

"I spent a bit of time there today. Interesting."

There was a certain intensity in the way he said it. "Anything you want to share with me?" she asked.

He switched off the iron and hung his shirt in the closet, then turned to face her. "Yes. Let's sit down."

They sat, and for half an hour Kathy listened without speaking. Finally he said, "What do you think?"

She took a deep breath. "I think it's brilliant. You must tell Brock."

"Oh no." He shook his head firmly. "I got burned the last time, Kathy. You can take this to him if you think it's worth it, but leave me out of it. That way he may give it a fair hearing."

"No. If you believe this then you've got to tell him yourself.

And I'm going to be there and I'll make him bloody listen." She got out her phone. "Okay?"

He bowed his head and, after a long pause, agreed.

Brock was still at the office, Kathy found, and hadn't had an evening meal. "How about Mexican?" she asked.

"I'm not very keen on Mexican."

"You'll like this," she said, and gave him the address of the place in Brompton Road.

They watched him come, look around, then respond to her wave. He shook hands with John and sat down, taking the menu the waiter gave him.

"I can never remember what these things are," he grumbled, looking down the list. Kathy made some suggestions and poured him a glass of wine.

"Well," he said, sitting back. "Cheers. It's been a beautiful day to be out and about, and not stuck indoors like us. What have you been up to, John?" It sounded as if he was trying to be neutral and polite.

"John's been working too," Kathy said. "He's got an interesting story to tell you, Brock. He told me, and I thought you had to hear it, all the way through, without interruption."

Brock looked at her in surprise, then gave a quiet smile. "Excellent. I enjoy a good story. Fire away, John."

So John cleared his throat and began.

Half an hour later the enchiladas lay cold on Brock's plate, untouched.

"So that's about it," John concluded, looking at him warily.

"Import–export," Brock said at last with a chuckle. "Well, it's a very good story, John. Why can't I find detectives with that sort of imagination?"

Kathy looked at him to see if he was being sarcastic, but he seemed genuinely impressed. He began attacking the enchiladas without apparently noticing them, his mind clearly still fixed on John's account.

"Circumstantial, of course, but we can fill in some of the gaps. Kathy, what do you think?"

"Quite interesting."

"*Quite* interesting? It's bloody brilliant."

"You think there might be something in it?" John asked.

"I think it may be exactly what I've been looking for." Brock chewed for a moment. "This isn't too bad."

FORTY

THE INTERAGENCY MEETING RECONVENED on Monday morning at eleven a.m. The same people were there from the Home Office, Foreign Office and the police, all except Brock, who had taken Kathy's place at Commander Sharpe's side.

"A wrap-up session, then," Sir Philip opened the proceedings. "Shouldn't take too long, I hope." He looked pointedly at his watch. "Commander Sharpe, a brief summary? We have all read your report, I take it."

Sharpe outlined the circumstances surrounding the arrest of Toby Beaumont and his team, and made some recommendations about what should be released to the press. His account was accompanied by chuckles and raised eyebrows from the Foreign Office man.

"Excellent," Sir Philip said. "No international ramifications, almost all of Moszynski's millions recovered, first-class result all round. Any comments?"

"Just a small rider," Sean Ardagh said, "regarding the human remains found in Beaumont's suitcase."

"Oh yes?"

"Our lab has completed tests and they support Beaumont's

story—probably a young German soldier from the First World War."

Sir Philip shook his head sadly. "Disgusting. I think we'll keep that quiet, don't you?"

"What about the strip of material with the bones?" Brock asked.

"Collar of his uniform," Sean said.

"Really?" Brock looked puzzled.

"Something worrying you, Chief Inspector?" Sir Philip was gathering up his papers.

"Well, I didn't realize the Germans went to war in rubber uniforms, Sir Philip."

"Rubber?" Sir Philip stared at him. They all stared at him.

"Yes. Our lab also carried out extensive tests on those bones before MI5 removed them, and they came up with rather different results. They say that the skull belonged to a man aged about fifty, rather old for an infantryman on the Western Front one might think. Also that he died no earlier than 1950. And the strip of fabric was of a rubberized material, very like the collar on a 1950s Heinke diving suit. There's one in the Imperial War Museum."

"Diving?" A ripple of astonishment went round the table. Only Sean Ardagh, lips pursed, wasn't looking at Brock. "What are we supposed to make of that?" Sir Philip demanded.

"Well," Brock went on, "it's interesting that Toby Beaumont's father, Miles Beaumont, was in the Special Operations Executive during the Second World War, and in Operation Harling in occupied Greece in 1942, against the German supply lines for the Afrika Korps. He was a qualified diver, and is understood to have taken part in limpet mine attacks on shipping in Piraeus harbor."

"You think Beaumont was carrying his father's remains?" Sir Philip said.

"No. Miles Beaumont died in 1956, at about the right age certainly, but of a self-inflicted gunshot wound to the temple. There's no sign of such a wound on our skull."

"What then?"

"Well, it's only speculation at this stage, but there was another diver fatality in that year, 1956 . . ."

"If I may suggest, Chairman," Sean broke in. "What Chief Inspector Brock is about to raise may touch on national security, and some of our own concerns. I would request that this meeting be closed and the last comments of DCI Brock deleted from the record so that we and the police can confer."

Sir Philip looked a little put out. "Just when it was becoming interesting. Very well, Sean, if you insist. Commander Sharpe?"

"We're always happy to talk to our colleagues in MI5." Sharpe looked upward at the ceiling. "But we won't suspend our inquiries for vague hints of national interest. We will need to understand Sean's reservations, in detail."

"No problem," Sean said, looking unhappy. "Perhaps we might have a few words, after this meeting."

"Right." Sir Philip jumped to his feet, snatched up his papers and name plate and said, "Let's leave them to it, shall we?" and swept out of the room, followed by the others.

"Well," Sean said, looking across at Sharpe and Brock balefully. "That was a fuckin' ambush, yeah?"

"Of your own making, Sean," Sharpe said affably. "Let's have no more obfuscation, shall we?"

"Very well. Care to tell me how your mind is working, Brock?"

"In early 1956 a man called Lionel Crabb, nickname Buster Crabb, was summoned to a meeting with the First Sea Lord, Louis Mountbatten, who asked him to undertake a special mission organized by British and American intelligence agencies. Crabb was a war hero, a frogman who had fought against the Italian underwater forces attacking British convoys and naval ships sheltering in Gibraltar, but by 1956 he was retired, drinking too much, a bit out of condition. Nevertheless he agreed to do what was required of him, to carry out an underwater inspection and photography of a Soviet cruiser, the *Ordzhonikidze*, which was due to bring an official delegation of the top Soviet hierarchy to the UK in April. The ship was of interest to the British and Americans because of its extreme maneuverability, thought to be due to underwater turbines. On April the nineteenth Crabb dived into Portsmouth Harbor near the Russian cruiser, and was never seen again."

"Yes, yes." Ardagh looked bored. "Everybody knows the story. So what? How can you connect this to Chelsea Mansions, for goodness' sake?"

"In June of the following year some fishermen near Pilsey Island, about ten miles east of Portsmouth Harbor, found the badly decomposed remains of a man wearing a Heinke two-piece diving suit, similar to the one Crabb had been wearing. However the head and hands of the corpse were missing, and identification was difficult. Nevertheless, an inquest determined that it was Crabb, cause of death unknown, an open verdict returned."

"So?"

"There's very little information about what Toby Beaumont's father did after the war. Toby told us he was in import–export, which sounds to me like a euphemism for spooks. I think he was involved in Crabb's death, and Nancy Haynes heard about it from her mother, whose husband had been the American intelligence liaison officer on the case, just before she died. And Nancy probably thought it would be tremendous fun to go to London and tell Toby, whose father had been the senior MI5 man, and Mikhail Moszynski, whose father had been their KGB contact, about this fascinating bit of Cold War history that tied them together. Except that Toby idolized his father and would do anything to suppress the story, and Moszynski saw it as a way to blackmail Toby into selling him the hotel. How does that sound?"

"A bit far-fetched," Sean said. "Why would the CIA and MI5 have the KGB involved?"

"I don't know, but that photograph of them together outside Chelsea Mansions proves they were. There have been theories that Anthony Blunt, the British Soviet spy, was involved in the Crabb story. Maybe Miles Beaumont was a Russian agent too. The first step will be DNA tests with Crabb's relatives to see if that skull really is his."

"Oh dear." Sean examined his fingernails. "You know that the files on Crabb are locked away, classified until 2057, do you? Speculations like this, flying around the Met, could make a lot of people very uncomfortable."

Sharpe said, "Who else is party to your *speculations*, Brock?"

"DI Kolla, and a Canadian consultant, John Greenslade. He's signed the Official Secrets Act. It won't go beyond them, provided I'm satisfied that we've got to the truth."

Sharpe turned to Ardagh. "Well then, what do you think?"

Sean sighed. "All right. Let's get together again later today. I'll tell you what I can."

THEY MET AGAIN IN Sharpe's office at five thirty. This time Brock brought Kathy, and Ardagh too was accompanied, by Vadim Kuzmin, who gazed around the room with the keen eye of a public servant picking up clues of status in the size of the desk and the quality of the leather chair behind it.

Sean cleared his throat. "I'd like to warn you that we may discuss matters that are covered by the Official Secrets Act 1989."

Sharpe said, "What about Mr. Kuzmin?"

"Vadim has signed the Act, Commander. He is a consultant to MI5 and MI6. I'd like to invite him to speak."

Kuzmin continued looking around the room. "Do you have a drinks cabinet, Commander Sharpe?"

Sharpe frowned. "I do."

"I'd like a small Scotch, if you don't mind. Just as it comes. No ice or water." Then he added, when Sharpe got to his feet, "But not too small."

"Anyone else?" Sharpe glowered at them. Kathy and Sean shook their heads, but Brock said, "I'll keep Mr. Kuzmin company."

Sharpe handed out the tumblers and sat down again.

Kuzmin tasted, nodded approvingly, and began. "One day, when Mikhail was down in the cellars, directing the men working on the latest building stage, I made a joke. 'Mikhail,' I said, 'what is going on? Is this where the bodies are buried?' He looked shocked and hurried me away upstairs. 'What do you mean?' he said. 'What have you heard?' Eventually I persuaded him that it was just my little joke, and he relaxed and told me a story. When his father Gennady was in his final days in the Marlinsky Hospital he was haunted by bad dreams. During his life he had had many dark experiences. For two and a half years he had endured the siege of Leningrad and witnessed terrible things—bombing, starvation, cannibalism—and he had killed Germans. But there was one death in particular that bothered him, not in St. Petersburg, but in London. He told Mikhail of a house in London where he had murdered a man with his bare hands. The house was Chelsea Mansions, he said, and the body was still there. By this stage Gennady had returned to the Orthodox faith, and he was convinced that the victim's body would rise up and drag him to hell if it was not given a proper burial.

"Mikhail said that this was why he had bought the house, to carry out his father's dying wish. But although he had torn the building apart, he had found no body, and he had become convinced that the old man was delusional.

"Then, from nowhere, an American woman comes to him and tells him that she also is Gennady's child, and Mikhail's sister. She too has been told old stories by a dying parent, stories of a love affair in San Francisco and of spies in London, and of something secret and terrible that happened in 1956, the year she went to London with her parents. This woman has photographs to show Mikhail, including one of Gennady and her family standing outside the house where this secret thing happened. It is the house belonging to the man who took the photograph, an English spy, and Mikhail recognized it as Toby Beaumont's house, the only part of Chelsea Mansions that he had not been able to acquire.

"Mikhail told me about this the same day the woman told him. Unfortunately he had already spoken to his mother about it. She was very angry, and he wanted me to calm her down, but when I went to see her she said it was all lies and wouldn't discuss it. Later I went back to her room to speak to her again and found her with Sir Nigel Hadden-Vane. She seemed to be demanding something from him and he looked very agitated, and she slammed the door in my face when I made to go in.

"The next day I had to go to Russia on business, but when the American woman was murdered Mikhail phoned me in Moscow and told me that he was afraid that his mother might be responsible, to avoid disgrace for Gennady. I thought this could be possible, arranged for her by Sir Nigel. Then when Mikhail was killed I thought he must have quarreled with Sir Nigel, who had had him killed too."

"But you didn't tell us," Brock said.

Kuzmin shrugged. "I had no evidence. It was only a theory."

"And it left you in control of Mikhail's fortune. Did you tell Sean Ardagh here about your theory?" Both men were silent. "You both knew about the connection between Nancy Haynes and Mikhail Moszynski after they were murdered, but you said nothing to us."

"We decided that it wasn't relevant to their deaths," Sean said.

"No," Brock objected. "You were terrified that it might lead us to the truth about what happened to Lionel Crabb back in 1956. So terrified that when you heard Kathy was in America asking about a picture of Nancy on her sixteenth birthday in London, you hopped on the first available transatlantic plane to drag her home."

Sean looked as if he'd bitten into something sour. "We had two priorities. The first was to protect Vadim, who is a particularly valuable asset of ours, and is rather vulnerable at the present time. The second was, yes, to avoid reopening an old scandal that still has the power to cause trouble."

"I think you'll have to explain that to us," Sharpe said.

Sean shifted in his seat. "Before the war, Nancy's father—Ronnie Elgin was his name—was a commercial attaché in the State Department who was also clandestinely involved in gathering foreign intelligence. When Gennady Moszynski visited San Francisco in 1939 with a party of Soviets, Ronnie cultivated him, and even encouraged the infatuation that he saw developing between the Russian and his wife, Nancy's mother. Although a committed communist, Gennady was an idealist; he believed in a brotherhood of nations and was appalled by what Stalin had done during the thirties. The three of them promised to remain friends, and after the war Ronnie made contact with Gennady again, and they exchanged low-level commercial information, with the aim of improving understanding between their two countries. Then, in 1956, after Krushchev's speech denouncing Stalin, they had the chance to meet up again in London, hoping that the Cold War might be coming to an end.

"Ronnie was also friendly with his UK counterpart, Toby Beaumont's father Miles, who had joined MI5 after he left the army at the end of the war, and he facilitated their meeting in London.

"But Miles was ambitious. He wanted to persuade Gennady to give them much more. He argued that the time was right, that the old Stalinist hardliners in the Kremlin were being challenged by Krushchev, and he wanted to offer Gennady a prize to gain his masters' trust.

"Now through his old diving friends he had heard that MI6 had hatched a risky plan to send a frogman down to investigate the cruiser that brought the Soviet leaders to the UK. The whole project was flawed. Apart from anything else, MI6 weren't supposed to operate within the UK, that was our remit, and there was a lot of bad feeling about it in MI5. It seems that Miles Beaumont got it into his head to turn the tables on MI6 and betray the plan to Gennady. The Russians captured the frogman."

"Commander Crabb," Brock said.

"Yes. According to what Gennady told Mikhail, they took him to London, to the basement of Miles's house, where Gennady was supposed to carry out an initial interrogation of Crabb, before he was smuggled back to Russia on one of the Soviet airliners that had come over for the visit. But Gennady was too rough. Crabb died. They buried him there in the basement. Later the body was exhumed, and all but the head and hands were removed and dumped in the sea near Portsmouth, as you said, Brock."

"Did Miles Beaumont have authorization from MI5 to do this?" Sharpe asked.

"Hell no. He did it completely off his own bat. He was a bit of a loner, by all accounts. An arrogant bastard. He never reported it afterward."

Brock was watching him closely. "But it was discovered?"

"After a while," Sean said reluctantly, "suspicions were raised."

"There was a cover-up."

"All the same, this is old history," Sharpe said. "Is it really so vital that it's not made public now?"

"That an MI5 officer arranged the kidnapping and murder of an MI6 officer by the Russians? Toby Beaumont thought so, and so do a number of other people who were around at the time."

"Well," Sharpe said, "you'll have our cooperation."

"We'd appreciate it."

When Ardagh and Kuzmin had gone, Sharpe gave a little smile. "Money in the bank, Brock. He'll have to pay for our silence."

Brock drained his glass. "Case closed then."

FORTY-ONE

TOBY BEAUMONT GATHERED HIMSELF up and stood rigidly to attention—like a prisoner of war, Brock thought, that's how he sees himself now, ready to give his name and serial number and nothing else. But he looked exhausted; prison was doing him no good, the effort involved in maintaining his front becoming too hard.

"I brought you some reading matter," Brock said, and placed a small parcel of books on the table between them. He watched Toby open the package and peer at the titles: a new history of Napoleon's campaigns, a reprint of Richard Burton's 1855 book, *Personal Narrative of a Pilgrimage to Al-Madinah and Meccah.* Toby looked pleased, until he turned over the third book, *The Buster Crabb Mystery.*

"You've probably read that one," Brock said. "I imagine you buy each one as it comes out, wondering if they've finally discovered the truth. Well now they have, Toby, thanks to Nancy Haynes, though we won't be reading about it. Like you, they prefer to keep it buried."

Toby's expression was unreadable behind the dark lenses.

"Tell me about your father. He must have been a remarkable man."

Toby remained silent.

"I'm told he wasn't a team player."

"He was a team *leader*."

"Why did he kill himself?"

Toby sniffed, but didn't answer.

"Did he change his mind about what he'd done? Did he realize that he'd never be able to explain to his friends how he'd betrayed a fellow officer to the Russians? Was he riddled with guilt at how it had turned out, once that brute Gennady got his hands on Crabb?"

Toby still said nothing.

"It was while you were away, fighting on the Suez Canal, wasn't it? I wondered if there was some connection. So I checked your army record, and discovered that you weren't up at Catterick Camp on the twenty-sixth of April 1956 as you said. You were on leave." Brock leaned forward. "You were there, Toby, weren't you, at Chelsea Mansions when they did it? You were part of it, helping. And I wondered if your father killed himself out of a feeling of guilt for having involved you? Or was his suicide the price they demanded, when they finally worked out what he'd done—the price to keep you out of it, to let you continue in your military career?"

Toby took a deep breath and spoke in a low voice. "It's a matter of loyalty, Brock. In the end that's the most important thing, loyalty to your kin."

Brock rubbed his beard thoughtfully. "Apparently an unknown woman looked after Crabb's grave for twenty years after he was buried. His family denied it was any of them. I wondered if it might have been your mother."

Toby got abruptly to his feet. He picked up the first two books, but left the one on Crabb lying on the table, and turned and marched away.

FORTY-TWO

BROCK DUCKED HIS HEAD through the low doorway of the old pub, steadying the tray of drinks in his hands. Across the dappled lawn, in the shade of a large oak tree, he saw the three of them around a table, heads together, discussing a photograph. They had met at one of Suzanne and Brock's favorite country pubs on the way to Battle, and Brock paused for a moment in the sun and took a deep breath, thinking what an enormous relief it was to be out of London, like escaping from an airless room.

Suzanne was making a great fuss of John, teasing information out of him, gauging his temperament, clearly enjoying his company. Yes, within ten minutes she'd decided that she genuinely *liked* him, Brock realized, and it made him aware that he hadn't even reached that stage yet. With anyone else he would have formed his assessment long ago, but with John he was lost, the burden of old memories too great.

He had at least made his apologies to the lad, for the Crabb business, and most of all for doubting his judgment about the authenticity of the letter. He felt ashamed of himself, remembering how he would have felt if his father had dismissed him like that.

Watching them now, laughing easily together, John's hand on

Kathy's arm, Brock thought how open and exuberant he looked. It seems, he thought, that I have things to learn from this young man.

Suzanne turned her head and saw him standing there and gave him a smile and a wave. He set off across the grass toward them.

It was that night I heard the ghost in the chimney. I was tucked up in the old-fashioned hotel bed, so high off the floor, unable to sleep. On the small table beside my pillow was the present that Uncle Gennady had given me, his war medal, the most precious thing he owned, he had said. I thought how strange it was that he had given it to me, and with a tear in his eye, but Pop had just smiled when I asked him, and said that he was a Russian, a very emotional race, given to spontaneous, generous actions.

I was thinking about this when I heard the sound, a strange, distant cry, almost inaudible. It came again, a little louder and more urgent, and it seemed to me that it came from the direction of the fireplace. I got out of bed and made my way toward it. I knelt down and bent my head toward the grate and felt a breath of cool air brush against my cheek. And then I heard it again, a scream of agony, echoing down the chimney from far, far away. I gasped and rocked back on my heels, terrified. All around me the room was dark and still. I jumped to my feet and ran back to bed and buried myself under the blankets. It was a cat, I told myself, up on the roof, yowling at the moon.

The next morning at breakfast I asked Daphne, the owner of the hotel, about the cries from the chimney. She seemed quite alarmed that I had heard them, and then explained that a ghost haunted Chelsea Mansions. I didn't believe in ghosts, but this was England, and things were different. Everyone seemed very subdued that morning. The happy mood of the previous day had vanished, as if the ghost had sent a chill through all our lives.